Brother Botolph
and
The Abbess

by

D.S. Pepper

i

This is the First Edition of "Brother Botolph and The Abbess."
It was first published in Great Britain in August 2014
by Earlsgate Publishing
Post Office Box 721
FOLKESTONE
CT20 9EY.

ISBN 978-0-9567508-1-5

Typeset in Book Antiqua / Papyrus.

To my family.

If you require a further copy of this book,

or any other books by the same author

please email your order to

botolph@virginmedia.com

or visit the website at botolph.info, or write to:-

Earlsgate Publishing,

PO Box 721,

Folkestone,

CT20 9EY.

Other books by D.S. Pepper:-

BOTOLPH,
(Volume I of the Botolph Trilogy)
published in December 2010.

Provisional titles of other books which are in the pipeline:-

A VOYAGE AROUND BOTOLPH CHURCHES (A gazetteer)
BOTOLPH, SAINT OF ICANHO (A biography)
ABBOT BOTOLPH OF ICANHO (Part III of the trilogy)

**Please note: there is a comprehensive Glossary
at the back of the book together with notes on such
matters as the book's historical accuracy.**

Acknowledgements.

I am grateful to all those who have helped in the publication of this book. My dear wife Zina has been most supportive as always and has born the more boring parts of my research with equanimity while (I hope) enjoying the more exciting times.

In April 2012 we travelled to Faremoutiers Abbey, which lies just east of Paris, and were greatly assisted by our friends, Jean-Marie Hennebelle and his charming wife Babette, who acted as intermediaries and arranged for us to meet Prieuse Clothilde who is in charge of the nuns who run the abbey. The Prioress, kindly, in the pouring rain, conducted us on a tour of some of the abbey grounds and of the twelfth century Saint Sulpice church which stands on the site of a former church which was dedicated to St Stephen (Saint Etienne). My grateful thanks to Jean-Marie, Babette and Prieuse Clothilde.

Thanks also to Daniela Nava for her initial review of *Brother Botolph and the Abbess* and to Patricia Taylor, Ray Beaglehole, Helen Barker, John Krakwcyz, Duncan Hopkin, Zina and my younger son Tom for their proof reading - and to my elder son Rob for help with some of the artwork.

The feedback I received from the previous book indicated that my readers would like me to be more ambitious with my scenarios and I inevitably 'over-egged the pudding' initially. I hope my proof-readers were not unduly shocked and that they will find this 'softened' version to their liking.

Thanks also to Jo and Lee Robinson who have taken over the marketing of my books, the website for which can be found at www.botolphbooks.co.uk.

An Apology

The first book in the Botolph trilogy was published in December 2010 and I had every intention of publishing the remaining two books within the next couple of years. Indeed this (second) book was 'finished' by April 2012 but I was keen to chase a route towards perfection.

I wanted to follow the more traditional publishing channels because I knew that this would hone my skills as a writer by making me 'jump through hoops of fire'. I therefore sent the draught to a reviewer who, three months later, had still not looked at it. After some delay and a little persuasion he returned the copy together with the advance which I had sent him. I tried again and sent it to another reviewer who, conversely, was extremely helpful and encouraging. The manuscript was returned speedily and I implemented some of her advice. I say 'some' because, like all good people, her advice was not infallible. By this time it was the end of 2012.

Having tidied the book further I set about finding a Literary Editor but they are few and far between, have their well-established clientele and (quite naturally) are reluctant to accept other clients unless they are sure that they have a winner.

Sadly, twenty six Literary Agents decided that an author who writes about an obscure monk living in an obscure century was not one of these. I did however receive two particularly encouraging comments, - although neither of the Literary Agents who gave these was prepared to 'put his money where his mouth was.'

By the summer of 2013 I was attempting to interest publishers directly but this also proved to be difficult as most required the approach to be made through a Literary Agent - a classical 'Catch 22' situation.

During this period, - from January 2013, - I had started a course for an M.A.(Biography) degree at Buckingham University. Naturally my subject was Saint Botolph and this will lead to a non-fiction publication (provisionally entitled '***Botolph, the Saint of Icanho***') which will, I hope, become his definitive biography.

Many of you will already have joined the **Society of Saint Botolph** (for those who have not - it is free of charge and application forms can be found at **www.botolph.info**) and have received the newsletters. Each of these monthly emails contains a feature on a different 'Botolph Church'; an expanded form of these will constitute a future publication. This will be a gazetteer (provisionally entitled '***Voyages around Botolph Churches***') which will, I hope, delight the ecclesiologists amongst you and be of great help when planning your tours around this elite group of institutions.

In spite of my difficulties with Literary Agents and Publishers I am delighted to note that Botolph has a great following as evidenced by the number of people who have 'badgered' me for the next book. I felt it was only fair to explain the reason for the delay and to promise that Volume III of the trilogy will not take so long.

Æ   (Known as an "ash").   In the interests of simplicity, I have sometimes chosen to reduce this to a simple "E" as from Æthelbert to Ethelbert and sometimes I have favoured the "A".

Ce   In Anglo-Saxon pronunciation (as in modern Italian) where "C" is followed by an "e" or an "i", the "C" is pronounced as "Ch".   Thus, for example, Ceolbert is pronounced "Cholbert" and Ceaster (as in Hrofsceaster, the Anglo-Saxon for Rochester) is pronounced "Chaster".

Contents

x

Characters in the Trilogy so far:-
(Those in bold type are real historical characters.
All dates are A.D.).

Abraham	Tubby Irish monk at Evoriacum.
Adulph	**Botolph's elder brother.**
Alfrid	Bandit at Bonoriacum.
Aliz	Wife of Bonitius.
Anna	**King of East Anglia 636-654.**
Antonio	Prior of Faremoutiers monastery.
Arnaud	Farmer who helped Queen Nanthild.
Ash	Luka's son.
Athelwald	**Sub-King ruler of West Kent, 616-?**
Atheran	Husband of Botolph's sister, Matild.
Augustine	**Saint sent from Rome in 597 to re-introduce Christianity to England. Founded the abbey at Cantwarebury.**
Audomar	**Saint and Bishop of Sithiu 637-670. Also known as Saint Omer.**
Balthild	**Former slave owned by Erchinoald and eventual wife of King Clovis.**
Berchar	**Duke of Laon.**
Bernard	"The Pot-Stirrer," friend of Botolph at Evoriacum.
Bertha	**King Ethelbert's Queen and Eanswythe's grandmother.**
Bertin	**Monk at Sithiu who met Botolph and Luka on their arrival.**
Bertille	**Pretty nun from Jouarre who became abbess of Chelles.**
Betta	Torrel's wife at Cnobersburg.
Blado	6-year old slave boy rescued by Luka.
Blue-Eyes	Captain of Sigeberht of East Anglia's guard.
Bonitius	Bandit chieftain.

Botolph	**Central character of this book. During thelatter years of his life, reputed to be the wisest and holiest man in England. (See next section).**
Brantome	One of the Bonoriacum gang.
BurgundoFara	**Abbess of Faremoutiers 620-655.**
Caelin	Master-at-arms at Burgh Castle.
Cedric	(4 years old) Feya's brother.
Ceolbert	Travelling monk, based at Cantwarebury.
Chagneric	**Burgundo-Fara's father.**
Chagnoald	**Bishop Faro's and BurgundoFara's brother.**
Chlothar I	**French king 511-561. Son of Clovis I and great-grandfather of Dagobert. Husband of Arnegunde.**
Clarisse	Archdeacon Gaubert's stepdaughter .
Clovis I	**King of Gaul 466-510. Became King of all the Franks.**
Clovis II	**Younger son of Dagobert. King of Neustria and Burgundia 639-657.**
Dagobert I	**603-638. Father of Sigebert III and Clovis II.**
Denis	**Third century saint. Bishop of Lutetia and Meaux.**
Eadbald	**King of Cantium 616-640. Eanswythe's father.**
Ebertram	Monk at Sithiu.
Ecci	Boatman near the Bloomery.
Eanfled	**Daughter of Aunt Ethelburga. Married King Oswiu.**
Eanswythe	**618-640. Abbess of Folcanstane. Daughter of King Eadbald.**
Ecberht	**King of East Anglia.**
Eligius	**King Dagobert's counsellor. Also known as Saint Eloi.**

Ella	Slave girl with the high cheek bones.
Eluhan	Hairy giant at Bonoriacum.
Eormenred	**The elder of Eanswythe's two brothers.**
Eorcenberht	**Younger brother of Eanswythe. Succeeded Eadbald as King of Kent.**
Erchinoald	**French nobleman. Eventual mayor of Neustria and Burgundia. Father of Queen Ymme of Kent.**
Ethelbert	**560-616. First Bretwalda-king of all England. Eanswythe's grandfather.**
Ethelburga	**Abbess of Liminge. Eanswythe's Aunt.**
Ethelburg	**Daughter of King Anna of East Anglia.**
Fara	**Abbess of Evoriacum. Also known as BurgundoFara.**
Faro	**Bishop of Meaux. BurgundoFara's brother.**
Fauve	Skinny monk at Meaux.
Feya	(13 years old) Slave girl rescued by Luka.
Fiebras	One of the Bonoriacum gang.
Fulkh	Foxy villain who helped Botolph and Luka.
Fursey	**Irish saint and Abbot of Cnobersburg.**
Gaubert	Wicked archdeacon of Meaux.
Godefroi	Catechumen at The Grand Baptism.
Guberna	Head of the Bloomery.
Gunder	(6 years old) Slave boy rescued by Luka.
Gurnard	The Master Ostler at Villa Calae.
Hansa	Boatman's son on Rumniae Marsh.
Haymo	**Duke of Ponthieu.**
Helgot	Bonitius's son.
Hereswith	**Sister of Hilda of Whitby. Nun at Chelles.**
Hessa	Carter who took the boys to Gippeswic.
Honorius	**Archbishop of Canterbury 630-653.**
Hwanna	Young Clovis II's wet nurse.
Ivan	Monk in Cantwarebury Scriptorium.
John	Tonsurer at Evoriacum.

Kera	Botolph's mother.
Lartan	(7 years old) Slave boy rescued by Luka.
Leofric	Botolph's father.
Leudesius	**Erchinoald and Leutsinde's idle son.**
Leutsinde	**Erchinoald's late wife.**
Lubaia	Wife of Gaubert. Mother of Clarisse.
Luka	Central but fictional character. Botolph's friend.
Magburga	One of the twin nuns from West Kent.
Malger	One of the Bonoriacum gang.
Marcus	Capellanu to Dagobert.
Margaret	Disgraced nun at Faremoutiers.
Markan	Tall monk-teacher at Cantwarebury.
Martha	Wife of Folcanstane fisherman and daughter-in-law to Eric.
Martin	**Saint who gave half his cloak to a beggar at Samarobriva.**
Mata	(8 years old) Slave girl rescued by Luka.
Matild	Botolph's elder sister.
Matthew	Prior of Cnobersburg.
Modegisile	**Bishop of Tours. Keeper of the key of Saint Martin's Cloak.**
Montey	Measurer at the Bloomery.
Mosel	Farmer from Apuldre.
Mummolin	**Brother at Sithiu who became Abbot.**
Nanthild	**Dagobert's second wife. Mother of Clovis II.**
Nelburga	One of the twin nuns from West Kent.
Oswan	One of the tree men at Bonoriacum.
Odo	(8 years old) Slave boy rescued by Luka.
One-eye	Slave trader who captured Luka.
Pedra	Prioress of Faremoutiers Nunnery. Sister of Archdeacon Gaubert.
Penda	**King of Mercia.**

Radingus	**Irish Bishop / Eveqcomte of Caesaromagus.**
Renier	One of the Bonoriacum gang.
Ricberht	**King of East Anglia 627-630. Father of Balthild.**
Richbert	**"Lanky-Boots" trainee monk at Cnobersburg.**
Samuel	Father of the footing vaults at Meaux.
Saethryth	**King Anna's foster daughter.**
Sigebert III	**Young King of Austrasia 634-655. Son of Dagobert.**
Sigeberht	**King of East Anglia who became a monk.**
Silvius	Bandit who became known as Scarface.
Sweyn	Disgraced monk at Faremoutiers.
Theodochilde	**Abbess of Jouarre.**
Theudebert	**Eanswythe's maternal grandfather and friend of BurgundoFara's father.**
Torrel	Sailing master at Cnobersburg.
Uffa	Eadbald's chief cook.
Willelma	Farmer's wife who helped Nanthild.
Ymme	**Eanswythe's mother.**

Foreword to the whole trilogy.

Saint Botolph
(c.620 - c.680)

Botolph was a real person who was renowned for his mildness and kind disposition.

He was born at a very exciting time, only twenty-three years after Saint Augustine had been sent by Pope Gregory I to revitalise Christianity in England. Like many of his countrymen, Botolph saw hope and love embodied in the new religion and he was inspired to spread this spirit of optimism throughout his known world. As a result he became one of the greatest of the seventh century English missionaries.

Most Benedictine monks lived a static life confined in their monastery. Botolph however was allowed to satisfy his desire to travel, and thus became revered as the patron saint of travellers from the time of his life until later medieval times when he was supplanted by Saint Christopher. Nevertheless there remain many edifices which give testament to his renown. The four gates of London each had churches dedicated to Saint Botolph and three of these still remain.

There are nearly seventy other churches in England which bear his title and the name of the town of Boston in Lincolnshire is believed to be a corruption of "Botolph's Town".

His name even features on the sign of a Public House on Romney Marsh in Kent called "Botolph's Bridge Inn" ... but more of Botolph's Bridge in a later book, although mention must be made here of another Botolph's Bridge in Peterborough. His travels and fame spread across to the continent, not only to France but also to Denmark where the festival of Botolph's Mass is still held each June.

Comparatively little is known about his life because of the destruction of records by later raiding parties. Many historians and writers have simply copied and followed the guesswork of their predecessors. There are, however, sufficient historical facts that give us a skeleton of Botolph's life; imagination and surmise flesh out the rest

His origins are unknown (although there are several theories) but I have chosen to have him come from humble beginnings, the son of an iron worker living on the Kent/Sussex border.

His name is written variously as "Botulph, Botolf, Botwulf" etc; (my gardener, Norman, insists on calling him "Bolt-off"). I have elected to retain the second "o" because I think the enunciation of the word flows better than it would with a "u". Although normally an advocate of simplicity, I find that retention of the "ph" does justice to its owner by giving the name a more holy and noble appearance than the hard, primitive and rugged "f"!

Botolph was, I believe, a very special person living at a very special time. Although the tales of his activities are liberally dramatised, I have done my best to ensure that they are as historically accurate as they can be in regard to the locations in which the stories occur and the historical characters he meets.

I hope you enjoy reading of his travels, trials and tribulations.

Prepare yourself for the Seventh Century

People often only read the foreword to a book when they have finished and enjoyed it. They then turn back to study this part which they should perhaps have read first. They do so because they are now hungry to devour every last morsel that has dropped from the writer's pen whereas at the start they were uncertain of how enjoyable their prospective literary journey would turn out to be.

In some ways I hope that you are doing that.

In other ways I hope you are not. I hope that you are reading this part first to prepare yourself for the story that will follow. To acclimatise your brain. To set the scene in your mind.

It is difficult for us, in this modern age, to conceive what our England was like in Botolph's time.

On the visual front you will need to drive from your mind the concept of roads; neatly ordered and bordered fields; lots of open spaces; rabbits; potatoes; tomatoes.

On the mental front you will need to eliminate the concept of peace and security and the certainty that your status quo will remain the same in the near and distant future. Many of your peers will be dying unexpectedly, sometimes for no apparent reason. Others of them will be snatched in raids to end up as slaves in faraway lands.

Even discounting the threat from human attack, your culture assures you that you are surrounded by elves and goblins and beasts and fiends who are as much of a danger to you as raiders or illness.

Your life is completely subject to the will of the gods. Superstition is the rote by which you live. Spells, charms, curses and witchcraft are the stuff of everyday life.

Apart from that, life in the seventh century A.D. for those who are rich, is probably better than you might have imagined: a plentiful supply of good food; strong warm clothes and soft leather shoes; good company and happy family life; but interspersed by tragedy and disaster which you must learn to take in your stride. Indeed things are rather better now than they were one hundred years ago when foreign raiders were a constant problem.

When you travel, you will usually do so on foot, or if you are lucky by mule or pony. Maybe you will hitch a lift on a wagon drawn by oxen or horses. You will generally not travel more than ten miles from your own family. If you travel further it will be because the family is migrating, ... often to get away from danger. The path you take will either be one of the remaining Roman Streets, or narrow tracks which criss-cross the countryside. The tracks will either have been made by travelling humans or by cattle or both. In open country the paths will only be wide enough for humans to travel in single file. Much of the countryside will not be 'open' but covered by dense forests of oak and ash. The lack of light on the forest floor will have reduced the vegetation. Tracks cut hundreds of years before and used on a regular but perhaps infrequent basis, will have remained passable. Glimpses of the sun will be rare and the forest will be cold.

People you meet will be suspicious of you and you of them. Dwellings you come across will be inhabited by souls who have been attacked before and will suspect you of the same evil intent. Travellers you meet may seem friendly at first, but if they suspect you of having more than they do, may kill and rob you at the first opportunity in order to better their own lot.

In these early days, there has been little silting of the rivers and the countryside is indented by masses of watery inlets which either have to be forded or swum or crossed by ferry. Bordering the rivers are marshy areas which can be fatal for unwary travellers, the wisest of whom keep to the high ground.

There are few signposts.   Planning for travel is difficult but your life may depend upon it. People you meet on the journey will give you news of what lies ahead of you in return for news from you of the areas through which you have just passed.   Much of your direction of travel will be influenced by the position of the sun by day or, if you are rash enough to walk abroad at night, by the moon and the stars.   You have to persevere in honing your sense of direction and must consign to your memory the landmarks of your trail so that you will recognise them at another time.

Surprisingly, crossing the English Channel is neither out of the question nor unduly dangerous. At least no more dangerous than it is going to be for the next thousand years. Plenty of craft cross the water, some carrying cargo and others specifically carrying passengers.   Such travel is expensive and, since the Romans left two hundred years ago, there is little coinage.   The only available currency is gold, salt or goods such a clothes, spearheads or arrowheads.   If you are a man of God like Botolph, and the boatman is a Christian he may choose to give you free passage in the hope that he will find his place in heaven.

Talking of God, your world is in a state of flux. Christianity is the new and up-and-coming religion. Paganism (the religion of peasants) is becoming unfashionable.   There is a strong movement to promote Christianity and to consign the lesser gods to the bonfire. Nevertheless, Druidism and other pagan rituals are still being defended (sometimes violently) by their practitioners.

There is a clearly-defined class system in your new life. It consists of Thanes, Churls and Thralls. As a man of God you are pleased to avoid having the onus of a Thane to answer to, as you would if you were merely a Churl.   You are certainly pleased to avoid the desperation and poverty of being a Thrall.

The Churls are farmers who rent land from their Thane and it is their fields that fill the open spaces between the forests. They grow cereal crops: wheat, barley and rye. They also grow vegetables in the form of parsnips, cabbages, carrots, celery and peas. Available fruits are apples, raspberries, blackberries and sloes. Livestock includes sheep, goats, cattle and pigs. Farmers have to work hard during the summer in order to produce enough food for their families to survive during the long hard winter. In the autumn, the cattle are slaughtered and the meat is salted for later consumption.

In the twenty-first century, we tend to forget that slavery has been with us since prehistoric times. In the time-context of this story, slaves may also be known as Thralls or Serfs. They are often Britons who have been captured by the Saxons in battle. Many of them will have been sent abroad where there is a good market for white Britons. Others will be the property of farmers, kings or even monasteries where they will be expected, for example, to do the hard building work of digging deep pits in the chalk for the placement of the wooden poles that will support a new building.

There are artisans too. Potters now use a wheel for fabrication whereas, until recently, all pottery was made by hand. Blacksmiths, bronzesmiths, goldsmiths, silversmiths, jewellery-makers and bone and wood carvers can all be found if you know where to look.

The topography of the countryside is already changing continuously but subtly. It is only ten thousand years or so after the end of the last major ice age and the routine logical effects of, first the ice and then the water movement that attends such a melt is still in its infancy.

Many rivers are still wide and deep. The hills are higher and more pointed than today. The erosion that occurs with melting and drying has certainly started and the silt produced by this erosion is being carried by the rivers towards the sea. Much of it does not get that far however but falls onto the river beds and the process of progressive shoaling has just begun.

This is the different world in which you will live as 'young Botolph.'

So, noble Thane or Thaness ... read on!

Denis Pepper,
Folkestone, November 2010.

Volume II
of
The Botolph Trilogy

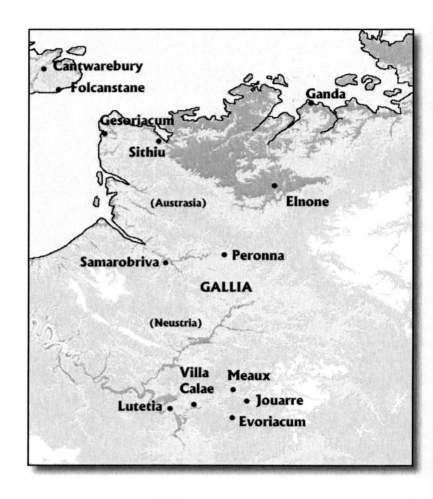

Fig 1. Gallia in the seventh century.

CHAPTER 1
Lost

Luka remained crouched and full of fight as he assessed his surroundings. The appalling scene had been taking place on a pallet of straw. Next to the pallet was a thatched mud and wattle hut; wisps of smoke were curling through a hole in the roof.

He looked back at the girl. She was lying on her side – her body wracked by convulsive sobs.

"A blanket," he thought. "She needs a blanket."

He crabbed towards the hut wondering if he ought to finish the arse-bleeder off as a matter of kindness. He flicked the catch off the door, threw it open and looked in.

"Christ!" he said again.

--o--

The search party found the river's edge and Botolph and one of the guards dismounted and, in the lights of the flames they carried, tried to analyse the tracks. It was hopeless. Not only was the darkness a problem but others besides themselves had passed that way and it was impossible to see which marks were Luka's.

"It's no good," said Botolph to the guard, "let's mount up again."

"What are we going to do now sire?" asked the other guard.

"Well I think we'd better make our way back to where we last saw him and see if we can find any clues. He might be lying injured somewhere. Who knows? He can't just vanish!"

They cautiously picked up speed again, with Botolph calling "Luuuka!" whenever it seemed appropriate. From time to time they would stop and listen and Botolph would call again. Annoyingly at one such point when Botolph was listening intently for any sounds of Luka groaning in the undergrowth two of the guards' horses kept whinnying and their noises hampered his efforts.

"Shut those horses up," he snapped uncharacteristically, not really considering just how the riders might be able to do that. But then there came the sound of an *answering* whinny.

In the blackness they could not see the narrow forest path previously followed by Luka. The burning torches helped by illuminating the trees but hindered by compromising their night vision. Botolph urged his horse through the scrub in the general direction of the sound – the animal tripped and stumbled several times on unseen rocks and holes. Eventually they reached the trees where the ground was flatter. They stopped and Botolph called Luka's name again and was rewarded by an immediate neigh in reply.

He dismounted and made his way through the trees followed by the two guards. As he approached, the horse shied at the burning brand he was carrying and Botolph passed it back for one of the guards to hold while he calmed the beast and examined the saddle and the surrounding ground.

He could see nothing untoward. He peered into the depths of the forest and, cupping his hands to his mouth, called: "Luuuuka."

He waited ... more in hope than expectation.   His only reply was a mocking rustle of leaves as a shimmer of night breeze wafted through the branches.

"I'm sorry sire," said one of the guards, "but there's nothing we can do now.   We'll leave a piece of the horse's bridle here to mark this spot and get Gurnard to organise a larger search party in the morning."

Botolph could see the sense in this so with a heavy feeling in his belly and with Luka's horse in tow they returned to Villa Calae.

--o--

Six pairs of eyes stared at Luka through the smoky gloom of the hut doorway.   As his vision adjusted he saw that the children were all fettered and chained together. They ranged in age from about four to ten summers and, as far as he could make out, there was an equal number of boys and girls, but they were so begrimed and their hair so unkempt that he could not be sure.

They stared vacantly at him with silent insolence, standing as he was bespattered with blood with his seax ready in his hand.   The tallest boy's eyes suddenly opened wide ... and the last thing Luka felt and heard was a cataclysmic blow to the back of his head as he was pitched into black unconsciousness.

--o--

Instead of taking the well-worn road from Lutetia to the south-east, they had headed *due* east.   The excitement of a different route had added spice to their sudden sense of freedom.

4

"We're going *away* from the river," Luka had called. "Where're we going to cross? Evoriacum's on the other side isn't it?"

"Don't know. I'll go and find out." Digging his heels into his horse's flanks, Botolph had steered her out and alongside the trotting mounts of the two guards.

"Where're we going to cross the river?" he asked.

"We're not," came the reply.

"Not?"

"Well not today anyway. You're going to spend the night at Villa Calae. The king felt you should have a good night's rest before arriving at the abbey!"

Botolph dropped back to relay the news to Luka but, with ears like a bat, he had already heard and was grinning like a madman.

"Great!" he crowed. "Another night of freedom! I've heard about Villa Calae. It's the old palace that's been used by French kings for centuries. There are bound to be some tasty wenches there and we'll have another night of revelry. Good old King Dagobert. He said he'd be forever in our debt!"

Botolph groaned inwardly seeing this as yet another delay. He comforted himself with the thought that one more night could surely do no harm.

They had been riding at a steady trot through a thick forest. To each side like guards of honour stood lines of tall trees. Behind those were legions of brother trees stretching into the gloom of the forest's interior. After a while the leafy ceiling lightened and they dropped down a hill and into the daylight. The regular jarring of hoof on road contrasted with a softer sensation as the horses plunged into *marshy* ground. Ahead of them, their guides splashed slowly through the bog until their horses reached firmer footing

5

whereupon they jerked up a slope and turned sharply to the right onto a narrow path that skirted a wood-covered hill.

A few miles later the path gave onto a river. Botolph guessed that they must now be well upstream of the same River Marne that encircled the new monastery they had spent the previous months helping to build in honour of Prince Clovis.

Their horses were tiring and the guards had slowed their pace since crossing the bog in order to allow the animals time to cool down. Botolph turned and looked back at the forest noting the sun dropping quickly towards the treetops.

"Will we arrive before nightfall?" he called.

"Yes, we're nearly there now. Once we're clear of these trees, you'll be able to see Villa Calae up on the hill."

This prospect had been too tempting for Luka who had immediately dug his strong sturdy heels into his mount's flanks and the surprised beast took off along the riverbank spooking the guards' horses as he scraped past. The shouted oaths were lost on his retreating form.

"Where's he off to?" one asked crossly.

"Don't worry," said Botolph, "he hates plodding. He'll drive his horse hard until he sees your promised villa and then come galloping back like a madman. You'll see."

"We should really go with him," said the other guard. "We were told not to let either of you out of our sight."

"That's not easy with Luka," said Botolph. "Never fear, he'll be back shortly."

But the minutes had passed and there had still been no sign of him. They rounded the corner of the trees and one of the guards pointed, "There's Villa Calae. D'y' see it atop that hill? But where's Master Luka got to?"

6

"I'm blessed if I know," said Botolph, an unexpected panic suddenly coursing through his body and peaking as a violent shiver.

The other guard pointed down to the fresh hoof prints in the damp fronds of grass by the edge of the riverbank.

"There are his tracks. He was travelling fast at this point."

"Well perhaps his horse had more life in him than he thought and he's decided to press on. We'll probably find him sitting on a stone with a big grin on his face in a moment."

They carried on at a leisurely pace following the river. The outlines of Villa Calae had grown ever larger and climaxed like a flaming beacon as the last of the evening sun glistened on its walls. Sadly, the beautiful sight was lost on Botolph whose mind was filled with seemingly unreasonable apprehension. As the sun abandoned its display and sank into hiding beyond the horizon it brought dusk over the sloping pathway that led to the villa's gates. With the poor light and the drier ground it became impossible to identify any of Luka's tracks; besides which, the travellers were not now alone. A constant stream of people plied to and from the villa.

The massive structure had been built on the site of an old Roman fortress of which plenty was still in evidence. They passed through the tall gates and into a bustling reception area with stables on one side and a paddock on the other. Two slaves held their horses' heads while the guards dismounted. Botolph remained stubbornly in his saddle.

"We've lost one of our party," he called down to a slave. "We're looking for a young British monk who should've arrived in the last half an hour."

The slave gabbled a half unintelligible reply of which the only words that made any sense were "... Master Ostler."

Botolph dismounted reluctantly and his horse was taken from him to be rubbed down, fed and stabled.

He turned to the guards: "Where will I find the Master Ostler then?"

"Ah that'll be Gurnard," came the reply, "... this way."

Gurnard was a leather-booted and aproned man with a wild beard and florid face who was busily directing the groom-slaves. He was of medium height and had rich brown eyes which shone like the brightest polished walnut wood. His leather apron matched his boots. Both were stained black at the edges, and in the centres were black scars mapping previous encounters between the man and his work.

He was so pre-occupied growling orders into the distance and giving brusque answers to questions from people queuing at his elbow that at first he failed to notice Botolph. Being head and shoulders in height above most of the crowd, Botolph was scanning the area for Luka. Eventually there came a gap in Gurnard's directives and his countenance changed from one of gruff efficiency to that of a dutiful host as he turned to the new arrival and said respectfully, "Good Evening young sire and welcome to Villa Calae, what can I do for you?"

Botolph was somewhat taken aback but comforted by this sudden change in attitude and said "My name's Botolph and we have come from the palace at Lutetia but have lost one of our party. I was hoping you might have seen a young novice monk dressed like myself but about two cubits shorter?" Botolph held out his hand in the position where it would have rested on top of Luka's head, had he been standing there.

"No. Can't say that I have," replied Gurnard, "just a moment." He shouted into the far end of the stable. "Anybody else arrived from Lutetia in the past hour?" Some sort of reply came rumbling back and he said, "No, sorry, it doesn't look as if he's reached us yet."

The two bodyguards were standing nearby listening to this exchange. Having lost half the party they were supposed to be protecting they were beginning to feel distinctly uncomfortable. The torches had been lit and were casting flickering shadows all around.

"We'll 'ave to go back and look for 'im," said one of the guards. "Gurnard, - can you lend us a couple of local men to help us search and give a bit of protection?"

Gurnard sighed and went off to fetch three fresh horses and a couple of mounted soldiers-at-arms. Tired and saddle-worn as he was, Botolph clambered eagerly onto the new nag, and the five riders, each carrying a burning brand, trotted briskly back down the path towards the river.

CHAPTER 2
The Forest

Botolph was right, Luka *had* been getting bored and as soon as he knew that the king's villa was around the next corner he could not resist spurring his horse into a gallop to go and see for himself.

He loved speed and relished the sensation of the wind blowing up his sleeves and streaming back his hair as the horse thundered along the river bank. He rounded the edge of the forest and delighted in seeing the villa as predicted. But it was all too soon. His mount had gained its second wind and was enjoying the burst of activity as much as he was, so, slowing his pace only a little, he cantered on around the next corner and onwards until his horse began to tire. Detecting the animal's change of pace he reined the beast in, letting out a great whoop of pleasure as he fell forwards onto his mount's neck slapping its withers in gratitude.

Shaking its head, the horse snorted in response and obeyed the pull of the reins as Luka turned him back towards his friends who were still well out of sight.

As he rounded a bend he saw a narrow track leading off to the right where it vanished amongst the trees. Ever the practical joker, the child in him stirred as he identified an ideal ambush point that could not be resisted. He urged his horse into the foliage and pressed on behind the tree-line where he could not be seen.

The walk had enabled the animal to recover from its run and it stood peaceably enough as Luka peered ahead waiting for a sign that would indicate that the time was right for him to begin his charge.

The forest had been quiet apart from the rustling of the leaves. A thrush called from the scrub ahead. But then came another sound from behind him and to his left. He turned in the saddle and listened. Keeping his head to one side he tried to focus his ears. There it was again. It had an urgent edge. Abandoning his previous plan he slipped silently to the ground and tethered the horse whispering *"Stay quiet"* in its ear before creeping away into the trees.

Was the sound from an animal or from a human? Although the sun was low, ample shards of light were still filtering into the leafy glade and this enabled him to avoid treading on broken twigs and branches that would otherwise signal his presence. His acute sense of hearing picked up the sounds from a long way off. By now he had been walking for a considerable time and had become enfolded deeply within the forest

Piercing the silence, from his right there came a sharp scream followed by distraught sobbing and raucous laughter. Luka froze and twitched his nose as the sweet smell of burning wood brushed past him. He saw a distant clearing and as he moved softly towards the edge of the trees the source of the cries became apparent. Two burly men were holding a struggling girl on a bale of straw. Between her legs a third man, with his breeches round his ankles, was savagely raping her. The rapist gave a climactic roar before collapsing forwards, his ardour sated. He rested, panting, for several moments before withdrawing and pulling up his breeks with an air of macabre triumph.

After a gruff exchange his companion, who had been holding the girl's ankles, let them go to allow him to move away. She rolled to one side bringing her knees together and her body was wracked with sobbing as she wept uncontrollably. It seemed to Luka that, for a moment, the leaves stopped their susurrations and the whole forest held its breath in shocked silence.

But there was more to come. The brute who had been holding the girl's arms strode jauntily forward and turned her on to her back again, wrenching her legs apart. She tensed and arched her back screaming "Noooo! ..." as he dropped his breeks.

Luka had been transfixed with horror. He had never seen anything like this before. The thought of returning to his horse and summoning help never crossed his mind. He had always been impetuous and acted on instinct without considering the implications. The girl needed help and needed it *now*.

He deftly unsheathed his seax-knife and launched himself from the trees as silently as he could. The men's attention however was fully occupied by their deeds. The first hint they had of his presence was when he plunged the sharp seax deeply into the cleft of the rapist's pumping buttocks. Even before his victim could give voice to his pain the seax was withdrawn and flashing in the last rays of sunlight as Luka shouldered the second man to the ground and then pressed the long knife into the belly of the third man who was holding the girl's arms. His eyes opened wide as Luka twisted the seax upwards in his trademark thrust allowing loops of steaming bowel to come tumbling out.

He felt an arm go around his neck as the man who had been holding the girl's legs finally regained both his senses and his feet. Shooting his elbow into the man's chest Luka dropped onto one knee and pulled hard on the arm. The body flew over his shoulder and, with a resounding crack, the head came to rest in a rocky groove.

Luka jumped back and crouched, tossing his seax from one hand to the other as he glared at his opponents and waited for a counter-attack. The girl had rolled onto her side and was sobbing piteously; Luka's horror increased when he saw that she was only about thirteen summers old.

His second victim was also lying on his side but surrounded by blood and steaming guts. He was making futile weak movements as his life ebbed rapidly away. The other man was still standing but bright red blood was pulsing from his rear where the seax had penetrated. He was groaning and squirming as he tried unsuccessfully to reach and stem the copious flow. The third man was lying unconscious with his smashed and bloodied face still on the rock.

"Christ!" Luka had thought, "what do I do now?"

CHAPTER 3
Capture.

Botolph's first night in Villa Calae had not been the happy one that King Dagobert and Queen Nanthild had planned for him and Luka.

After surviving a sea journey to Gaul culminating in the second shipwreck of their lives, the paths of the two aspiring monks had fortuitously crossed with that of the retinue of the great King Dagobert. They had enjoyed his protection during their long journey through a countryside plagued by murderers and thieves. When only a few leagues short of their destination however the king had forbidden them to continue. Their tongues were the culprits.

It was not that their words had been subversive. On the contrary, it was their joyful stories of monastery life that had been their undoing. King Dagobert had decided that they were the ideal enthusiasts to oversee the construction of a new monastery that he was building in honour of his fifteen-month-old son. He decreed that they would remain in Lutetia until the work was completed.

Botolph and Luka, being only eighteen, were surprised that anyone, let alone a king, should feel that they had any advice worth giving. They had become used to thinking of themselves as pupils rather than teachers. On reflection they realised that King Dagobert had a point; they *had* learnt a lot in the previous six years; it seemed that the time had come to put their knowledge into practice.

It was not that staying in Lutetia had been any hardship. They were fed at the king's table and able to enjoy themselves rather more than was perhaps appropriate for a couple of hopeful young monks. It did from time to time occur to Botolph that so much enjoyment might be sinful. He questioned how they would manage to re-adapt to an austere way of life if they ever *did* manage to reach the abbey of Evoriacum.

Luka, typically, would only discuss the matter so far as to say that their good fortune was clearly a gift from God so in his view it would be a sin *not* to enjoy it.

Botolph was at his happiest when they were working on the river site and doing physical work such as unloading building stones from the mule carts and hauling timbers up to the roofs. In the early days much of their time had been spent poring over drawings in company with the king, his counsellor Eligius and Queen Nanthild.

"Where should the doorways go? How many rooms ought there be? How big shall we make each room?"

Botolph had pointed out that much of this depended upon the number of monks it was intended to accommodate. He and Luka had been part of a very large community at Cantwarebury but of a much smaller one at Father Fursey's monastery in Cnobersburg.

His words fostered more questions. What number would be ideal? Botolph tried to give constructive answers to the group. At the start Luka would make useful suggestions too but after a short while his gaze would become transfixed on a blank space of wall and Botolph knew then that he was on his own.

They had good accommodation sharing a room which, although small and tucked away, was far more luxurious than Botolph had ever experienced. Both boys came from noble stock but Botolph's parents had fallen on hard times and he had grown up in a thatched mud and wattle hut in the Weald of Cantium on a bloomery site occupied by ironworkers. Luka, by contrast, had enjoyed the privileges of aristocratic surroundings. Botolph felt that *his* childhood had been much better than Luka's. He had had a very happy family life and he loved his parents, brother and sister dearly. By contrast Luka hated *his* family - could not wait to get away from them - and hoped he never saw them again!

King Dagobert's tall elegant counsellor Eligius had helped to select the site upon which the monastery was to be built. The rocky outcrop they had chosen lay in the middle of the gurgling waters of the River Marne. Perched above the rocks were the crumbling foundations of an old Roman fortress called Bagaudarum. The plethora of tiles bricks and stones that were already in place made the whole project much easier since fewer building materials had to be carried from afar. As the monastery progressed the castle moat complimented the structure and gave it an appearance of grandeur as well as offering greater security.

They endured several months of hard work and it was late summer before the time came when the young men could at last take their leave. Pleased as Botolph was to be on the move, he had grown very attached to the royal household. He would miss Eligius's wise words and his witty, droll ways; he had learnt a lot just by being in his presence. The brave adventurer Luka had no such reservations; he was animated and raring to go.

"Shall we travel by boat? Are we going via Meaux? How long d'you think it'll take us?"

Botolph thought they should head straight for Evoriacum on the basis that they could not afford any *further* delays. Skilled sailors as they were their experiences with boats had not been happy ones and Botolph thought they should see if their feet would still work. Luka looked puzzled for a moment, glanced down at his feet and then gave Botolph one of his 'I don't think that's very funny' leers.

They collected their few possessions, stuffed them into their leather scrips and retrieved their walking poles which had been gathering dust in a corner. It was time to say their "God-be-w'ye's" so they headed for the refectory where everyone would be breaking their fast As they made their way through the dusty passages it occurred to Botolph that the palace seemed extraordinarily quiet. When they turned the corner into the dining room they understood why.

Everybody was there and a great round of applause and cheering broke out as they entered. King Dagobert, goblet in hand, climbed onto one of the tables and, in a stentorian voice, gave a stirring homily thanking them for their wise counsel and wishing them well. Raising his goblet on high he proposed a toast to their long, successful and happy life.

"A long and happy life," the crowd repeated and cheering broke out anew. A goblet of mead was thrust into Botolph's hands and he felt his stomach rebel at the sight and smell. He was rescued by the arrival of a throng of people who all wanted to pat him on the back and give their blessings; he thankfully abandoned the goblet on a nearby bench.

Luka gleefully downed his mead in one go and gladly accepted another. He was full of bonhomie as he played the role of the departing hero.

Jumping down from the table, King Dagobert put his hand on Botolph's shoulder. Looking towards Luka he said how much he regretted the fact that he could not show his gratitude by giving them any gifts since they would have to give up all their possessions on entering monastic life.   He was however lending them two good horses and an armed escort to ensure that they arrived at Evoriacum safely and quickly.

He wished them Godspeed and told them that he and his family would be forever in their debt.

To more cheering they were summarily ushered out of the palace and into the courtyard.   They both kissed little Prince Clovis who had formed a strong bond with Luka since being rescued by him at Samarobriva.   They kissed the hand of Queen Nanthild (whose eyes, Botolph noted with surprise, were brimming with tears).   They kissed the hands of the king and Eligius.

Their horses were waiting and they had mounted up and, led by the bodyguards to the sounds of more cheering, the humble habit-clad grinning figures had turned onto the Pons Magnus and made their way out of the city... but now Botolph was here in Villa Calae ... without his dear friend.

--o--

The custodian of the villa had received orders to provide a good meal, musical entertainment and the attention of six nymphettes.

Botolph felt sure that the nymphettes would not have been good for Luka's soul.   The avoidance of that conflict was the only bright part of the evening from Botolph's point of view.

Food was placed in front of him and music was played but Botolph had neither the stomach nor the heart for either.   He ate a little and drank absent-mindedly knowing that he had to fuel his strength and wits for the morrow's search but his belly felt sick with apprehension about what they might find.

As soon as he could excuse himself he left the refectory and walked out onto the peristylum, crossed the garden and leant on the balustrade. He stared south towards the river. His gaze veered westwards and he wondered if Luka was out there now similarly eyeing the lights of the villa. He desperately hoped he was. Perhaps he was lying injured? Perhaps he was thinking unholy thoughts about the company of nymphettes?

Botolph sighed. He turned and made his way back past the garden's central fountain and across the mosaics into the atrium where he skirted the rain-pool and emerged on the northern terrace. He stopped and his unseeing eyes stared into the distance - his joyless heart appreciating nothing.

A series of horse-noises rose from the stable block below and the familiar smell of the animals provided a little comfort as torturing thoughts twisted and turned within him.

Where *could* Luka have gone? It was not like him to vanish in this way. He was unpredictable it was true but ... a short sally into the distance and then a dramatic return in a cloud of dust; that was typical Luka. We had the first part - but what happened to the second?

He turned his head to the northeast gazing into emptiness. His eyes slowly focussed on the chapel and his feet started to move towards it.

Through the doorway there were two candles burning on a plain altar. They drew him towards them and he knelt on the altar steps. Putting his hands together he turned his eyes upwards and fixed his gaze intently on the very centre of the wooden cross.

"Dear Lord, I'm here again," he said, simply.

There was no flash of lightning or clap of thunder - nothing.

His head dropped in a mixture of despair and tiredness before he turned it upwards again.

"Take care of him, Father. Give him Your help to get out of whatever trouble he is in. Guide *us* tomorrow. Keep him safe. Amen."

After a minute he stood, genuflected and made his way back to the terrace. His prayers, he knew, were inadequate but they would have to do for the moment; his brain was in turmoil. He staggered dazedly back to the peristylum, found his bed and lay down ... to think ... and eventually, to sleep.

--o--

A muffled grating sound disturbed Luka's injured subconscious; it gradually became louder; it was metallic. His nose itched and he tried to move his hand to rub it but the hand would not obey his brain's command. He made an effort. His eyes snapped open.

His head hurt. He tried to move it. Every attempt was painful. Although his eyes were open - he could not see. Everything was a hazy blur. A distant red fuzzy glow attracted his attention. He watched, fascinated, as it came closer – but then stopped when still about two cubits away. He realised that it had not really moved at all. It was a joke played by his half-dead body as it started coming back to life. He numbly made a mental note that he did not think it was a good joke. His head hung down and he could only see the redness by turning his eyes upwards as far as they would go. He stared as the glow became less fuzzy before it slowly sharpened revealing itself as embers in a central hearth. He remained still - partly because the slightest movement hurt and partly because he realised that he had been very effectively immobilised.

The events of last week, - or was it last night? - came back to him and he recalled the sight of the six children before the world went black.

On reflection, he was rather surprised to find that he was still alive. At least he *supposed* he *was*. If this were Hell, he reasoned to himself, the fire would be bigger. Ever the optimist he numbered his blessings. He had fought alone against three men so he really deserved to be dead but life spawns hope.

A second bonus was that he was sitting and relatively comfortable.

But there the positive aspects seemed to end. His wrists were tied and they were stretched up above him. His ankles were also tightly lashed together and he could not move his feet. His palate felt like an encrusted riverbank parched by the sun and a growl came from his empty stomach.

He listened. Was he alone or were the children there too? The rasping sound came again but it was from outside his field of view. He listened intently. There were no sounds that would suggest the presence of others. The thought crossed his mind that he was perhaps locked in a sealed pit and that daylight had already blossomed above. He looked forwards straining his eyes and wondering if that was the outline of a door that he could just discern in front of him. If door it was, no light came from below it. Perhaps dawn had not yet broken then?

He wanted to start planning his escape but, bearing in mind his current circumstances, there did not seem to be much profit in that.   He would have to see what daylight brought.   Always supposing of course that his new acquaintances were not planning his summary execution.

--o--

Botolph had slept fitfully and at the first sign of dawn he was up and heading for the latrines.

As he stepped outside his cell he was accosted by one of the villa's servants who asked him if he wished to bathe.

"How do you mean?" said Botolph.

"Well sire, the villa still has the Roman hypocaust and thermal baths so you are welcome to use them if you wish."

Botolph had heard of such baths but his needs at that moment and until they found Luka were only very basic; he declined.

After leaving the latrines he walked briskly down the path to the stables where he found Gurnard already working and preparing the day's orders.

The Master Ostler looked up as he arrived "Ah, young Botolph.   Glad to see you're early.   I take it your friend didn't turn up last night?"

"No," said Botolph, "but that's a point. I suppose we ought to check he's not bedded down elsewhere in the villa before we mount another search."

"I'll send the lad," said Gurnard calling over a slave and giving him instructions to find the custodian's secretary.

"I can see you're worried, and so would I be.   I detailed four soldiers last night when you came back empty-handed.   The men should be here at any moment, together with King Dagobert's guards.   I'll be coming along too so there'll be eight of us altogether.   That should be sufficient to conduct a good search and to handle any trouble.   Don't worry my lad, I'm sure we'll find him."

Botolph could but hope he was right.

--o--

It seemed to Luka that he had been staring at the shadow for hours and hours willing dawn to define it. Nature's unstoppable cycle eventually granted his wish and surprise flitted through his mind as he marvelled at how much pleasure daylight brought. The pleasure was short-lived however as, no sooner had the shadow's edges sharpened than the door was wrenched open and trouble stood silhouetted in the grey morning light.

Luka could not see the man's face but would not have recognised it anyway since when last he saw it, it was half-buried in a rocky cleft.

The image came and crouched before him.   A calloused palm pushed roughly under his chin forcing his head upwards so that he was compelled to stare into the fellow's one good eye.

His attention flickered sideways a little and he saw that, where the other eye should have been, there flared an empty socket with a graze of fresh blood over eyebrow and cheekbone. It looked, Luka thought sadly, as if the missing eye had been lost in a long-ago encounter rather than as a result of his own efforts.

The graze extended down the right side of the face to include both upper and lower lip and "One-eye" snarled at Luka.   His fetid breath stole offensively through the black clots lining a recent gap in his craggy dentition.

"So you're back with us then? A fine mess you caused last night. Both my father and the drayman are dead and I'm short of two teeth ..."

He stood and smashed his fist into Luka's face, perhaps in hope that it might even the score.

Even as his head jerked to one side and the pain seared into his brain, Luka felt strangely encouraged. He had a battle-tally of two and if he could only get his wrists free, One-eye might soon make his score up to three.

The ugly face looked at him for a few long moments and then turned and Luka watched as the misshapen unfortunate loped out of the hut, slamming the door behind him. Luka was puzzled. Why had he only punched him the once. He might have been mistaken but Luka was good at reading people and he felt that he had seen in that eye a mixture of uncertainty and confusion.

Luka's own eyes had only just had time to grow accustomed to the gloom again when the door was flung open and he winced as daylight flooded back in. Through the doorway he could see a haywain to which was hitched an elderly horse. It was not the cart that drew his attention so much as its contents: the older girl who had been raped the previous night and six silent dispirited children. All were still fettered and chained; the six children were standing and the older girl was lying on her side facing the back of the wain.

They watched dispassionately as the thug went into the hut and smashed Luka in the face once more. He stepped back and watched as blood started to drip from Luka's eyebrow. From his belt he pulled a short knife and Luka lifted his head and stared insolently into the other's face as he braced himself for death. The one eye stared back and the knife rose, slicing through the lashings that strung

Luka's wrists on high. He fell face forward onto the earthen floor, his wrists still bound together before him. He lay still, trying to spit out gritty soil. His captor pushed a knee into the small of his back and, after slicing his wrists apart, wrenched them roughly behind his back. He felt the twine bite into his skin as the lashings were retied. He reflected that the half-wit might not have *much* going for him but he *could* tie decent knots. Like a sack of corn he was dragged out to the wagon and thrown in against the recumbent girl. The hinges creaked as the backdrop was pushed up and he heard the click of the pegs as they were locked into place.

All Luka could see was the girl's foot. He felt the wagon tilt as One-eye climbed onto the driver's seat. The wain lurched as the old horse jerked it forwards and a couple of the children promptly fell on top of Luka and the girl. As they wriggled to untangle themselves the wagon moved off and Luka wondered where in the name of Hell they were going to now.

CHAPTER 4
The Hut

The search party soon found the leather thong that had been tied to the tree where Luka's horse had been, and they left it in place as a central marker. There was no sign of any pathway through the forest at this point; the original track seemed to peter out as soon as it reached the trees. Gurnard decided that they would divide into pairs and fan out to see what they could find. He sent one pair of the villa soldiers to cover the left flank and the other pair the right flank. Dagobert's men he sent half left and he and Botolph went half right.

"Shout if you find anything," he instructed, "but if we are too far away, one of you stay with whatever it is and send the other to try and find me. If you have no success by noon, head back here and we'll decide then what to do next."

They split up accordingly and Gurnard led Botolph through the densely packed trees. At one point they heard noises and veered off to the left to investigate only to find that it was Dagobert's men who had strayed to the right of their allocated route. Gurnard's thick eyebrows danced as he cursed at the wasted time and led Botolph off to the right again. After nearly two hours they had seen nothing but trees and even Gurnard's sense of direction was becoming compromised.

"We still have another couple of hours before noon," he said, looking at the sun glinting through the trees, "but I think we'd better head back and start a box search from that marker. He surely can't have come this far."

They turned their horses and headed south but going back was no easier than getting there and in spite of studying the vegetation intently Botolph could not recognise any features from their outward journey. After an arduous time crashing through thickets in the most dense part of the forest they found they were running parallel to a worn track and they moved over to take advantage of the easier route.

"The direction looks about right," said Botolph, "but clearly it doesn't go as far as the river bank or we'd 've seen it yesterday."

"No," agreed Gurnard, "I've no idea where we are but this will at least give us some speed. Come on!"

He spurred his horse into a quick trot and Botolph did likewise. The track was only just wide enough for a narrow cart and it looked as if it had been used by one recently as the grass was still indented by wheel marks. It took a while before the track ended at a clearing where they found a hut outside which were two bodies. As they approached, a cloud of evil blue flies rose and buzzed furiously into their faces.

"Well there's no doubt they're dead," said Gurnard, holding his nose as he used his foot to roll over the thug with the ruptured abdomen.

"What the hell's happened to this one without his breeks? There's blood all over the place. What do you make of it?"

Botolph remembered the stories about the fighting techniques that Luka had used in the defence of Folcanstane two years earlier. He was not too sure whether he hoped this *was* Luka's handiwork or not.

He lifted the latch on the door of the hut and cautiously heaved it open. Gurnard immediately noticed the hooks and spikes driven into the walls and said "Slaves. This is a slave transit post"

"What?" said Botolph.

"There's a slave route which passes here running from the coast to Rome. It's a distasteful business but slave-trading's a way of life. The country couldn't run without them. They're part of the reward and finance of war. We assert our strength and dominance by border raids and then get a good price for selling prisoners as slaves. That helps to finance further raids and it's how our country grows. The fact that this hut is so tucked away, suggests to me that it's either a trading post or a staging post; it looks as if your friend Luka might have stumbled across it and tried to put the world to rights singlehandedly."

"I do hope you're wrong," said Botolph going into the hut. "What are these iron pegs and rings for?"

"They're for chaining the manacles and fetters to. Traders'll sometimes leave their victims in a hut like this for several days while they go and collect some more and then take them all off to the slave market in one fell swoop."

"Do they leave someone with them?" asked Botolph.

"Not always. It depends how many there are in each gang. However many there were in this one there are two less now; in my view that's no bad thing but murder's still a capital offence."

The place smelt of urine and faeces. Botolph backed out saying "The fire's still hot so they can't have left long ago ..."

His words tailed off and he stumbled as his ankle twisted on a cloven rock a yard or two outside the door. He almost fell completely but at the last moment managed to regain his balance. He glanced back at the stone that had nearly been his undoing and as he turned away a flash of light made him look back again.

"Gurnard, lend me your dagger a moment will you?" He pushed the blade in at the bottom of the cleft and then flicked it upwards. The handle of a seax lifted into the light and then defiantly dropped back into the cleft again.

"Gurnard, I'll flick it and you catch it." It took two more tries before the knife finally wrested from its cheated grave. Botolph, still squatting, balanced it on his fingers and said "Luka ... what *have* you done?"

CHAPTER 5
The Barn

Every time the wagon lurched Luka used the momentum to shift his position until eventually his body was vertical and resting against the backdrop of the cart. He looked down into the big but expressionless eyes of the previous night's victim and she stared blankly up at him. He gave a ghost of a smile and after a few moments he was rewarded when she gave an even ghostlier one back. The rest of the children just stared, either too tired, too weak, too shocked, or too depressed to make any movements or noise.

He soon found out that there was another reason why they were so quiet when he leant towards the girl and said quietly "My name's Luka." There was suddenly a crack and a searing pain in his chest as One-eye flicked his whip with uncanny accuracy and issued a volley of commands of which Luka understood the gist but not the words which seemed to finish with something that sounded like "it'll be the worse for you."

Luka considered the prospect of trying one more gambit in trying to point out that he was a friend of King Dagobert and if One-eye did not release him at once it would be the worse for *him* too. The sight of the whip, now back in its holder waiting its next mission, and the language difficulty persuaded him that he should save that for later.

He started to think. There was no doubt that he was in a bit of a fix. He was not prone to dramatising a situation – indeed he had often been told that he would make a joke at his own burial. There was no denying however that one moment he had been having a pleasant ride along the river's edge with every prospect of a night of debauchery in the renowned Villa Calae, when suddenly the picture changes and now here he is, trussed up in the back of a hay cart with a load of sullen smelly children on his way to a slave-market or worse.   It needed a bit of thinking about did that.   He had to have a plan.   Escape would be a priority.   How was he going to do that though, trussed up like a chicken as he was? Not easy.

What he needed was for Botolph to come and rescue him but Botolph had no idea where he was.   He wondered if he might manage to stick his head up over the high sides of the wain as they passed through a hamlet.   He had a distinctive face.   Somebody might see him.   If Botolph *did* come looking, then he would at least know that he was following the right trail.

He started pushing against his heels and working his body up the side of the wagon to try to reach the position where his head would show over the top.   One-eye seemed to sense this however, and glancing round, he grabbed the whip and Luka felt a searing pain in his cheek as the flagellum found its mark.

He abruptly bent his knees and shrank back down, listening for evidence of the outside world.   He concluded that the track they were following was a solitary one with few areas of habitation; he would have to think of another tactic.

Luka and food were usually never parted for long but the last time he had eaten or drunk was on the ride from Lutetia when they had stopped for a rest

The cart had been on the road for several hours and his stomach was telling him that he was more likely to die from starvation than from One-eye's efforts.   The sun had been blazing but the strength had gone out of it now and he sensed the change of incline as the cart came out of the trees and gathered speed as it rolled down a hill. One-eye was continually heaving on the brake and it struck Luka too late that in such circumstances he would not be able to handle both brake and whip.

Too soon they reached the bottom of the hill and splashed through some marshy ground and, he guessed, maybe a ford before they started to climb on the other side and became surrounded by trees once more. The cart turned to the right and promptly stopped.

One-eye hitched the reins to one side, jumped down and came round to the back of the wain, pulling out the pegs as he did so. Luka knew what was going to happen and tried to adjust his position but he was not quick enough and he followed the falling backdrop and landed hard on the ground. He did not, for the life of him, feel that it was half so funny as One-eye seemed to think.

One-eye's mirth was short-lived. They were at a farm and the children followed as he dragged Luka into a barn. One-eye motioned everyone to sit down while he took hold of a long iron chain which was attached at one end to a ring high up on the wall. He threaded the chain through the children's fettered legs and then through Luka's before locking it to another ring. Going back to the doorway he shouted unintelligibly into the distance and a woman and a skinny downtrodden man with a scarred face scurried in clutching some food.

The farmer's wife looked a lot younger than her husband but had a surly appearance. They brought bread, cheese and water into the barn and portions were placed on the straw in front of each captive. Nobody spoke or moved until One-eye motioned them to eat whereupon there was a general scramble.   Luka remained motionless, half-lying, half-sitting, his wrists still pinioned behind him.   One-eye leered at him and picked up the flagon.

Luka felt a spark of hope but this was extinguished when One-eye emptied the contents over Luka's head.   He put out his tongue and tried to catch the water that was dripping off his nose;   each drop tasted like nectar.

One-eye laughed mirthlessly and turned to leave.   As he did so he heaved a kick at the young girl's thigh, shouting something unintelligible at her whilst gesturing at Luka. With that they were plunged into semi-darkness as he slammed the door.   They heard the cross-bar being dropped into place.

CHAPTER 6
The road to Meaux

Botolph fixed the seax to his horse's saddle and he and Gurnard started to walk the route marked by the tracks of the wheels. Once it became clear that there was only one way that the cart could have gone, the two horsemen stopped to make a plan.

"How about if I follow the tracks," said Botolph, "while you go back to the rendezvous point, collect the others and then come and catch up with me."

Gurnard was happy with that and wasted no time talking further. With a wave of his hand he spurred his horse southwards into the trees whilst Botolph headed north up the narrow track. He pushed his horse as fast as he dare bearing in mind the uneven surface and the fact that he did not know how much stamina the beast had nor how far he would have to ask it to go. It was over a league before he reached the crossroads where he dismounted and studied the ground trying to work out which route the cart would have taken. It looked as if they had turned to the right, besides which, he reasoned, the new road showed signs of being well-used and ran east-west and was probably therefore the road from the coast to Rome that Gurnard had mentioned earlier.

Quickly remounting he urged his horse eastwards and began calculating. How much of a lead would they have on him? He guessed that they must have left at daybreak whereas it was now coming up to noon. They would therefore have already been on the road for half a day and could now be as much as six leagues ahead of him. Assuming ... he ducked to avoid a branch ... *assuming* ... his horse stumbled ... *assuming* that they would keep going until nightfall it could be as much as twelve leagues from here to their next stop.

No sooner had he formulated these thoughts than his horse began to slow. He kicked her onwards and began calculating again. As long as he could maintain a good speed and nothing went wrong he ought to be able to catch up with them sometime in the late afternoon.

He came over a ridge and then the track started to drop down a hill. This gave his horse some relief although he realised she had already nearly had enough; pushing her too hard would defeat his purpose. The ground flattened off and he emerged from the forest into an area of wide open fields; in the distance the roofs of a village pricked at the flat horizon.

He returned to his thoughts. They might not keep going all day; he might have miscalculated; their destination may be closer; he would have to be alert to the fact that he might over-run them.

What he would do when he found them? Would there be a gang? Would Gurnard and his men have caught up with him by then? Indeed *was* Luka *in* the cart or had he been killed or taken somewhere else?

Botolph began to wonder if he had perhaps been too hasty. Maybe they should have looked more closely at the hut in the forest clearing. In Botolph's mind there was only one way of dealing with a crisis to which he saw no obvious solution.

Ignoring a voice which told him that he must keep going as fast as he could, he reined his horse to a stop and slithered to the ground. Flicking the reins over its head he tied them to a sapling; the animal immediately began to feed on the long grass.

He knelt where he was, facing to the east which was coincidentally the direction in which he believed his quarry lay. He closed his eyes, raised his clasped hands and began to pray. He pushed the sense of urgency to the back of his mind as he felt he was now in a different time scale and he did not hurry his prayers. Purposely and methodically he covered everything and everyone from his parents and siblings to his mentors and priests at Cnobersburg, Cantwarebury and Sithiu. He remembered Eadbald and Ymme and the dear Lady Eanswythe and Dagobert and Nanthild and their children. He slowly and precisely recited the Pater Noster. Only then, when he felt that he had gathered all the love, wisdom and holiness of his life-friends around him did he take a deep breath and broach the subject of Luka's disappearance. He asked for guidance, help, skill, wisdom, inspiration and for the Good Lord to keep Luka safe wherever he was and to give him courage and hope. He finished by saying the Grace and then stood and crossed himself and gazed into the distance for several long minutes.

He looked around him. The birds were singing. The horse was grazing. He was otherwise alone. Nothing had changed. He looked again at the track ahead then briskly walked to the horse, retrieved the reins, clambered onto its back and spurred it onwards again feeling re-armed and ready for whatever the good Lord might throw at him.

CHAPTER 7
Feya

As the cross-bar slammed into place Luka heard him call to the farmer. Several phrases followed and he recognised the ending of the last one "...it'll be the worse for you."

Luka smiled grimly to himself and then rocked his head sideways mimicking his captors favourite expression, "It'll be the worse for you ...!" There was initial silence and then the children giggled. The ice was broken.

Encouraged, he shuffled towards the girl, dragging the chain behind him inevitably knocking his bread out of the way. The girl had been watching him. In what he saw as a gesture of friendship she turned towards him so that the group became crescent shaped with the younger children in the middle.

"What's your name?" he ventured to the girl in English.

"Feya," she replied instantly, "what's yours?"

"Luka ... and these other children ... are they related to you?"

"Only the little one." She nodded to a blond-haired little girl in the centre who immediately cast her eyes down and concentrated on nibbling at her piece of bread, "he's my brother."

"Ah!" Luka forgave himself for his mistake on account of the long curly locks and big eyes. "How old is he?"

"Four, and his name is Cedric."

"What about the rest of you?" asked Luka, looking at the boy sitting next to Feya. There was no response. Luka had assumed, that being captives in Gallia, they were likely to be foreigners to the country and therefore, as likely as not, to be British. He had initially been relieved to find that this seemed to be the case. Now however, it began to look as if they were a mixed bag; unless the boy was deaf or dumb.

Luka, hampered by the inability to use his hands, nudged his head towards his left shoulder and said "Looka!" and then jerked his chin in the boy's direction and opened his eyes and his face expectantly hoping that this drama would convey the right message. There was an instant's reflection when it passed his mind how such contortions would have made Botolph laugh and, after a heartbeat's pause, a light dawned in the young lad's eyes and he pointed to his chest saying "Odo".

"Ahah," said Luka and decided against pushing his luck to ask his age; he looked about eight.

He moved on to the next one who was rather smaller but looked like another boy; he responded "Blado". The third, a girl of eight or nine, was called "Mata"; then a slightly shorter boy called Larten and the final boy who was sitting next to Luka and whose name was Gunder.

"Right," said Luka rehearsing it again, "Feya, Odo, Blado, Mata, Larten, Cedric and Gunder. I think I should be able to manage all that."

They had started by speaking in hushed whispers but their voices had gradually gained confidence and strength. Luka felt that he had made good progress in spite of his parched throat and empty stomach. He had just one more question for the moment and he said "Briton?" and swung his head from left to right, looking at each of the five unknowns with his 'questioning face'. They shook their heads and said something unintelligible.   He gave up and concentrated on his next objective: the crust of bread.

"Feya," he said, "if I knock my piece of bread in your direction and you move towards me as far as the chain will allow, I might be able to stretch out this end of the chain in the same way and then perhaps you would be kind enough to hold it to my mouth?"

It was not easy and the other children were squashed between them as he made desperate attempts to bite into the bread.   It was Larten who finally understood the exercise and, being in a better position than Feya, was able to help Luka to eat.   He was struggling though because the dry bread was sticking in his parched craw and he started to gulp.   Feya saw his problem and passed her own flagon to Larten who carefully dribbled it into Luka's mouth.

They all jumped guiltily at the sound of the cross-bar being lifted outside the door which was flung open to reveal the twilight.   One-eye stood there, reeling slightly, and then lurched towards Luka.   He put his face close and Luka winced at the odour of stale blood, onions and wine as he leered at him and uttered some garbled words.

He released the chain and slid it back through Luka's legs before relocking it to the wall-ring.   He then dragged Luka across to the other side of the barn and ran another chain between his arms and legs before securing it to another ring.

He stood back and surveyed his handiwork and there came more nonsensical garble.   Eight pairs of eyes watched silently as he staggered out of the door.   Luka hoped that the wine might have befuddled his brain enough for him to forget the cross-bar but his hopes were not realised.

Obviously, Luka thought to himself, One-eye was not as daft as he looked on three counts.   Firstly he had only left them alone long enough for them to eat and even if Luka had managed to get himself untied, he would still have been securely locked in the barn.   Secondly he had separated Luka a long way from the others.   Thirdly he wasn't as drunk as he had hoped he might have been.

Luka lay where he had been thrown and started to make plans about what he was going to do next.

--o--

Botolph pushed his horse as hard as he dare for the next hour but kept losing time by having to ask everyone he met whether they had seen any signs of a cart full of slaves. From his first enquiries he discovered that he was heading towards the city of Meaux. Many carts passed up and down that road and although many had been seen, nobody remembered seeing one full of slaves.

Half a league later a horseman riding in the opposite direction replied that he had recently passed a high-sided haywain that he had noticed was full of children.   With increased optimism Botolph spurred his horse round the next bend and up the hill.   On reaching the crest he could see a cart half a league ahead of him.   There was only one driver and the horse was keeping up a good pace.

Botolph hurtled down the hill in hot pursuit.

--o--

Gurnard regrouped with the other six guards and, after relating what he and Botolph had found, led them back through the forest to the clearing. Here they spread out and searched to see if they could find any other clues of relevance.   Once he was satisfied that they had missed nothing, they remounted and took the track to the north finally emerging on the Meaux road.

Like Botolph before him, Gurnard kept stopping to ask other travellers for news of the road ahead, and in particular if there had been sight of a fast-riding monk on horseback - but many of the travellers were struck dumb by the impressive picture of the squad of six mounted guards, led by the old warrior and merely shook their heads.

CHAPTER 8
Botolph in Meaux

Botolph's horse had warmed to the occasion and they drew up alongside the cart in a cloud of dust. The driver turned with a startled expression. The would-be monk was suddenly lost for words when he glanced into the wagon and saw it contained nothing but four piglets.

He hesitated – searching for words but no inspiration came, so he waved a salute and spurred his horse onwards. Mid-afternoon came and went by which time he had inspected several more wagons but none of them held anything of interest and before long he found himself at the foot of a bridge that led to the gates of a city which he guessed was Meaux. Reigning his horse to a standstill he gathered his thoughts while he took stock of the scene.

He noted how the river did a tight loop - virtually encircling the city leaving it as an island in the centre. Access was via the bridge which was full of horses, wagons, ox-carts and pedestrians flowing back and forth across it.

"Oh well, here we go," he said to himself reluctantly and muttering a short supplication for the Lord's aid he clicked his teeth and dug his heels into his mount's flank. As the beast's hooves crushed the fresh dung left by the animals preceding it the not-unpleasant cattle smell drifted into Botolph's nostrils helping to neutralise the other less pleasant odours that rose from the waters beneath.

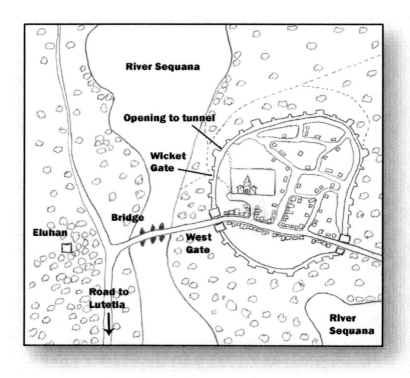

Fig. 2. The City of Meaux

As he passed between the city gates the grey stone walls closed in on him and he called to one of the watchmen, "I'm looking for a cart carrying some slaves.   Have you seen them?"

The gate-keeper was hot and tired and had been on duty all day and all he wanted was to go home, so he was disinclined to say anything that might impede his departure.

"We get loads of slave carts everyday passing through on their way to Remi.   There've been several through this afternoon.   Go and ask at the abbey," and he turned away.

"Where's the abbey?" called Botolph to his back.

Irritated he turned round again "Eh?"

"Where's the abbey?"

"Up the road and first on the left."

Botolph wanted to ask him if he knew of anywhere that he could stay for the night but decided against it.

He soon found the abbey, outside which stood a thin fresh-faced monk with his hands on his hips; Botolph noted the unusual pose. The strange figure at least represented someone to whom he could direct his questions; he slipped down from the saddle.

"Welcome brother," said the monk in a high-pitched voice, his hairless nostrils flaring as he spoke. "Whither are ye bound?"

"Well," said Botolph, "I'm not really bound anywhere at the moment.   I am looking for a consignment of slaves."

"Oh aren't we all?," said the monk rolling his eyes. "And what do you want me to do about it?"

"Well I wondered if you might have seen any," replied Botolph obviously.

The monk sighed and rubbed his right hand around one of his generous ears. "Lots of slaves have come in today. At the moment they're being fed. They'll sleep in the crypt tonight. What are you looking for - a man or a woman? If you're offering a good price you might get one today, - otherwise they'll be off to Remi in the morning. You can come and have a look if you like."

"I'm not here to buy," said Botolph, horrified, "I'm looking for a brother monk who's missing. There's a suggestion that he might have been captured."

"Oh poor thing," said the strange monk. "Was he taken in battle and sold on? Once he has been bought you know it'll be very difficult for him to get his freedom back."

A moment of panic hit Botolph. "No, he wasn't taken in battle. He is a novice monk like me and we're friends of King Dagobert. He's just vanished!"

"Oooh! Friends of King Dagobert eh! Just hark at you! What's he like, this friend of yours. Is he big and strong like you are?" The monk sidled up to Botolph and prodded one of his biceps.

"Well - no he's rather short actually, - about yea high – but he *is very* strong."

"Oooh!" said the monk again. "I like strong monks. Is he a dwarf?"

"No he's not," said Botolph bristling, "He's just unusually short."

"He'll fetch a good price then."

"What?"

"He'll fetch a good price! Unusually short people are very popular in Rome just now. The boys there are always looking for something different."

"Now look ..." said Botolph, tiring of the conversation, "he's *not* going to be sold as a slave. He's been

45

captured illegally and his destiny is to be trained as a monk in Abbess Fara's abbey at Evoriacum."

"Oh, Abbess Fara ... why didn't you say so before?"

"Well does that help?" said Botolph.

"Well it helps me young man 'cos the name of Abbess Fara's not welcome here so I am afraid I can't talk to you anymore. God be w'ye!" and with a false smile and a nod of the head he backed inside the abbey door and tried to slam it shut but Botolph quickly put his foot into the gap.

"Why not?"

"Get off! How dare you push on this door? Leave at once!"

"Why not?" he insisted. "What's the problem with Abbess Fara?"

"You'll find out soon enough and I'm not going to be the one to tell you so take your foot out of the door!"

With that he turned and stamped his heel on Botolph's foot which was already becoming painful as the door crushed it against the jamb. The extra pain made Botolph wrench it free of the gap and grabbing the foot in both hands, he hopped around in a circle of agony as the heavy oak door crashed shut behind him.

CHAPTER 9
Escape

Luka lay thinking and tried to pull his wrists from the ropes that bound them behind his back. His skin was already chafed and pulling against his bonds achieved nothing but make the pain worse.

"Feya!" he whispered.

"Yes?"

"I need something sharp." Silence. "Do you have anything?"

"I'll look."

He could hear the straw rustling as she cast around herself in the darkness.

"There's nothing."

He heard something fall as she continued to search.

"Ah. Just a moment," came her voice.

"What have you got?"

"The flagon." He heard a sharp crack as she smashed it.

"How did you do that?"

"On the chain."

"Oh, good girl. Find a nice sharp piece and then throw it across."

He heard a soft sound as it landed in the straw nearby and he squirmed over to get to it. Using his heels he kicked it behind him and then shuffled back closer until he could reach it with his right hand. He dug it out of the straw where it was threatening to bury itself.

His wrists were crossed but he found he could hold the shard in one hand while he rubbed it on the rope; it did not seem to be making much impression. He reversed until his back was against the wall of the barn and then started to slide along sideways feeling the wooden base of the wall until he found what he was searching for; a groove in which to hold the shard steady. He pushed the broken fragment into place and backed up to it again and began to rhythmically slide the cord up and down. He felt the fibres beginning to part but cursed suddenly as the piece of earthenware fell out of its slot.

He tried again, now stretching at his wrists to keep the rope taut. His hands started to come free and at last he managed to pull a wrist out. He lost no time in flicking the rope off the other wrist as he brought it round in front of him and rubbed life back into them both. Retrieving the faithful chard he set to work on the rope that bound his ankles. Sadly its edges had become dulled by use and he made slow progress. The action was warming his hands though and the numbness had now left his fingers. Although he was unable to see anything, he managed to feel his way around the knots and he gradually unravelled the bonds. On the principle of retaining anything that might be of use he coiled the rope loosely and tucked it into his belt.

Relishing at least *temporary* freedom he stood and stretched. The next question was how was he going to get out of the door. He felt his way across to it and then all around the frame but there seemed to be no possibility of getting through it. There had to be another way. He wished it were not so dark so that he might see better. His hand found the chain that linked the children together. He knew that one end was locked but this other end just vanished somewhere under the eaves. It was too high for him to see, let alone release.

He changed his tactics and headed towards the left side of the door, feeling his way around the walls in order to see if he could find some inanimate allies. On the way he came across two pieces of timber which he dragged back to the doorway. One, he estimated, was about Botolph's height and the other was a couple of feet longer.   Without any particular plan in mind he placed the longer one at an angle to the wall and just below the origin of the chain. He looked up into the darkness and pushed against the beam giving a satisfied grunt.   Warming to the germ of his new idea he positioned the shorter one a foot or so away from the first at a similar angle.

"Feya," he hissed.   "I'm going to need your help to get onto that beam.   I want you to lean against it making your hands into a cradle, so that I can stand in there and then on your shoulder. Alright?"

They tried that but short as he was, Luka was too heavy for the girl's hands, so he got her to brace herself in such a way that he stood on her knees and then her shoulder. She had to bite her lip to stop herself screaming out with the pain of his weight on her thigh. For his part he was holding onto the chain which was cutting into his hand as he was trying to pull himself upwards. To Feya's relief his weight came off her thigh but she nearly screamed anew as his right foot crushed her shoulder.   With a superhuman effort he pulled on the chain with his free hand and managed to get his right foot onto the top of the short piece of timber. He rested there for a moment and heard Feya wisely move away from being directly beneath him.

He squinted into the darkness.   He could see now that the chain was hooked over an iron spike just under the eaves.   If he were able to stand on top of the long beam he should just be able to get to it.   The problem was that he needed the chain for support and he could not hold onto the chain at the same time as taking it off the spike.

There was nothing for it, - he was going to have to go up to the next level.   He heaved on the chain pushing off with his right foot, and after swinging wildly sideways, managed to stabilise himself again before hauling himself up to the top of the longer beam.   He was now well within reach of the spike.

"Right," he muttered, taking his recent bondage out of his belt and talking to it, "you can do something more useful now."

He had a sudden vision of Torrel at Cnobersburg and his training in the art of knots and splicing and, in a most un-Luka like way, he instinctively fired off a prayer of thanks. "I must be going soft" he thought as he managed with his left hand to knot the rope on the spike under the chain.

His right arm was tiring but he laid the rope loosely on his shoulder before passing his left hand under his right armpit and taking two turns under the chain but round the spike.   He pulled the rope tighter and leant backwards to test it.   It held.   He was now lashed to the spike and could let go the chain.

"Now!" he said to himself.   He knew what was coming.   The chain was a heavy one and there was a dead weight of about twelve cubits of it.   He would have to lift it up a hands breadth before it would be free of the spike.   Not only that but as he lifted it, the spike and the rope would be taking the combined weight of his body and the chain and there was a good chance he was going to make an unplanned-for and undignified descent.

He grasped the top two chain links with both hands, took a deep breath and heaved.

CHAPTER 10
Gurnard arrives at Meaux

Botolph could not believe the monk's rudeness. He had never met the like before. What sort of place *was* this?

He looked up at the black buildings and felt his goose bumps rise as a blanket of evil seemed to fall on top of him. A huge shiver twisted his body and he wondered whether he should cross back over the bridge to escape the aura. The sun was already dropping towards the horizon though, - so going back to Villa Calae was not an option. He assumed that Gurnard and his party would arrive shortly; they were all going to need somewhere to stay for the night.

Overcoming his apprehension he made his way back to the west gate and approached the watchman who had just relieved his grumpy partner. With some trepidation Botolph asked for a recommendation of lodgings adding that he was expecting the imminent arrival of seven horsemen.

To his great relief the new fellow was as helpful as could be but recommended that he tried the abbey.

"Whoa now," said Botolph, "I have already tried that and had the door slammed in my face."

"Oh?" said the Watchman, "I *am* surprised. The monks are normally only too keen to have visitors as it helps them swell their coffers for no expenditure at all. "Who did you see?"

"No idea what his name was," replied Botolph. "Thin pasty-faced fellow with a high-pitched voice."

"Haha, Brother Fauve," said the watchman. "He's a law unto himself. Sharp as a dagger and will stab you in the back with it if he has a mind to. Be very careful if you've upset him. He is as vicious as a hill cat."

"Thanks for the warning," said Botolph "I'll bear it in mind. Now about these lodgings; where else could we go?"

"Well I don't know where else to suggest for so many. You could split up I suppose. There are several alehouses in the city that could take a couple each."

"Alright, thanks," said Botolph and turned his horse to explore the city. He rode up to the church which seemed to be on the highest point. On his way he passed some shops and a busy alehouse which had attracted its customers by planting a pole outside the door tied to which was the traditional green bush to show that a new brew was ready.

He also found the farrier and handed over his horse for the farrier's lad to give it a good rub down and temporary stabling. He had no money with him but guessed that Gurnard would take care of that when he arrived. All the time as he walked he was hoping that Luka would suddenly appear around a corner; sadly that did not happen. He went back to the alehouse where he searched out the Mistress and related the story of his dilemma concerning Luka and the fact that they would need eight beds for the night.

The Mistress seemed quite relaxed about his questions until he mentioned slaves and King Dagobert whereupon she started to look distinctly nervous and then suddenly clammed up.

Thwarted, he made his way back to the West Gate where he arrived just as the last of the sun dipped behind the trees. It was a warm evening and he settled himself down on the grass inside the city wall against which he rested his back; he closed his eyes.

It seemed only moments before his shoulder was being shaken and he looked up into the face of one of Dagobert's guards behind whom stood seven steaming horses and six riders. He jumped to his feet and took the head of Gurnard's horse.

"Any luck?"

"No, none at all. Plenty of traffic including carts but not a sign of one containing slaves. How about you?"

"No. Nothing. What are we going to do Gurnard?"

"Well we'll have to stay here the night and certainly we must return to Villa Calae in the morning. The cart may have stopped off at another staging post in which case we might meet them coming the other way tomorrow."

"There's something else," said Botolph. "I get a strange feeling about this place. I have met some very odd people and they seem to be ... to be ... well ... nervous"

"Nervous? How do you mean?"

"Difficult to explain," said Botolph, "you'll have to see for yourself, but I went to the abbey where I met a young monk. He was initially pleasant enough but as soon as I mentioned Abbess Fara his attitude changed and he ended up slamming the abbey door in my face."

"Hmm," said Gurnard, "well you're right, we'd better go and see for ourselves."

"I found the farrier's," continued Botolph. "Do you want to place your horses there while we go to the abbey?"

"Well no not really. We should be able to find stabling at the abbey which'll be free of charge."

"Ah. I left mine at the farriers and he'll need paying."

"Not if you go and collect him now, he won't. I doubt they've done anything more than rub him down and they won't mind doing that for free for a penniless monk."

When they arrived at the abbey door it was still firmly closed. Gurnard rapped hard on it and it slowly creaked opened to reveal an elderly monk. Gurnard asked to see the Abbot. The six guards waited outside while the monk led Gurnard and Botolph along some corridors and up some stairs to a wooden door upon which he knocked once.

"Venite!"

The monk opened the door which gave onto a small room and a large desk behind which sat a portly monk with greying crinkly hair which matched his grey habit. He put down the quill he had been holding and rose. There was a palpable silence as he tilted his head back. Cold blue eyes looked down the length of his nose as he examined each of them with an unsmiling stare. Botolph felt that he had been waiting for them.

"Good evening brothers," he said finally, with a curl to his lip that had the effect of turning his words into a snarl," and what can the *humble* monastery of Meaux do for you today?"

--o--

At the first pull, Luka could not quite manage to get the weight of the chain over the spike, so he let it slip back and took four or five deep breaths before he steeled himself and heaved again. This time he was successful and there was a satisfying clatter as the heavy links met each other on the straw.

Luka was about to release the slip knot and start his own descent to the ground when he felt a draft of night air brush his face. The draft was coming through a gap under the thatch. He inched along towards it. There was just enough room for him to get his body into the space but he was unable to turn himself so that his legs went over first There was no alternative but to crawl over head down. He readjusted the rope that he had hooked over the spike, making it into a stirrup which he then used to push himself upwards. A portion of thatch obligingly gave way and he felt himself emerge into the fresh black air. He took a deep breath of triumph before he addressed the other minor problem: he was hanging head down. He reflected that from this position, if he was going to escape he either had to perform a somersault in mid-air with the hope of landing on his feet, or just drop with the risk of landing on his head and killing himself.

Moving his right arm sideways he felt under the eaves past the roof truss and hooked his arm into the next gap on the top of the wall. He wriggled his legs up and over the top whereupon he was at least now the right way up even if he was perched somewhat precariously. By pushing with his feet he gained a purchase with his left arm too and paused to take a few more breaths.

"Good job I'm small," he thought. "Botolph would never have had a hope in hell of getting through that."

He looked down. As far as he could see the ground below him was clear of obstacles.

"Oh well, here goes," he thought and pushed himself away from the wall and poised his feet for a hard landing.

His landing, on the contrary, was soft but very smelly. He had landed in a manure heap and compounded the felony by rolling over in it.

"Shit!" he said appropriately.

He lay still for a moment, looking and listening for signs that he might have been heard but there were none. He shuffled backwards out of the messy dung heap and went across to the barn where he silently lifted the cross bar out of its crutches and eased open the door.

The ever-resourceful Feya had already taken the initiative and unthreaded the newly-released chain from between children's legs. The ironworks on their legs clinked alarmingly as they shuffled into the open. Luka scratched his head. How was he going to have any hope of getting these children to safety when the fetters hardly allowed them to walk, let alone to run?

CHAPTER 11
Fauve and the archdeacon

"Good Evening, Bishop," began Botolph, only to be interrupted almost before he had started.

"Forgive me young man, but I am not the bishop. I am the Oculus Episcopi," he said intimidatingly. "My name is Archdeacon Gaubert."

"I beg your pardon archdeacon," said Botolph refusing to be intimidated. "I've never heard that title before, - you are the ... *Bishop's Eye*?"

"Indeed I am," replied the archdeacon. "I am charged with observing everything that goes on and reporting it to the Bishop. Now what can I do for you?"

He placed his hands on the desk, sat back in his chair and looked down his aquiline nose with obvious distaste. The large gold-set ruby ring on the little finger of his left hand matched the colour of his cheeks which were criss-crossed with red veins as was his nose which also had a bluish tinge. He had a large black mole in an unfortunate position above his upper lip but immediately beneath his left nostril. At first Botolph did not realise that it was a mole but thought it was something nasty that had recently escaped from his cruel nose.

In fact he was unable to tear his gaze away from it. He wished the man would use his sleeve to brush the thing away. He wondered if he should lean across and do it himself. The archdeacon suddenly seemed to become aware of the focus of Botolph's attention; the situation was clearly not new to him. He leant forwards, looked Botolph straight in the eye and flamboyantly brushed his sleeve across his face.

The mole remained as did the triumphant sneer on the archdeacon's face as he leant back in his chair. Botolph flushed in embarrassment and tried to collect his thoughts.

His memory was fresh from the unnerving experience that had befallen him when mentioning the name of Abbess Fara earlier. He decided to avoid a repeat performance so started with the subject of the king.

"For the past three months, my friend Luka and I have been guests of King Dagobert in Lutetia. He sent us to Villa Calae in company with two bodyguards to ensure our safe passage."

Botolph paused for breath, wondering how he should formulate the next part of the tale. The archdeacon interrupted again however.

"I take it that this is Luka," he said, indicating Gurnard.

"No, Father, this is Gurnard, Keeper of the King's Horse at Villa Calae. He and four Calae guards have been helping me search for Luka who has ... er ... got lost."

"Lost?" the archdeacon raised his eyebrows while giving Botolph a penetrating stare. "Perhaps you had better tell me the whole story."

At this point Botolph rather hoped that the archdeacon might suggest that they should all sit down. Their discomfiture, however, seemed to be the Archdeacon's primary aim, so Botolph began his tale.

"Luka became separated from us yesterday as we rode along the river bank. He went on ahead and ... well that's the last we saw of him. We sent a search party out last night and found his horse tied to a tree in the forest but no other sign of him so we tried again at first light this morning."

"Go on."

"Well there were eight of us searching and we seemed to be making no progress at all until Gurnard and I came across a small clearing in the forest where there was a hut served by a narrow track along which a cart had obviously recently passed."

Botolph paused and there was a silence.

"Was that all you found?"

"Er, no. We found two dead men. Gurnard said that the hut, in his view, looked as it had been used as a staging post or trading post for slaves."

"So what did you make of that then as far as your friend Luka was concerned?"

"Well, we didn't know what to make of it really. Gurnard said that there is a fashion now for taking children as slaves and if Luka ..."

"There is nothing illegal or unusual about trading in children," the archdeacon snapped. His face had suddenly flushed red. "Any children that are captured in battle are quite legitimate targets for the slave-traders and always have been. How do you think the country would survive if there was not a steady supply of slaves?"

Botolph was taken aback by the archdeacon's outburst. The subject was obviously a touchy one as far as he was concerned. Botolph decided that the less he said the better so he remained silent.

The silence hung above them until the fire began to leave Gaubert's cheeks whereupon he prompted further conversation.

"So what do you think this had to do with your friend Luka?"

"I really don't know," said Botolph noncommittally. "All I know is that there were two dead bodies, an empty shed containing the warm embers of a fire, signs that a cart had driven away recently and no Luka."

"And what do you expect *me* to do about it?" glowered the cleric rising to the attack again and echoing the other monk's question earlier in the day.

Botolph was beginning to dislike this man intensely. He knew it was a sin but he could not help it, and he an archdeacon too!

Botolph answered crisply, "We need somewhere to sleep tonight and somewhere to stable our horses. If you have sight or sound of my brother Luka, I would be grateful if you would send word to Villa Calae."

"Well," the archdeacon countered smoothly, - with a trace of a leerish curl to his lip, "you and your men are welcome to bed down in the crypt and your horses may stay in our stables. I will tell you this though ..."

"Yes?" said Botolph.

"If it transpires that your friend Luka killed those men and they are shown to be legitimate slave-traders ..."

"Yes?"

"It is very likely that he has already been arrested and is on his way here for trial on a charge of murder whereupon we shall almost certainly hang him. So I would not waste too much of your time by looking for him." He walked over to the door and gestured them out. "Good Night."

--o--

"Wait!" whispered Luka and disappeared back towards the barn. He worked his way round some other outbuildings and a few minutes later came back triumphantly clutching an axe which he had found in a woodshed. It was a starry night but there was no moon. Luka could not make up his mind whether this was good or bad. He considered the prospect of trying to reunite the horse with the cart but decided that would be noisy and would take too long and increase the risk of discovery.

The door of the barn gave an alarming creak as he pushed it closed. He glanced nervously around as he quietly dropped the cross-bar into place.

"C'mon," he said and started to lead the way up the track but as he glanced back he saw how painfully his group was shuffling after him. It was going to take forever just to get back to the road. He had a dilemma. He had realised from the start that one of his first priorities would be the removal of the children's fetters and it was for this reason that he had searched out the axe. He was going to need a rock or some hard wood to use as a base; he also needed enough daylight to see clearly what he was doing.

He decided it would have to be done in three stages. First he would get them far enough away from the farm to be able to make a little noise in safety. Secondly it would be quicker and perhaps safer just to break each chain so that the children could take longer strides and the whole party could move further away more quickly. Thirdly, when he had daylight, time, a decent rock and some solitude, he could spend time removing the fetters completely.

He reckoned it was about halfway between midnight and daybreak so they had quite a while in which to find some cover, but it was going to take an hour or so of that time to split off the chains. He groaned. It seemed hopeless. "Help me God," he said and went back to Feya who was carrying Cedric and leading the rest of the children.

"Keep following the track," he said. "It leads up and round to the right. Wait for me at the corner."

He ran up the path into the wood and then turned right up towards the road. "This isn't going to do any good," he thought to himself. "That is the way they would expect us to go. He ran back to the corner. He could see the children fifty yards or so away so turned to his right stumbling across the edge of the path and into the wood. He did his best not to cause too much damage to the vegetation and thereby leave a track. It seemed to him that this was the better way to go. He returned to the path, and found the children were just arriving. He took Cedric from Feya and placed him on his shoulders and held out his hand for Feya to take. She in her turn took the hand of Mata and all the children linked up in the same way and they started an agonisingly slow trip between the tree trunks. Luka was aware that for anyone with even a minimum of tracking skills, they were leaving a clumsy trail, but there seemed to be no alternative.

--o--

One-eye was also up-and-about early that morning in spite of a severe headache caused by the excessive number of times he had lifted a flagon to his lips.

For this reason his senses were even blunter than usual when his one good eye cast its glance at the cross-bar on the barn door. If he had been a little more alert, he might have looked up and seen where the thatch had been lifted on the eaves, but he did not. He foisted his old mare out of her stable, slung himself over her back and trotted briskly up the path and onto the road to Meaux.

It was only a short ride and he went straight to the archdeacon to discover what he wanted him to do about the murdering dwarf.   After listening to his story, Gaubert hurried him down to the crypt where they found that they had just missed the departure of his eight guests.   They caught up with them in the stables however and Gaubert introduced One-eye to Botolph and asked One-eye to repeat his story which, being a man of few words, he did very succinctly.

Gurnard translated his words for Botolph's benefit and he gave a grim nod of comprehension.

Botolph did not like the archdeacon and he liked One-eye even less.   At least he now knew what had happened to Luka and that came as a blessed relief.

"*How* many slaves did you say?" asked Botolph.

"Seven," replied One-eye - sulky at being interrogated by a boy-monk.

"Seven!" repeated Botolph with foreboding.   "And what sort of ages would they be, pray?"

"Well then, there was one older girl and six little ones."

"God Almighty!" expostulated Botolph swinging round to the archdeacon, "and you condone this sort of thing?"

The archdeacon stretched himself to his full height, which was still a foot or more shorter than Botolph, but he still managed to tilt back his head and look disdainfully down his nose while saying silkily,

"Slavery, my dear young man, as I have said before, is a fact of life.   Children might just as well get used to the idea early.   Come, let's go and inspect this consignment and I shall be able to cast my eyes over your double-murderer friend.   We'll take the Constable along with us for good measure and bring them all back to the abbey. I suggest you saddle up your horses and wait for me at the West Gate."

CHAPTER 12
Removing the fetter chains

Luka's intention was to keep going in a straight line and put as much distance as possible between himself and the farmhouse before he started his attack upon the fetter chains. They crossed the top of a gulley and the ground started to slope downwards. Luka stumbled on a rock and the extra weight of Cedric on his shoulders nearly made him lose his balance. Regaining his equilibrium he hefted Cedric to the ground and went back to look at the rock; he could hardly make out its dusky outlines. He ran his hands over the hollowed top and decided it was just what he needed.

He asked Feya to sit down with one foot on each side of the rock and arranged the chain so that it stretched over the centre. "Close your eyes," he ordered, partly to quell her fear and partly in case chips flew up from the rock. It wouldn't do, he thought cryptically, to add blindness to his group's handicaps. He swung the axe and it hit the chain with a resounding thwack. He felt the chain; it was grooved but not broken. He set it in place again. "Close your eyes". Thwack!

Curse it! He had missed the target and now there was a second groove further along the chain. He turned the chain over and hit it on the opposite side. Still no success. He lined up the axe again and hit the chain rather harder. The rock itself broke this time leaving a small indentation into which the link fitted more snugly. Luka could see the link better now too. He took a harder swing. The link still did not break but, looking closely at it, he could see that the metal was significantly thinner. He pulled the link across a groove in the rock and tapped it smartly in the middle with the axe. The link bent. He turned it over and tapped it again. It broke! He was jubilant and so was Feya. Luka was also pleased that the work had not seemed too noisy.

He worked away on the fetter chains of the other six children and success seemed to come more quickly each time. He considered carrying the project on further and perhaps removing the ankle irons too but decided against being too greedy of his success. He hoisted Cedric back onto his shoulders. It was easier this time because the young boy could now splay his feet more widely. They set off and made good progress following the line of the gully.

In spite of their freer movements the children were tiring quickly, partly from lack of sleep and partly because they had to move their limbs awkwardly in order to avoid the leg-irons crashing into each another; for them it was painful progress.

As soon as he saw the first glimmer of daylight, Luka sat them down to wait while he dropped into the gulley to explore it. At the bottom was a small stream which was overgrown with brambles. He used the axe to chop these back and then bent down and scooped the cool clear nectar into this mouth. It tasted better than the best mead! He followed the stream downwards for half a mile and then crossed it and came back on the other side. He thought he saw what he was looking for and climbed a steep part out onto the exposed roots of a large oak tree. Working his way around the trunk he jumped down on the other side where the roots had clearly originally extended over the ground but where the winter rains had washed the soil out leaving a curtain canopy.

He reckoned that the cave-like niche behind it would give adequate protection for the children. It had the extra advantage of offering a good view across the stream which would give them plenty of warning should searchers come from the same direction as they had. A party approaching from the east would be a different matter though and Luka resolved to explore in that direction at his first possible opportunity. There were other priorities at the moment however; he must, as quickly as possible, get the group under shelter, start removing their leg-irons and find some food.

--o--

The archdeacon looked somewhat incongruous on his horse but he seemed to be an able rider. The constable was a gruff looking man, dressed in black with a large well-trimmed and impressive beard.

Their party seemed to be forever growing as One-eye and the archdeacon led the way out of the gate closely followed by the Constable, then Botolph and Gurnard with the six guards behind them.

They broke into a fast trot and commandeered the road scattering everything before them. It seemed no time at all before One-eye led them down the side track into the woods and round the bend until the party came to rest by the dung heap.

The archdeacon called one of the guards over to hold their horses whilst he, One-eye and the Constable headed over to the barn. One-eye lifted off the cross-bar and triumphantly threw open the door.

Disbelief showed on his face and he rushed inside and searched all four corners before he was able to accept that his captives had gone. He picked up the loose end of the chain and stared at it incredulously.

"Well," said the archdeacon, walking across to Botolph where he still sat on his horse. "Your friend Luka seems to have even more crimes to add to his record now. He would appear to have stolen seven slaves."

"Well you can't hang him twice," retorted Botolph irreverently. "C'mon Gurnard, we'll get back to Villa Calae."

"Wait!" said the archdeacon. "I demand that you and your six guards come with us to search for the fugitives."

"I don't think so," said Botolph.

"You have no choice. I demand it in the name of Bishop Faro in whose diocese you stand."

"I don't think so," repeated Botolph. "C'mon Gurnard, let's go."

"I warn you," screamed the archdeacon. "You will live to regret this."

Botolph did not stay to argue the point but dug his heels into the horse's flank and took off down the track, hoping that Gurnard and the six guards would follow him. He was relieved to hear the sound of their horses behind. As they turned the corner, leaving a seething archdeacon with his two companions staring into the empty barn, Botolph noticed, at the edge of the path, that there was some flattened vegetation leading into a wood.

--o--

Botolph kept silent, riding alongside Gurnard as they took the road back. When they reached the crossroads it was time for Dagobert's guards to take their leave and head

69

straight on to Lutetia. Botolph thanked them for their support and they asked what they should tell the king about Luka.

"I am afraid you'll just have to tell him the truth," said Botolph. "He'll hear soon enough anyway. I'll send a message to Eligius as soon as I know what's happening. Thanks again. God be wi'ye."

The guards carried on down the road while Botolph's party turned left, arriving at the stables in the early afternoon. In the time since they had left the villa, Gurnard and Botolph's friendship had blossomed and the older man kept close to him after they slid from their horses.

"What are you going to do now?" he whispered. "Is there any way I can help?"

Botolph had been pondering his next move all the way back from the barn. His silence had been filled with a mixture of prayers and planning and he had been grateful that Gurnard had seemed to understand and kept his silence too. Little did he realise that the old warrior had been doing his own planning.

"We need to talk," said Botolph. "Let's walk round the paddock where we can't be overheard."

As Gurnard closed the paddock gate he said, "What's to be done then?".

"I need someone discreet who's a skilled tracker. I know where Luka is. He's in that wood somewhere but he'll have gone to ground and I'd have no chance of finding him without shouting and calling and that would draw unwelcome attention.

I need someone who is used to hunting the king's stags. I don't care whether he is one of the king's men or a poacher as long as he knows his job. But I need him *now*."

"Now?" said Gurnard. "You're not thinking of going back this afternoon are you?"

"Well I would," said Botolph, "but by the time we get there it will be too dark even for a skilled man to find enough clues to make sense of. No, I want to leave at midnight so that we arrive at the barn at first light before anyone's about. Our man will then be able to start tracking from where they entered the wood. Did you mark the point?"

"Aye, I did," said Gurnard. "It was all too obvious. I felt like going back and trying to cover it up."

"Well if we both saw it, there is no doubt that our evil archdeacon will have seen it too and you can wager your life that if it's not happened today, there will be a search party on Luka's tail tomorrow. That's why I want to get there before they do. For one thing we'll be able to find Luka and give him his seax and some food, and for another we'll be able to lay a false trail to give him more time to get away."

"You're sure he is going to have to get away then? You don't think the best thing would be to try to get King Dagobert to arrange a pardon for him?"

"I think our ignoble archdeacon would hang him first and worry about the consequences afterwards. I gained the impression that there's more to this slave-trading than meets the eye. I think the archdeacon and probably Bishop Faro somehow have a vested interest in it. The archdeacon was more furious than one would normally expect unless he had some personal involvement. I suspect that, somehow, Luka's actions will result in him losing money. That's how I read it anyway."

"Yes, I think you're right," said Gurnard. "Right, I know just the man for you but you'll have to be discreet too. This man has no love either for King Dagobert or for Bishop Faro and his cronies; in fact he hates them both with equal venom so it's going to be better not to mention that you are the king's friend. You're also going to need some money as his services won't come cheaply."

"Ah!" said Botolph, suddenly deflated. "That was one thing I hadn't thought of ..."

CHAPTER 13
The Cave

Luka went back and collected his little band and, this time trying not to leave so obvious a trail, took the group down to the stream where they had their fill of the cool refreshing water. They then climbed back into the wood and around the oak tree and into what they came to call the "Cave".

"I'm hungry," said Cedric and Luka looked at him helplessly.

"I'm afraid you're going to have to *stay* hungry for a little while," he said. "I don't know what I am going to be able to do about that."

Cedric started to cry.

"Don't worry," said Luka hastily, "I'll think of something. Now the first thing I need to do is to get these leg-irons off. C'mon Odo, I'll start with you. Feya, you keep the children quiet and tucked into the back of the cave. On second thoughts, while I am doing this, perhaps if Mata stays with Cedric, you, Blado, Larten and Gunder could start to collect some greenery to disguise the opening of the cave. But you will have to collect it carefully without making any obvious disturbance or that alone will show that someone's been here. Do you understand?"

Feya nodded and Luka led Odo back into the wood searching for a suitable rock upon which to work. Being unsuccessful he returned to the gulley and climbed further up towards its head until he found what he was looking for. This left him rather more exposed than he would have liked but there was nothing for it as this seemed to be the spot that God had chosen for him.

"God," he thought, "God!" He had hardly thought about God since they left Lutetia. He knew that Botolph would be constantly chatting away with Him, asking Him this and thanking Him for that but Luka excused himself with the fact that he really had been just too busy. Here he was though, on his way to becoming a novice monk and yet slave-children were now featuring more in his life than God was.

He motioned Odo to stand by the side of the rock whereupon he twisted the leg-iron round so that the flanges rested on the rock's surface. He placed the axe between the two flanges so that it rested on the rivet. He turned and picked up a heavy stone which he had laid nearby. This would serve as a hammer. He prepared to strike the top of the axe with it. Odo's eyes opened wide in fright.

"Don't worry," said Luka "this won't hurt ... " - and then as a silent mutter to himself ... "at least it won't hurt *me!*"

He was trying to behave in a matter-of-fact way when underneath he was full of foreboding knowing that he was about to undertake a procedure at which he was completely unskilled, on a child who had suddenly become his responsibility.

He withdrew the axe, set down the stone and pointed to the ground gesturing Odo to kneel, which he did. Luka knelt beside him, grabbed the boy's hands and placed them together in an act of supplication. He wagged his index finger at him admonishing him to stay still and then used the same index finger to point skywards. Odo was a bit mystified by all this but tilted his head in the requisite direction.   Luka placed his own hands together and, also looking upwards, prayed:

"Jesus, God, - whoever You are and wherever you are - we're in a bit of a fix and would very much like your help. Please show me how to get these bl ... , these ... these leg-irons off without crippling anyone and then show me where to get some food and ... and then help us get out of this mess. And, ... er, we ask this in and through the name of your Son-Jesus-Christ-Amen."

Odo was still stricken looking silently skywards so Luka poked him and said expectantly, "Amen ... Amen."

"Amen amen," said the child and Luka said "No, not Amen amen, just ... oh never mind, stand up again!"

They reverted to their original positions and, showing more confidence than he felt, Luka struck the top of the axe with the stone.   Nothing much seemed to happen other than the fact that there was a shiny point on the surface of the rivet but it had not snapped in half as Luka had so fervently hoped.   He tried again with the same result.

"Either the prayers weren't strong enough or I'm not good enough," he thought, replacing the axe for the third attempt.   This time the rivet seemed to bend slightly and thus encouraged he tried again.   Suddenly there was a pinging sound and the top half of the flange flipped off the head of the rivet.

Luka then realised that by forcing the blade between the end of the chain and the flange, he had been stretching the rivet against the other flange and the head of the rivet which had been peened over had now become un-peened and had slotted back through the flange.

He looked skywards, "Thanks!" he said grimly.

He could now pull on the flange and open the gap wide enough for Odo to pull his foot through.   He rewarded

Luka with a wide grin and then to Luka's consternation he threw his arms around his neck. Luka was quite overcome and reflected "What have I done to deserve this? Here I am in the middle of a foreign country, leagues from home, with an eight-year-old lad who speaks no English, cutting leg-irons off!"

He shook his head. "C'mon," he said, "let's have the other leg." This time Luka concentrated on what was happening to the rivet head as he forced the blade inside the flange and he soon saw the quickest and most efficient way to work. The second iron was off in no time. Laying the axe and his hammer-stone by the side of the rock, he stood up and took Odo's hand and led him back to the cave.

Feya looked up as they approached and waited while he inspected the progress they had made with the camouflage. He was very impressed with her inventiveness and the way she had twined the branches round each other to make a screen. She smiled a little and blushed with pleasure at his approval.

"Who's next?" he said. "C'mon Larten."

Once Larten's legs were free, the fronds around the cave were finished. He took all the children up to the rock with him in order that he could demonstrate how he was going to remove their fetters so that they would not suffer the same fright as Odo had.

He started with Feya and once she was finished she told Cedric that he had to be a brave boy and go next. The four-year-old was as good as gold and that gave encouragement to Mata, Blado and Gunder and in no time at all they were all joyously rubbing their fetter-free legs.

Luka brushed down the area in an attempt to disguise what had been happening there and he stuffed the fetters and chains under the roots of a tree so that they could not be seen and they started to walk back to the cave.   Luka had sudden inspiration as the morning light filtered through the trees and into the relatively treeless gulley.   He told the others to wait while he dropped down over the edge and found just what he was hoping for.   Brambles!

The children scrambled down after him and they were soon enjoying the succulent black fruit which stained their faces and fingers.   The stream was at hand to wash everything down and by the time the little band made their way back to their hiding place, the emptiness in their stomachs had been somewhat sated.

Luka looked skywards "Err ...   Thanks again!" he said.

CHAPTER 14
Fulkh

Botolph was aware of the necessity of adequate food and rest to fortify him for the rigours of the night ahead. Leaving Gurnard to make what arrangements he could, he headed back up the slope to the chapel of Villa Calae. Here he knelt and prayed for guidance in the matter of rescuing Luka and in the matter of raising money to fund it.

Calling into the kitchens he asked tentatively for some bread, cheese, fruit and a flagon of mead. As an honoured guest he should not have been so apprehensive and the victuals were willingly given. He took them out onto the peristylum where he could sit in the shade and eat while looking over the garden. He was deep in thought when he became aware of someone standing on his right and he looked up to see Gurnard.

"All arranged," he said. "You are to meet him at the stables at midnight. His name is Fulkh."

"Fulkh?" said Botolph, "that is appropriate. Fulkh the fox, eh?"

"Yes ... and foxy, wily and cunning he certainly is, but he knows his job and he will be loyal to us. His family owes me some favours."

"What about money?" said Botolph.

"Don't worry about that, he's asked for half now and half when we can get it. I have a small amount of savings and I'll pay him his first half. I am sure that given time you'll be able to raise funds for the second half and will no doubt pay me back too."

"Of course," said Botolph, knowing that this was what he was going to have to do but not too sure how he would set about it. Money and possessions, it had been instilled in him, were things that were unnecessary for a monk to have. He was now finding that life was not quite that simple.

He thanked Gurnard who left him to make his final arrangements and said that he would see him at the stables at midnight.

Botolph tipped back the last of his mead and returned the empty flagon to the kitchen, where he obtained another four loaves of bread and enough cheese and fruit to serve eight hungry people. The food was wrapped into two bundles in cloths which he would be able to drape over his horse's withers. In addition he commandeered two leather bottles full of water.

He then went back to his cell, curled up on his pallet and slept.

--o--

When he awoke it was dark and he was afraid that he had overslept but relaxed as he realised that Gurnard would have come to wake him if he had missed the appointment at the stables.

He slung the food bags across his shoulders and clutching a leather water bottle in each hand, made his way out through the atrium and down the path to the stables where one light was flickering silently.

Gurnard stepped out of the shadows to greet him.

"Am I early or late?" asked Botolph.

"Neither," came the reply, "you're in nice time. Fulkh's just arrived. Here he is. Fulkh meet Brother Botolph."

--o--

Unbeknown to Luka, it was nearly noon before his escape was discovered and his worries about any noise that he had made whilst removing the fetters was therefore somewhat unfounded.

By the time their absence was noticed, they had been securely settled in the cave for at least three hours but during that time Luka had been expecting the arrival of a search party at any moment.

Noon came and went and Feya and Luka took it in turns to sit behind the fronds at the front of the cave looking and listening while the children sat back deep in the shadows.

One-eye and his gang's strict insistence on the silence of their charges, played into Luka's hands at this point because the children had been so cruelly subdued by the slave-runners that their instincts told them that any noise or movement would result in a lash of the whip.

Mid-afternoon also came and went with no sound other than the birds in the trees and the odd rustle from an animal in the undergrowth.

As dusk began to fall Luka realised that it would do the children good to stretch their legs and to go and visit the brambles and the stream again. He felt it would be safe now but, even so, he stood outside the cave listening intently before letting the children run freely.

Luka thought to himself that if he had been confident that the wood was going to see no unwelcome visitors that day, he might well have tried to increase the distance between himself and his followers. On further reflection though, he felt that it must have done the children good to rest and get used to their newly lightened limbs. At the same time he was puzzled as to why there had not been an instant hue and cry. From what he could see of the wood it was quite a small one. Perhaps the slave-runners had it surrounded and were just waiting for him to break out. They were bound to realise that food would soon become an urgent necessity. He was not too sure what he was going to do about that. The bramble bushes could not feed them forever. He supposed he would have to go back to One-eye's farm or find another farm where he could steal whatever he could find. It was not a pleasant prospect and there was every chance that One-eye would be waiting for him.

After an hour of the children running around, drinking from the stream and feeding on the berries, Luka called them back into the cave and they settled down for the night. His first thought was that he would keep a night-time vigil but he had always needed his sleep and he realised that it was important for him to have his wits about him the next day. So he asked Feya to stand the first watch telling her that as soon as she began to feel tired or if she heard or saw anything suspicious, she must wake him. She nodded and he settled down on his back using the axe-head as a pillow.

--o--

Fulkh was a short wiry man with big eyes and a hooked nose overshadowing thin lips which showed no sign of a smile. In fact he looked *grim*. In his belt was a dagger and round his chest was a baldric supporting a quiver full of arrows on his back; in his hand he held a short bow. He nodded at Botolph.

"He speaks no English or Latin," said Gurnard, "so you'll have to get on as best you can. I went to see him at his house this afternoon and we agreed that he would come along prepared to ride his horse to Meaux but there's been a change of plan."

Botolph's heart sank. "What is it?"

"He has arrived in his wagon because, having given it some thought, he's convinced that there is no time to be lost and it's important both to find the escapees and get them out of the area *at once*. There'll be no second chance."

Botolph had to agree. He had been wondering how he could possibly get food to Luka on a long-term basis if he remained holed up in the wood.

"The other thing," Gurnard continued, "is that you have to get Luka out of the diocese of Meaux. It's no good bringing him here. You have to get him closer to Lutetia but you can't afford to take him into the city itself or to let him be seen because Bishop Faro has spies everywhere. He'll have lost face due to Luka's actions and he's nothing if not vindictive. He'll stop at nothing to secure Luka's death."

"So where does the diocese end?" said Botolph. "Where can we take him?"

"The diocese ends more or less here at Villa Calae," said Gurnard. "Everything west of here is in King Dagobert's personal realm. One of Fulkh's less savoury friends is a scoundrel called Bonitius who holds sway over a gang of robbers that inhabits the woods halfway between here and Lutetia. It's an area that no sensible traveller would pass through without an armed escort. I'm afraid that's where your friend Luka is going to have to go for the moment. Fulkh's vouchsafed that he'll do his best to take care of him and the other slaves but Bonitius is a law unto himself and he might cut Luka's throat just as quickly as Bishop Faro would."

"Wonderful!" said Botolph, thinking that he was going to have to spend all his time on his knees if Luka was going to stand any chance of survival.

"One more thing."

"Yes?" said Botolph.

"Fulkh brought these clothes for you to change into so that you're not so recognisable."

He passed over a rough coat with a hood which Botolph put on.

"The place where the barn is, is known as Ruten Wood and when you get there Fulkh'll slip off into the trees. He wants you to carry on driving the cart towards Meaux. Just before you reach the city there is a road to the right that will take you down to the river. Follow that until you come to a ford. Go through the ford and wait on the other side for Fulkh to return. Have you got that?"

"I have," said Botolph, thinking that it did not sound like a bundle of fun.

They went over to Fulkh's cart which was half full of vegetables ready for the market. Fulkh jumped up into the driving seat.

"Good Luck," said the Master Ostler as Fulkh flicked the wagon into motion and Botolph swung himself up onto the seat beside his latest taciturn friend.

--o--

Luka was in the depths of a dream when Feya shook his shoulder.

"Mmm? Huh? What's up?" he spluttered automatically reaching for the axe.

"Nothing! You just said for me to wake you when I was tired. I'm frightened that I won't be able to keep my eyes open anymore."

"Good girl," he said. "Well done. You go and get some sleep and leave it to me 'til morning."

He stretched and yawned and felt rested in spite of his sudden awakening. He walked back and forth a couple of times in the limited space to exercise his legs and then, putting the axe beside him, settled down at the entrance to the cave.

All was quiet except for the wind occasionally zephyring through the trees. There was no moon but it was surprising how much light came from the stars on such a summer night. He was glad it was not winter.

Two hours went past.

Suddenly his head shot up and animal instincts took over. A shiver went down his back and goose-bumps exploded on his right thigh. He stayed rock still, his head turned towards the place from which the noise had come. His right hand instinctively clutched the handle of the axe and he was ready to fight as soon as he could see his quarry.

There came another sound; the slightest cracking of a twig but it made the hair stand up on the left of his neck. His eyes bored into the darkness searching for the enemy ... and then there was a movement to his right ...

CHAPTER 15
Ruten Wood.

The journey on the cart was not a happy one as far as Botolph was concerned. He had never been afraid of the dark but this was something different. Unbeknown to him, he repeated to himself the same thoughts that had just occurred to Luka, ... how surprising it was that so much light was being shed by the stars. And yet in Botolph's case, since they were moving through woods much of the time, the light was intermittent.

They saw nothing of people or traffic on the road although animals occasionally crossed in front of them; once a fox and another time a young deer. And yet Botolph had the feeling that they were being watched. He did not feel afraid but it was eerie and he peered into the darkness, straining his eyes trying to identify where the watchers might be. The road was quite straight and the horse seemed to know where he was going. From time to time Botolph recognised various landmarks from his own journey the previous day but most of the time he had absolutely no idea of where he was.

He studied Fulkh's driving techniques; particularly he noticed how he leant on the brake bar as they went down a slope to stop the cart from driving the horse. Botolph had never driven a cart before but it looked fairly easy. He hoped it was!

It took them half the remaining night to get to the wood. They had previously crossed a stretch of open country and Botolph was fairly certain that he could see the black loom of the wood coming up.   Sure enough, Fulkh pointed ahead and handed the reins over to him,.   Botolph nodded and Fulkh slipped off the right hand side of the cart. Suddenly he and his bow, baldric, quiver full of arrows and dagger were gone and Botolph was on his own ... except of course for the horse, which continued to plod along as if nothing had altered.   Botolph reckoned that the animal knew however because his ears had suddenly twitched backwards as Fulkh had left.

It was still very dark but soon they came out of the wood and the shadow of the city rose out of the gloom ahead.   The novice cart driver began to worry that he might miss the turning.   He was getting very close to the city walls by this time but he knew the junction must be somewhere before the bridge.   Suddenly he realised that he was on top of it and he yanked the reins hastily around to the right.   It was rather too hasty for the horse which was used to going straight on to the market.   The animal became confused; it stopped and would go no further.   Botolph tried slapping him with the reins and clicking his teeth at him - all to no avail.   The last thing Botolph wanted to do was to create a disturbance in the middle of the night so close to Bishop Faro's city gates.   He slipped down from the driving seat, went to the horse's head and pulled on the bridle.   The horse lifted his head and stiffened his forelegs.

"Come *on!*" said Botolph, feeling a mixture of panic and frustration - and then more soothingly " Come on. It's alright, Fulkh told me to bring you this way, ... come on." The horse looked at him doubtfully but Botolph kept up the pressure on the bridle and eventually the animal surrendered and submitted to being led down the muddy path.   Botolph nearly slipped over several times but managed to save himself by maintaining a firm hold on the bridle.   He contemplated the possibility of falling flat on his back and being run over by a wagon load of vegetables. That might ruin everything, he decided, so he hoisted himself back onto the driver's seat.

A little while later they reached the ford which was, as promised, unmistakeable, and after the horse had splashed his way through, Botolph reined him to a standstill but stayed in the driver's seat. Dawn was beginning to break and he could just make out the edge of the river bank. The realisation struck him that the advantages of better visibility might be outweighed by the disadvantages of others being able to see him too. He looked across towards the city but was relieved to note that he was hidden from sight by the edge of the wood. Elsewhere was just a bleak and desolate vista. Even so, he felt exposed and half expected an early morning search party of soldiers to round the corner and come trotting down the track.

--o--

Two little pink eyes looked up at him in surprise as the young wild boar found a stranger in his territory. Luka froze – as did the boar and they stared at each other for several moments. It turned its head slightly from left to right sniffing the air as it did so. Then it put its nose down to the ground again and went snuffling on its way. Luka gave a sigh of relief and relaxed a little. He wondered what would be happening in One-eye's world. He wondered if they would bring dogs.

How many men would One-eye be able to raise? Was there any chance at all that he and the children could remain undiscovered? He began to lose faith in his plan. Perhaps he could stay outside the cave and act as a decoy, so that if it looked as if the hideaway was going to be found, he could lead the searchers away. He might be captured but if Feya kept her head, the children might be saved. He decided that would be their only hope. He woke Feya and told her that he was going to find himself a spot where he could keep an eye on the cave from a distance. She was to remain there with the rest of the children and on no account to come out; particularly if she heard sounds of a chase and a fight. Today all the children must remain quietly in the cave right up until dusk. Did she understand? She nodded and he told her to go back to sleep.

He crept out of the cave, replacing the fronds behind him and made his way further into the wood. There was an old gnarled tree that he had noticed earlier. It had a hole in the trunk which would have made a fine hide at night but would be hopeless once the sun was up. He wondered if he might be better climbing up the tree. Searchers notoriously only ever looked downwards. But if they brought dogs it would be a different matter.

He was now beginning to have second thoughts about his second thoughts. Acting as a decoy was a forlorn hope really. Once he had been caught the searchers would no doubt return to the woods and discover the children and all would be lost.

A short while later dawn broke and found him still sitting in the trunk of his tree pondering which was the better of the awful choices that lay in front of him when he jumped with fright as a crouching figure crept silently past him. Without sparing time to think he launched himself onto the man's shoulders and flattened him on the ground with his arm around his throat and his left arm twisted behind him.

"Oof!" said the figure.

Luka wondered what he was going to do next and stayed alert to the possibility that this victim had brought friends with him.

"Atoolf!" said the figure again.

The creature was very wiry but he was no match for Luka who had the upper hand in every sense of the words. He would have to kill him – but how? The man lay very still. Luka hoped he was not already dead. He relaxed his grip a little on the man's throat which allowed him to rasp out "Batoolf". The word had a familiar ring about it but was so out of context that Luka could not at first place it. "Batoolf!" the voice insisted. Luka cautiously relaxed his grip further but kept him face down with his arms pinioned firmly behind his back.

The light dawned.

"Botolph?" Luka said incredulously. "Do you come from Botolph?" The head nodded vigorously. Luka took his knee out of the man's back and pulled him to a kneeling position but kept his arms pinioned. He thought for a few moments. The fellow was dressed like a huntsman with a quiver of arrows that Luka had all but destroyed and a bow that now lay on the ground. He did not look like part of a search party in fact he looked very much like a loner. Luka decided it was worth taking a chance and he let go his arms. The man dusted himself down and stood and picked up his bow. It was only then that Luka noticed the dagger and wondered if he had made a terrible mistake but the hunter seemed to bear him no grudge. He beckoned Luka to follow him. Luka retrieved his axe from the side of the tree and did as he was bid.

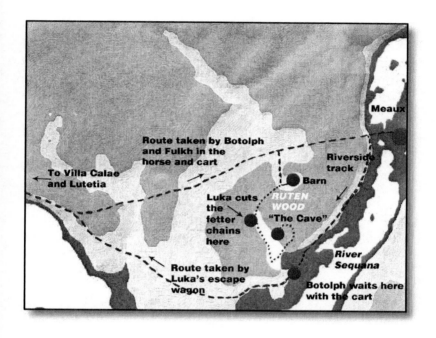

Fig. 3. Ruten Wood.

It took them ten minutes or so to scramble down the gorge to the curtain edge of the wood where the huntsman gestured towards a horse and cart standing on the opposite side of a ford. Sitting on the cart was someone who looked incredibly familiar.

Luka felt a surge of exhilaration and was at first inclined to rush across to his dear friend but he resisted the temptation and turned and ran back up the edge of the gorge towards the cave. He heard a noise behind him and was surprised to see the huntsman hard on his heels.

He wasted no time in pulling back the fronds and called "Feya, come on, - bring the others ... quickly."

Out they all came and Luka sent them back down the hill with the hunter while he spent a few moments replacing the leaves so that their hiding place would not be quickly found. He rushed after the group, sweeping Mata into his arms as he went. They entered the gulley and crossed the stream and followed the other side of the ridge down to the last of the trees where they broke out of the wood and ran to the cart.

Botolph jumped down from the driver's seat whereupon Luka put Mata onto her feet and he and Botolph clasped each other for a long moment.

"Come on," said Botolph, "there's not a moment to lose. Get up into the back of the cart with the children. You'll all have to lie down and cover yourselves with the vegetables. It won't be a good disguise or a comfortable ride but there's nothing else for it."

Luka did as he was asked and the others followed suit while Fulkh drove the old horse as fast as he would go along the desolate path by the river. Three quarters of a league later he stopped the cart and went to inspect his merchandise, covering them over as best he could so that the cart looked for all the world as if it was full of vegetables that had been purchased at the market of Meaux.

Fulkh regained his seat and they carried on at a more leisurely pace. A few moments later, Botolph understood Fulkh's tactics as they re-joined the busy main track from Meaux to Lutetia. The hunter nudged Botolph and gestured that he should put his hood up. Once done, they did their best to adopt the appearance of two tired peasants wending their way home at a steady but gentle plod after an early trip to the city. Botolph felt anything but relaxed. He wanted to get Fulkh to whip the old nag back into the brisk trot that it had managed along the riverside path. He knew in his heart though that Fulkh's pace was likely to attract the least attention even if the butterflies in his empty stomach did not seem to agree.

CHAPTER 16
Bonitius

An hour before the escape, the pompous archdeacon had been strutting up and down the Meaux precincts, chivvying the constable and his search party to get mounted and be on their way. The delay had been due to the late arrival of the dogs and their handlers. Eventually everybody was ready and with the archdeacon on the leading horse, the nine searchers trotted briskly out of the gate and down the Lutetia road with the two dogs lolloping alongside. Half an hour later they arrived at the barn where they tethered their horses and started a noisy, clumsy, systematic line-search of the wood from North to South.

It was not long before one of the dogs found the hidden fetters. A soldier carried them triumphantly back to the barn where the archdeacon was waiting, confident of having the fugitives brought to him within the hour. At the sight of the fetters his face turned spectacularly scarlet and he nearly exploded with fury. He threw the fetters on to the ground and followed the soldier back into the wood, eager to witness his prey's discovery and looking forward to boxing that infernal dwarf around the ears for costing him even more in blacksmith's money.

It was just as they caught up with the search party that the cave was discovered and the dogs, now in full cry, followed the scents down the gulley. The archdeacon puffed along after them until they reached the stream whereupon the dogs became confused. Their handler urged them to the other side where they soon found the scents again.   The great noise and excitement would have suggested to any watcher that the searchers were right on the heels of their quarry and indeed the archdeacon was anticipating imminent triumph.   The dogs increased their speed again dragging their handlers down the track that led to the edge of the wood and out to the river's edge.

Here, mud-splattered and breathless, everyone stalled while the dogs went round and round in ever-widening circles trying to rediscover the trail.

Once he had recovered his breath and his wits, a less confident archdeacon scanned the horizon in all directions, hoping to see signs of life in the desolate area ... but there were none.

The constable called him over to an area where, all too plain to see on the muddy ground, were the marks left by the wheels of Fulkh's cart.

Gaubert's face began to turn red again. He opened his mouth but his ire was so intense that, for a moment, he could not speak.   The others held back – watching him apprehensively – each maintaining statuesque immobility in the hope that they would escape his notice.   One or two of them winced visibly before the roar of frustration suddenly burst from his mouth and he jumped and writhed lashing out with his horse whip at anyone and anything within range.   He chased the soldiers and constable back to their horses bawling at them to find the wagon and, if necessary, pursue it right through the gates of Lutetia.   As the constable's horse started to move away the horse whip found its mark on the animal's rump and the rider nearly became unseated as the beast reared in surprise. Gaubert resolved that his victims were not going to get away this time.   He felt personally affronted by the events of the previous few hours and would willingly go through the gates of Hell or the gates of King Dagobert's palace if that is what it would take to get his revenge.

--o--

When the pursuers regained their horses and left Ruten Wood, Fulkh's cart was still quite a way from the Meaux-Diocesan Border and it seemed to Botolph that they were travelling painfully slowly. By contrast at Ruten Wood the pursuing horsemen had whipped their charges into a frenetic gallop. They wasted no time asking people on the road if they had seen a covered wagon. Speed was of the essence and caution was thrown to the wind as the alarming cavalcade overran everything in its path.

A short while later Botolph took a routine glance over his shoulder. For the previous hour they had been travelling along a straight track passing through treeless cultivated fields so they could see behind them for several miles and regular glances behind had revealed nothing untoward. This time Botolph was shocked by what he saw; he was unwilling to believe the evidence of his eyes.

"They're coming!" he said quietly to Fulkh.

"Hein?"

Botolph gestured behind and Fulkh took two seconds to look at the threatening cloud of dust before he whipped life into the old nag. The horse was a willing servant and certainly did his best but they were going up a hill at the time and the animal's rear bucked and shied as its four legs made pitiful efforts to hiccough their way towards gaining some speed. Once he reached the top of the rise the going became easier and the old horse bounded away as fast as his sturdy little legs could carry him.

The change in speed had alerted their passengers and Luka stuck his head out of a pile of turnips and cabbages to say "What's happening?"

"I'm afraid they're onto us," shouted Botolph above the noise. "I think we're actually on King Dagobert's land now, but it doesn't look as if that's going to help us much."

He looked around him and pointed to a woodland area to the right of the road.

"Fulkh, - make for that wood. It's all we can do.

"Luka - as soon as we stop, jump down and, fast as you can, take the children into the trees while Fulkh and I keep the archdeacon occupied."

As soon as the words were out of his mouth, he thought to himself 'And how am I going to do that?' There was no answer.

He leant across to Fulkh and pointing, said again "The wood, - make for the wood."

Little did he realise but, by a stroke of luck, that was the particular wood that Fulkh had been looking out for all along and he needed no encouragement to head towards it at full speed.

As Botolph turned back his hand caught on something deep in the folds of his habit. He retrieved it and leant over the back of the seat and tapped Luka on the shoulder, handing him his seax. Luka's eyes lit up!

"Don't kill anyone else with it!" admonished Botolph.   Luka grinned wickedly.

The children had by that time cast off their camouflage of vegetables and were kneeling down and hanging on tightly as the wagon careered along the rut-scarred track. Two horsemen came over the hill well in advance of the others and were now closing on them fast. As they approached Odo picked up a turnip and threw it at them. It landed well short but the horse spooked slightly as it bounced on the road in front of it. Thus encouraged, the rest of the children and Luka armed themselves with produce. Luka told them not to throw until he gave the word. The first horseman was nearly on them now and Botolph could do nothing but watch in horror, wondering how the rider would stop the cart but then realised that his aim would be to overtake and grab the nag's head.

Luka said "Ready ... NOW!" and the children hurled the vegetables at the unfortunate rider. A good-sized turnip makes useful armament and Luka was not throwing for fun. His turnip caught the rider fair and square under the chin and his horse shied as Feya hurled a cabbage at its head. The rider momentarily lost his balance which was enough to unseat him and he fell sideways. His horse simultaneously shied and fell and the second horse crashed straight into it throwing the second rider into a ditch.

The children all cheered and started to prepare their next fusillade but they had drawn level with the wood and Fulkh swerved the cart to the right up a tortuous track which he knew well, and finally entered a clearing where he reined the horse to a standstill.

Botolph jumped down and plucked the pins out of the backdrop which fell with a crash and Luka and the children spilled out.

"Quick now! Run!" said Botolph pointing into the wood as they heard the thunder of hooves approaching. The escapers did not await a second bidding. Luka took off in the lead carrying Cedric. The older children sprinted bravely behind him and Feya brought up the rear, urging the younger ones along in front of her.

Botolph and Fulkh ran back to the narrower part of the track where they arrived at the same time as four horsemen and the constable.   A furious argument broke out between Fulkh and the horsemen in a language that Botolph did not understand.

Fulkh was shouting at the top of his voice and waving his arms to spook the horses which, having galloped for a long distance, were only too happy to meet and obey someone who wanted them to stop.

"For God's sake," screeched a voice from the back of the melee, "What are you, - soldiers or children? Push those vagrants out of the way and get after those slaves!"

The pompous little archdeacon on his pompous little horse, pushed his way to the front and would brook no obstruction.

Botolph and Fulkh gave up their efforts.   They had tried so hard and had perhaps gained a little time but it seemed to Botolph that Luka would hang before nightfall. The soldiers dismounted and crashed past them into the woods.

--o--

The children were running as fast as they could. Every so often, one would fall over, then another would help him or her up but they could hear the soldiers gaining on them.   Luka realised that he was going to have to fight but he knew that he would have to choose the right moment.

The soldiers were upon them now and suddenly came a scream.

As Luka turned he realised he had left it too late. One of the soldiers already had Feya and had lifted her off her feet.   She was kicking and biting but could make no impression on the burly man.   Another soldier had Mata who was looking silently terrified.   Luka took Cedric off his shoulders and put him on the ground with Blado and Larten and then crouched and moved round to his left, drawing his seax as he went.

The other four soldiers had now arrived and were strung out in a line facing him.

"You might get me in the end," said Luka "but some of you are going to die in the process.   Who wants to be first?"

--o--

"You've no right to do this," said Botolph to the archdeacon.   "You're outside the Diocese of Meaux."

"I know that," came the silky reply, "but if you think that bothers me then you're even more stupid than I thought you were.   As soon as the men have recovered my property we'll put them in your cart and they'll be back over the border in no time at all.   *Then* we shall see who is in charge. *Then* we shall see your friend Luka swinging from a gibbet. You'll be able to come and watch."

For the umpteenth time, Botolph wondered how a nasty little man like the archdeacon had ever come to be so high up in the service of God.   It was a riddle he could not comprehend.

Suddenly however the two so dissimilar men of God came at the same time to the realisation that the sounds of shouting and crashing soldiers had abruptly stopped.   The woods had gone silent.

"God Almighty," the archdeacon said for the second time that day, "what on earth are they up to now?   Do I have to do everything myself?" and he dismounted from his horse and pushed roughly past Botolph as he marched off into the forest in the direction in which his soldiers had gone.

Botolph and Fulkh followed on behind, dreading what they might find.

It did not take long before they found seven gagged and trussed bodies tied back to back in a tight circle. There was no sign of Luka or the children.

The archdeacon stopped and stared, lost for words. After a few seconds he spluttered, "What? I don't understand ... What's happened?"

Botolph was as mystified as he was. The archdeacon managed to collect what little was left of his composure and strode up to the constable and pulled the gag from his mouth. "How did this happen?"

To the archdeacon's consternation, the constable said nothing. His eyes were widely opened and it was as if he had been struck dumb. Botolph and Fulkh looked on with amusement as the archdeacon's face became redder and redder. "Speak to me man! Dammit, speak to me or I'll have you strung up with that infernal dwarf so help me I will."

"Actually," quipped Botolph happily, "it doesn't look as if you're going to be stringing Luka up tonight after all."

"Shut up, monk! Now look here constable, I pay your salary and I demand that you tell me ..."

There came a soft laugh from behind the archdeacon's left shoulder and he swung round to confront a large grey-bearded man.

"He won't talk to you archdeacon, because he knows that there are ten arrows aiming at his throat and if he or his comrades utter a single word the arrows will find their targets."

"Bonitius!" faltered the archdeacon, the blood rapidly draining from his cheeks. "Bonitius!"

"Yes, it's Bonitius my nasty little slug-faced, worm-gutted crooked apology for an archdeacon ... it's Bonitius!"

"W- what are you g-going to do?"

"Well you're right of course archdeacon. I couldn't let you go without some sort of sign that would let Meaux know that Bonitius still rules in Bonoriacum, now could I?"

The archdeacon had visibly deflated and closely resembled a gibbering idiot as he retreated to the only protection he could think of. He whimpered as he crossed to Botolph and grasped his habit, curling round in front of him away from the gaze of the forest-king.

"Don't let him kill me," he pleaded, looking up into Botolph's eyes. "I'm not a bad man. I've a job to do like everyone else."

"Ha!" roared the new interlocutor. "Ha! So you have a job to do, do you? Take off your clothes!"

"What?" screamed the archdeacon.

"You heard me, take them off or I shall get my men to take them off for you and you won't like that I can promise you. Take them *off*!"

Gaubert backed away and under the malevolent stare of the man of the woods, the archdeacon danced about shedding his clothes until his little fat white bepaunched body stood glistening in the sunlight as he held his hands over his private parts.

"Don't bother to cover it with your hands," said the big man, "it's too small for us to see anyway!" There were guffaws of laughter from invisible watchers amongst the trees.

Bonitius went over to the soldiers. "In a moment I am going to cut you loose and remove your gags. I am sure that you won't try to do anything stupid. You'll find your two other colleagues at the edge of the woods with your horses.   Take your pathetic archdeacon away with you and don't ever let me see you in my woods again or you'll pay for it with your lives.   D'you understand?"   The ring gave a group nod and were released.

Bonitius, Fulkh and Botolph followed and watched as the dispirited soldiers re-mounted their horses.   The archdeacon had been forced to remove even his shoes and he hopped about comically as he trod on the sharp cones of the forest floor.   It came as a relief when he was at last on his horse's back and all he wanted to do at that point was to get away.   He squealed at the other riders to stay round him as the group trotted off.

Bonitius, Botolph and Fulkh watched until they reached the summit of the hill whereupon they stopped and the watchers saw the soldiers donating various items of clothing to cover the archdeacon's modesty.

Once he was re-clothed, he turned and stared back in their direction - suddenly brave again.   The sound of his screech came to them across the wind, but he was too far away for them to make out any words.   Then he and the horsemen cantered over the brow and were gone.

CHAPTER 17
Back to Lutetia

Luka had been nearly as shocked as the soldiers were. The trees behind the soldiers had suddenly grown hands and arms which neatly, efficiently and almost in unison, clamped the solders' mouths shut and forced them to their knees.

Luka put his seax back into his belt and gathered the children around him while they watched the tree-men silently stuff gags into the soldiers' mouths and truss them into a circle. He saw one of the men go up to the constable and talk to him quietly in a language that Luka could not understand but from the man's gestures towards the trees and the shaking of his bow, the gist of what was being said was clear.

The man, who Luka found later was called Oswan, then waved his hand and the other tree-men melted back into the forest. Oswan beckoned Luka and the children and they followed him in the other direction, leaving the seven terrified would-be bounty collectors to their fate.

The walk was a long one and Oswan did not look back but kept up a brisk pace dodging in and out of coppices and turning left here and right there, until they came to the edge of the wood where they saw a farmstead set up on the hill commanding wonderful views over a rolling countryside.

It all looked very homely. Sweet-smelling wood smoke spiralled from a hole in the thatch of the largest building and a portly round-faced lady came through the door and waved a greeting. She was clearly a motherly soul who was used to dealing with the unexpected. The children took to her at once and she picked up young Cedric and made all sorts of cooing noises at him that made up for the difference in their languages. She soon rustled up a flagon of water to slake everyone's thirst and busied herself setting up a table with bread, cheese, fruit and great chunks of meat.

Some time later Bonitius arrived with Fulkh, Botolph and half a dozen men. He was a man of few words and Botolph could not quite work out whether his men were overawed by him, just respected him or were frankly terrified of him. He certainly exuded quite a 'presence' and was not the sort of person you would want to meet on a dark night or to upset. He rarely smiled.

"Dejeuner!", he announced. "Eat first. Big talk afterwards!"

Both Botolph and Luka thought that sounded ominous.

--o--

The meal was sumptuous and a great delight to Luka and the children. Botolph and Luka caught up on the news of what had happened to each of them since they had parted. Luka was full of apologies for upsetting Botolph's plans but Botolph was magnanimous in his response that he had no doubt that Luka had done what he considered right at the time. As far as both Botolph and the children were concerned, Luka was a hero!

"That's not the way the archdeacon sees it," retorted Luka.

"No, therein lies the problem," agreed Botolph, lowering his voice.

"What do you think I should do?" whispered Luka.

"Well for a start I think we'll have to listen to Bonitius's ideas. We are, after all, in his power at the moment."

"It's not only me, but the children that we have to plan for. Bonitius might have saved us from the archdeacon but I'm not sure that he's much better than the two rapists I killed. It wouldn't surprise me to find out that he was a friend of theirs. All in all, I think I have landed us in deep ... – perhaps we should seek the help of King Dagobert?"

"I've thought of that and talked it over with Gurnard, but ..."

"Gurnard? Who's he?"

"Oh yes of course, you haven't met him. He's the Master Ostler at Villa Calae and as honest a fellow as you would care to meet. He seems to know everything and everyone; it was he who found Fulkh to come and rescue you."

"So what did this Gurnard suggest?"

"Well, it all seems to revolve around the boundaries of Bishop Faro's territory. The bishop is, apparently, very powerful and holds great sway with all the lords and nobles in the area who are often in conflict with the king. His main interest is in getting more power, money and influence and he doesn't seem to care too much how he comes by it. I haven't met him yet but if he's anything like his archdeacon, he's going to be a nasty piece of work."

"So where does Faro's land finish?"

"Well, here in Bonoriacum we are just out of them. You crossed the border just after you passed the road which led to Villa Calae."

"So Villa Calae is *within* his see?"

"Yes, unfortunately, so that's why you couldn't be taken there."

"But the villa's been used by Gallic kings for ages?"

"True but Faro's influence is getting ever greater and even the king has to use his discretion. The see also extends right across to Evoriacum."

"What? So your abbess is under Meaux' influence too?"

"Yes, but apparently Abbess Fara has some hold over her brother. In fact he seems to be frightened of her and so leaves her and her abbey alone most of the time."

"Ah, so in that case I could still come to Evoriacum with you."

Botolph's face clouded over and he was silent for a long while. "As things stand at the moment I don't think you could, Luka. You'd always be in danger from the archdeacon as well as from Bishop Faro. Perhaps God is telling me that *I* shouldn't go to Evoriacum. Perhaps we *both* ought to head back to Britain where you'd be safe?"

It was at that point that they were interrupted by Bonitius standing and calling for silence. The big man strode up and down the hall between his men, occasionally kicking at a leg that got in his way. He spoke in the language that the boys did not understand but they had come to the conclusion that it was a sort of peasant dialect. Some of the words and intonations were similar to Gallic, of which they had now learned a good smattering. From the reactions of the bandits and the similarity with words they knew, they gradually became able to understand the gist of what Bonitius was saying.

He started off by pointing at the children and at Luka and saying that they had these strangers in their midst and they had to decide what to do with them. The first option was an easy one, they could kill them and that would mean they did not have to feed them and it would reduce the danger of the archdeacon making a renewed attack to get his revenge on Luka.

The second alternative was to sell the children as slaves. They would bring in a good price and provide some much-needed money. He was not too sure what they were going to do with the dwarf though. Like as not his story would be told around camp fires for many months to come and the many who hated Bishop Faro would consider the dwarf a hero.

"It's a mess," he said, kicking savagely at a dip in the earthen floor of the hall, so that soil sprayed into the faces of some of his listeners.

"The last thing we want is to have children around. They'll be a nuisance and get in the way and it's more mouths to feed."

He turned to Botolph and spoke in Latin. "However we might appear to you at the moment, we've no desire to be thought of as *nice* men. Here we are, close to the city of Lutetia, with the forest behind and a good view of the countryside in front. Over there lie the marshes and, if necessary, we can vanish into those at a moment's notice and never be found. We can't do that if we have children to look after. We won't be able to move with the speed that we need to ..."

He turned to Luka "as you've already found out,". Luka nodded reluctantly.

"We're robbers, murderers and bandits and *proud* to be so. We live by stealing from others. Those you see here are just a small number of my people. This small area contains a very large portion of the scum of Gallia. I rule here with a mighty fist. Many of my own men would like

107

to kill me and take command - but I have lasted for sixty-three years and I'll do so for many more."

He paused and glared at the gathering.   Eyes and heads turned away from his stare.

"We're outside the law and there's a price on nearly every man's head here. We enjoy the way we live. We enjoy attacking travellers on their way to Meaux. We enjoy seeing the rich squirm and as a result of it we eat and drink well."

He grasped an earthenware flagon and raised it high in the air.   There was a spontaneous cheer.   He smashed it down on the table and it broke into a thousand pieces.

Early smiles vanished.   Bodies jumped at the splinters and nerves stretched taut again.

Luka and the children were in no doubt that they were on trial and that their lives lay in the palm of the big man's hand.

There was a long silence whilst everyone waited for his next word.

He swung round and pointed at Botolph.

"It's done!"

Botolph gulped.

"One moon!"

"For one moon, I will keep these children while you find some way of taking them off my hands. If you've not done that within a moon then they'll either be killed or taken to another part of Gallia and sold.   I'm offering this on one condition."   He turned to Luka.

"I'm offering it on the condition that your friend Luka promises to stay and fight under my command for at least two years."

Botolph gulped again and looked at Luka.

Bonitius continued.   "My men have told me how this little man here faced those six soldiers and the constable and threatened to kill them all. They said that he had such fury in his eye that he might well have got four of them but he'd never have managed all six. If he's going to lose an arm or his life, I want it to be in my service. Those are my conditions. Either take them or be gone by nightfall."

He waved his hand and the men hastily rose from their seats and vanished through the open door. Bonitius remained gazing at it - his back to the newcomers. He swung round.

"I'll leave you three to talk," he said. "I'll be back shortly when I'll expect your decision," and he swept out of the door.

Fulkh rose twitchily, shrugging his shoulders and waving his hands abstractedly and then said in broken English "Wagon ... 'orse ... you want? ... you 'ave," and followed Bonitius through the door.

The children had already gone outside and the shrieks of laughter of their playing drifted into the hall. Botolph and Luka sat gloomily opposite each other.

"I'm sorry, Botolph," said Luka.

"Aaah, it couldn't be helped. It must be some sort of destiny. What d'ye think?"

"Well," said Luka, perking up a little. "I don't mind staying here for a while. You know I've always enjoyed a good scrap and if it means the children's lives will be spared it'll be worth it."

"Yes," said Botolph, "but you realise that although *their* lives will be spared, you'll be expected to kill many other people on Bonitius's behalf. He wants you as a *fighter* not as a cook."

"Well, I'll only kill those I think *deserve* to be killed," said Luka naïvely.

"I don't think it'll quite work out that way."

"Hmm. Maybe not. So what'll *you* do?"

"Well, I'll have to go back to Dagobert and explain the situation and try to get a pardon for you. I'll ask him and Eligius for suggestions as to what I can do about the children. Maybe he'll be able to put them in service with others of his lords and nobles. I don't know how he feels about Bishop Faro and his lot. It'll be interesting to find out.

"But what about Fara and Evoriacum?"

"Ah well, that'll depend upon what Dagobert says. If he thinks there's any chance of us getting safe passage back to Britain then maybe that's what we should do."

"No!" said Luka.

"No?"

"No. You've set your heart on going to Evoriacum and God's guided you here. I'm not letting my actions stand in the way of that. Besides which, Bonitius is expecting an immediate answer and it'll be days before you'll get to talk to King Dagobert. If we were to decide *now* to head back to Britain, our priority would have to be to make arrangements for the children and that would probably take all of the moon that Bonitius has offered."

Botolph turned and with a smile, peered closely into Luka's eyes.

"Those children are important to you aren't they my friend?" he laughed.

"Well," said Luka, shuffling and going a little red, "Well, they're young and defenceless and ..."

"Ha!" said Botolph grinning. "I never thought to see your soft side," and he threw him a playful punch.

"Well ..." said Luka again.

"Right," said Botolph cutting his short and getting serious again. "Time is running out. So you're prepared to guarantee Bonitius that you'll stay here for two years.   I'll get Fulkh to take me to Lutetia ... Ah ..."

"What?" said Luka.

"I have to find some money to pay Fulkh," he said. "He didn't mount your rescue out of the kindness of his heart. Gurnard has already paid him half and I have to find the other half and pay Gurnard back."

"Oh Christ!" said Luka.

"Luka!"

"Yes?"

"On your knees."

Down Luka went and mumbled away his usual prayers of penitence and then, brightly rising to his feet again said, "At least I won't have to keep doing that every five minutes with you in Evoriacum and me here."

Botolph was not to be mollified.   "God and your conscience will stand in for me and you'll have to offer your act of penitence whenever you blaspheme.   T'would be a better idea if you didn't do it!"

"Alright, alright," said Luka, "I know you're right. Maybe when I go on successful raids, I can persuade Bonitius to pay me a little so that I can pay Fulkh and your man at Villa Calae?   Anyway, leave it to me."

"Perhaps I can also talk to Dagobert about it. He said he'd be forever in our debt."

"Yes, well that was before he knew how much debt was going to be brewing up. You'll have enough to do with settling the children somewhere. You concentrate on that."

"Alright," said Botolph "if you say so.   I'll be off to Lutetia shortly and who knows how long it'll be before we meet again?   It might be possible for me to come back when the children are collected but it might not work out that way.

"For God's sake and mine, take care of yourself, Luka. Don't get yourself killed. Try and stay happy and healthy and *remain a servant of The Lord.* I shall pray for you every night ... and probably during the day too."

They embraced and memories of dramatic times they had shared together flashed through both their minds. In spite of the differences in their characters, their brains remained so well attuned.

They went through the door into the sunlight just as Bonitius arrived back. "Well?" he said.

"You're on!" said Luka.

"Good! Right young Botolph. One moon. By the next half moon I expect you to be back here to collect these wretched children and take them out of my sight. In the meantime I'll do my bit in protecting them and I shall expect Luka here to protect me. Fulkh's waiting for you down at the Gateway. He'll take you to Lutetia and drop you at the end of the Pons Magnus. He can't take you into the city because he's not welcome there ... as he isn't in many other places," and he gave one of his rare laughs.

"The Gateway?" said Botolph.

"Yes, that's what we call it. One of the boys will take you there. Off you go now. Luka and I have some serious talking to do."

Luka and Botolph embraced again and then Botolph turned to Bonitius and attempted to embrace him too, trying to find words of thanks. Bonitius responded gruffly saying, "That's enough, - be off with you now. I can't remember *ever* embracing a monk!"

--o--

Botolph followed the lad towards the forest. Before the trees enfolded him he turned and waved at Luka and

Bonitius who were still standing by the Hall door. Luka waved back and, with a heavy heart, Botolph turned and followed the boy through the trees.

It took several minutes to get to the Gateway and although they saw nobody else on the way, Botolph sensed the eyes that were watching him. He looked up into the foliage and peered inquisitively round the corners of tree trunks but no other soul was visible.

Fulkh and the old nag were patiently waiting. Botolph glanced into the back and, amongst the remaining vegetables, saw the two unused leather water bags and the food he had been given at Villa Calae. In the pandemonium he had completely forgotten about it.

Fulkh offered a curt nod and Botolph climbed up beside him whereupon, without more ado, Fulkh clicked his teeth and away they went. Wordlessly he handed the reins to Botolph and then snuggled up against the backboard of the driver's seat, closed his eyes and promptly fell asleep.

Botolph was not sorry. He quite enjoyed driving the old horse now and was relieved to be left with his thoughts; he had plenty of them.

Some while later Botolph saw the familiar sight of the Pons Magnus. Fulkh had awoken earlier but had made no effort to take the reins. When they reached the bridge however, he leant across, took them out of Botolph's hands and pulled the horse to a standstill. Botolph had little doubt that this was Fulkh's way of saying that here was as far as he was prepared to go. Thanking, as well as he could, the strange little man with whom he had shared so many troubles and so much danger, he dropped down onto the track and watched distractedly as the cart turned back towards Bonoriacum. He turned and started across the bridge.

The grey cobbles and parapet reflected the greyness in his heart as he walked towards Dagobert's palace. By now, he and Luka should have been well ensconced in Evoriacum and that indeed is where the king would expect them to be. Botolph felt that he was returning to the king with his tail between his legs having failed in the mission in which King Dagobert had so willingly supported him by providing both horses and guards to speed him on his way.

He wondered how he was going to be able to explain all this to Dagobert and what favours he dared ask. By the time he reached the palace gates, he had decided that Eligius was the first person he needed to find.

CHAPTER 18
Alfrid

"Right my young felon," said Bonitius, "you come along o' me and I'll show you your sleeping quarters."

Luka did not know whether to be pleased or offended by being called "a young felon", but on reflection he decided that, in the circumstances in which he found himself, it had rather an attractive ring. He followed Bonitius into the wood ...

It took several minutes before they reached a thatched wooden hut that showed no sign of occupation. Bonitius lifted the latch and swung the door open. When his eyes became accustomed to the darkness Luka saw the usual central hearth and four straw palettes.

"This is your billet," said Bonitius. "I'll introduce you to your companions later. You won't be spending much time here as mostly you will be out watching the perimeter or on a raid. Each night we eat together at the hall. We do it in two shifts. The first meal starts an hour before sunset and when you're on night watch, that's when you take your dinner. After dinner you go to relieve the day watch and they come in to dinner. You got that?"

Luka nodded.

"Obviously if you are on day watch, you stay at your post until the night watch comes to relieve you."

"So if I am on day watch, will my companions in the billet be on day watch too?"

"What?" asked Bonitius looking puzzled.

"The other three people in the billet. Will they be on the same watch as me?"

"It's not a case of the *three* other people in the billet my little felon, - there are *seven* other men billeted in your hut."

"Seven?" said Luka. "But there are only four palettes."

"Well why would you want more?" said Bonitius. "Once the night birds come off watch and get their heads down, the day birds are up in the trees. At the end of the day the night birds lift themselves out of their pits leaving the straw nice and warm for the day birds to crawl in. It works very well."

"Yes, I s'pose it would," said Luka. "So will I be on night watch some times and day watch at others or do I stick to the same watch all the time."

"You're full of questions aren't you?"

"Well I just want to get it straight."

"Well you can change around from time to time but most men tend to stick to the same watch. If you change you have to stay awake for twenty-four hours so that discourages most people from changing too often."

"So, will I be day or night?"

"Well, you're going to have to do both watches for a while, until you know what you're up to. During that time you'll be with several others who'll explain what to do, how to communicate and in what order to fight."

"What order to fight? Surely a fight is a scrap and you just get on with it?"

"No. Doesn't work like that. Normally there are only ten or so involved in a raid. The others are all tucked back out of sight in the trees but watching the skirmish and probably keeping their arrows trained on the opposition.

Still others will be well away from the frontline, watching other parts of the forest perimeter as well as the hall and the farmhouse villa. Over yonder is a watch tree on a hill where the keeper can see any movements elsewhere in the forest. We've never yet been overrun but it could happen. In that case, there are special paths which you'll have to learn. These take us out into the marshes where we can easily pick off anyone who's stupid enough to follow."

"You've got it all sewn up as tight as a prior's scrip then?" said Luka.

"Hmm. That sounds about right. Our lives depend upon everyone doing their jobs properly. You'll need to learn to recognise every part of the forest; to be able to melt into the trees so that you can't be seen; to communicate silently or by bird and animal calls with the other men, and to be able to move quietly through the undergrowth or at height from tree to tree."

"What about raids?" asked Luka. "When will I go on the first one?"

"Whoa there young felon. Not so fast. You've got a lot to learn before I can let you loose. Sometimes a raid'll get too hot, such as if some of the king's guards turn up unexpectedly. Then you won't know which way to run. I don't want you killed in your first moon!

"That's enough talk about what *might* happen. Let's get you started. We're going to take a walk around this part of the forest and I'll show you the other huts. While we do so I want you to keep your eyes open and see how many watchers you can spot."

Luka did not really understand what he meant, but nevertheless, he followed him through the trees, looking up in anticipation of seeing a foot or arm or hearing a rustling that would indicate the presence of one of Bonitius's men.

By the time they reached the first hut he had seen nobody at all.   Bonitius threw open the door and Luka saw that the hut was really very similar to the billet that he would occupy. Once again there were no occupants, and after a grunt, Bonitius closed and latched the door again and then turned to Luka and asked "Well then, how many watchers did you see on our way here?"

"None!" confessed Luka.   "Were there any?"

"Well there should have been seven or eight on that stretch, but I must confess that I only saw signs of four of them myself.   C'mon, we'll retrace our steps and I'll point them out to you."

After a short distance Bonitius paused by a tree and pointed up into the leaves.

"There," he said "d'ye see?"

Luka moved closer to Bonitius's shoulder and looked along the length of his arm towards his extended finger.   He stared at the trunk looking for any movement that might betray human presence.   Gradually he realised that what he had originally thought was a leaf, was in fact a foot and his gaze followed the foot until it became a leg and then a body with arms supporting a bow, and above that a grinning face topped by a green hat.

"Ah!", he said triumphantly, "I see him".

"Well done," said Bonitius, "that's Alfrid.   He's the one who'll be showing you the routines.   Come down Alfrid and meet your new friend Luka."

There was a rustle of leaves and a slithering and the foot was joined by its partner and within what seemed to Luka like no time at all, both feet were beside him on the ground and the grinning face was close to his.

Luka had time to take in Alfrid's pixie-like appearance. The pointed upturned nose, the high eyebrows, the sharp chin and stickie-out ears. His teeth were white against the colour of his weather-beaten face and Luka guessed that the boy was only a few years older than himself.

Bonitius introduced them.

"This is Luka," he said. "He killed two of Bishop Faro's slave drivers a few days ago so he finds himself compelled to hide with us."

"Hah," said Alfrid gleefully, "any enemy of the Bishop's is a friend of mine! Well done young Luka. Good to know you!"

"Alright, don't get carried away," said Bonitius, "back up that tree with you, you'll have enough time to talk at dinner tonight."

As they turned away, Luka saw Alfrid swing lightly onto a branch and merge into the arboreal back-drop.

CHAPTER 19
Eligius

Botolph nodded to the guards as he passed through the city gates. He followed a passageway round to his right and headed for Eligius's quarters where the counsellor had given him and Luka hospitality on their arrival in Lutetia four months earlier. He found a slave at the bottom of the steps and asked if Lord Eligius was within. The slave led him up the winding stairway to Eligius's study.

The golden man rose from his seat by the window and with a warm but puzzled smile welcomed the young monk back into his life.

"I thought you were in Evoriacum," he said. "What brings you back here so soon?"

The slave left and Eligius motioned Botolph to the window seat where he joined him.

"You look troubled, my young friend. What's amiss?"

Botolph spilled out the whole story and Eligius listened silently apart from the odd grunt and occasional wide opening of the eyes and raising of the eyebrows. When Botolph had finished, Eligius remained silent for some considerable time.

"Well it seems to me that your problems are threefold," he said eventually. "You have to find the money you owe to that little weasel Fulkh ..."

"You know him?" interrupted Botolph.

"Oh, yes, I know him alright. He and his family have been a thorn in the king's side for many years. I'm glad to see that he's done something useful for a change, but to continue ... your second problem is Luka's confinement. I'm not sure that casting him into the clutches of Bonitius was a terribly wise move ... and then you have the problems of the children.

Botolph stared miserably at his hands. "I really don't know where to start," he confessed.

"Well, I suppose that is why you came to see me?" said Eligius gently.

Botolph felt a shred of hope as he looked into Eligius's eyes. "I am sure we will be able to work something out. First things first: the money. That won't be a problem. I shall arrange for it to be made available from the palace coffers and I've no doubt that King Dagobert will be pleased to help you in this way, even if the money will be going to a scoundrel like Fulkh. If, as you say, Gurnard has already paid the first half, I assume that he will be able to arrange settlement with Fulkh?"

"I think so," said Botolph, suddenly feeling guilty that he had perhaps done Gurnard a disservice by exposing his association with the underworld.

Eligius seemed to read his thoughts. "Don't worry," he said, "Gurnard's an honest fellow and seems to know everything and everyone. He's greatly valued by the king who's even been known to consult him himself on various delicate matters".

Botolph heaved a sigh of relief.

"Now," continued Eligius, "Luka's confinement. How does your friend feel about being held hostage?"

"Well, he isn't really being held against his will. In fact I think he was rather relishing the prospect of being part of a brigand gang for a while."

"He will of course be in perpetual danger. King Dagobert's not the only one who'll be doing their best to kill him. The second is that he'll be regarded as a particular threat to the king and the royal family."

Botolph suddenly sat upright. "But Luka would never do anything to harm the king!" he protested.

"He'll not have any option. He's Bonitius's puppet now and when Bonitius says 'jump', then jump he will."

Botolph was horrified.

"There's another problem."

Botolph looked questioningly.

"The relationship between King Dagobert and the Bishop of Meaux is not a happy one."

"Oh?"

"The king's strong in influence and popularity at the moment and the one thing that the bishop and his cronies hate is a strong royal hand. It's unlikely therefore that Faro could be persuaded to give any concessions to the king such as granting Luka a pardon. So you'll see that, sadly, the king is not as all-powerful as at first sight he may appear. It would seem therefore, that certainly for the moment, Luka's probably in the best place."

"What about the children?" Botolph said.

"Ah, well that might be different," replied the counsellor. "In fact King Dagobert might be quite pleased to score over the Meaux nobles by relieving them of a few slaves."

Botolph brightened at this prospect which would be a major burden taken off his shoulders. Although, he reflected, the burden was not so much on *his* shoulders as upon those of Luka.

"So what should I do?" he asked.

"Tell me about the children. How many are there and what are their ages?"

"Seven. Two girls and five boys. Feya is the eldest; she has thirteen summers and the other girl is about eight. The boys range from Odo who is also eight to Cedric who is only four."

"My life!" said the counsellor grimly, "what a terrible time they must have had, wrenched from their parents, whom they probably saw put to death, and then they themselves being shipped off to a foreign country. Do you have any idea where they come from?"

"A mixture of British and Saxon, I think."

"Well, it sounds as if the thirteen year old might make a good serving wench for Queen Nanthild. I'll have a word with the queen and see if I can persuade her to see them. You'll need to get them cleaned up and smelling sweet before you present them though. The king's away at Saint Denis at the moment but as soon as he returns I'll talk to him about Luka; though I'm not very hopeful.

Now how about you? We need to get you off to Evoriacum as soon as possible or the Abbess will think you've returned to Britain."

"I can't really go until I have done all I can for Luka and made sure the children are well provided for," said Botolph.

"Yes, I suppose that's true," responded Eligius pensively, "so we'd better make arrangements for you to stay here for a couple of days. You can bed down where you and Luka were before. Then first thing tomorrow you'll have to come and talk the matter over with the king and make arrangements to bring the slaves into the palace."

"It's quite a way for the little ones to walk," said Botolph. "Is there a chance that I could borrow a cart?"

"Hmm. The problem with that is that you'd never be able to persuade any driver to go within arrow distance of Bonoriacum. Just a mention of the place instils fear into all the local people."

"If I could borrow a cart and horse I could take it there myself to bring the children back," said Botolph eagerly.

"You've added driving to your list of talents have you?" teased Eligius.

Botolph blushed and Eligius laughed.

"I'm sure we'd be able to arrange that. Now off with you and prepare your billet and I shall maybe see you in the Refectory Hall later, or if not, come and see me first thing tomorrow morning and we'll arrange this audience with the king."

CHAPTER 20
Eluhan

Luka was settling into his new life quite happily. Alfrid was good company but the rest of Bonitius's men were very variable to say the least. "The scum of Gallia" Bonitius had happily called them and Luka began to see what he meant. Without exception they had all been involved at some stage in carrying out a multitude of crimes and were being sought by kings, bishops, tribes or offended husbands. They had common interests in that they were all lacking in morals, manners, and consciences. They lived for themselves alone and the biggest and strongest persecuted the smallest and weakest.

Luka's arrival caused a fair amount of contemptuous mirth - particularly from an evil-looking, black-bearded, mountain of a man called Eluhan. He was sitting alone in the Feasting Hall when Luka and Alfrid came in and he greeted his first sight of Luka with a great roar of laughter.

"What have you got there, Alfrid?", he said. "What in Jupiter's name is Bondy thinking of, taking in a scrap like that?"

Luka gave Alfrid no time to answer but in a few quick paces was at the table where he picked up Eluhan's trencher and smashed it into his face.

"Why ..." roared the great giant rising to his feet and leaning across swiped his great paw at Luka's head. Luka saw it coming and ducked at the last moment so that the force of the blow was taken by the window frame.

"Shit! ... Come here you little varmint ... You'll pay for that."

He effortlessly upended the table in Luka's direction. Alfrid could not see how his new friend was going to avoid being crushed but Luka skipped sideways as the bearded mountain moved towards him. The beard, Luka noticed with satisfaction, was flecked with particles of food that had been forced into it by the untimely arrival of the trencher.

Luka might have been quick but the mountain was also surprisingly nimble for his size and as he passed the hearth he grasped the iron fire-stoker and moved towards his adversary. Luka made no attempt to run but stood at one end of the hall his legs planted firmly apart with his seax glinting in his hand.

"Huh! That's the way of it is it?", said the beard. "Going to kill me are you? Hah! We'll see about that."

The fire-stoker came crashing down from one side. As Luka crouched to duck the swinging iron he thrust the seax's point into the earthen floor in a mixture of instinct and bravado. The mountain reversed his swing and aimed at Luka's legs. Luka leapt over the hissing steel and took the opportunity whilst Eluhan's arm was wide, to slide under it and in one movement grab his victim's sleeve whilst issuing a kick with his heel behind the big man's knee.

The result was spectacular. The knee buckled and with a howl of rage and pain, the man collapsed floorwards. Luka's body completed a circle as the great bearded head descended to a level where he could at last reach it and putting all his weight behind his clenched fist he hit the jaw where the beard merged with black flowing locks of greasy hair. His victim's head jerked to its right and then smashed onto the ground. Luka was not finished. He knew exactly where his seax was and, without taking his eyes from the fallen mass, he took the handle and leapt onto Eluhan's back and grasped his hair with one hand whilst raising the seax with the other.

"No!", came a deep authoritative shout from a darkened corner of the hall. "Leave him!"

Luka was reluctant and still fired up and panting from his exertions but the sight of Bonitius striding towards him temporarily quelled his ardour.

"Get off him," ordered the rebel leader. Luka hesitated for a moment but then with one swift stroke from his seax, sliced the shock of oily hair from his victim's head, and still holding the hair in his left hand, stood to one side. He looked across at Alfrid who, with his arms folded, was leaning, smirking, against a wall beam.

"I can't have you killing my best fighters," growled Bonitius. "If you are going to stay here you are going to have to work *with* the rest of my men; not *against* them."

"It wasn't *my* fault," said Luka. "He was the one who started it ..."

"I know, I know," softened Bonitius. "A bit of fighting is good for a newcomer. The word'll get around and you'll have made your mark. It's unlikely that anybody else'll challenge you now but if they do ..."

"Alright, I know," said Luka. "... Don't kill 'em!"

"Quite."

Bonitius kicked at the prostrate body which stirred and then rose with a roar, shaking the still food-encumbered beard. When the eyes focussed on Luka, standing sturdily with his feet apart and arms akimbo, Eluhan made as if to continue the fight but met the restraining arm of Bonitius.

"This is Luka," he said. "I would introduce you properly but it seems you have already met. He will be on your team Eluhan so in future I want you fighting back to back not slaughtering each other.   Is that clear?"

There was a heavy silence as the mountain glared for a long time at his recent adversary who glared back with equal venom.   He then tossed his hand in apparent acceptance and shuffled off through the door.

CHAPTER 21
Collecting the children

Eligius had been as good as his word and organised an audience with King Dagobert, who, in his turn had greeted Botolph warmly and listened to his problem with concern.   He had readily accepted the prospect of accommodating the children.   When Botolph reiterated his wish to collect the youngsters himself his face clouded over for a moment.   Botolph had not been sure whether this was because he was fearful for his safely, because of his hate and mistrust of Bonitius, or because he was apprehensive of Botolph's skill as a wagoner.

Nevertheless, all had been arranged and Botolph now found himself approaching "The Gateway" which had changed but little since he had left it a couple of days earlier.

He drove as far as he could into the forest and tied the horse's bridle to a tree.   As he turned back towards the wagon, he almost collided with one of Bonitius's men who had materialised silently behind him.

Although startled, he was unsurprised since he had assumed that, once enfolded in the forest, he would automatically be conducted to Bonitius and so it proved to be.

His guide took him through the trees to the clearing by the Refectory Hall and then down to the water's edge where he found Bonitius gazing thoughtfully across the mere.   When the big man turned, it seemed to Botolph that he looked at him somewhat contemptuously.   They were of similar height but Bonitius won hands down in terms of girth.

"You've come for the children then?" he said. "You didn't waste much time. I reckon I'm doing Dagobert a favour by swelling the ranks of his slaves. What's he going to pay me for them?"

Botolph was taken aback. "Pay?" he said. "You told me to get back here as fast as I could and take the children off your hands. You didn't say anything about payment!"

"Ah, well I have been thinking about it since and I reckon they're worth quite a bit. So what's he going to pay me?"

Botolph suddenly realised that he was going to have to change his tactics. Having at first assumed that his mission was that of a simple collector it now appeared that he had become a negotiator. The frightening thought occurred to him that the lives of the children might depend upon the success or failure of his negotiations. He groaned inwardly. It had all looked so straightforward. A simple matter of collecting the children and taking them back to the palace. Botolph's silent prayer for help was interrupted by a growl from Bonitius.

"Well?"

Botolph turned and looked straight into the eyes of the rebel chief.

"I came here to collect the children and that's what I'm going to do. Unless, of course, you decide you want to keep them in which case just say so and I will be on my way."

There was a fury-filled silence as the young man of God and the pagan barbarian fought a dual with their eyes. A feeling of inner strength accompanied by a touch of annoyance surged through Botolph. He was determined that he would not be the first to break eye contact. At last

Bonitius grudgingly conceded and said "Take them then!" and, turning his back on Botolph, strode into the forest.

Botolph looked around him. He seemed to be entirely alone. A quick prayer of gratitude that he was at least back on track and he started to make his way over to the refectory. He had hoped that he might see some sign of Luka but it looked as if his hopes were not going to be realised.

He pushed open the refectory door but the place was empty; he turned and walked towards the larger of the adjacent huts. They were similarly deserted and he stood perplexed, wondering what to do next. A faint cry came from the distance. He strained his ears. It came again. Was it the sound of children playing? He fervently hoped it was; he headed towards it.

The volume of the cries gradually increased until, at last there they were, playing a game of tag near a spring that emanated from the hillside and began its tortuous passage through the trees and down towards the water where Botolph and Bonitius had talked. Feya was the first to spot his approaching figure and he noted her initial concern change to relief as her guard relaxed and then to joy when she recognised him.

She ran down the hill stopping a little way off – apprehension lining her young face.

"Have you come to get us?" she asked tentatively.

"Certainly have. Are you ready to go? Do you have anything to collect because if not I think we should leave as quickly as possible ... before Bonitius changes his mind." He added the last part softly to himself.

Her face broke into a vision of joy and Botolph felt its warmth as if the sun had emerged from behind a cloud. The other children had stopped in mid-play, frozen wide-eyed in tense anticipation, realising that Botolph brought momentous news and wondering how it was going to affect their young lives.   Feya gathered them together and, with her arms spanning them protectively, the group set off down the hill towards the mid-afternoon sun.

They saw nobody on their walk.   The wood was deserted and it occurred to Botolph it seemed a wonderfully *spiritual* place on such a summer's day with the birds singing above and the occasional animal scurrying into the bushes as they pressed on towards 'The Gateway.'

To Botolph's surprise and satisfaction, his sense of direction seemed to be working well and they found the wagon without difficulty.   On the driver's seat a wicker basket had appeared containing plenty of bread, cheese and fruit for them all.   Botolph looked at it in wonder and then gazed left and right into the forest in the hope of glimpsing a sight of their retreating benefactor.   Could it have been Luka?   Or was it perhaps Bonitius's wife?   Or maybe even Bonitius himself?   For all his gruff blustering, Botolph felt sure he had a soft heart inside him.

Although they did not realise it at the time, the wagon ride to Lutetia was something that the children would remember fondly as being the first major step in their liberation.   The horse plodded evenly along and Feya softly started to sing a song which, although Botolph did not recognise it, the children did and joined evermore enthusiastically into the chorus.   The song finished rousingly and they all burst into giggles of laughter while the older children begged Feya to sing them another.

She demurred however and insisted that they first eat the provisions and promised that she would then sing again.

Thus they steadily made their way towards the beginning of their new lives in the palace, none really knowing exactly what lay in store for them.

CHAPTER 22
Evoriacum

It was another two days before Botolph was able to take his leave of Lutetia for the second time and, with the same two bodyguards that had escorted him and Luka on their first departure, he arrived at the stables of Villa Calae and clasped the arms of Gurnard as he was welcomed back.

Ever mindful of the needs of others, Botolph was relieved to find that Dagobert had been as good as Eligius had said he would be and that both Fulkh and Gurnard had been more than adequately recompensed for the expenditure involved in Luka's rescue.

His stay at the villa was destined to be brief however and early the following morning he and his guards found themselves following the less familiar road towards Evoriacum.

They kept up a good pace, the young soldiers being keen to accomplish their mission before any other unforeseen disasters befell them. There was a delay of an hour or so at the riverside while they waited for the tide to fall sufficiently for them to be able to wade across, but they were soon over, their horses trotting briskly through fields of summer vines bursting with grapes. A short while later an impressive-looking building poked its roof above the treetops. The guards told Botolph that it was another of Dagobert's residences known as "Villa Latiniacum". Then came the joy of a steady canter through a cool forest after which they broke out into a wide area of open grassland before plunging back into another dense wood.

When they finally emerged from this the leading guard stopped his horse and waited for his colleague and Botolph to join him before pointing into the distance where a stone tower could be seen breaking the skyline.

"Yonder's your destination!" he announced triumphantly.

Although the sun was high in the sky, Botolph still had to shield his eyes as he concentrated on the shape and absorbed his first sight of the *alma mater* of his ambitions that had eluded him for so long.   He thought to himself that perhaps it should have been called "Elusiacum" but he kept the witticism to himself.   Instead he took a deep breath and filled his lungs with the air of the Gallic countryside;   he thanked God for his safe arrival.   He *deeply* regretted that Luka was not with him to share this triumph but guessed that his Father must have *some,* at present hidden, reason for separating him from his dear friend.   As they set off again over the open fields towards the distant tower, Botolph continued to wonder what God's purpose might be for him and Luka.   Was it for Luka's sake that they had been separated ... or for his? Had Luka been consigned to the clutches of Bonitius to learn something from life that Abbess Fara could not teach him?   Or was God's purpose that Bonitius and his band of brigands should learn something from Luka?   Was there some point in Botolph being on his own at Evoriacum?   Would Luka have been a distraction?

All these things were whirling through Botolph's mind as the tower of Evoriacum Abbey grew ever larger. The guards and horses also seemed excited to arrive and they cantered right up to the monastery gates.

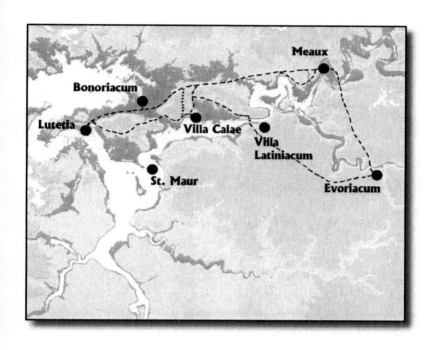

Fig. 4. Lutetia to Evoriacum.

It was just after noon and as soon as the clatter of hooves stopped, Botolph could hear the sound of chanting pervading the air as the office of Sext took place in the abbey church. Although there were clearly many people in the chapel, the grounds were also full of bustling activity and Botolph began to wonder just how many souls called this enormous site their home.

The gatekeeper and two slaves held the horses' heads while the three dismounted. The bodyguards looked questioningly at Botolph.

"We'll go and find somewhere for the horses to be fed and watered and then we'll make our way to the refectory. I'm sure there'll be some food there," he added encouragingly, recognising hunger in their looks.

This brought a couple of smiles. Botolph turned his head to the gatekeeper and asked for directions.

"What'll you do about my horse?" Botolph asked the guards as they led the horses towards the stables.

"He'll come back with us on a leading rein," came the reply. "I doubt that we'll manage to get across the river tonight so we'll have to stay at Villa Latiniacum and then press on to Lutetia tomorrow."

"I could probably arrange accommodation here if you wanted," said Botolph.

He noticed one guard sharing a glance with the other who replied "That's very kind but I think the company at Villa Latiniacum might suit us better than that of monks and nuns," and they both laughed at a hidden joke.

With excitement brewing in his heart, Botolph followed the gatekeeper's directions to the stables where he found an ostler sitting on a straw bale eating his lunch. The man, startled, jumped up and, wiping his face with the back of his hand, finished chewing his last mouthful as he crossed to take charge of the new arrivals.

Botolph patted his horse's withers in thanks for a safe journey and handed over the reins. The guards followed suit. Botolph asked where he could find the refectory.

They headed down a winding path which led them to an open doorway through which wafted a delicious smell.

"This'll be it," grinned Botolph as they went inside. Centrally placed was a massive iron cauldron, suspended from the beams above an open fire. The sweet-smelling smoke pervaded the hall before the surplus found its way out through a hole in the apex of the roof. Standing beside the cauldron and stirring its contents with a great iron ladle was a young tonsured monk wearing a long woollen apron.

He raised his concentrated stare from the bubbling liquid and greeted the newcomers with pleasure and surprise. "Pax vobiscum ... and to what might we ascribe the joy that brings you to us today?"

"Pax vobiscum brother," Botolph repeated. "My name is Botolph and I carry letters of introduction to Abbess Fara from Bishop Honorius of Cantwarebury."

"From Cantwarebury eh? Greetings and welcome. I am Brother Bernard, and ..." he added with a twinkle, "it is my job to stir the pot!"

Both Botolph and the guards were quite famished after their long ride. Brother Bernard recognised this but was momentarily unsure of what he should do.

"It'll be some time before Sext is over," he pondered, "although the soup is ready now. I'm sure the abbess won't mind my feeding three hungry travellers before the main repast but you'll have to sit outside and eat."

This suited them very well and Brother Bernard called a slave to bring some bowls which he handed to each of his three guests before ladling steaming soup into them. The slave was sent back to the kitchen to get some chunks of newly-baked bread which the trio grasped gratefully and headed out of the hall searching for a tree under which to enjoy the tasty fare.

They had been up since daybreak and once their bellies were full tiredness fell upon them as the hot rays of the afternoon sun flickered hypnotically through the foliage of their tree. They stretched themselves out and all were soon snoring loudly.

It was in this ignominious position that Abbess Fara found them. Botolph was drawn out of his slumber when the world suddenly went dark as his new abbess's shadow fell across his face. His eyes opened to the view of a black silhouette surrounded by a brilliant halo of sunshine.

He jumped up, embarrassed, guessing who stood before him and then re-descended to kneel before her, saying "Mother Abbess, your servant Botolph."

"Stand up young man. I know quite well who you are. Pax vobiscum. You have taken long enough to reach us. Where's your friend Luka?"

Botolph stood. "Et pax in terra, Abbess. I regret that Luka has asked me to bring you his apologies. I'm afraid that he has been further delayed. Indeed ..." he stuttered and felt a lump grow in his throat, "... indeed, I'm afraid his ... delay may be ...um ... permanent."

"Permanent?" The formidable Abbess glowered at him. "Where *is* he then?"

"He's ... He's at Bonoriacum."

"Bonoriacum! Bonoriacum is a foul nest of pagans and robbers. What in Heaven's name is he doing *there*?"

"It's a long story Mother," said Botolph.

"I look forward to hearing it in minute detail," she replied acidly.

By this time the guards had also awoken and they struggled clumsily to their feet and stood sheepishly to one side listening to Botolph's interrogation. Suddenly she spun round and turned her penetrating gaze onto them.

"And *you* two. What are *you* doing here?"

One bodyguard at first responded proudly and strongly, "We are the young monk's escorts sent by King Dagobert, my lady and are due to return to the palace at Lutetia ... so ... err ... so ..."

His confidence waned under her steely unblinking stare and his voice trailed away. He cleared his throat and shuffled his feet finishing feebly, "... I suppose that ... um ... with your permission we should be on our way?"

She seemed to soften a little and raised her hand in blessing saying "Go in peace" and turning on her heel walked briskly from the dishevelled trio.

"Rather you than me!" whispered the first bodyguard to Botolph, nodding in the direction of the departing Abbess and with a chuckle he and his colleague turned likewise and scuttled off to find the ostler and make their escape.

CHAPTER 23
Bernard the Pot-stirrer

Botolph was rather non-plussed by these events and remained standing under the tree glancing first in the direction in which the Abbess had left and then at the retreating shoulders of his former bodyguards. Suddenly he felt very alone. Unbeknown to him, his thoughts reflected those of Luka a few days earlier. Here he was, in the grounds of a foreign abbey where he knew absolutely nobody. His only acquaintances were in the process of leaving and heading back to Villa Latiniacum which he guessed held secrets about which he was better remaining ignorant. His dear friend Luka seemed lost forever and now ... he did not even have a horse! He stared at his sandals and thought that at least he had his health and his two feet; he tried moving the left one and watched dispassionately as it pushed forwards in the general direction of the abbey church. As it disappeared beneath the hem of his habit the other popped forwards and then similarly disappeared.

"Well brother ... ?"

Botolph jumped and then turned and looked into the eyes of Bernard the Pot-stirrer.

"You look lost, my friend."

"Lost? Well, yes I suppose I feel rather lost. It's been my ambition for so long to reach this abbey but now that I am here ..."

" ... you wonder if you've made a mistake?" the monk finished for him.

"A mistake? Oh no! I am sure I'm in the right place. I've no doubt that I was meant to come here and that God has many plans for me ... It's just that ... Yes, as you said, I feel rather lost at the moment."

Bernard laughed good naturedly and said "Come. If you feel lost let's walk around the abbey grounds and see if we can help you to find out where you are."

They turned onto the path taken some minutes ago by the striding abbess.

"You know what doves do when they arrive in new surroundings. They circle in the air and get a good view of the layout before they land. We'll wander round the abbey like the doves so that you can see what's here before you become 'unlost' and finally roost in your new dovecote. On the way I'll give you a brief description of my history and you can tell me yours."

As they walked Bernard told him of his home town of Ganda in northern Gallia and an inspirational man called Bishop Amand who had influenced his life. Botolph was always fascinated to hear tales of far-away places and listened intently.

"So Ganda must be a big place then if it's got a bishop," said Botolph.

"Well it is," admitted Bernard "but Amand was not bishop of Ganda, he was actually Bishop of Mosaetraij - another town further to the east but he was never one for being confined; he believed his calling was to travel and in doing so to spread the word of God."

"So he travelled to Ganda and spread the word to you and that's why you're here?" offered Botolph.

"Yes, more or less. I first met him in Ganda when I was eleven summers.   I was a growing boy with a healthy appetite and I had many brothers and sisters."

He laughed. "I think my parents were quite pleased to put me under the bishop's protection so that they had one less mouth to feed! We travelled south at first and stopped at a place called Elnone where we were given a great welcome by the village folk. While we were there, King Dagobert turned up and there was a big row which ended up with Bishop Amand being told he was no longer welcome in Gallia!"

"King Dagobert?" said Botolph. "That doesn't sound like him. We travelled from Sithiu with him earlier this year and he seemed very mild-mannered."

"Ah well I think he's mellowed a bit now but a few years ago he was living a riotous life of which Amand did not approve and he unhesitatingly told him so. The king was offended and promptly told him to leave his country and never come back."

"And did he?"

"Oh yes. We left straight away and headed towards Lutetia with a view of going to Rome. During our journey I told the bishop that I wanted to become a monk. He insisted that we spent a lot of time praying about it. Finally he decided that the most important thing for me was an education. So we pressed on past Lutetia until we arrived here in Evoriacum which even then had a great reputation as a seat of learning. He left me under the care of Abbess Fara gaining from her the promise that when I was ready she would send me back to a monastery in the North."

"And where's the bishop now?"

"Well I don't really know but from what I gather, after we parted company he travelled thousands of leagues to the east. The word is that he has spent the past few years bringing the word of God to the pagans there. I then heard that he was in Rome but a few months ago word came of his return to Gallia and news that he was building an abbey at Elnone.

"But what about Dagobert's banishment order?"

"Oh, that's all been forgotten. In fact King Dagobert invited him to act as tutor to his son but Amand declined."

"That must have been for his eldest, Sigeberht. He lives in Metz; Clovis would have been too little. I know that the king worries about Sigeberht living so far away from the family and I can see that someone like your bishop would have made an ideal guardian."

"Not Amand's style though," said Bernard. "The last thing he'd want would be to be stuck in an out-of-the-way place like Metz teaching an arrogant child the rudiments of Latin grammar."

By this time they had walked past the paddock where several horses were grazing contentedly. One looked up and stared hard at Botolph but then seemed to decide that he was of no consequence and returned its attention to the more pressing grassy meal.

Bernard pointed out three large halls which served as dormitories for the monks and then they were strolling through the vineyard and admiring the fine crop of grapes.

"We're proud of our wine at Evoriacum," said Bernard. "One thing about it here, you'll eat and drink well. Abbess Fara is unstinting in ensuring that our bellies never go unfilled."

Botolph laughed and thought how well that would have suited Luka. They strolled on in silence as he remembered his friend's baking prowess and the wonderful bread he used to bake at Cantwarebury and how the prior had chastised him for making it too tasty. There would be none of that sort of conflict at Evoriacum. Oh how Botolph missed Luka's smiling face and happy-go-lucky disposition.

He wondered what was happening to him; what friends he had made; whether he was still alive; whether he had killed anybody else. Oh dear, they had been such a good pair together and Botolph worried about him getting himself into even more trouble. He wondered if he was still swearing as much. With a crowd like Bonitius's lot, cursing and swearing would be the language of everyday life ...

"... Botolph?"

"Ah! Sorry, I was leagues away. What were you saying?"

"Over there. Those are the nun's dormitories."

That would bring joy to Luka's face, thought Botolph as he replied "Oh ... Right!"

"And on the other side of them is the kitchen garden where all the fresh vegetables and herbs are grown. Over here is the infirmary. You'd better hope that you never end up in there because the only way you'll come out is dead. Unless that is, Brother Abraham's herbs do you any good."

A tubby monk was wobbling up the path towards them having just passed through the gap in the box hedge which surrounded the kitchen garden.

"Brother Abraham, this is Brother Botolph," said Bernard. A broad smile broke across the little monk's face as he wiped his soil-covered hands on his habit and warmly clasped the newcomer's arms in greeting.

"Pax vobiscum brither and welcome to our hoomble abbey of Evoriacum. May y'r stay be happy healthy and full of the joys of britherly love," he intoned, his voice and demeanour having a sincere ring.

"Thank you brother. I hear that it's the herbs of your tending that serve to keep the abbey healthy."

"Oh indeed it is, indeed it is, wi' the Lord's help," came the reply.

145

"So would you be from Ireland?" asked Botolph.

"Now whatever makes you t'ink that?" grinned the monk. "Might it be that Oi still have a little accent left from me days in the Emerald Oisle. T' be sure oi t'ought oi spoke wi' a Gallic accent now."

"Not Gallic enough," laughed Bernard. "In fact we have great difficulty in ever stopping him from talking. He's always getting into trouble from the abbess for his loquaciousness during mealtimes. In fact that's why she sent him off to tend the herbs in the kitchen garden, - so that he can talk to them all day instead of disturbing the rest of us."

Abraham grinned good-naturedly. "Ah to be sure, but don't we grow the best herbs in Christendom as a result of all the Oirish talking I give to them?"

"Well I must admit," laughed Bernard, "that since Abraham has been in charge of the garden it has flourished and prospered and so generally has the health of our inmates. The infirmary has never been so little used!"

"D'ere we are d'en. 'Tis the Oirish d'at does it, d'ere's no doubt about it. But Oi can't stand here all day wastin' toime wi' ye. Oi've got my manure to spread, so oi'll be wishing you a good day and look forward to seeing ye tomorrow," with which he raised his hand and wobbled his way off towards the vineyard.

"His accent reminds me of Father Fursey," said Botolph.

"Who's that then?"

"Oh, he was the abbot of our monastery in Cnobersburg before we had to flee to avoid being murdered by King Penda."

"You've had an interesting life already then?"

146

"Hah! That's one way of putting it. There've certainly been a few challenges but I suppose that's God's way of making us strong?"

Brother Bernard came to a standstill. "That pretty well concludes our tour of the abbey grounds," he said. "But the rest of the abbey estate stretches for leagues around. I expect we'll all be called out into the fields soon, helping to gather in the wheat which is nearly ready."

And thus it was that Botolph was introduced to the Evoriacum Abbey. As the days passed he gradually came to feel more part of the community and less of an outsider. Certainly he should *not* have felt an outsider since there were many other Britons there. The common language was Latin and he had no problem with that and continued to enjoy listening to tales of distant countries and meeting people from all walks of life.

"Distant" was the way that Abbess Fara also remained for quite a long while but Botolph grew to love and respect her. She maintained an aura of arrogance but it was clear that she was devoted to her people and wanted the best for them and for God.

True to her promise at their first meeting, she laid aside some time for Botolph to tell her the whole of his story; about how he and Luka met and their escape from Waif Island and Luka's narrow escape from death. He told her about Princess Eanswythe and King Eadbald and Martha the fisherman's wife and even about Farmer Mosel and his family.

She listened intently to all he said and her only interruptions consisted of "Mm" and "Oh?". As Botolph concluded his tale he found his stomach filled with butterflies as he told of how he had had to leave his dear friend Luka behind.   He fell silent and could not raise his eyes from his hands.

The abbess too remained silent and when Botolph finally looked up he was surprised to see a tear rolling down her cheek.   The mature abbess and the young man gazed at each other for a long moment and then she said simply, "I understand."

After that, he could do no wrong.   She pushed him and worked him hard.   He laboured in the fields - in the kitchen garden - with the pigs sheep and cattle - in the scriptorium - in the kitchen - in the chapel.   When the ague hit the monastery she had him working in the infirmary but in spite of the fact that he tended half the monastery including the abbess herself, he never succumbed to the illness and all his patients recovered.   Brother Abraham maintained that it was the prophylactic herbs with which he supplied Botolph that kept him healthy and that it was the medicinal ones that he supplied for Botolph's patients that enabled their recovery.

Botolph had been tonsured the day after he had had his talk with Abbess Fara.   He had been surprised and said as much to John the tonsurer as his hair was being chopped.

"Why are you surprised?" asked Brother John, "You are a monk now!"

"Yes ... but I am *not*!" he had replied.   "I am a *novitiate* and won't be a monk for several more years."

"Ah - you don't understand how it works here," said John.   "The abbess makes her own decisions and her own rules.   She'll have had a long talk with you.   Am I right?"

Botolph made the mistake of nodding his head and he cried out as the tonsurer's blade dug into his scalp.   John leapt back and then grabbed a towel to stem the flow of blood that his blade had produced.

"Now that was a silly thing to do," he said crossly, "Next time you're tonsured you'd better make sure you remember to say "Yes" and "No" and otherwise keep your head still; otherwise you're going to die an ignominious and premature death from loss of blood."

"Yes, I'm sorry," said Botolph.

"Well I'm sorry too," John grumbled. "Don't go telling the others or you'll give me a bad reputation. Now what were we saying? ... Ah yes, so you've had your chat with Abbess Fara. Well there we are then. She's weighed you up and considers that you've all the right qualities to be a monk and so a monk you now are even though at present you're an *'inexperienced* monk;' it's that which she will change over the coming months. There you are. All done. Off you go. I can hear the bell tolling for Vespers."

CHAPTER 24
Silvius gets burned

Luka had also settled into his new way of life. He had become completely at ease with the rogues who were now his comrades-in-arms. He and Eluhan had not exactly become close friends; they kept a wary eye on each other and neither actively sought the other's company but nor did they find any need to avoid it.

Theirs was a large community and they had no produce to sell in order to support its maintenance. As far as Bonitius was concerned 'business' meant robbing and thieving and those were the activities that he directed. Raiding parties were regularly sent out into the countryside and they would return with whatever was on Bonitius's shopping list plus any other opportunistic possibilities that turned up at the time.

All the cattle sheep and pigs that gave sustenance to the bandits had, at some time or another, been stolen from local landowners.

Bonitius's attempts at animal husbandry were not very skilful and those animals which were slaughtered or died had to be replaced; cattle rustling therefore was a routine and essential activity. Every so often one or two farmers would become indignant about their losses and would gather their friends together in an attempt to recover their property.

Bonitius's guard system was well set up however and so the attempts were, without exception, never successful. Luka's conscience had no problem with fighting battles to defend Bonitius's property, nor initially did the cattle rustling bother him.

One night two farmers who had pushed their chances too far ended up getting themselves killed. Bonitius decided to use the event as a warning to other locals not to try the same thing. The following day he put Luka in charge of a particularly disreputable group with orders to return the bodies to their families and to bring back whatever other loot presented itself and then to burn the homesteads.

Amongst the group was a pair to whom Luka had already taken a particular dislike. Both were short and stocky and the most evil of the two was inappropriately called Silvius.

Luka set off with a feeling of unease which was not alleviated when they arrived at the first farm. As they burst out of the cover of the woodland, the farmer's children ran to the protection of their mother and the little family cowered at the entrance to their hut. Luka, as the lead horseman, looked down at them and tried to feel like the bandit he was supposed to be. The farmer's body was tossed at the widow's feet whereupon she burst into a cacophony of wild wailing and fell sobbing upon it. Two of the party dismounted and Silvius entered the hut and came out with a burning branch that he had taken from the hearth. He held it under the eaves to fire the thatch.

"No!" shouted Luka. "Enough! Mount up!"

The surprised bandit turned and looked insolently towards him for a moment; he then turned back and defiantly applied the torch to the eaves. The yellow of the flame as the straw caught fire was interrupted by a flash of silver as Luka's seax flew through the air and pinned the man's sleeve to the wooden doorpost. He dropped the burning branch and tried unsuccessfully to wrench his arm free.   The flames licked down and set fire to his hair.   Luka leapt from his horse and, using his own cape, smothered the flames from both hair and thatch.

He pulled the seax from the wood as the man fell to his knees holding his face and sobbing.   Luka hauled him back to his feet and felt a glow of what struck him as unreasonable pleasure as he kicked him towards his horse saying mercilessly "Now do as you're told in future.   Mount up!"

Still rubbing his newly-acquired short singed stubble, the man stifled his sobbing and climbed onto his horse. Luka mounted up too and with never risking a glance at the family or his followers led the way to the next farm. Here a similar scene was enacted but with less drama.   A more-disciplined team returned to the camp empty-handed.

Bonitius was furious and subjected Luka to a torrent of bellowing that looked as if it might last forever.   Luka stood his ground defiantly and let his master rant and rave without interruption.   The half bald Silvius was unwise enough to whinge at Bonitius before the master's anger was spent and received a cuff on the left side of his head to match the burn on his right.

Eventually after what seemed to Luka like an age of pacing up and down Bonitius decided he had no more to say and waved his hand in dismissive disgust saying "Get out of my sight, all of you," and they discreetly sidled away to their various forest lairs.

CHAPTER 25
Feya and Nanthild

The children settled in well at Dagobert's court.

Nanthild was as gracious as ever and Clovis was gaining in confidence and becoming quite a handful. As soon as Dagobert had heard about Feya he had earmarked her as a potential handmaiden for his queen. When he saw how Feya cared for her 4-year-old brother Cedric, he knew he had not been mistaken.

This in itself had posed a problem. Feya would not be separated from Cedric and the king was uneasy about his younger son growing up with a commoner who might acquire ideas above his station.

His fears were allayed when Nanthild told him how, without a word from her, Feya had immediately started to tutor Cedric to be Clovis's little henchman.

The other children were offered no such favours and had been scattered throughout the household to earn their board and lodging but there were no complaints and the whole group was able to keep in touch through Feya who had total freedom of movement throughout the palace.

That is not to say that Feya's life was easy. Although she had many privileges she was at Queen Nanthild's beck and call and the queen was a demanding patroness. There was many a time when Feya would have liked to point out that she had only one pair of hands and could not be in two places at the same time. In spite of her youth she was wise enough to know that she must hold her tongue and endure her tribulations with a sweet smile.

By contrast, Nanthild had found life much better since Feya's arrival. Although there was a vast difference in their ages Feya was very easy to talk to and Nanthild relished the close female companionship that she had previously lacked. The demands of Clovis were also easier to bear when they could be divided into two - or even into three ways if Cedric's involvement was taken into account.

In fact Nanthild mused that the boys were like two young puppies who were able to play and romp together rather than the single pup that Clovis had been, always looking for mischief with which to keep himself amused. Feya watched their games from the side-lines and soon intervened if she sensed that Cedric was overstepping the boundaries.

When the youngsters tired however she was also quick to take Cedric into her arms. He would lie back silently with his thumb in his mouth, the picture of contentment as his eyelids fluttered and he drifted off to sleep. Clovis would often remain a ball of energy and seem disinclined to let Cedric rest and even showed some jealousy at the attention Feya gave him.

It was then that *Nanthild's* wisdom came into play and she would entertain her son until he also succumbed to fatigue. Winter's afternoons saw the cosy picture of the lady and her maiden sitting in front of a log fire with their charges each snoozing on their laps.

Nanthild felt that she had become a better mother since Feya had joined her. She had been sad when her elder son Sigeberht had departed for Metz but was forced to admit to herself that she had, in some ways, been relieved to see him go. She had been much weakened by her second pregnancy and Clovis's demands for her breast milk drained her emotionally as well as physically. She had found the long journey through Austrasia and Neustria quite exhausting and it came as a great relief when they were at last settled in Lutetia again.

This however brought more stresses in the designing and building of the new monastery; by the time that Feya arrived Nanthild was reaching her wits end. To her pleasure all that had now changed and even winter evenings that were usually so tedious had taken on a new and valued lustre.

CHAPTER 26
Ella and Erchinoald

In a Neustrian palace much further to the north of Lutetia another drama being played out. This drama would affect the lives of Gallia as a whole but in particular it would affect the family of King Dagobert.

The characters involved were a fifty-six year old widower called Erchinoald and a ten year old slave girl by the name of Balthild.

Balthild had been born in Britain. Her father was Ricberht, the stepson of Raedwald, King of East Anglia. Ricberht was hard, cruel, ambitious and full of resentment as a result of his step-father considering that he had no kingly qualities. When the old king died, Ricberht's half-brother took the crown - as previously decreed by their father. Ricberht fumed both silently and publicly and looked for a chance to turn the situation to his advantage. At long last an opportunity arose whereby he was able to dispose of his half-brother without any repercussions and to take the kingdom for his own.

This heralded the start of three years of pagan debauchery in East Anglia during which time one of the many children that Ricberht fathered by a multitude of different concubines was the little Princess Balthild.

As was bound to happen, the debauchery finally turned inwards on itself and instead of preying on others, dog fought dog and Ricberht became one of the casualties. The young princess was sold to a Gallic trader in the East Anglian port of Gippeswic from whence she was exported to

Gesoriacum and sold on twice more before she arrived as a toddler in the Neustrian palace of Lord Erchinoald.

He bought her as an investment and apart from treasuring the evidence of her provenance took very little interest in her as she grew up with the other slaves of his household.

Erchinoald was not a bad man and his wife Leutsinde was as ambitious as he was. They had a son, Leudesius, who was a fat and pampered brat upon whom the couple doted. When Leutsinde suddenly died, the old nobleman was distraught.

As time went on, he became more and more lonely in spite of his large court. His son had always been worse than useless and since the death of his wife Erchinoald had found him impossible to handle.

Erchinoald yearned for the sex, security and comfort he had found in his wife and began to turn to his slave-girls in search of the former. They soon became wary of his regular prowling ventures into their domain and did their best to avoid him. There were several that he particularly favoured and even some who favoured *him*.

One morning when dawn was just breaking, he rose from his bed with a lust that he could not contain. Gathering his cloak around him, he made for the slaves' hut. They were just rising from their straw pallets and in the half-light he found the pretty fifteen-year-old with the high cheek bones. He grasped her wrist and shouted "Out, out, all of you - out," as he swished his cane at them. Some screamed but others giggled as they emptied the hut, leaving him to draw the young girl back to her pallet which, he noted with satisfaction, was still warm from her night's sleep.

Ella looked at him wide-eyed but this was not her first time with him and she knew what was expected of her.

The first time had come after he had groomed her over several weeks, taking her into the palace, dressing her in fine clothing and feeding her well with exotic fruit. She had been pampered and favoured and the older girls had warned and prepared her for what was going to happen.

She was not surprised therefore, when, one night, well after the time when she would normally have left, she had found herself alone with him in his sleeping chamber. That night she had lost her virginity to a man who was nearly four times her age. And yet she did not resent it. He was her lord, after all and he had treated her with tenderness and respect. Clearly he was experienced in the art of making love. The Lady Leutsinde must have taught him well how a lady's body should be used. Strangely, far from feeling defiled, she felt a new respect for her lord and for the now dead lady whose place she had, at least temporarily, taken. She wondered if she was the first he had had since her death and guessed that she was. What would happen now? Would he work his way through the servant girls or would she be able to keep him for herself?

"How are you?" he said.

"How *am* I?" she replied. "That is a very odd question. I am fine thank you. Why wouldn't I be, having been loved by my lord?"

Now it was his turn to be surprised.

"Hah!" he said. "I knew you were a good girl but I didn't know you were *that* good. Will you forgive me for my actions this night?"

"I will, my lord, and I thank you for your kindness."

"What?" he cried, with a great guffaw of laughter, "you really are full of surprises. Now though," he had said, becoming serious again, "Now though young Ella. Don't you start getting ideas above your place. Because you have shared my bed it does not make you my queen. You are still just the same as the other slave girls. Do you understand?"

She had nodded contentedly.

"Now! We must get you back to your hut. I may come for you again ... or I may not ... or I may come for one of the other girls. You must not get jealous or treat me with any undue familiarity; things must stay the same as they always were. Right?"

"I understand, my lord," she had said demurely but hiding a smile knowing that they could never be the same again.

The following morning she was besieged by a panoply of questions which she answered with a serene and secretive smile whilst assuring her colleagues that all was well and that she had not been violated.

To herself she wondered if that were true. Of course she *had* been violated by an old and singularly inappropriate man. But it did not feel like it. Although she felt a slight inner soreness and was rather trembly at the knees she felt generally wonderful. She wondered if she were pregnant. After the tutoring she had been given by the other girls, she assumed in her naïvety that she probably was and she wondered what it would be like to have a baby.

But as time went on, it became clear that she was not pregnant. Erchinoald called for her regularly but he took his selection from three of the other slave-girls from time to time too. He continued to treat Ella with respect.

And so that early morning arrival of her lord in her hut, was no more than a slight variation to the usual proceedings. He had never laid with either her or any of the other girls in their hut before. Clearly his need that morning had been desperate. Maybe he found that laying the vixen in her own den was more exciting than devouring his prey in the palace.

CHAPTER 27
Gold Bullion

Silvius had not only lost some hair but he had also lost his name since he was known as "Scarface" for the rest of his life by friends and enemies alike. Most of his hair grew back but he retained a vivid red flush of knotted skin on his right cheek where the flames had done their work. The scar was a constant reminder to the other inmates at the camp that Luka was not a person to be crossed. In spite of Bonitius's long-term fury at his orders having been ignored that day, Luka from then onwards became his first choice of leader whenever raiding parties were needed. He knew that he could trust this complicated dwarf to bring some sort of order to his unruly gang of bandits and at least to lead them back alive, even if his orders were not always carried out to the letter.

One day, Scarface disappeared and in spite of Bonitius questioning all who might have known of his plans, no trace could be found of him. Bonitius secretly wondered if his festering hate had finally erupted and he had been unwise enough to make some sort of attack on Luka as a result of which the dwarf had perhaps eliminated him. It was unusual. Such things did occur but there was normally a body - even if nobody took any responsibility for it. Bonitius questioned Luka many times on the subject but, drunk or sober, he persistently denied any involvement in Scarface's disappearance.

The daily running of the camp became more difficult as autumn turned to winter. Bonitius was beginning to regret his actions towards the local farmers. He began to realise that he had overegged the pudding. His severe treatments and killings had resulted in there being fewer local farms for him to raid and he was having to send his rustlers further out into the forests to find more distant farms in order to bring in a regular supply of meat.

As a result of a mixture of fear and prudence, even well-guarded travellers were now avoiding the Bonoriacum road when travelling from Lutetia to Meaux and were taking the riverside road instead. This was outside Bonitius's operating area and did not offer a quick and easy escape back into his forest refuge. With winter now fast approaching, there would be even fewer travellers and funds and stock were running low. Bonitius was worried. Something had to be done.

Salvation came in the form of intelligence regarding a consignment of gold that King Dagobert was sending from his palace to Meaux. Bonitius guessed that this would have to be done before winter really set in.

The news came to Bonitius's ears one night when they were feasting in the main hall and his eyes lit up greedily in the reflection of the flames from the hearth. Here was the solution to his problems that, if successful, would get them through the winter. If unsuccessful they would be dead anyway.

It was a dangerous prospect. The wagon would be well-guarded and would, no doubt, take the riverside road. Bonitius and his men had never conducted a raid so far from Bonoriacum and this would give the royal planners a false sense of security. Other smaller gangs who might hear of the consignment would be put off by the enormity of the task of facing a large array of palace guards.

It turned out that the information had come via Meaux rather than Lutetia and Bonitius immediately set about ensuring that the small group who were around him when the news was delivered kept silent about it. In the meantime he infiltrated the two cities with his spies in order to discover more precise details. But time was short. He needed to act quickly.

CHAPTER 28
Magburga and Nelburga

Botolph's time was passing peaceably at Evoriacum Abbey. Although it was a very relaxed way of life, every day was full. He enjoyed helping with the harvest: first the barley, then the wheat and finally the grapes. As each crop came in, monks, nuns and slaves, under the farmer's guidance would be involved in sorting, trimming, threshing, storing, milling, treading, mashing, and washing and it was all a great joy to Botolph.

Abbess Fara ran a well-disciplined but free and easy institution. Botolph began to get to know the other monks and nuns. Chatter was firmly discouraged but a blind eye was turned to discrete conversation, even that between monks and nuns.

Naturally it was the English-speakers who engaged Botolph first. There were two nuns from East Anglia - a couple of monks from Mercia - a monk from Deira and three nuns from Gippeswic; it gave him much joy to discover that there were also two nuns from Cantium.

He had his first chance to have a conversation with the latter when they ended up in the same haymaking team. Their names were Magburga and Nelburga and they came from the western part of Cantium of which Botolph knew very little. He had travelled through it on the way to the Tamesis river crossing when he and his brother Adulph had journeyed from Hrofsceaster to Cnobersburg. They had been rumbling along in a fish wain and that had not given him much chance to appreciate the area – beautiful or otherwise.   He struggled to remember the name of the wain's driver on that momentous day and after a while it came back to him ... yes ... "Hessa" of course.

His silence whilst he reminisced had the advantage of bestowing some decorum on his interchange with the twin sisters ... for that was what they proved to be.

It was their brother who had sent them to Evoriacum. His name was Athelwald and he, Magburga proudly told Botolph, was king of Cantium.

At that moment Botolph was in the midst of pitching some hay onto the back of the cart but the girl's comments made him stop in half pitch.   Both hay and fork dropped unceremoniously onto the ground.   Botolph swung round towards the two nuns: "*Eadbald* is king of Cantium" he said.

"Oh no ..." Magburg started to reply but then lowered her eyes in submission as she and her sister abruptly returned to their task of gathering the hay into stooks.

Botolph looked over his shoulder to see Abbess Fara and Prioress Pedra descending upon them.

It was the Prioress who had charge of the nuns. She was tall and her countenance was always severe.   Like the abbess she wore the grey undyed woollen habit of the monastery with a white scapula and veil but unlike her superior she exuded coldness and Botolph felt an involuntary shiver as she passed.

The time had come for Vespers however and Botolph would have to wait for another day before he would be able to find the answer to the mystery of who King Athelwald might be.   It did however perplex him to the point that he had difficulty in concentrating on the nuances of the antiphons during the evening's devotions.

In fact it was several days later when they were out in the fields again before he was able to get close enough to

Magburga to ask her what she meant about Athelwald being king of Cantium.

"He is!" she insisted.

"Well he wasn't when I left Britain," said Botolph, "King Eadbald of Folcanstane ruled Cantium."

"Oh!" giggled Magburga, "Eadbald's our half-brother and it's true that he rules the eastern side of Cantium but it's our other half-brother, Athelwald, who has ruled the *western* side for many years. Eadbald is the senior king but he rarely, if ever, visits the west."

"Oh I see," said Botolph. "So you and your half-brothers share the same father but have different mothers?"

"Yes," said Magburga. "Our father was King Ethelbert and the boys' mother was Queen Bertha but *our* mother was his second wife who was less than half his age when he married her."

Botolph was silent for a few moments, recollecting stories that he had heard many months previously.

"So," he said carefully, taking care not to cause offence, "your mother ... was the lady King *Eadbald* married ... after Ethelbert died?"

Magburga bit her lip and nodded.

"And that caused a great furore within the church in Cantwarebury who were incensed that the new king had married his father's widow?"

Magburga nodded again. "Eadbald was young. He had always rebelled against Christianity and wanted to go back to the old pagan ways so he was happy to upset the church in any way that he could."

"That's why he left Cantwarebury and went to Folcanstane," interrupted Nelburga. "He set up a new community there taking the new widow as his bride."

"But it was not long afterwards that he *divorced* your mother?"

"Yes, - he realised that, to be an effective king, he had follow the new religion so the church brought a Christian bride over from Gallia for him."

"Queen Ymme."

"Queen Ymme," they chorused, nodding and laughing again.

"So what happened to your mother?"

"When Eadbald married her he didn't realise that she was already pregnant." They giggled.

"So," said Magburga taking up the story, "clearly our mother couldn't stay in Folcanstane, so she was sent to live in our brother Athelwald's court in West Cantium.

"So that's where you were born and grew up?"

They nodded.

"Are Athelwald and Eadbald alike?"

"Athelwald's younger," said Nelburga, "but he didn't really want to be king. He'd rather spend his time hunting than having to look after his court; he likes the easy life."

"But Eadbald insisted," said Magburga, "he said that it was impossible for him to rule both ... ," - she broke off suddenly and Botolph glanced behind him to see Prioress Pedra striding purposefully towards them.

CHAPTER 29
Balthild and Erchinoald

Ella, the slave girl with the high cheek bones continued to be one of Erchinoald's favourites but another year had passed and he was looking towards the future.

The youngster, Balthild, whom he had bought as an investment, was now approaching puberty. She'd grown up to be a pretty little thing with those finely-sculptured white marble features which were typical of her kinfolk. It would be another year or two before she was ready, but now that she had ten summers it was time to start grooming her for his bed.

It fell to Ella to notice what was happening and, seeing that nothing could be done to stop it even if Ella had wanted to, she felt it her duty to prepare Balthild for the future that might be awaiting her.

The tall-for-her-age Briton with her puppy-fat breastlets was at first uncomprehending and then astonished when she was told "You're the next you know".

Her noble heredity was instantly awakened and as soon as all became clear she tossed her head and said "Oh no I'm not!"

"You must," Ella told her. "He's your lord and if he's chosen you, you'll have to obey."

"I don't think so," she said.

"*You* don't think so! *You* don't think so! Who are *you* to even think *anything*?"

"I'm a British princess," she retorted "and I'm not going to be defiled by some dirty old Gallic farmer."

168

"Whether he's a farmer or not my girl, he's your master. He *owns* you and whatever he chooses for you to do, you are going to have to do it so I suggest you get used to the idea," she snapped. "Anyway, he's not dirty ... and believe me you could be defiled by someone a lot worse."

She quietened, thinking back to a couple of weeks earlier when the lord's son Leudesius had decided that he wanted some of what his father had been having. He was a totally different prospect to the old man and was entirely lacking in any social niceties. He, for all his youth, *was* dirty and smelly and fat and unmanly and rough and ignorant ... she tried to extend the list of his shortcomings but ran out of suitable adjectives. She had been alone in one of the animal huts, when she had heard a noise behind her and swung round to be confronted by his cruel grey staring eyes bearing down on her.

He had said nothing but grasped both her wrists and in one movement turned her round away from him, bent her over and lifted her shift over her head. She was face down in some smelly hay while he wreaked his painful degrading havoc. There was nothing she could do and when he had finished he hissed in her ear "Tell my father and I will kill you."

After vaguely trying to tidy her state of dress she had collapsed onto the hay and sobbed and sobbed until all her tears had been exhausted. She hoped Balthild would never have to endure anything like that. Knowing Balthild, she would put up a fight and probably get beaten as a result.

But Balthild did not have to put up with anything like that. Forewarned of Erchinoald's intentions she made an art out of avoiding him. That did not mean that she could avoid him forever and he tried several times to approach her with a view to luring her back to his quarters. Eventually he succeeded in voicing his invitation but failed entirely to achieve the desired result.

She simply put her nose in the air, gave an imperious "No!" and then turned and strode quickly away, before his astonished puckered lips could complete the "Why ever not?" that had formed in his voice box.

He was at once frustrated and yet, being a reasonable man, quite amused at the little creature's resistance. As time went on, he did, somewhat half-heartedly try several more times; each with the same result.

CHAPTER 30
Attack

The consignment was leaving Lutetia in three days. They would set up an ambush by the riverside near where Luka had taken his fateful journey into the woods. It was at this point that the trees ran close to the river and they would be able to wait hidden in the forest until the caravan of horses was sighted.

Bonitius formulated his plans for the attack and then called in his henchmen for a round table discussion to decide on the finer points. The evening meal was foreshortened so that the meeting could be held in the Feasting Hall. It went on well into the night.

It was an eerie gathering. A map had been drawn in the earthen floor and surrounded by candles. The six men crouched together studying it and then Bonitius grasped one of the candle holders, and, using the flame's light, pointed out with his staff the tracks, hazards and other features of the campaign.

He proposed that they took twenty men which, he said, should easily outnumber those travelling with the coach of which there would probably be a maximum of twelve; a vanguard of four, four others with the coach and four rear-guard; there would also be the driver and grooms but they could not be expected to put up much of a fight.

Luka was not happy.

"There's going to be one hell of a scrap Bonitius," he said. "This isn't going to be your average hold up of a cart containing four frightened people protected by two incompetent guards. We're talking here of a major gold consignment protected by twelve – and it may be even more – *twelve professional* fighters. We need more men."

There were mutterings of agreement and Bonitius glared across at Luka: "And just where do you think I am going to get more men?"

"Well there must be other bandit groups in the area?" said Luka.

"Yes there are but I wouldn't trust any of them to look after my grandmother."

"Oh, they're villains are they?   Not decent honest citizens like us?" Luka crowed to the amusement of the others.

"That's not what I mean. We have to keep this quiet to avoid our plans leaking.   If we were to involve other groups, the word would get out and it could end up with *us* getting ambushed instead of the king's gold."

"So what are we going to do then? We need more men," Luka repeated.

"Well I suppose we might be able to draw in another ten or twelve from some of the farming community that owe me allegiance."

"What about the forest guards?" asked one of the others.

Bonitius was getting edgy as he began to realise the enormity of the situation and his frustrations suddenly boiled over: "We can't leave the camp unguarded you stupid shit," he erupted. "What's the point of going out on a raid and coming back to find we've been raided ourselves?"

His roar was greeted by a silence.

"Well dwarf?" he said with a sigh, when the silence became untenable, "Where do we go from here?"

"We *have* to do this raid I suppose?" said Luka.

"Well, put it this way, if we don't, you won't be eating in the middle of winter."

"Well then. I think the answer is we'll just have to amass as many trustworthy men as we can and follow the original plan."

"Great!" said Bonitius.

"I haven't finished. We must wait in the woods and assess how strong the opposition is. To be safe we need two of our men for every one of theirs. If the odds are worse than that we must abandon the idea."

"What then?"

"Well we will just have to let them go and hope that we find some other rich pickings before the winter sets in."

There was a pause in the proceedings as eye met eye and moved on.

"So be it," said Bonitius capitulating with a sigh. "I'll see if I can rouse out more men tomorrow and then we'll run the plans past the rest of the group tomorrow night".

--o--

By the time of the general briefing Bonitius had found only three more men to add to his party but he made it clear to the gathering that if the odds did not seem to be stacked heavily in their favour the attack would be aborted.

The information that he had received from Meaux and Lutetia indicated that the consignment would be leaving Dagobert's palace at first light on the morning of September twentieth. It was about nine leagues between the two cities, so they would plan to arrive in Meaux before dark. In spite of Bonitius's hopes to the contrary, his intelligence told him that the party would be following the river towards Villa

Calae before turning inland. They were going to have to make their attack when the coach had been travelling for a quarter of a day. By that time, Bonitius surmised, the guards would be more relaxed and less alert than earlier. They would also be nearing Villa Calae and this might give them a false sense of security too. It seemed a good plan.

That same morning soon after first light, Bonitius's twenty-three men left the safety of their woods in three separate groups. It was only two leagues to the ambush point so they were in position in plenty of time.

Four of the bandits were detailed to leave their horses hidden in the woods with the main group and make their way on foot to the western edge of the forest where they could look out over the river crossing. As soon as the wagon was spotted, two of the men were to take the news to Bonitius whilst the other two were to stay in position until the convoy was well past them so that they could ensure no nasty surprises in the form of after-guards.

The others stayed hidden within the confines of the trees. They were all nervous in spite of their years of experience. This they knew was a big prize and the fight could be hard and long. They spent their time chatting in low voices, their horses' reins lashed loosely to various trees.

Bonitius was leaning on his horse and patting its flank as he talked quietly to his two sons, Aubry and Helgot. Luka was sitting at the base of a tree, whittling a sapling with his seax. He noticed that his one-time adversary, the big brute Eluhan, was sitting on a rock and seemed to be casually passing the time of day with Alfrid. Luka was just reflecting how thin and tiny Alfrid looked when placed alongside someone as large as Eluhan, when there was a crackling of twigs underfoot as Brantome and Malger arrived to announce the arrival of the convoy.

"How many guards?" whispered Bonitius.

"Ten," came the reply.

"Ten, - is that all?   No after-guard?"

"Not when we left but Fiebras and Renier will be back in a minute."

No sooner were the words out of his mouth than the two other watchers arrived and confirmed that there were no other outriders.

"Hah!" said Bonitius, punching his left hand with his clenched right fist.   "It will be a walkover."

He looked at Luka who caught his eye and grimaced, tilting his head doubtfully.   He did not like the feel of it.   If it really *was* a large consignment of gold, ten guards did not seem very many.   Perhaps the cargo was worth less than they had been led to believe.

He peered through the trees at the corner around which they expected to see the first horsemen and sure enough, here they came; but then Luka had a shock.   Where he had expected a rough strong wagon to be following, it was a royal coach.   He glared across at Brantome thinking that he should have had the sense to impart that information, but there was no time for recriminations because they were suddenly off - galloping after Bonitius and roaring their cries of attack.   As had been planned, four of the bandits leapt off their mounts and grabbed the heads of the leading horses while Bonitius and his other men made short work of the two leading riders.   Luka's men had engaged the four rear-guards and were battling with the driver and the soldiers on the coach.

The ferocious noise of battle had passed its climax and was now gradually quietening.   While his men were busy snuffing out the lives of the unfortunates, Bonitius and Luka met at the door of the coach.

"Well that was easy wasn't it?" said Bonitius with a grin. "Best we have a look and see what we've got for our troubles."

They swung themselves down from their mounts and Luka pulled on the door of the coach while Bonitius stood, seax in hand ready for any last errant guard that might come leaping out at him.

Luka's seax was also raised aggressively in his left hand as Bonitius wrenched at the blanket that had been covering the window.

Luka gave a gasp of shock and nearly dropped his seax as the blanket, torn from its fixings, revealed the coaches unexpected occupants.

... "Nanthild!" he yelped ... "and Prince Clovis!"

"Luka", she said, suddenly recognising him. "Oh Luka - thank God it's you."

Luka looked helplessly at Bonitius. "What're we going to do now?"

"Christ Almighty," he said in exasperation. "I presume that's the gold in those boxes they're sitting on. Get them out of there while Aubry and Helgot help me to see how much there is. If there's not too much we can put it in the panniers; otherwise we'll have to take the coach".

The queen was too frightened to do otherwise than pass Clovis into the arms of the only friend there and Luka changed roles to handing her royally out of the coach and hurrying her away from the scene of gore, death and action to the edge of the forest. He thrust Clovis back into her arms and with a brusque "Stay there," ran back to mount his horse. Bonitius and his sons were still busily unloading the gold and Luka was just about to go off and retrieve one of the loose horses for Queen Nanthild when the world erupted around him.

Knife-wielding horsemen seemed to come at him from every direction. He hardly had time to draw his seax from his belt before the first one was on him but his enemy's speed was his own undoing. Luka held the sharp seax up in a posture of defence and the luckless horseman fell against it and met his Maker. The horse collided with Luka's and the man's body fell against him. Once more Luka blessed his short stature as he ducked under it at the same time as he heard an axe from his next prospective opponent sink into the torso's shoulder. He dug his heels into his horse's flanks and wheeled round to face the next two attackers, driving the horse at them whilst swinging his blade to left and right. The noise of the shouting and screaming of men and beasts as they clashed time after time was horrendous. Luka caught a glimpse of Bonitius and his sons fighting back to back against tremendous odds. They were totally outnumbered by three to one and half their men had been slaughtered already.

He gave a gulp of anguish as he remembered Nanthild and Clovis and looked across to the place where he had left them. They were gone. Probably dead, he thought and a rage built up inside him. He turned his horse and with a roar of ire and indignation raced her back into the furore swinging his seax in flashing curves. He was gripping the horse with his knees and wielding a dagger with his left hand as he worked the seax with his right.

His roar had attracted the attention of the few remaining Bondies and they rallied behind him fighting furiously. He caught Eluhan's eye as they fought side by side and more than once Eluhan parried a blow that had been meant for Luka. All the Bondies were shouting now and fighting like men possessed driving their attackers back along the river path from whence they had come. Suddenly there was a bugle call or a shout or something that made the remaining fifteen or so raiders turn and flee.

Luka stopped the pursuit.

"Whoa," he said, "back to the coach. Let's clear out of here before they return with reinforcements."

Truth to tell his main worry was Nanthild and Clovis and he dearly wanted to find out what had happened to them. He felt as if his whole life and sanity depended upon it. He had always felt a great respect and fondness for the queen; regal and demanding as she could be. And young Clovis? Well there had been a bond between them ever since they had had their adventure amongst the foundations of Samarobriva Castle.

When they arrived at the coach they found an apparently-dead Bonitius lying by the side of a definitely-dead Aubry.

Luka glanced at the empty boxes lying on the floor of the carriage. "The bastards got all the gold then," he said.

"No they didn't," said Alfrid pointing to a pair of panniers slung across the flank of his horse. "Aubry had already given me this one to carry before the attack came".

"Oh, well that's something I suppose," said Luka dismounting and placing his hand on Bonitius's chest.

He thought he felt a movement and gently slapped the old man's face, calling "Bonitius; Bonitius; wake up. Can you hear me?"

He slapped again and the head moved and the chest started to heave but then stopped in half-motion and the mouth cried out in pain.

"Quick," said Luka, "help me get him on a horse".

The others dismounted and one went off to capture a nearby wandering mare while another two lifted their master out of his contorted position and then sat him onto the beast.

He lolled forwards with his head on the horse's withers and they lashed him as best they could. He had recovered a modicum of speech and kept asking where Helgot was. At his behest they searched thoroughly amongst the bodies but in vain.

The day was still young and not yet noon. It occurred to Luka that so many lives had been changed in the previous hour.

Out of their original twenty-three, only thirteen were still alive.

CHAPTER 31
Considerations

Nanthild had also been horrified when the battle started anew. Horsemen had appeared from all directions including from the forest behind her and they all spurred on towards the coach in which she had been a passenger until a short while previously. She saw Luka join battle and decided that her best option was to make herself scarce so, pulling Clovis behind her, she turned and ran into the woods. In the split second before she did so however, she noticed one of the riders point in her direction and another, seemingly at the first's command, power his way back towards her.

Fear for her life and that of her young son gave her heels wings and she scooped Clovis up into her arms and with her heart thumping she fairly flew along the forest path ever mindful of the sound of the pursuing horseman breaking his way through the branches that conspired to defend her.

In spite of her hopes she could not expect to outrun him and the rider leered a laugh as the horse inevitably overtook and nudged her off the path so that she crashed painfully into a tree and fell to the ground cradling Clovis against injury.

Even so the shock of the fall frightened the young lad and he set up a ferocious howling. She let him out of her arms as they both struggled to regain their feet and then scooped him up again and made another break for freedom as the rider slid from his horse. Ducking under his outstretched arm she ran on but after a few yards she fell again as she tripped over a malevolent tree root and in a trice he was on top of her pinning both wrists to the ground as Clovis ran some yards further on still screaming loudly.

She struggled and squirmed and hurled curses at her assailant but he just laughed and she realised that she was no match for him.

"Well now my fine lady," he said. "You feel and smell a lot better than most of the other wenches I've had. And since I'm ordered to kill you, I might as well have you first don't you think? It would be such a waste otherwise.

She glared at him from her undignified position.

Clovis howled from his.

The assailant considered his prospects. How was he going to satisfy his lust on this she-wolf? At present he was sitting astride her but he needed to lift his garments and hers whilst at the same time getting between her legs. She had a pretty face and he was loathe to smash his fist into it to subdue her. Or was it all worth it? Should he perhaps just cut her throat or strangle her and be done with it?

"Now look," he said, "you do as I say and I'll be nice to you. I'm going to let go your wrists and if you stay still you won't get hurt. Understand?"

She gave a sudden enchanting smile and nodded.

He released the pressure and started to lean backwards when with a sudden movement she brought her thighs up under his backside pitching him forwards again and then threw a punch in his face with her puny fist. It was not so much the force of the action as the speed with which it occurred and the fact that her fist had made contact with a particularly tender burn scar on his face.

As he had done so many times since that fateful day when Luka's seax had pinned him to the burning thatch, he automatically raised his hands to his cheek to ease the searing pain.

Nanthild seized her opportunity whilst he was unbalanced and tipped him off sideways. Rather than taking the opportunity to run again, she rolled over after him and leapt onto his back biting hard into his left ear. He roared and bucked pitching her further forwards onto her hands, the right one of which settled on a large stone. She instinctively clutched it and raised it high in the air and then smashed it hard onto his skull. His body went limp, but the stone was still in her hand and fury in her mind, and she smashed it again and again into the wet red soggy mass that had been his head.

Clovis had stopped crying and was sucking his thumb. The forest was quiet although the sounds of continued fighting could still be heard coming from the edge of the trees. Scarface's horse was standing quietly grazing. Nanthild was exhausted mentally and physically but instinct told her that she still had to get away. She dragged herself from Scarface's inert body and pushed her hair back from her face, adjusting a couple of hairpins to keep it in place. She looked behind her but nobody was coming. They were safe for the moment. She picked her son up and sat him astride the horse and then mounted behind him. The horse was a little large to what she was used to but she was a competent horsewoman and the beast was compliant.

Digging her heels in, she urged him up the forest path, pushing the sounds of fighting further into the distance.

--o--

Bonitius's thirteen survivors had made rich pickings from the bodies of their dead enemies. They had lost most of the gold, except for the pieces Alfrid had in the panniers.

The carriage was too wide to take up the woodland path so, wasting neither time nor sympathy on the bodies of their foes, they collected their own dead and the wandering horses and with Luka in the lead and Eluhan bringing up the rear, they headed as quickly as they could for home.

It was to Luka's surprise that they came across the bloodied body on the footpath and Luka called a halt while he dismounted and ran to it. He knelt down and felt it but it was cold. He rolled it over and recognised the damaged features of Scarface. He withdrew the seax from the belt and tucked it into his own and then rolled the body onto the verge out of the way of the horses and they pressed on.

--o--

Nanthild followed the trail until it broke out onto the road. She had no idea where she was, nor whether to turn left or right. She used her womanly instincts and decided that "right" looked more friendly, so she turned towards the east.

She felt sick and light-headed. Her heart was thumping in her chest. Clovis started complaining that he was hungry. As a feeling of panic began to overcome her she saw a distant farmstead and spurred the horse towards it. Two souls were toiling in the garden and they looked up surprised as she approached. The woman called to her husband and they ran towards the strange bedraggled horse-lady who was about to fall from her mount. The husband caught her just in time and she and her begrimed fretful son were hurried into the farmhouse.

The farmer laid the fainting girl on a pallet and the wife found some milk and bread for the youngster. It did not take long for Nanthild to recover her spirits and once the boy had been fed he promptly went to sleep. Nanthild roused herself and she and the child changed places as the wife invited her to sit at the table.

"So what's yer story then?" said the farmer.

"Hush, hush husband, - let the poor girl rest – she can tell us her story later."

"No, - really, it's alright," said Nanthild. "I feel better now," and she took a long draught at the warm milk that had been placed in front of her. It increased the feeling of nausea but settled her nerves.

The farmer glanced at his wife as he said "What's yer name then? What should us call ye?"

"I'm Nant... – I'm Nan," she replied and, looking at the wife asked "what about you?"

"Me name's Willemma and this 'ere's me 'usband Arnaud. So me poor pet, what's been 'appening to you then?"

"Nan" had had little time to think how she should explain her circumstances. She started by telling of the attack by Scarface. When Mistress Willemma asked her how she and her son came to be in the forest in the first place, she took refuge in exhausted tears. She saw Farmer Arnaud place a restraining hand on his wife's shoulder and the farmer and his wife led her back to the straw pallet where she fell into an exhausted sleep beside her son.

Further questions could wait until the next day.

--o--

The watchers at The Gateway realised there was something wrong as soon as they saw the first horseman. By the time the dispirited and bedraggled riders reached the woods kind and willing hands were ready to help them down from their mounts and to tend their wounds. The womenfolk fussed around and helped the walking wounded back to their billets. Whilst some of the men remained on guard, as many as could be spared attended to the horses' needs. They now had rather more horses than potential riders.

Bonitius's horse was led to his farmhouse where he was cut gently down and laid on his bed. In spite of her grief at the news of the death of her eldest son and the capture of her youngest, Aliz started immediately to tend her husband's wounds. She called upon her two daughters to help and the trio worked efficiently to clean the old man.

Bonitius himself was too weak to take part in the proceedings other than to look into his wife's eyes and raise his eyebrows and nod his head in acknowledgement that the outcome of their jaunt had not been a good one.

Luka, tired as he was, was concerned with other things. It was he who had led the party back and it was he who, in the absence or indisposition of the male members of Bonitius's family, was now effectively in charge.

He selected those two vastly different characters, Alfrid and Eluhan as his lieutenants and set about the job of getting everything cleaned, tidied and re-organised from the point of view of security. Even since Luka's arrival at the camp it had fluctuated in numbers. People like Scarface had suddenly left but new people were constantly arriving. It had never, however, been quite so depleted in numbers as it was now. Luka was acutely aware of his new-found responsibilities and the possibility that, if the information leaked out about Bonitius's injuries and the camp's depleted strength, there might be an opportunistic attack from either the archdeacon's group at Meaux or King Dagobert's army at Lutetia, or indeed a rival bandit group.

It was with this in mind that he secreted the gold and oversaw the attention that was needed for the new horses and lent his thoughts to the guarding rosters. He arranged for a special meal to be provided that evening and ordered that everyone who had fought that day, should have an early night.

It was whilst relaxing after the evening meal that the discussion inevitably turned to the day's events.

"Everything was going so smoothly," said Eluhan, "until those bastards descended on us. Who were they and what were they doing there?"

"I've been thinking about that," said Luka. "Did you recognise any of them?"

"Not really," Eluhan replied, "but I sort of ... got the feeling that they were the archdeacon's lot."

"Hah! So did I," said Luka, "and that body in the wood was Scarface's who used to be one of us."

"Oh was it indeed?"

"I think," said Luka, "that we were set up. The archdeacon's an unforgiving and vicious man and he's probably been looking for an opportunity to avenge the indignity of being sent home nude on his horse. I suspect that he's never forgotten that day and has spent the last moons plotting a way to get his own back on Bonitius. Scarface also bore a grudge against me and seeing him there makes me guess that he had perhaps combined his forces with somebody else's in order to achieve our downfall. I think the archdeacon may well have been that other person. *He* would have known about the gold shipment to Meaux and Scarface could well have been able to tell him about Bonitius's fading fortunes. Between them I reckon they hatched out a plot to leak the information to trap us in their spider's web. I had a feeling that something was wrong. The feeling increased when the ambush seemed to go so easily."

"But why were the Queen and the prince there?" said Eluhan.

"Well I expect that was just an unexpected bonus for the archdeacon. Perhaps they wanted to go to Villa Calae and took the opportunity to travel on a well-guarded bullion coach that was travelling along a short, safe route?"

"What's going to happen now though? If the queen and her son have made it back to Lutetia, they will have told him that it was us who stole his gold and Dagobert is likely to be after our heads!"

"You're right!" replied Luka gloomily. "It has all fallen into the archdeacon's hands very nicely. Although we have *some* of the gold, more than half of it vanished during that second skirmish and it seems likely to me that it's now lining the archdeacon's vaults. He'll make sure that we get the blame for stealing the lot! Yes, very clever I must admit. The next move the archdeacon is likely to make is to persuade King Dagobert to mobilise his army and come and attack us here to retrieve the missing bullion. Bonitius has been a thorn in King Dagobert's side for years and this would be a good excuse for him to overrun the camp and eliminate us all. I only hope that Queen Nanthild and Prince Clovis *have* reached the palace safely, or we shall be blamed for any harm that comes to them too!"

"So what's to be done?"

"I think, bearing in mind the circumstances, that our best plan would be to give *our* half of the gold back as a gesture of good faith and to convince the king that the archdeacon has the rest. Let's face it, it's no good keeping the gold if we are all going to get ourselves killed because of it."

"We could hold a *little* bit of the gold back," said Eluhan. "That way it would turn the tables on the archdeacon and he would be blamed for all the gold that's missing. The small amount that we keep would get us through the winter."

"I didn't hear that," said Luka "and kindly don't mention it to me again. If I am going to end up negotiating with the king I shall want to do so with a clear conscience so I will assume that whatever gold is in the panniers is the total amount we have. Right?"

"Right!" said Eluhan staring Luka straight in the eyes and giving a nod and a wink.

"So the next thing we have to do is to communicate with the palace and check that the Queen and Clovis have arrived back safely. We can then make a clean breast of things before the army suddenly turns up on our doorstep."

"How are you going to do that then?" said Alfrid joining them. "None of us outlaws can afford to come even within *sight* of the palace walls."

"I've no idea," said Luka. "If Botolph were closer I'd ask him to do it, but in the time it'd take me to contact him it'd probably be too late. I'll have to think about it. I'm off to get my head down now. I'll see you two in the morning. Wassail to you both."

"Wassail," they replied.

CHAPTER 32
Helgot's Capture

Nanthild awoke when it was still dark and it took her a few moments to realise that she was not in the palace. All was quiet except for some snoring which she guessed must be from Farmer Arnaud - or maybe from his wife? She wondered where Clovis was, but trusted that Willelma had taken good care of him.

She lay there reliving the horrible events of the previous day and drifted in and out of sleep until at last the new dawn stole into the room. When it became light enough she could see the farmer's cot by the door.

She watched as he stirred and stretched before rolling himself into a standing position. He grasped an iron poker and riddled at the logs in the hearth, brightening their red glow to a vibrant orange before he added further kindling. New long yellow flames flared, highlighting black shadows which flickered round her head. The new life of the hut's interior was short-lasting as he placed another log dulling the flames of its source.

Between the lights provided by the dawn and the fire she had been able to make out Mistress Willelma in her own cot with her arm wrapped around Clovis who was still sound asleep.

It only took a few moments though before everyone began to stir and Willelma was soon scurrying around preparing the dough for the new bake and warming yesterday's bread to complement the eggs and cheese.

A still-sleepy Clovis staggered from Willelma's bed to Nanthild's and crawled into her warmth, placing his arm round her neck before promptly going to sleep again.

She lay there for a while wondering what the day would bring and how they would get home. Might it be better to go back to Lutetia or on to Villa Calae which, after all, was where they *had* been going and which was now undoubtedly closer.

Still undecided, she swung her legs over the edge of her bed and swept Clovis into her arms and took him out into the cool morning air. Mistress Willelma had already placed a bowl of fresh-from-the-well water on a nearby bench, and to her young son's noisy disgust his mother insisted on dipping her hand into it and washing his face. Having now gained the benefit of his full attention she pulled off his shift and Willelma stood by smiling as he stamped his little feet up and down in reluctant nakedness while she washed the rest of him. The farmer's wife handed her a coarse woollen cloth in which she wrapped the little boy and cuddled him warm again. When his shivering stopped she placed him on her hip while she washed her own face and then borrowed the end of Clovis's cloth to dry it before going back into the house.

To her surprise, Farmer Arnaud did not seem too determined to start his day early and they broke their fast together sitting around the central hearth. When Clovis felt the warmth of the fire, he wriggled free of both the cloth and Nanthild and wandered around naked until Nanthild called him back and placed the shift over his head.

"So how are we going to get you back to your family my lady," asked Willelma, "and where indeed might your family be?"

They had been so kind that Nanthild felt it was time to share the whole truth with them and so she told them the story.

"My!" said Willelma when she had finished. "To think: our queen in my bed and I have seen the prince naked!" They all laughed and then Willelma became deadly serious.

"But your husband must be worried stiff about you. They'll be scouring the countryside for your bodies!"

"Well, maybe," Nanthild replied reluctantly. "But the king will not know of our disappearance unless he received a message from Meaux that the gold consignment didn't arrive. And in the normal way, Meaux would not be too concerned because they might just think that there had been a delay in its departure.

"Regarding my return, - this is the street to Meaux is it not? I suppose I could just take the horse and ride there but to tell you the truth I feel somewhat nervous about the prospect of riding on my own."

"I should think so too," rejoined Farmer Arnaud. "No, that's not the answer. I'll take you into Meaux in the haywain if that's where you've a passion to go. Otherwise I could take you back to Lutetia?"

"Well my passion, as you put it, was to go to Meaux but, in the circumstances, I feel we should return to Lutetia so that I can explain to my husband what has happened."

"Lutetia it is then," said Arnaud. "I'll go and prepare the wain. Are you coming too, spouse?"

"I reckon I am. Be nice to see the city again ... 'n I might even meet King Dagobert!"

--o--

Helgot had been kneeling down holding open the second of the horse panniers while Aubry and Bonitius were transferring the gold from the boxes in the coach. It was his low stance that had saved his life when the attack occurred. His brother was felled instantly by a single spear thrust. Bonitius dropped the gold he was holding and was in the process of drawing his seax when another blade whizzed over Helgot's head and penetrated his father's chest and he fell, his head cruelly crashing onto the carriage wheel as he did so.

Helgot drew his own seax and stood to face the next wave of attackers, his action protecting the inert bodies of his father and brother. As he fought he hoped that they would both regain consciousness and come to his aid. Out of the corner of his eye he could see other Bondies fighting desperately but the odds were overwhelming; black capes seemed to be everywhere. He glanced down at his father but saw no movement and came to the reluctant conclusion that both he and Aubry were probably dead. Most of the assailants had dismounted and were fighting on foot. Two more attackers ran at him and as he moved towards them and away from the coach with the idea of giving himself more swinging room, he was grasped from behind, his arms pinioned and his seax wrenched from his hand.

"We'll keep this one," said a voice. "Tie his wrists and ankles and lash him to a horse while we finish the job. Fill this pannier with the rest of that gold and then put it on my spare horse."

Helgot's two captors thrust him to the ground and knelt on him while he was trussed. He could do nothing to resist and concentrated on trying to spit the mud and grass out of his mouth as he lay with his face buried in the mire. He was hauled up and carried ignominiously sideways for a few yards before being wound around a horse's flank. Instead of the taste of mud he now smelt the hot mustiness of the animal's coat as they tied him in place.

Once secured, they left him and as he viewed the battle upside down he heard Luka's unmistakable Battle Cry and twisting his head further to the left he saw the flash of steel as Luka, followed by two or three other Bondies came crashing into the fight scattering the Black Capes as they did so.

The latter clearly decided that enough was enough and they ran for their horses. Helgot felt his horse start as another rider tugged on its halter and the beast took off at a gallop.

Soon the pace slowed to a gentle trot which for Helgot, in his unaccustomed riding position, was only slightly less uncomfortable. The horse stumbled and he felt his centre of balance shift as his head slid towards the ground. A few more horse-paces and his face slid under the belly and his body dangled dangerously between the hooves. He had a moment of panic realising that if the rope broke he would fall to the ground and be trampled.

"Oi!" he shouted without any effect. "Oiiii!"

There was the sound of more hooves and he felt a rider draw alongside. His horse was pulled out of the line and stopped; with no words being spoken, he was roughly rotated back to his earlier position where he was lashed more securely before his horse rejoined the train.

It was another half a day before their hooves clattered on the Meaux cobbles and they rode into the abbey precincts.

Helgot was cut down and his ankles untied before he was manhandled through the abbey door and down into the dungeon-like crypt where he was thrown into a stone cubby and its iron door clanged shut behind him.

CHAPTER 33
Sweyn and Margaret

Arnaud harnessed the pony to the wain and he and Nanthild climbed onto the driving seat while Willelma and Clovis settled down in the back and prepared themselves for the half day drive.

Willelma had brought some amusements for Clovis to play with as well as some fruit, cheese, milk and bread.

They saw few other travellers, all of whom would be taking the more-popular riverside route. After a while, just as Arnaud was in the process of telling Nanthild that they were passing The Gateway of the infamous bandits' den, they saw a dust cloud indicating that a rider was coming out to them.

Arnaud sensed Nanthild tense.

"Don't 'ee fret m'lady," he cooed. "I know the Bondies well. My farm's on their patch and I have an understanding with Bonitius so we need have no worries there."

"Do you know Luka?" she said.

"Oh ah! I know the little dwarf alright. 'E's a real character. Rules Bonitius's men with a firm rod but 'e's fair, 'e's fair. I 'ave no problem with 'im ... Wassail Alfrid!"

"Wassail Arnaud! Wondered who it was trespassing on our road. You off to Lutetia then?" and turning his gaze past Willelma to the other lady he had a sudden thought that he recognised her from the previous day. He looked into the back of the wain and the sight of Clovis confirmed his suspicions.

As his horse trotted alongside the driving seat, he raised his hand in salute to her. "Salve Regina", he said.

"Salve, salve," she replied. "Have you come to rob us?"

He grinned. "No, Regina," he said, "but Luka will be pleased to hear that you and the princeling are fit and well. He has been worrying about you all night."

"Well, that's gratifying to hear I'm sure."

"In fact I know that he'll want to talk with you himself so perhaps you might care to ... "

"I don't think so," she replied anticipating him whilst at the same time recovering her imperiousness. "I must get back to Lutetia without delay."

"Very well my queen," answered Alfrid courteously, much to her surprise, "I'll get straight back then and tell Luka of your journey which I trust will be a safe one."

He wheeled his horse round and with a wave of his hand galloped back up the road from which he had come.

"A pleasant young man!" said Nanthild. "I'm touched that he called me 'my queen'. I didn't think that unruly bunch of bandits recognised *any* authority."

"Ah, ye'd be surprised ma'am," said Arnaud. "They're much softer now than they used to be."

They were crossing the desolate marshes that led to the Pons Magnus when Willelma warned of another group of riders approaching fast behind them. Arnaud's heart leapt into his throat at the prospect of an attack just as a safe haven was showing on the horizon. He cracked the reins hard and leant forwards urging the pony faster.

--o--

There were four of them and Willelma sat up in the wagon clutching Clovis to her as Arnaud did his best to get the wain closer to the city gates in the forlorn hope that some of the guards might be alert enough to ride out to their assistance.

It was hopeless though; the distance was just too great and with horror Arnaud realised that he had a horseman on each side of him and that one was calling him to stop. He surrendered to inevitability and pulled steadily back on the reins.

"Arnaud!"

"Luka!" Nanthild cried joyfully.

"Luka," growled Arnaud, stopping the wain entirely. "My life! You *did* give me a fright."

"I'm sorry," said Luka but I wanted to catch you before you reached the bridge. My lady I am pleased to see you looking so well. I was fearful for your safety."

"So was I," she admitted, "but our dear God was looking after us and led us to the protection of these good people. But what're *you* doing here? You're close enough to the city to be captured and gibbeted."

"Yes, I know. We won't tarry long but I come to ask you to bear our apologies to the king, - together with this ..." He heaved the double pannier off his horse's flanks and dropped it into the back of the wain.

"The whole attack was a terrible mistake. We should never have done it and I doubt that we would have done so, had somebody not set us up and made it look so attractive that it seemed too good an opportunity to miss. We'd no idea that you'd be travelling in the carriage; we thought it was just a consignment of gold."

"And now ten of my husband's best men are dead." She stared at him sternly.

"Luka ... Luka, why oh why have you got yourself mixed up in a group like this?"

"You know I have no option ma'am.   There's a price on my head.   If you could only get a pardon from the king for me and my friends, we'd give up our banditry tomorrow."

"Would you indeed?" she said with half a hint of a smile on her lips. "We'll see. I'll try to have a word with my husband.   In the meantime might I hazard a guess that these panniers contain the gold you *accidently* stole?"

"Yes my lady ... well ... actually no – this is all the gold *we* have.   The rest was taken by the other attackers and we have no idea who they were."

"Very well.   I'll do what I can.   Now get off home before you get yourselves arrested.   Thank you for your concern.   Come on Arnaud, I want to go home too."

--o--

It was 8th October 638 and Botolph had been at Evoriacum for two moons but it felt like a lifetime.   It also felt like a lifetime since he had seen his dear friend Luka. Apart from praying for him every night he tried not to dwell on his loss and he occupied his mind by fully joining in, both spiritually and bodily, with the activities of the abbey.

The Abbess Fara continued to rule her monastery sternly delegating as much responsibility as she could to her two priors.   While Prioress Pedra controlled the nuns, in charge of the monks was Prior Antonio: a tall elegant man with a heavy Genoese accent. The Rule of Columbanus by which the abbey abided, was very demanding.   There were however over one hundred people to supervise and even with the help of her two priors, Fara could not keep an eye on everybody all the time. Once in a while, ever since the abbey had been founded, the bodily desires of one or other of the monks or nuns overtook their strict training and discipline had to be enforced in a dramatic fashion to discourage the others from similarly descending into evil ways.

It was the time of the grape harvest and, once again, all the occupants of the monastery from the lowliest slave to the abbess herself, were called upon to help in the picking.

The weather was glorious and the work not unduly hard so the atmosphere was one of relaxation and fraternisation in tune with the festive occasion.

Botolph had noticed that the tall handsome Brother Sweyn from Jutland, seemed to be more interested in talking to pretty sixteen year old Sister Margaret than he was in filling his sac with grapes. Although grape-pickers were left unsupervised during this period, the abbess and her priors would walk around on regular inspections whereupon inappropriate discourse would abruptly cease.

Sweyn was four years older than Botolph and had already been at Evoriacum for two years, - so although Botolph felt the brother was becoming indiscreet bordering upon being sinful, he was somewhat in awe of him and therefore felt unable to chastise him. A few days later however he wished he had, since the story sped around the establishment that Brother Sweyn had been caught with Sister Margaret behind the vine-thresher; - she with her habit round her waist and he between her legs and "really tucking in"; or at least that is what Botolph *thought* his informant had said.

Sixteen-summers-old Margaret had been stripped in her cell by the merciless hard-faced Prioress Pedra and her screams had been heard around the abbey as she was scourged with willow canes.

When she was too bloodied and too weak to move, she had been locked in her cell from which constant sobbing was heard as darkness drew in. There were stories that giant bat-like shadows had been seen flitting around the walls eerily calling her name.

Early the next morning the prioress had taken her a special porridge which, they said, had smelt like rotting parsnips.

The story went that she professed that she was not hungry but the prioress forced spoonful after spoonful into her mouth in spite of her constant retching and screaming. When the last spoonful had gone she rolled on her side and sobbed her last.

All in the monastery were chastened by what had happened and they went about their work in absolute silence, crossing themselves whenever they had to pass the young nun's room.

At noon, the prioress returned and unlocked the cell. When she came out she left the door wide open and it remained that way all night.

The following day, the body was wrapped in a black shroud and taken on a farmer's cart to a field outside the monastery where it was buried in unconsecrated ground. It was later said that at every major festival flames could be seen coming from the ground where the body was buried and that these flames were signs of devils still leaving the body.

Brother Sweyn's punishment was not to die although he would dearly have liked to. The guilt for what he had done was deemed punishment enough and he bore the sign of anguish on his face for as long as Botolph knew him.

The event cast a black cloud over the abbey.

Two weeks later it was Samhain. Abbess Fara hoped that the bonefires and celebrations would help to raise her people's spirits but they did not seem to.

CHAPTER 34
Journey to the Synod of Meaux

A few days after Samhain, a horseman arrived at the abbey bearing a message from the abbess's brother commanding her attendance at a synod to be held in Meaux.

It was not Fara's style to be commanded by any earthly mortal, least of all by a brother who had once in her childhood tried to murder her. Nevertheless, the timing was ideal for all sorts of reasons so she swallowed her pride and set about making arrangements for the journey.

She decided to take the twins with her together with Bernard the-pot-stirrer and the new monk Botolph; she would also take Prioress Pedra. Prior Antonio was to be left in charge of the monastery.

Botolph was delighted about the prospect and managed to persuade the abbess that he and Bernard should ride on horseback rather than in the farmer's dray as was her original intention.

"You'll stay close to us though," she had said. "The reason I've brought you two is to lend a manly hand from time to time and to give us protection. I don't want you both riding over the horizon. Make sure you stay in sight."

The journey had been cool but pleasant and both the boys were pleased to have the freedom of a horse beneath them rather than a bumpy dray.

"The dray might do the prioress a bit of good," said Bernard, "- shake a few cracks out of her face." Botolph decided not to rise to the bait so simply replied, "Why do you think the abbess has brought her along?"

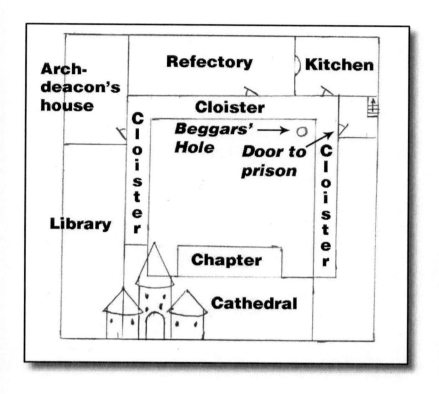

Fig. 5. Plan of Meaux Cathedral.

"Well partly to get her out of the abbey to give Prior Antonio a chance to cheer things up a bit and partly to see her brother."

"Why would the abbess want her to see Bishop Faro?"

"What? ... No, - not to see the *Abbess's* brother, - to see her *own* brother, - the archdeacon."

"She's the archdeacon's *sister*?"

"Certainly is."

"A fine pair those two make."

"Exactly. Have you met him then?"

"Once. The last time I saw him he had no clothes on and was squawking like a frightened chicken."

"What?" laughed Bernard, slapping his thigh.

Botolph told Bernard the story as their horses walked along behind the dray where its occupants were also in deep conversation.

After they had forded the River Morin it was another half a day before they came within sight of Meaux. By the time they arrived at the last ford the flood was well underway and the water came above the axles of the dray causing much giggling and 'oohs' and 'aahs' from the twins. It was mid-afternoon before they arrived, hungry, thirsty and tired. The sound of the horses' hooves on the cobbles reminded Botolph of his last visit. He hoped that this time his stay would be a happier one.

--o--

Meaux, 14 November 638.

On their arrival at the city gates, the abbess announced that she and her nuns would walk the last part to the abbey church. Botolph and Bernard were sent off at a trot to warn the bishop of their impending arrival and to request quartering for the three horses and the dray.

By the time the ladies reached the abbey the bishop and archdeacon were standing waiting at the great door in company with the effeminate Brother Fauve.

"Salve sister," said the tall bishop silkily, his lips giving a smile that was betrayed by his eyes. "This is indeed an unexpected pleasure. I hope you've had a pleasant journey."

"Pax vobiscum brother," she replied, kneeling and kissing his right hand. "The journey was a pleasant but uncomfortable one and I have no wish to repeat it for a few days. Can I crave accommodation?"

"Of course. We shall be pleased to have your company. Archdeacon, you know the abbess."

Archdeacon Gaubert in his turn bowed and kissed the abbess's right hand.

"I've brought your sister to see you Gaubert. I wish you joy of reunion."

She stood to one side and the prioress moved towards her brother and kissed him. She then turned sullenly and knelt and kissed the bishop's hand. Their entourage, as befitted them, kept well back from these formal introductions but Botolph noticed a glint of recognition in the eyes of both the archdeacon and Brother Fauve when they looked in his direction. He met their gaze unfalteringly and thought he sensed the strength of his righteousness overcome what he felt sure were their weaknesses of guilt and apprehension. He felt empowered and confident. But for what motive he was unsure.

The sound of their shuffling shoes resounded from the sandstone walls as the group made their way through the precincts to the Refectory Hall which they found initially empty but which soon filled.

Slaves bearing food and drink appeared from all sides and the company sat and talked amongst themselves. The bishop called over one of the slaves and then sent him off to arrange their accommodation.

Before they retired that night, Botolph asked the abbess's permission to take the horse and visit King Dagobert at Lutetia the next day.

"Why on earth do you want to go there?" she had asked coldly. "We have only just arrived *here*."

"I crave your indulgence, abbess," he had replied. "I really need to go to ask the king to arrange a pardon for Luka. If I don't go now winter will set in and it'll be spring before there's another opportunity."

"Very well," she said. "For how long do you expect to be away?"

"Only two days mother," he had replied. "I really just need a 'yes' or a 'no' and maybe a document that I can bring back to Bishop Faro to show that Luka's been reprieved."

He left at daybreak the next day and, after an uneventful ride, crossed the Pons Magnus as daylight was beginning to fail. Having stabled his horse, he went straight to find Eligius and tell him of his plans. What Eligius had to tell him was not good news.

--o--

Bernard missed Botolph, and for some reason that he could not discern, felt ill at ease in the Bishop's Palace. He would have liked to accompany his new friend to Lutetia, but it was out of the question. He was in Meaux to give support and protection to his abbess and that is what he would do. He could see that Fara and her brother shared no great family affection but, for some reason, it appeared they had plenty to talk about. The prioress was occupied with the archdeacon so that gave the twins and Bernard plenty of free time. The twins were content just to sit and chatter, so Bernard set about familiarising himself with the building.

His monk's habit gave him anonymity and authority of passage so he went unchallenged from room to room and stairway to stairway. His explorations eventually took him downwards and he was amazed to find that there was more of the palace below ground level than there was above.

He descended several floor levels through a series of tunnels, the steps becoming rougher and the walls wetter until he reached a chamber where the roof was supported by great stone pillars piled through a sandy floor. The sand was soft and wet and as he explored he felt as if he were walking through a quagmire which was forever trying to prise off his sandals. Occasional beams of orange light came through ventilation shafts and he stood under one of these relishing the cool fresh air and hoping that he would be able to see blue sky but the shaft was curved and all he could see was the redness of the rock. There seemed to be no way out other than by returning the way he had come but as he turned to leave he thought he saw a movement to his right. A feeling of unease washed across him making the hairs stand up on the back of his neck and goose-bumps pimple the tops of his arms.

He must have been mistaken.

"Anybody there?" he called.

His voice came echoing back to him but otherwise there was no response. He felt a strong urge to get away. There was definitely something creepy about the place. He tried to stop the rapid breathing that had developed in his chest and took deliberate long deep breaths as he endeavoured to walk slowly with a confidence that he did not feel back towards the broken steps.

There it was again, - to his left this time, just beyond the pillar.

"Hello?" he called. He retraced his steps pulling closer to the pillar and looking around it. As he did so he felt goose-bumps now spring up on his right flank. There was nobody there.

He turned back, his rising panic conflicting with his attempt at deep breathing. The wet sand was leaking into his leather sandals. He reached the steps and started up them using his hands to steady himself as the steps changed direction. Before turning into the tunnel he crouched down to take one last look and felt the hairs on his lower back rise again and then ripple up towards his neck; but there was no one there.

--o--

Bernard did not tell anybody else about his experiences in the underground tunnels. He thought he would wait until Botolph returned and then share them with him. In the meantime he decided to make a proper job of inspecting the whole house. Although he was three years older than Botolph and well-established in Evoriacum, he had already acquired great respect for the newcomer and determined to do all he could to help him in his project – whatever that may be. In any case, he had a lot of time on his hands so he felt he was following a Christian premise by spending it usefully.

His next mission was to find out more about the archdeacon. He had taken an instant dislike to the pompous little cleric although he had not mentioned it to Botolph or anybody else because he had been wracked with self-guilt about such unchristian feelings.

Archdeacon Gaubert's quarters were in the northwest wing. Prioress Pedra had chosen to stay there with her brother rather than joining the rest of the Evoriacum party in the guest-quarters. The next day whilst the remainder of the visitors were breaking their fast in the refectory, Pedra was eating with the archdeacon. When Fara asked him to take a message to the archdeacon's sister Bernard jumped at the chance to spy further.

The nature of the message was inconsequential. It was Fara's simple method of ensuring that her staff were kept roped together and provided a subtle reminder that they had left their individualism behind them when they took their vows.

He left the refectory and walked out into the courtyard where he stood for a moment taking in several lungsful of cool November morning air before heading into the cloisters and along to the archdeacon's door.

At his knock the door was opened by a pretty but scruffy maid with a shock of red hair. On asking to see Prioress Pedra the maid's pretty face was replaced by that of the archdeacon.

"What do you want?" he enquired crossly.

"The abbess has asked me to give a message to Prioress Pedra," he replied.

"What is it?"

Bernard was not going to make life any easier for either this nasty little man nor for his objectionable sister.

"I've been asked to deliver it to the prioress herself!"

Bernard sensed a couple of people passing behind him and from the archdeacon's face guessed that they too were peering inquisitively into the room.

"You'd better come in then ... sit there ... I'll get her."

Bernard did as he was bid and scanned the room trying to take in as many details as possible whilst at the same time pretending to look disinterested.

The archdeacon's wife whose name turned out to be Lubaia, was short, plump and sullen, whereas his daughter was tall, heavy-boned and ungainly and had more to say for herself than Bernard thought was useful. His son on the other hand, although only a boy of about fifteen years, was flabby, expressionless and apparently pampered. As Bernard watched them, he wondered at the diversity of family units and not for the first time, blessed the fact that he had become a monk.

His feelings were confirmed when the ungainly sister suddenly took it into her mind to put on an exhibition making it clear that it was she who ran the household. Jumping to her feet she started to issue a plethora of instructions to the young red-headed girl whose name proved to be Clarisse.

For the next few minutes it was "Clarisse fetch this ... and Clarisse do that ... ," and Bernard wondered how she would know what to do first . As, in pursuit of her orders, she ran past the sister, the ungainly wench reached out and issued a hefty cuff to her right ear. The girl cried out, stumbled and nearly fell, but regaining her balance ran through the doorway with the cackling of her sister's crow-like laughter ringing in her ears. The older girl looked across at Bernard as if in the hope of a glance of admiration. She received nothing but a look of disgust.

The prioress appeared in the doorway and came over to him.

"Yes?" she said tersely.

"Sister Prioress, Abbess Fara requests you attend her in the church as soon as you've broken your fast."

"Very well, I'll be there.   Is that all?"

"Yes, prioress."

"In that case you may leave," and she escorted him to the door.

CHAPTER 35
Botolph and Eligius

"I'm afraid you've had a wasted journey. The king's not here. He's gone to Metz," said Eligius.

"Oh no," said Botolph, totally dismayed.

"Why so distressed? What was your purpose in seeing him?"

Botolph explained in a torrent of non-ending words, how involved Luka was becoming in Bonitius's camp; how Botolph lived in constant fear of Luka's being captured or killed; how what was needed was the king's pardon ratified by the bishop; how winter was coming which would inevitably slow down the whole pardoning procedure; how Botolph's visits could only be infrequent; how this had seemed a God-given suitable time to sort out the horrible problem; how he had to get back to Meaux tomorrow; how ..." Botolph looked miserably at the floor.

Eligius rose and placed his arm around him.

"There there, my son. Don't despair. All will be well. Our God is clearly doing this for some reason which ultimately will bring nothing but good. You must trust Him."

"I do," said Botolph "but here I am trying to help God towards what I'm sure must be the fulfilment of His plans, and what happens but the Devil sends the king off to Metz!"

"Yes I know it's frustrating," said Eligius, "but there's something else too."

"What's that?"

211

"I am afraid that Luka's no longer the king's favourite person. In fact he's more than a little displeased with him."

"Oh? Why?"

"You've obviously not heard the story of the gold theft."

Eligius motioned to a stool and Botolph sat down heavily while Eligius brought him up to date carefully including the fact that Bonitius's share of the stolen gold had been returned.

When he had finished, Botolph stayed silent, thinking furiously.

"But it's not Luka's fault – it's Bonitius's. Luka has to do what he's told and the reason he's trapped in this situation is all the fault of that infernal archdeacon. If he hadn't put a price on Luka's head then Luka wouldn't have had to join Bonitius, and he and I would be together at Evoriacum just where we're supposed to be!"

"I know," soothed Eligius, "and I'll do all I can to help. When the king returns I will, as diplomatically as I can, pour some oil on troubled waters and lay your problem before him and try to make sure he gets on and signs a document for Luka's pardon. I'll then take it to Bishop Faro myself to get it ratified. Will that suit you?"

"Well ... yes," said Botolph, a reluctant smile coming to his lips again. "That'd be wonderful. It means my journey's not been wasted after all."

"Indeed not," said the golden knight. "Now let's make arrangements for your accommodation and you can tell me all about Evoriacum and Abbess Fara and everything that's been happening to you over the past couple of months."

It was late on the Sunday evening before Botolph arrived, dusty and tired, back at Meaux. He made his way to the palace refectory and was just in time to rescue the last dregs of soup before it was tipped into the pig swill.

The abbess and the twins had already retired for the night but Bernard was still in the hall and just about to leave when Botolph arrived. He turned back with his friend. After Botolph had collected his bowl of gruel and a hunk of still-warm crusty bread and bowed his head and given thanks, he started hungrily to slurp it down. One advantage of the late meal was that it placed them beyond the laws of silence and Bernard was bursting to tell his friend every last detail of his discoveries in the palace.

Both finished (Botolph his gruel and Bernard his discourse) at more or less the same time and Botolph, feeling replete, sat back and wiped his lips with his sleeve.

He thought silently for a moment whilst Bernard waited expectantly.

"There are still plenty of mysteries to be solved here then," said Botolph.

"I don't like it," said Bernard. "This place has a really creepy atmosphere and the people themselves are no better. I keep getting the feeling that I'm suddenly going to discover something really awful."

"I know what you mean," replied Botolph "even though I haven't spent much time here yet. What's happening tomorrow? Has the abbess any particular plans?"

"Ah yes," said Bernard, "she asked me to tell you that we have an early morning audience with the bishop to discuss the see's arrangements for Evoriacum during the next year."

"Are we to be privy to these discussions then?" said Botolph, amazed that he and Bernard as lowly young monks should be included.

"I don't think we will be invited to give our views," smiled Bernard. "We'll be there to give the abbess support and to act as witnesses."

CHAPTER 36
Fauve and Helgot

17th November 638. Early morning.

The following morning found the two of them in the chapter house amongst a mass of new faces. The building was already half full of be-robed dignitaries, both clerical and secular, and their servants. The place, Botolph thought, would have been cold and bare if it had not been for the gathered throng which gave it warmth and colour. At the north end was an altar-like table around which sat a group of clerics with Bishop Faro at its centre.

He was tall, formidable, grey and unsmiling but Botolph did not sense the same evil emanations from him as he did from the portly archdeacon who sat on his right.

Those at the table seemed to be the court officials of the chapter, whereas the others in the body of the hall were the hangers-on. Amongst them, Botolph could identify both knights and abbots as well as ordinary monks, nuns, servants and slaves.

The hustle and bustle went on for some time as more people arrived and a medley of chairs and stools was brought in to accommodate the higher echelons; the hangers-on would have to stand. Eventually the inward flow reduced and then stopped and people jostled for positions of comfort either leaning on the walls or propped up in doorways.

Botolph noticed something peculiar about a small group over to his right but then his attention was distracted as Faro rose to his feet and the archdeacon banged on a gavel to quieten the crowd.   When he looked back again the peculiar group were no longer where he had last seen them but on looking behind him he caught a glimpse of one of them leaving by a side door.   It crossed his mind that it was strange that they should have taken the trouble to turn up at the synod and then leave before it had even started.   He turned his attention back to the proceedings which were settling in to what looked likely to be a long session.

The bishop spoke with his silky tone; all his actions were smooth and coordinated.   He had, Botolph realised, a perfect sense of timing, choosing just the right moment to interject during a discussion whilst at the same time, letting the talk run on when it was appropriate.

Botolph became in some awe of him as he watched the bishop intently.   There was something about him which did not ring true but he could not put his finger on it.   It was some sort of evil – of that he had no doubt and he gave a shiver.

Bernard looked at his friend in alarm.   "You alright?"

Botolph nodded.   "Just someone walking over my grave."

--o--

Mid-morning.

There was a cold November breeze blowing and the three were glad of the excuse to keep their cowls over their heads.   As they passed an oaken door, one tried turning the iron ring but in spite of a clank as the lever lifted inside, the door remained firmly locked.

They moved on past the kitchen from whence savoury smells of newly-baked bread were emanating. They looked through the refectory doorway and noted the bare furnishings. They pressed on past the archdeacon's quarters and grimaced at the raucous shouts of a woman's voice followed by the cackling laughter of another. They noted the ditch of evil-looking water that flowed under a stone slab which supported the corner of the next building which subsequently proved to house the Library and Scriptorium. The halls would normally have been full of scribes working away at their desks but today everybody was in the chapter house.

So where on earth could he be? They had already looked in the guests' quarters and the monks' dormitories but there was no evidence of the presence of the one they were seeking. They had thought it would be so easy but the very fact that had made the period of their visit seem so ideal - the holding of the synod - was now working against them since everybody was in the chapter house leaving nobody who might be able to give them a clue as to where he might be.

They had been right round the courtyard and were now back at the refectory door which was ajar.

Luka put his head to the gap and listened for sounds of movement. He heard none so he cautiously pushed the door open until it was wide enough for him to be able to slip in. The place was empty. The others followed suit and silently closed the door behind them.

A mouth-watering yeasty aroma led them compulsively into the kitchen where, joy of joys, they found racks of still-warm newly-baked bread. Luka tossed one to Bonitius and another to Alfrid and they tore into them as they continued their search.

"Over here," came Luka's hoarse whisper, as he put down the remains of his bread and upended to his lips a flagon of beer which promptly spilt and ran down onto his neck.

Alfrid had already found some cheese which he brought over; Luka exchanged the flagon for this and it was passed on further as they each drank deeply of the refreshing liquid.

Bonitius had only taken half of what he would have liked when they heard a murmur of voices and the sound of footsteps approaching the kitchen door. Scooping up their plunder and sweeping tell-tale breadcrumbs out of sight, they quickly left the kitchen area and crept back into the refectory, pressing their bodies against the separating wall as two cooks entered the kitchen.

Bonitius nodded to Luka who edged silently along the wall until he reached the corner and then, with the others following, repeated the process along the second wall until they made it to the door which he noiselessly unlatched. As he pulled it open the hinges gave a silence-defying creak which was mercifully covered by the simultaneous sound of crashing in the kitchen. The noise made them all jump but they took their advantage and sprang through the opening pulling the door closed behind them.

One of the cooks heard the click made by the latch falling. He put his head round the corner and into the hall but turned back to his colleague and said, "Nobody there brother. We've a little while yet."

--o--

On the archdeacon's right, sat the old prior of Saint Genevieve. Botolph had never visited the abbey itself but he knew roughly where it lay on the outskirts of Lutetia. Next to him was the new young abbot of St Maur. Botolph had met both of them at the consecration of Nanthild's new monastery.

At the end of the table was seated a familiar figure whom Botolph had at first struggled to recognise. Once he heard him speak however, he immediately remembered the lilting voice of Evequecomte Radingus whom he and Luka had first met on their journey through Gallia. Although now speaking in Latin, his native Irish lilt turned his voice into distinctive music.

Botolph turned his attention to the opposite end of the table where, in a position of honour, sat his abbess Fara and two other ladies. One of the ladies was of a similar age to Fara whereas the other was rather younger and Botolph could not help noticing that she was rather pretty.

The meeting droned on for ages and he was, for once, glad that Luka was not with him. He smiled inwardly when he thought of how his friend would have been fidgeting and complaining. In fact a fair amount of both was going on all around him and many of those who had been standing were now sitting on the floor; some were asleep.

Eventually the morning session reached its end and Bishop Faro got to his feet closely followed by the rest of the gathering. With the archdeacon trotting at his side the bishop led the way to the church for the office of Sext.

Abbess Fara came over to where Botolph and Bernard were standing with the twins Nelburga and Magburga. She brought with her the elderly lady and the pretty nun and introduced the former as Abbess Theodochilde of Jouarre and the latter as Sister Bertille.

"Sister Bertille," she intoned, "has been at Jouarre Abbey for the past eight years and is highly valued by Mother Theodochilde."

"Saints in Heaven," thought Botolph, "she must have been an infant in arms when she arrived. She looks barely fourteen now."

It transpired that Sister Bertille had withstood the passage of time well since, as became apparent during further conversation, she was in fact *twenty* years of age; two years older than Botolph.

"I hope," the abbess concluded, "that we shall be granted the blessing of a visit from these good Sisters-in-Christ at Evoriacum from time to time."

The other abbess inclined her head in acquiescence.

Botolph would have liked to talk further with the pretty nun but the Abbess of Jouarre swept her away to one side of the great church while he and the others followed Fara to the other side.

--o--

A hiding place

As the hooded group of three left the refectory they heard the ringing of the great bell marking the end of the office of Sext and they guessed that there would soon be a flood of people pouring into the courtyard.

They knew that their time was running out and wondered if they should cut their losses and run out too. The sounds of the tall vertical bolts being thrown on the great doors of the chapter house echoed across the courtyard.

Luka suddenly had an inspiration. Taking his companions' arms he propelled them urgently towards the archdeaconry.

"Stand still and cover me," he hissed, drawing them close to the stone slab by the ditch. They followed his cue and stood as if in deep conversation, their habits billowing in the wind and forming a helpful screen while the stocky one sank to his knees and crawled under the flagstone.

A moment later there was a "Psst! Come on you two," and with a quick glance around to make sure that nobody was watching, the skinny one spread his habit open as the bigger fellow took his opportunity and ducked down into the gap. The chapter house doors were wide open now and the thin one froze as he saw the first of the monks come out and look directly at him. The monk then turned away to talk to his neighbour and the thin one took his chance and shot into the hole.

The monk at the chapter house took a breath in his conversation and looked back to where the thin one had just been standing and then looked briefly away again; he suddenly jerked his head back and stopped in mid-sentence so that his companion said, "Botolph, Brother Botolph, what *is* the matter? You have gone quite pale. You look as if you've seen a spirit."

"I ... it ... it's nothing," said Botolph. "I thought I saw something but I must have been mistaken."

--o--

Their new accommodation, although cramped, was adequate for their needs. A little light filtered down through the gaps in the boarded floor of the room above, but most illumination came from between the wooden palings at their side. They had to crawl on their knees and elbows but at least they were out of the wind and could relax for the first time since they had entered the city.

They threw back their cowls whereupon Luka hissed jovially "Well well well, - if it's not Bishop Bonitius and Prior Alfrid!"

Alfrid grinned but Bonitius scowled. "What are we going to do now?" he said.

Luka put his fingers to his lips and shushed him as the sound of approaching voices reached them. Through the gaps in the palisade they saw the robes of two clerics.

"... Nice and juicy? What sort of talk is that for a monk?"

"Never you mind archdeacon. *I* know what I mean. In fact I think I'll go and see him now if you'll be kind enough to get me the keys."

The older voice grunted and Luka heard the door swing open above him. The archdeacon called to someone as his steps plodded over Luka's head and were joined by steps coming in the opposite direction. There was the sound of jangling metal as some keys were handed over.

--o--

A little earlier.

Helgot's prison was on one of the lower floors but not in the depths of the footing vaults. It was Brother Fauve to whom the duty of his supervision had fallen. The archdeacon did not want to soil his hands in dealing with what he regarded as scum.

As Fauve had walked back from the church with the archdeacon, he had asked him what he intended to do with Helgot.

"He's a nice strong young man," Fauve said appreciatively.

"Well *you* may do with him whatever you like," the archdeacon had replied, "as long as he stays fit and well in that prison cell until I am ready to use him to curdle Bonitius's blood."

"I hear he's been unwell," said the monk.

The archdeacon turned sharply. "The boy? Unwell? What do you mean?"

"No no archdeacon, ... not the boy ... his father Bonitius," cooed Fauve, taking every advantage of the opportunity to rile his superior. "Apparently somehow, I can't imagine how, - he managed to get a sword wound recently and was near to death."

"Hah! Fancy that!" said the archdeacon, "I must pray for his improved health. I can't have him dying and depriving me of the sweet joy of revenge."

"Ooh," said Fauve, "what exactly do you have in mind for young Helgot then?"

"You mind your own business," the archdeacon replied, "anyway I haven't fully decided yet, - I am still honing my plans. You just make sure that he's kept pink and in good voice so that his father will be able to appreciate his screams. What sort of age is he?"

"I really couldn't say. I'll ask him when I next go down. About sixteen summers I should think. Nice and juicy anyway."

"Nice and juicy? Nice and juicy? What sort of talk is that for a monk?"

"Never you mind archdeacon. *I* know what I mean. In fact I think I'll go and see him now if you'll be kind enough to get me the keys."

Once they were securely tucked into his girdle, the monk went to the kitchen, obtained a pitcher of mead and put half a loaf and some cheese and a couple of small fish in a wicker basket. He walked through the cloisters and across to the heavy oak door which he unlocked, went through and then locked securely behind him. Selecting the thickest taper from an iron basket which lay just inside the door, he lit it from one of the burning brands that permanently illuminated the stair-well. Looping his left arm through the handle of the wicker basket, he used his right hand to steady himself on the rail while his other also clutched the handle of the heavy pitcher and the taper.

It was not an easy transit but he only had to descend one floor and was soon walking the length of a passage towards another door, the sound of his sandals clip-clopping eerily on the echoing flagstones as he did so.

Before unlocking the second door he lit the nearest brand in the passage in case he lost the flame in his taper. He shivered at the thought of having to find his way back to the cloisters without a light. It was not the possibility that he might get lost, so much as the thought of unseen beings that might lurk in the shadows on the way. Stories were rife about evil fiends who lived in the Footing Vaults ... and Fauve was afraid of the dark.

He pushed the door open and went down the steps to another short passageway where the stench of human excrement made him catch his breath. He heard a movement in front of him.

"Hello?" said a frightened voice. "Who's that?"

He didn't answer but relished his temporary ability to instil fear and uncertainty in the mind of the prisoner. He tucked the taper up on an iron wall-bracket; the yellow glow of the flame contrasted with a blue-white mist of light coming down a ventilation shaft. The shaft, Fauve knew, gave onto the outside of the western wall of the library. He had often stood out there in the past, listening as the archdeacon's torturers practised their art. Such events always gave him a thrill.

He softly but quickly turned the corner and was greeted by the sight of an iron grill through which stared the wide eyes of the young captive who had not seen the light of day for two months.

"It is only your Brother Fauve," he said smoothly. "I have brought you some food. Would you like it?"

The half-starved boy did not answer but looked at him warily knowing that more was to follow.

"How old are you?"

"Thirteen."

"Hmm. Nice!"

"Remind me again ... what's your name?"

"Helgot."

"Hmm. *Very* nice! Well then Helgot. I want you to know that I'm your friend so I've brought you some lovely food and mead. Are you hungry?"

The boy nodded.

"Good, well here you are then," and he put the food down on the flagstones close enough for the youngster to reach.

"What's the catch?" said the boy warily.

"Catch? There's no catch Helgot. This is done in the spirit of friendship. There might be a few things that I'll want you to do for me sometime but don't worry your pretty head about that for the moment. There we are then. Eat when you're ready. I'll leave you to it."

In truth Fauve had all sorts of plans for the boy but he could afford to bide his time. The lad looked quite strong in spite of being only thirteen summers. Having had a close look at him Fauve was not sure that he could handle him on his own. He would perhaps have to arrange some assistance.

He turned away, regained the taper and went back through the door, feeling only a little frustrated. He had sown his seeds in one way if not in another. He would, he thought, invest his time in the boy before he invested anything else in him. Fauve could afford to be patient. It would all be worthwhile in the end.

CHAPTER 37
Under the floorboards.

Above him there started a cacophony of shoutings thumpings and bangs. Luka thought to himself what a noisy household this was and wondered how long they were going to have to endure its proximity. He was more intent at that particular moment however, on keeping his eyes on the key-bearer as he walked across to the kitchens. Luka crabbed his way further to the right so that he was closer to the palisade and had a better view of the archdeacon's companion as he threaded his way through the last of the clerics who were entering the refectory.

His attention was distracted for a moment by Bonitius and Alfrid crawling towards him so that they too could view the courtyard. He consequently missed the re-emergence of the monk from the kitchens. When he looked again he saw him with the wicker basket on his arm; he was standing at the same door that they had tried and found locked an hour or so previously. An insertion and quick turn of the key and the door swung open. Luka noted how he hesitated a moment taking a furtive look around him as if to make sure that he was not being watched before he slid inside, closing the door behind him.

"What *is* he up to?" wondered Luka aloud. "If that food's for Helgot, why would the skinny monk take it himself? Why not get a slave or someone else to do it?"

As the constant noises of the communal living of the clumsy family continued over their heads, Luka turned towards his companions and whispered, "At least we now have a pretty good idea of where Helgot's probably being kept."

"Assuming that's where the monk is going and that there's only the one prisoner," said Alfrid.

"That's true," said Luka.

"So assuming it is, all we need to do is get those keys and slide him out," replied Bonitius. "Why don't we get out of here *now* and make our way across to that door. As soon as it opens, we can push the faggot back in and slit his throat. That'll give us time to deal with whatever else we find down there get Helgot out and make a break for it."

It seemed like a sound plan and the other two nodded their assent and all three started towards the flagstone entrance. Suddenly there came the sound of chanting from the depths of the refectory. Bonitius was just about to duck under the flagstone and emerge into the previously-deserted courtyard when a procession burst onto the scene.

He looked wildly at Luka and Alfrid. The procession was coming straight at them. There was no way they could get across the courtyard without being seen. They gloomily returned Bonitius's gaze and Luka shook his head, as the first of the chanting monks came level with their hideaway. They watched helplessly as the oak door opened on the other side of the courtyard and the monk re-emerged, locking it securely behind him.

Their frustration knew no bounds as he walked directly towards them, waited a few moments for the procession to pass, and then stood outside the palisade and knocked on the archdeacon's door, his habit mocking them as he waited. They heard the heavy sister plod across the room and give a welcoming grunt as she opened the door.

"Tell the wench I've fed him today and she's not to give him any more food until I say so."

There were some more muttered words and a jangle from the keys as they were handed over and then he left.

Bonitius cursed and raved as silently as he could while the others shook their heads in disbelief. They had been so close. It had been a good plan but bad luck had meant that they had missed their chance. They withdrew into the lair and listened to the noises of the family above. In an attempt to see where the keys had gone, Luka tried pressing his eye against a gap in the floorboards but gave up suddenly when a footfall sent down a blinding shower of dust.

He slumped down ruefully rubbing his face and when his vision finally cleared, looked across at the other two.

"We'll have to wait until after dark," said Bonitius. "We're just going to have to get hold of those keys somehow. With any luck we should be able to make good our escape before anybody knows that Helgot's gone."

"What about the horses?" asked Luka.

"Oh they'll be alright. Eluhan knew we might have to wait until night-time."

"Yes, but what if we can't get the keys tonight? It might take several days ... and *we're* going to need food too!"

Alfrid grinned and Bonitius said, "You and your blessed stomach Luka. Can't you go *any* time without eating?"

Luka sent back his winning smile and, shaking his head endearingly, said "Nope!"

Shouting came from above their heads and footsteps stomped across the floor followed by a sharp crack, a cry of pain and the sound of a body falling. Then came sobbing and more shouting from the voice that they were all beginning to recognise as being that of the heavy sister.

The sobbing gradually eased and the ambient sound returned to an unintelligible mush of mutterings interspersed by the occasional louder noises.

They managed to work out that the room had five occupants. The archdeacon was constantly coming and going, issuing pompous remarks whilst there, and flouncing out from time to time to fulfil his clerical duties.

The "heavy sister" was the noisiest of the family. Although he had only seen her from below, and that was not a pretty sight, Luka imagined her to be very tall with masculine features. Perhaps, he reflected realistically, it was the angle he was viewing her from and the fact that she was just habitually heavy-footed and clumsy. He wondered if he would ever know. He concluded that either way he would not lose any sleep over it.

There seemed to be a young boy in the family too but he, by contrast, rarely spoke or moved.

That left two other women, one of whom they reasoned must be the archdeacon's wife. It was however clear that the "heavy sister" ruled the roost.

Then there was, as the skinny monk had put it, "the wench".

It must have been she who had borne the brunt of the heavy sister's chastisement earlier in the day.

The three villains half sat and half lay in their uncomfortable low-ceilinged prison, listening to the sounds from above and waiting for darkness and an empty courtyard.

CHAPTER 38
Luka?

Fara's party of the twin nuns and her two monks joined the end of the chanting procession as it made its way back into the chapter house for the beginning of the second session of the synod.

Botolph noticed that the numbers were reduced. Quite a few of the delegates must have left in order to return to their monasteries before darkness fell. He would be happy to get back to Evoriacum. He could not help noticing the constant but intermittent aura of weirdness that emanated from many of the people and buildings; excluding, of course, the emanations from Bertille.

There she was, sitting at the Bishop's table looking as demure and sweet as you like. Botolph felt a pang of guilt about Eanswythe as he looked at her. He felt drawn to them both. He wondered how Eanswythe was and how her nunnery had progressed in the moons since he had last seen her. He wondered about her father Eadbald and her mother Ymme and about Folcanstane itself. How was the fisherman Eric and his daughter-in-law Martha and had there been any more attacks from raiding parties?

Bishop Faro was speaking again and talking about the great missionary Columbanus who, Botolph knew, came from Ireland, was a compatriot of Father Fursey and whom his abbess had met in her childhood. Columbanus had prescribed ways in which monasteries should be run and the bishop was leading a discussion about how some of those ways might be changed.

231

The afternoon session finished without coming to any dramatic conclusions and at the sound of the Vespers bell, they trouped back into the church. Botolph did his best to edge his abbess closer to the Jouarre contingent but without success. After the office, the best voices of the choir led the synodists back out into the courtyard again.

As they approached the refectory, Botolph caught sight of the same three monks who had left the morning session early. They were grouped together near the kitchen doorway, their cowls obscuring their faces. One, who was particularly short, turned his head as they approached and Botolph caught what seemed like a familiar green flash from the shaded eyes as the cowl passed him and then turned further.

Bernard spoke and Botolph leant towards him saying "Sorry?"

"I was saying that we could catch our deaths out here, the time it always takes to get into the refectory."

Botolph looked back to the group of three again. They were still in the same position but appeared to be intent on their own conversation as the tide of monks swept past them.

"I'll catch up with you in a moment," said Botolph, "you go on."

He turned back and threaded his way against the tide towards the group of three. There was another party of five monks also deep in conversation, standing nearby. Botolph slowly made his way around the back of these, trying to make it look as if he was part of their group, until he was back to back with the smallest in the group of three.

He strained to hear their conversation but it was being drowned out by the others.

He turned a little more, his nose twitching like a dog's. Some primeval sense told him he was right; but *was* he? Or was it just something he wished for? He looked at the back of the cowl and said softly, "Luka?"

As the head started to turn Botolph held his breath wondering if he had made an embarrassing mistake.

CHAPTER 39
Clarisse

17th November 638 Late afternoon.

Bernard made his way to the serving counter, collecting a wooden bowl as he did so. He bowed his head in thanks as it was filled with broth and lifted the cloth from the wicker basket to pick up a chunk of warm bread. Finding himself a seat at one of the tables, he tried to arrange matters so that there would be space for Brother Botolph when he needed it. He put his hands together and closed his eyes in a silent prayer of gratitude for the food that was about to pass his lips.

No voices polluted the room. The only sounds were those of feet shuffling and food being served until the last person took his place, whereupon the reader commenced. Bernard reflected how well the deep bass voice complimented the flavour of the broth. He always enjoyed the readings even though they sometimes tended to make his eyelids droop.

Botolph had still not made his appearance and Bernard wondered what his friend was up to.

--o--

"Luka!"

Botolph felt the tears in his eyes begin to well up as he gazed at his dear friend's sweet smile in the depth of his cowl and they gripped each other's arms.

234

Botolph turned his gaze towards the face of the big man who stood on his left ... "Bonitius?"

"Aye, and this is Alfrid.   Pax Vobiscum Brother Botolph."

"And pax, pax, a thousand times pax to you too," said Botolph.

They were attracting no undue attention, enshadowed as they were by the other group of monks and the stream of those still passing.

"But what are you *doing* here?" asked Botolph.

"Shhh," said Luka, "keep your voice down or we'll *all* be in trouble. Bonitius's son, Helgot, is being held captive in the church cells and we've come to get him out."

A frenzy of thoughts whirled through Botolph's mind.   Here was his outlawed friend, for whom he would willingly give his life, bent on another of his crazy illegal missions in the company of one of the most notorious villains in the country, right here in the midst of a Holy Synod, the leaders of which would string all of them up on the gallows with barely a second thought.

"How can I help?" said Botolph disarmingly.

Luka gave him a grateful smile: "You can't dear brother," he said, "but we're grateful for your offer," – the others nodded.   "There are many things we need but you live on a higher cloud than we do and I'd not ask you to tumble from it for my sake. Just do what you're best at and pray for our safety and otherwise forget you've seen us. Now go and peace be with you my dearest brother."

"But ..."

"No! Go!" and Luka put down his head so that the cowl hid his face from Botolph's sight and Botolph knew he had been dismissed.

He looked again at the top of the cowl and squeezed Luka's arms receiving a long answering squeeze in return. After a moment's pause he turned away and with tears streaming down his cheeks he stumbled back towards the refectory, sure that tears were streaming down Luka's face too.

The group of three stood silently for several more minutes, the head of the little one remaining bowed. The moment passed and the big one gently patted his arm and the three regained their mobility and drifted off inconspicuously towards the flagstone by the archdeacon's house at which they arrived just as the last of the authentic monks entered the refectory.

--o--

Early morning the next day.

They were awoken by the howling of a strong wind and a heavy downpour of rain; they kept well back from the perimeter shuttering in order to avoid the splashes.

They could do nothing but watch and wait. Bonitius was getting more irascible and Luka was bored; always a dangerous condition in the case of Luka. Alfrid, by comparison seemed fairly content.

Bonitius cursed the fact that the skinny monk had banned all food going to the prisoner. He wondered why that was. Were they trying to starve him? What good would that do? He wondered why the archdeacon had not simply put Helgot in a slave train and sent him off to Italy. He had a nasty feeling that the archdeacon had a secret agenda and that keeping the boy in Meaux had something to do with his desire for revenge.   Nothing seemed to be happening.   They needed a break.

Their break came during the morning and as Luka reflected later, they could have starved under those floorboards for another week if they had been less lucky so perhaps God was a little bit on their side after all.

It was still early when the arguments, shouting and sobbing started again in the room above.   Bonitius had remarked to Luka that the bad weather perhaps made the heavy sister's temper bad too.   Luka had just given a concurring grunt when they heard the outer door open above them and saw a screaming object fall past the gaps in the shuttering and land heavily in a puddle outside, the muddy splashes from which burst into their space.   The body lay sobbing in the mud for some moments while familiar cackles of laughter came from the remaining occupants of the archdeacon's dwelling.   The door slammed shut.

Luka edged closer and watched as the girl raised herself on one elbow and continued to sob.   The rain eased a little and a brief shaft of sunlight swept across her.

"Each ray of sunshine reflects the colour of her hair," thought Luka.

He noticed how it changed from red at the crown, to auburn, russet and then dark brown as the mud from the puddle unjustly started to soak into it.   Her arm was covered in mud too. She wiped her eyes and pushed the hair from her face; she stood and looked around her. Nobody else was in the courtyard.   She sniffed back more tears and then suddenly, to Luka's horror, she walked straight across to the flagstone and with one lithe movement ducked under it ...

Mid-morning.

The bad weather kept Botolph and Bernard confined to the abbey. They would have liked to explore Meaux but the rain was unrelenting. They visited the library and the scriptorium; Botolph was unimpressed.

"Why?" asked Bernard.

"Well, they're only playing at it aren't they?" said Botolph. "It seems to me that the whole idea of a scriptorium is either to copy existing books to add to the library, or else to copy library books to sell to others. There are only these two doddery old scribes here; one can hardly see and the other's finger bones are so twisted that he can barely write. At Cantwarebury and Cnobersburgh, the scriptoria were the liveliest places in the abbey."

They joined the Meaux monks at Terce and in the chapter house afterwards, with the result that they started to become amalgamated into the Meldian community. They talked to one of the monks who told them that Meaux was called Iatiniacum during the first part of the Roman occupation; after that the popular name changed to Meaux after the Meldi tribe of honey gatherers who frequented the region.

CHAPTER 40
The Keys

The girl shrieked as her face nearly hit Luka's. He abruptly stifled her cry by putting his hand over her mouth whilst using his other hand to pin down her arm. Wide-open eyes peered over his fingers. Once he judged that she had recovered from her shock he took his hand away touching his index finger to his lips in a gesture of silence and giving his most winning smile as he did so.

She nodded and gave half a smile in return and he released her arm.

"Who are you?" she whispered.

"Luka, Bonitius, Alfrid," he pointed. "And you?"

"Clarisse."

"Clarisse. Hmm. Nice!"

She giggled.

"How long've you been living under our floor?"

"Two miserable days," growled Bonitius softly.

"Why?"

"The prisoner."

"You've come to rescue him?"

"That's the plan."

"You'll never do it. They'll kill you."

"Who's they?"

"My father."

"Your *father*?" jerked out Luka.

"Yes, the archdeacon's my father ... well, no ... he's my stepfather actually. When he married my mother I'd already been born."

"So that lump of lard that bounces around up above is your stepsister?"

She giggled attractively. "Really she's my *half*-sister. She was born to the archdeacon's first wife who died in labour."

"I'm not surprised," said Luka, "giving birth to a monster like that! And the boy?"

"He's my step-brother and was born to my mother when I was two summers."

"God, your family is nearly as complicated as mine," said Luka, "and I hate *them*!"

"I hate mine too," she confessed, "and they certainly hate me. I'm only there to cook clean and carry and even then I get cuffed round the ear for my pains. My father resents me and my mother's too weak to stand up to him so she resents me too."

"Come away with us then," said Luka impulsively.

"What?" Her eyes opened wide again.

"Come away with *us*. *I'll* look after you!" Luka had always been one to make instant decisions. He had only been wrong once in his life and that was when he first met Botolph whom he had wanted to beat to death. He had learned from that though, and these days found that his first impressions were rarely wrong. He judged that this little girl was a treasure to whom he could offer the world.

"You don't even know me," she protested, "and look at you; you're intent on getting yourself killed."

"No I'm not," said Luka, "I've never got myself killed yet and I'm not proposing to now. So what d'you say? Will you come? You're having a miserable life here. We're bandits but you'll have more of a family at Bondy than you'll get here in a million years!"

She laughed at this earnest young man with such a fetching smile. "I'm not promising anything but the idea sounds attractive I must say."

It had given Luka such joy to transform this weeping desolate rag-doll of a girl into the happy smiling creature he now saw before him.

Bonitius and Alfrid had been entirely non-plussed by his activities and they could but look on in silence and admiration with smirks of amusement on their faces.

"I used to come down here when I was a child," said Clarisse. "Nobody ever found me. I used to bring a doll that my real father made for me before he was killed. Even now, when I get a chance to sneak away I come here but this is the first time for moons. I shall have to go soon though, or I shall be missed."

"But they threw you out," protested Luka.

"Yes, I know, but they'll soon want their dinner and I shall get a real beating if they don't get fed. I'll save some for you if I can."

"You'll get us some dinner?" said Luka, even more impressed with this vision of loveliness who could also produce food. Bonitius and Alfrid were looking brighter too.

"What about Helgot?" said Luka. I know your sister keeps the keys but is there any way *we* can get hold of them?"

"They hang at her waist all day. I, of course, have them when I take food to the prisoner ... Helgot ..." (she smiled uncertainly as she realised that now he was more than just 'the prisoner') .... "but Fauve's forbidden me to take any more food to him, so I won't have them for a while."

"Fauve - that's the skinny monk?" said Luka.

She nodded.

"He can't deny Helgot food for long," said Luka. "Perhaps when you are next given them you will be able to get them to us."

She nodded doubtfully. "During the night my sister hangs the keys on a peg over her bed. I might be able to steal them."

"That'd be good. If we were able to get Helgot out at night, we'd stand much more chance of being able to escape. Let's work on that idea."

The rain started to ease and more stomping and shouting started above them. She giggled. "They do make a noise don't they? I must go. I'll come back as soon as I can."

She looked into Luka's eyes and he, enraptured, gazed back at her.

"I've decided," she said. "I really would like to come with you. Don't leave without me ... please."

"No chance," said Luka as they edged their way towards the flagstone.

"You see the hole over there where the waste water from our kitchen drops into the gutter?"

Luka nodded.

"I'll wrap some food in a cloth and then lower it down and throw it to one side so that it doesn't get wet," she said. "I might even be able to lower one of our smaller flagons through the hole but you'll have to catch it or it'll fall over and spill."

"Is there any chance you could get the keys tonight?" said Luka.

"I'll try but it depends on lots of things," she said. "I'll do what I can."

"Well, you're a caution to be sure," laughed Bonitius after she had left. "I've never seen anyone do his courting leaning on one elbow, nor have I ever seen it accomplished in such a short time.   Wait until she sees you standing up and finds you're only knee-high to a grasshopper!"

"I hadn't thought of that," said Luka.

CHAPTER 41
The archdeacon's meal

18th November 638 Early morning.

While the three bandits' attention was being taken by their bedraggled but pretty visitor, they missed the activity that was taking place on the other side of the curtain of rain.

Two rough-looking individuals shook the water from their cloaks as they ducked into the dry cloister and used their own key to open the oaken door before sliding surreptitiously inside.

It was the sound of the key turning in the lock of the second door that woke Helgot.

His immediate thought was one of terror that it was Fauve returning; he heard the door slam shut again and a couple of strangers came round the corner to peer in at him.

"So you're the prisoner then?" sneered the short one. Helgot did not answer.

"We're friends of Brother Fauve," volunteered the other. "We've come to look after you. We believe the dear Brother has plans for you that may necessitate our 'elp," and they both sniggered.

"I 'ope you're ready for it. He's got quite a big one," and they laughed again.

"'e likes us to inflict a bit of pain on his victims," said the other. "We over did it on the last one and 'e bled to death the following day. 'Ope that doesn't happen to you." They laughed again.

"C'mon let's find somewhere to make ourselves comfortable while we wait for Fauve."

"Pr'aps we could 'ave the youngster ourselves while we're waiting. That'd 'elp to pass the time."

"You're asking to get your balls cut off, you are. You know Fauve likes 'is meat kept fresh. Come on now, let's settle down. Bring a light and I'll give you a game of knucklebones."

The two disappeared and Helgot sank into his corner to await his fate which he felt sure would not be long in coming.

Soon afterwards.

By the time Clarisse pushed open the front door of the archdeacon's house, most of the rest of the occupants had forgotten the drama of an hour or so previously and they hardly noticed her return. Her mother though was unusually attentive and helped her daughter to change out of her wet clothes before ushering her into the cooking area to help prepare the day's meal.

The warmth from the blazing logs helped to drive the November chill from Clarisse's bones as she tarried a little longer than necessary whilst placing a cauldron of water to heat.

Her mother noticed her lighter attitude and Luka, in his sunken position, clearly heard the heavy sister say, "What's got into you then? Must've done you good sending you out in the rain. Washed all your bad temper away ehhh? We'll have to do it more often!" She turned to her brother to accept his approval which he dutifully gave with an adoring grin.

Clarisse ignored the jibes and kept her head down, carrying on with her work while thinking furiously how she was going to be able to do what her new friends had asked of her. In truth she was glad to have the opportunity to defy the household but terrified of her sister, - and not without good reason.   Even the *thought* of wilfully disobeying her made her legs turn to jelly and a knot form in the pit of her stomach.

Whenever her mother's back was turned, she pushed portions of food into a corner which she covered with a trencher held on its side by the weight of a drinking horn. She had already taken the precaution of putting on a woollen neck scarf, ostensibly to warm her up after the morning's experience. She now took it off and laid it by the trencher and searched out a small flagon which she filled with water from the bucketful that she had collected from the well the previous day.

The door burst open and the archdeacon entered accompanied by a shower of water and a wet Fauve.

"Lubaia, Brother Fauve'll be eating with us today," he announced. "We've things to discuss."

A sense of panic flooded over Clarisse as she realised that there was now going to be a conflict between the missing food and the increased number at the table. She wondered whether to put the stolen pieces back in their rightful position but decided she would take the risk. If all else failed she would go without food herself. While her mother went to help the two clerics with their wet cloaks and all attention was on the new arrivals, Clarisse took her chance and quickly wrapped the food in her scarf and, plunging her arm through the waste hole, tossed it sideways.

After a quick glance at the group drying themselves at the hearth, she grasped the flagon and thrust that through the hole too. Nobody took it. No hand came to relieve the weight. She desperately waved it sideways; to no avail. She let it go just as her mother reappeared saying, "What are you doing down there?"

"I ... I was just tidying up."

"Well get off your knees then and help me put this food out young lady. You're acting very strangely today."

The food was duly set out for the family.

"Is this all there is Lubaia?" asked the archdeacon.

CHAPTER 42
Rescue?

Luka was so busy untying the scarf that he had not noticed the flagon insistently swaying over his head. It was Alfrid who spotted it and managed to catch it as it dropped. They all heard the mother scolding her daughter for crawling around on her knees.

They tucked in right royally whilst trying to eavesdrop on the conversation that the archdeacon was having with Fauve but it was impossible to hear them clearly.

--o--

"Well ... Well ..." spluttered the mother, "I thought we'd prepared more than this. Clarisse ..." but Clarisse was busily pouring mead into drinking horns and maintaining a stare of total innocence. The moment passed and with the young girl's abstinence supplies were just sufficient and the paucity was forgotten. The archdeacon and Fauve were huddled in deep conversation.

Clarisse kept herself to herself for the rest of the day, aware that her sense of growing excitement was creating within her a rarely-experienced sense of optimism that might be discernible to the rest of the family. She had thought that she was doomed to live her life of drudgery and oppression for ever but now, out of the blue, came this unexpected opportunity to break free. She did not really care what happened.   She would rather die than let this chance slip through her fingers.

Little did she know that that was indeed what she would be facing.

--o--

Later that night when they had settled down in their pallets, Clarisse listened intently as sleep stole slowly over all except her. She was too excited to sleep. She could feel her heart hammering away at her rib cage and drumming in her ears and thought that its noise must be loud enough to be heard by everyone.

In the glow of the fire's embers she had watched her sister taking off the girdle that she wore over her tunic and putting, as she always did, the keys on the peg above where her head would lie.

In her mind Clarisse rehearsed what she must do; how she must slowly clutch those keys together so that they made no noise and then lift the ring over the peg whilst supporting it so that, when the weight was relieved, the ring did not fall over and hit the keys or worse still hit her sister's head.

She stifled a giggle at the thought but then her stomach growled once more to remind her that such a mistake would be a disaster.

She could hear the archdeacon snoring now and his trumpeting call was soon taken up by her sister as they joined in an unholy cacophony.

She waited until the snoring became regular and then she waited again.   Nearly an hour passed as the orchestra tuned and retuned before she felt it was safe to move.

Rolling over quietly she retrieved her sandals from nearby, and laced them on. She tucked her cloak under her arm and then crept to her sister's bedside and leant across the snoring face to retrieve the keys. Just as she touched them the snoring stopped and the body moved. She froze and held her breath. After what seemed an age the snoring re-started and, breathing again, she reached further and clutched the keys together. Keeping her thumb on the lower part of the ring to stop it turning, she lifted it off the peg. She refused to allow herself the luxury of a feeling of triumph and continued to creep cautiously past the snoring archdeacon to the door.

To her horror two black eyes flashed open and held her in a stare. She froze once more. The eyes blinked ... threateningly.

--o--

Luka could hear the snoring too. At one point he had to shake Bonitius awake when he threatened to add his own contribution. Alfrid was sleeping peacefully and Luka wished that he could join them but he was hoping against hope that Clarisse might get the keys tonight. There seemed no point in waiting any longer. He wondered how Helgot was faring. It was Luka's desire to pay off some of his debt of gratitude to Bonitius that bound him to the cause of Helgot's rescue rather than any particular liking for the boy himself - although he was a nice enough young lad.

--o--

At that very moment Helgot was awake. He had managed to sleep for a while. He lay still, thinking that he was glad that he had been spared Fauve's visit during the day although he was less than happy about the arrival of his two "cellmates". In fact they seemed a more dangerous prospect than Fauve himself.

He could hear them both snoring so they offered no threat for the moment. Perhaps it was their snoring that had woken him. He was feeling so hungry. He had tried licking the walls during the day to try to moisten his mouth a little. It had temporarily slaked his thirst. He snuggled down and tried to go back to sleep.

--o--

They were the eyes of her mother. The archdeacon's snoring continued; the eyes continued to stare. It was bizarre; she began to think that perhaps her mother always slept with her eyes open. But there was no doubt that Lubaia was awake and watching her intently. Neither of them moved and not knowing what she should do, Clarisse did nothing.

And then, her mother smiled and gave a simple but unmistakeable nod of her head.

For a moment Clarisse froze, wondering if she had misinterpreted the sign. The smile and nod were repeated. Her mother knew. Her mother was wiser than she had ever guessed. In that brief moment Clarisse suddenly understood so much: her mother's love; her mother's inability to show that love as she would have wished; her mother's total, - well almost total, dedication to her husband's cause.

Clarisse returned the brief smile and the nod. She hesitated. She wanted to embrace her mother in a last 'goodbye' but the embrace had to be ethereal. She peered at her and watched as a tear welled up in her mother's left eye and, overflowing, crossed her face on its sideways journey towards her right ear.   Clarisse felt her own eyes fill.

Her resolve returned.   She crept to the door, raised the latch and was gone.

--o--

Luka was dreaming one of his unmentionable dreams when she shook his shoulder and he woke thinking that perhaps it had not been a dream after all.   It took no time at all before he was wide awake and rousing Bonitius who roused Alfrid and all four silently crossed the deserted blackened courtyard.

Luka wanted to take the keys and unlock the door himself but she had done it so many times before that she knew the feel of the lock and swiftly and silently they were soon inside.

"Shall I lock it?" she asked.   "I usually do."

"No," Luka said.   "Leave it undone.   I don't like the idea of being on the wrong side of a locked door.   This should only take us a few minutes and nobody is likely to try the lock before we come back ourselves.   Alfrid took a taper from the iron basket and lit it from the wall-brazier and they made their way down the passage to the next door.

Clarisse put the key in the lock and turned it but then frowned, "it's already unlocked!" she whispered.

Luka pulled the door open a little and listened.   All was quiet.   "Where is he?" he whispered.

"Down the steps and round the corner," Clarisse replied.

"Right, let's get 'im," said Luka   He pulled the door fully open and started down the steps followed by the others.   Suddenly a shape materialised in front of him and something hit him hard on the head. He blacked out and crashed to the floor dowsing the taper. The door slammed shut and sounds of shouting and screaming and blows being exchanged filled the pitch black interior.

"Alfrid, Luka, where are you?" Bonitius shouted.

"I'm here, with Clarisse," came Alfrid's reply from the other side of the passage and then after a pause, "Don't know where Luka is." Bonitius felt a movement on his left side and grabbed at whatever it was, - there was a shouted oath from a voice that he did not recognise so, whilst still holding the bunch of clothing in his left hand, Bonitius threw a hopeful punch with his right fist and was rewarded by a satisfying double contact as his opponent's head hit the wall. There came the noise of scrambling and the door was thrust open again flooding light into the arena. A figure hurtled up the steps and into the upper passage way with Alfrid in hot pursuit.

Bonitius's adversary was just a bundle of rags so he left him where he was and followed Alfrid. He arrived at the doorway just in time to see the other guard open the outer door and head into the courtyard. Bonitius cursed the fact that they had failed to lock the outer door but he called Alfrid back and they set about getting some light onto the scene.

Helgot had recognised his father's voice and Bonitius called Clarisse over to unlock the cage whereupon father and son joyously clasped each other's arms.

Alfrid shook Luka back to consciousness and he came round suddenly, shaking his head, saying "What hit me?" and staggered to his feet.

"You've been having another sleep while we've been fighting," quipped Bonitius.

They grabbed the unconscious guard and dragged him into the cage before locking the door again.

The sound of a continuously-tolling bell, filtered down to them.

"It's the alarm," said Clarisse. "They're calling out the guard."

"C'mon then, let's get out of here," said Bonitius and with Alfrid and Clarisse in the lead they ran up the steps into the inner passage. They had hardly gone more than a few yards when the upper door opened in front of them and in came armed guards followed by the archdeacon in his night attire.

They were trapped!

--o--

"What's that?"

Botolph and Bernard's sleep was shattered as the alarm bell penetrated the usual calm and quiet of the abbey. The bell was insistent and urgent, quite unlike the gentle peal of the bell that would within the hour have called them to Matins.

"The building must be on fire. Quick, let's get out into the courtyard."

They hurriedly slipped on their sandals and with an ever-growing throng of other bodies, made their way into the open. There was no smell of smoke nor any sign of flames but armed guards seemed to be everywhere.

"What's happening?" Botolph asked one of them.

"Not sure, but I think there's been an attack of some sort."

Abbess Fara and the twins appeared. "What's going on?" she said.

"I don't know mother," replied Bernard. "Some talk of an attack."

As sleep left his brain, it gradually dawned on Botolph that Luka might somehow be involved in all this. If this was the case then he really needed to know. He walked through the crowd towards the kitchens where the mass seemed to be at its most dense. Bernard had left the abbess behind and was following Botolph closely.

They pushed their way through be-habited figures towards the centre which consisted mainly of men-at-arms.

"What's happened?" he asked one of them.

"There's been a break out of some of the prisoners," he said.

"Prisoners? How many?"

"About six I believe."

"Where are they?"

"Well apparently they broke out into the courtyard but when the alarm bell sounded they ran back into the prison and slammed the door behind them. So it don't look like there's a problem. We'll just put a guard on the door and then smoke 'em out in the morning when we can all see wot we're a-doin of'."

The crowd started to break up as it became apparent that the night's entertainment was over. Botolph wondered what help he could give Luka. What would his Lord have wanted? Was it unchristian to aid a felon?

"You look concerned," said Bernard.

Botolph looked at him.

"I do have a bit of a problem," he said. "To be honest, I am not sure if it is fairer to keep it to myself or to share it with you."

"Well," said Bernard, "We're friends and there're plenty of proverbs about friends sharing problems and all of them seem to point to the fact that 'sharing' is the right thing to do, so tell me brother!"

"Come," said Botolph, "Let's go into the refectory where we can talk in privacy and out of this cold wind."

Once settled opposite each other in one corner of the refectory, Botolph started his story.

"You remember the story so far about my friend Luka?"

"Indeed I do. When last heard of he had a price on his head for the murder of a rapist and had joined a gang of bandits just outside Lutetia."

To his surprise Botolph found himself a little shocked at Bernard's concise and accurate summing up.

"Err ... yes, I suppose that's right," he said, "although saying it like that does make it sound rather stark. Anyway, he's here!"

"Here?" said Bernard.

"Yes, - he's one of the prisoners who escaped."

It was Bernard's turn to be shocked and he sat in silence for a full minute contemplating the implications.

"How did he come to be imprisoned in Meaux?" he asked.

"Ah, well, strictly speaking, he wasn't. I've had to take the mix of what I know and mingle that with what I've heard and come to my own conclusions. I've a hunch that the man-at-arms got his story a bit confused. As far as I understand it there was only *one* prisoner and he's the son of Luka's friend. Luka, the father and one other bandit had come to rescue the son and they were wandering around the precincts disguised as monks."

Bernard leant back and there was silence between them.

"So that's who you were talking to yesterday when I went into the refectory?"

"Exactly."

"So what's *your* part in this?"

"I have no part. As soon as I saw Luka I offered my help but he wouldn't hear of it, - he said that I was sitting on a cloud which was at a higher level than his and that I should stay there. I objected but he simply shooed me away."

"So where does the girl fit in?"

"Girl? What girl?"

"One of the guards told me that there was a girl involved as well."

"I know nothing about any girl. The man-at-arms story seemed to be wildly exaggerated so I expect they've added a girl to give extra flavour."

"Perhaps you're right. So what are we going to do?"

"Do? Well I can't see that we can do anything."

Another silence fell over them.

It was broken by the sounds of the distant ringing of the bell summoning them to Matins.

"Come," said Botolph. "Let's go and pray about it and see if the Good Lord can suggest anything. I don't want to do anything that is against the law but I *do* want to do what is right for Luka; if succour proves to be illegal but God tells me it is morally right, then so be it. I'll give to God what's God's and Caesar can have what's Caesar's. The trouble is at the moment I'm not sure whether Luka is God's or Caesar's!"

Bernard laughed grimly as they stood and headed for the door.

"Wait!" came a high-pitched voice as Botolph placed his hands on the door handle. They turned, startled, to see the cloaked figure in the darkness at the entrance to the kitchen.

"I heard every word you said."

Botolph's heart sank. Fauve! There was no chance of rescuing Luka now. His mind raced. There were two of them and only one of him. Was there any chance that they could capture him and bundle him away for long enough to allow them to release the prisoners? And yet they did not yet even have a plan for doing that.

It was life-changing decision. He would have to give up all hope of becoming a monk and he and Bernard would need to flee the country.

He could not involve Bernard. There was no choice but surrender.

"Brother Fauve," he said, noncommittally.

CHAPTER 43
Assessment of the Prison

The tear finally dropped off her cheek and was followed by several more as Clarisse's mother watched the door close behind her daughter. She hoped she would have a good life. She did not know the whole story but her instinct told her that she might have fallen in love. She assumed that the object of her affection was the young prisoner. She had so wanted to free her child from the drudgery and sadness of her life. She was a broken woman. She had no mind of her own. She did what was asked of her and that was all. She felt that she had never had an original thought in her life. It was a small spark of light and hope when she saw that Clarisse's character had matured to the point when she could take her own freeing decision. She thanked God for it and prayed that, whatever it was, Clarisse's plan would succeed.

It was a forlorn hope however, to which was added colour when the alarm bell started clanging just a short while later. She, like the rest, leapt out of her pit. The archdeacon was fussing and grumbling and trying to find his sandals; the heavy sister took a taper to the fire and used the flame to light a couple of oil lamps; the son's eyes were still closed as he stood, stretching, willing the urgency to go away. The archdeacon snapped, "Fire I expect. Bring a bucket," and she went to fetch one while he and the rest of the family tumbled out into the courtyard. In the corner there were two small buckets and one large one, the latter having been borrowed from the abbey kitchen earlier in the day.

She knew it was not a fire and that they would not need a bucket but she had learned that you do not question your husband but just do as you are bid, so 'bucket' it was, and if a bucket, then it might as well be a large bucket!

Carrying the useless bucket, she was soon an integral part of the pressing crowd and absorbing their conversations. Words like 'prisoners, girl' and numbers ranging from 'five' to 'twelve' were being bandied around. She could not see the archdeacon and the thought of her daughter being hauled out of the cell and being arraigned like a common criminal was something she hoped she would not have to witness.

It had all gone wrong then; just as she had thought that there was a glimmer of hope. She pushed her way through the chattering horde and made her way forlornly to the kitchen, in the hope of escaping the noise. She upended the bucket and placed it over another and then sat in a corner on a stool and leant forwards, her elbows on her knees, her head in her hands, and sobbed. When the tears had all finished, she rested her head back into the angle made by the walls and stretched her legs out straight and just sat and thought.

She heard Bernard and Botolph enter the refectory and began to panic when they came in her direction. It was ironic that they chose the thin wall to lean against which was the same wall as that by which she was also supported. Or perhaps it was *not* ironic. Perhaps it was the will of God. She could hear every word.

--o--

They slammed the door behind them and held it fast.

"Quick, the key," shouted Bonitius, and with trembling hands Clarisse felt for the keyhole in the dark and then inserted the big iron lever and quickly turned it giving them at least temporary security.

"What are we going to do now?" said Bonitius after the hammering on the door eventually stopped.

Luka assumed that the question was directed at him although in truth Bonitius had thrown it out as an expression of despair rather than expecting any answer.

"Well, let's see what we've got," said Luka, not really knowing where the conversation was going but feeling that he had to say something.

"We've five healthy bodies, one of whom is a wench." There was a groan from inside the cage.

"Six healthy bodies," said Bonitius, "well, six *bodies* anyway!"

"We've a bunch of keys," Luka continued, "a dark room and passage, a locked cell and a locked door."

"And a ventilation shaft," said Clarisse.

"Yes," said Helgot, "and a ventilation shaft, - but one which is only half a foot square at the end. I've been looking at that shaft for several weeks. It's not even wide enough for someone as slim as you to escape from. And the shaft is about six feet long which is the same width as the wall and there is no chance that we'd be able to make that hole any larger. It's only virtue is the air that comes down it although I've a feeling that there's another shaft somewhere because the smells in here get really bad sometimes. It's as if the smells come *in* from somewhere else and then perhaps *out* through that shaft. Another good thing it does is to let in some light during the day."

It was not letting in any light at that moment. The room was as black as pitch.

"Anybody got a strike-fire with them?" asked Alfrid.

"Yes, I have," replied the ever-ready Luka. "See if you can feel your way to getting one of those brands down off the wall Alfrid, and Helgot – stick your hands through those bars and collect a bit of kindling from your straw cell."

"'S not my cell anymore," said Helgot. "'Tis 'is!"

"Well don't get upset about it. Get some anyway!"

A flash went through Luka's mind that made him wonder if it had been a good idea rescuing Helgot after all. He was beginning to annoy him. Perhaps it was because they were all tired, not to mention stressed about the imminent prospect of capture and death.

The items having been collected, Luka set to with the flint and in a trice the kindling was alight, soon followed by the brand which was returned to its holder. From the new light they found the taper and used that to light another brand.

Taking the taper, Luka walked round having a good look at the walls and ceilings of the chamber in hope of finding a an escape route - but there was nothing. The only thing he *did* find was the other source of ventilation of which Helgot had spoken. In one corner down at floor level there were three grooves of about one hand's width each. When he put his nose near them, an unholy stench pervaded his nostrils. Recoiling, he returned to the fresher air where the others were sitting on the floor.

"Anything?" Bonitius asked, looking up.

"Nah, nothing."

"How long've we got?" said Alfrid.

"Only the few hours to daylight I guess," said Luka. "Then they'll be back."

"It's a good strong door," said Alfrid.

"Yes but sadly the hinges are on the other side," said Luka. "They'll soon cut those off and that will be that."

"Perhaps we'll stand more chance of escape *then*?" said Helgot. "I mean, even if we get out of here we still have to get back to Bonoriacum and we could be captured at any time. Why don't we just unlock the door, give ourselves up and take our chances?"

"Your only chance in those circumstances young man," replied Luka, "starts and ends with a rope round your neck. No, there's got to be a way out of this ... trouble is, I don't know what it is yet ..."

CHAPTER 44
Hope

She threw back her cowl.

"No brothers - it's your lucky day, - it's not the accursed Fauve - it's I, Lubaia, wife of Archdeacon Gaubert."

Botolph offered a lightning prayer of thanks, - but they were not out of the woods yet. An Archdeacon's wife could still make a lot of trouble for them.

"What do you want?" he asked cautiously.

"The same as you."

"What do you mean?"

"I want to help you release the prisoners."

Botolph began to feel uneasy again:

"Now why would you want to do that?"

"Because my daughter is amongst them."

"You're *daughter*?" they exclaimed in unison.

"Yes, it was she who gave the dwarf the keys."

"The redhead Clarisse!" said Bernard.

Botolph looked at him sharply.

"The same," said Lubaia, "she's my daughter."

Botolph shook his head disbelievingly.

"No," he said, "She might have given him the keys but Luka would never have let a girl go in there with them."

"She's in there," she insisted. "The dwarf offered her a chance of escape from this rotten place and she took it. You'll just have to trust me."

She suddenly gave a sad smile and said coyly, "I don't really think you have much alternative."

Botolph saw her point: "What's in your mind?"

264

"The hill the palace sits on is riddled by a series of tunnels."

"I know," said Bernard, "I've been down them."

"You have?" she said.   "Well I'm surprised you're still alive."

"Are they that dangerous?" asked Botolph.

"Certainly, if you don't know what you're doing. People who value their lives would never venture down there without a guide."

Bernard felt some butterflies suddenly start to dance in his stomach but ventured no further comment.

"So how can you help us?"

"Beneath the prison cell there's an escape tunnel and I can show you where it is."

"What's the catch?   If your daughter is your only interest, then why take us?"

"I'm neither big enough nor strong enough on my own."

Her countenance changed to one of seriousness.

"Are you with me or not, because there's no time to be lost?"

There came the sound of the bell ringing for Matins.

"I'll come," said Botolph.   "Bernard - you go to Matins and do your best to cover for me."

"No, - I'm coming too." said Bernard.   "With such a lot of people here at the Synod there's a good chance we won't be missed."

Botolph groaned inwardly at the mixed blessing of having so many loyal friends.   He opened his mouth to protest but the sight of Bernard's earnest face made him close it again and he just nodded in gratitude.

"The tunnels will be dark so we are going to need two or three oil lamps, a jug of oil and a fire-maker," said Lubaia.

"If we wait here until Matins is underway the place will be deserted. I can get one lamp from my house together with a jug of oil and a strike-fire if you can bring two more lamps from your dormitory. I'll meet you shortly just round the corner from the south door."

Time went frustratingly slowly as they waited for Matins to begin. Botolph eventually risked opening the refectory door. To his relief the courtyard was empty; the two monks sidled out unnoticed.

Unnoticed that is, except by one. Fauve was still standing in the shadows just inside the open doorway that led to the prison cell. He had decided to miss Matins in favour of spending his time trying to devise the most gruesome punishment for his prisoners when they saw the light of the next day. He snapped alert as, out of the corner of his eye, the movements of the two monks caught his attention. He watched as they made their way to the dormitory and went inside. He was still considering the possible implications of this when he saw another ghostly figure leave from the same door and creep across to the Archdeacon's house. What *was* going on? He pushed back deeper into the shadows and waited.

It was not long before his patience was rewarded as the figure re-emerged from the Archdeacon's house and made its way into the cathedral. Moments later the two monks came out of the dormitory and followed the same route. Matins was still in progress. Were they all simply late for the office or was there something more sinister? Instinct told him it was the latter.

He quietly closed and locked the passage door and stealthily followed in their footsteps.

--o--

A November fog had descended and was swirling around them as they followed Lubaia out of the precincts and across to the city wall. Each of them was carrying a full lantern from which they were taking care not to spill the oil. The path dropped down behind some bushes and they chased along the wall until they reached a narrow wooden door secured by a wooden bar. Their guide lifted off the bar and swung the door open, leading them onto another shrub-bordered path outside the city walls. After a short distance she stepped off the path and, crossing some grass, headed uphill, looking back every so often to make sure they were still following.

When she reached a stone buttress she grasped a branch of a bush which was climbing up the angle between buttress and wall. The bush yielded to her pull and fell away from the wall. She pressed through the narrow slit closely followed by the two monks.

The tunnel widened into an ante-chamber and Lubaia turned and said, "Time to light up while we can still see a little."

"All the lanterns?" asked Bernard.

"No, only two. We have to save the oil for as long as we can. I've brought a taper with me so that as soon as one shows signs of going out we can light another."

Lubaia led the way with the first glowing lantern and Bernard brought up the rear with the second, - both were holding a hand in front of the flame so that their forward motion did not extinguish it. Their eyes gradually became accustomed to the darkness.

A studded iron door appeared ahead of Lubaia's lamp. She pulled on a metal lever which clanked noisily heralding a grinding sound as the great door swung towards them revealing another tunnel.

She kicked at a small rock that was clearly there for a purpose and used it to pin the door open and then she set off again. After a short distance they stumbled up a few stone steps which led to another long level passage.   They made good speed and were able to see well enough to keep close behind their leader who suddenly stopped as they reached ... a complete dead end.

They were in a widened chamber which went nowhere.   In one corner was a dust-covered small sturdy table and a couple of chairs which looked for all the world as if they were waiting for a couple of gaolers to sit at them. But what would they be guarding, ... there was nothing.

Botolph exhaled in frustration as Lubaia slowly turned and faced them, the black eyes piercing the shadow's cowl.   Had they been led into a trap?

--o--

Fauve saw them leave the abbey and drop onto the grassy surround which led down to the river. He could not follow too closely for fear of being detected, so he did not see them disappearing behind the buttress. He carried on down towards the river and cursed in a most un-monk-like way as he stumbled on a boulder, his ankle turning painfully sideways as he did so. His anger was flavoured with fear as the ever-thickening fog swirled around him. Fauve did not like the dark.

It was not until he felt his left foot step into the muddy river that he realised he had come too far.   He had lost them.   He stopped and shook his arms with fury and frustration emitting a coward's sob as he did so. Turning he started back up the track but was terrified that he would miss his way in the dark and fall off the right hand side of the path from where there was a sheer drop down to the river. At one point the unseen path turned a little to the right and Fauve felt the long grass through his sandals.   He could see nothing through the fog and the darkness. Panic started to rise in his throat. He felt sick. He was lost. He stopped – panting. He retched and his heart hammered at his chest. He forced his breathing to slow.   He reasoned that if he could feel grass beneath his feet and kept climbing uphill he would be safe. He started to sob and then, holding his arms in front of him and with tears streaming down his cheeks, started to ascend the slope.

A shape loomed suddenly to his left and he gave a scream as it threatened to envelope him. His hand touched it. He screamed again and then lost his footing and fell and started to roll down the hill.   He flattened his arm on the ground and checked his descent. He rose to his knees and sobbed helplessly waiting for the creature to attack him. He hated the dark; this was his worst nightmare.

After a while when, to his grateful surprise, nothing had happened, he pulled himself together and rational thought returned.   All was quiet. Nothing harmful was there. He looked up and saw the shape. He recalled that it had felt dry and hard. He looked again, straining his eyes through the darkness. It was the city wall; he was safe.

He pulled himself to his feet and, with arms outstretched, walked forwards and upwards and suddenly it was there again but this time it was friend rather than foe. Encouraged he used it to feel his way upwards. The ground was constantly rising but steeper in some areas than others. At one point he nearly fell but grabbed at a bush which rose up the wall inside a buttress. As he pulled on it for support the bush came away from the wall and revealed a gap through which came a fetid smell which he recognised instantly.

"Hah!" he crowed triumphantly.

--o--

"What?" he asked.

"Up there," she said pointing above her. "You see those iron bolts? Slide them back."

Botolph reached across and put his lantern on the table and then peered above him. He was just able to reach the nearest bolt which he pushed on with all his might ... but it would not move. It seemed to be rusted into place. He tried again.

Lubaia went over to the table and placed the lamp on the floor. She dragged the table over to Botolph. "Here," she said, "stand on this."

The bolts still would not move so Bernard put his lamp down in order to help. As the lamp reached the floor it rested against a rock which Bernard picked up hopefully.

"Let me try with this," he said and Botolph moved to one side as Bernard clambered onto the table and hammered at the bolt.

--o--

They had reconciled themselves to the fact that when daylight came, they were going to have to give themselves up and hope for the best.

They were sitting on the floor of the chamber where the guards had been playing knucklebones only a few hours earlier. Their backs were resting against the walls and their legs were stretched out straight.   The eerie yellow glow of the brazier flames flickered the room with shadows.   They had heard no sound from the guard in the cell.   He was probably dead.   They did not care.   They had their own problems.

"Any ideas?" said Helgot turning to Luka.

"Not yet," he growled, annoyed at this pestering child.   "How about you?"

"*You're* the expert," came the ungrateful retort.

Luka looked at him and wondered if he should slap him there and then.   He looked across at Bonitius.

"Leave it, son," said his father.

Luka marvelled at the fact that here was a man who ruled a gang of bandits with a rod of iron but where his own flesh and blood were concerned, he was a weakling.

A sudden heavy knocking started underneath them.

"What in God's name's that?" said Luka jumping up, - as did they all.

Bonitius came and crouched beside him as the hammering continued.

"Seems to be coming from under here," he said. Luka moved forwards to place his ear to the floor when there was a sudden bang and a great chasm opened up where he had just been sitting.

Luka peered over the edge of the void.

"Who's that?" he said.

There came a delighted laugh from a mouth which then said "Botolph!"

"Botolph!   What the …? … How did you find us?"

"Never mind that," said Botolph, "Just get yourselves
down here."

Bonitius and Luka carefully handed Clarisse down to the rescuers first. Then it was Helgot and Alfrid's turn. Bonitius made a rather more ungainly exit but Luka did what he could to suspend him from above until Bernard and Botolph could support him from below. Luka was the last one out and was agile enough to swing from the edge by his fingertips until Botolph could guide his downward drop.

In the party atmosphere Botolph had almost forgotten that they owed their success to Lubaia and he turned to see her and the pretty little redhead hugging each other. His thoughts were interrupted when Luka said

"C'mon, let's get this trapdoor shut."

"You'll never do that Luka," said Botolph. "It's too heavy. It's solid stone set in an iron frame."

"We'll have a try," said Luka. "You never know when I might get imprisoned up there again and need to use it a second time!"

They all laughed.

"Anyway, closing it'll slow down any followers and give us a bit more time if needs be. Let's try. If it won't work, we'll leave it."

They pushed the table out of the way and with Luka on Botolph's shoulders and Helgot on Bonitius's they somehow managed to swing the heavy slab back and hold it there just long enough for Bernard to hammer the bolts back into place.

There was no time for niceties so as soon as the trap-door was closed they picked up their lamps and set off down the passage with Clarisse and Lubaia in the lead. As they reached the steps, Botolph's stomach leapt with foreboding as he saw a movement in the light of Lubaia's lantern.

"What's that?" he said.

The creature suddenly turned and ran down the tunnel. It went through the doorway and kicked out the rock that Lubaia had placed there. A head reappeared and watched mockingly as they broke into a run. It withdrew and the door's hinges creaked as the great iron structure gained momentum and closed with a vibrant clang, the echoes reverberating around the dripping stone walls. Then came the sound of the bolt being shot.

Too late, Lubaia had realised what was happening and had thrust her lamp into Clarisse's hands before bounding down the steps and running forwards with a cry of "No-o-o ... "

She collapsed against the ironwork of the door and started to shake and sob.

Botolph put his shoulder against the ironwork, and leaning at an angle, pushed as hard as he could but there was no sign of the slightest movement.

CHAPTER 45
Despondency

It was the middle of the night and Eluhan was awake. He was cold; he was tired; he was wet from this swirling fog that had come down overnight and he was depressed. It had been three days since they had arrived and there had been no sign or message.

He had become used to the ringing of the office bells as the sounds drifted out of the monastery but this bell's constant and urgent alarm was different and he wondered what it meant. It gave him hope.

He would have liked to have been able to go into the city yesterday and find out what was happening but that might have attracted unwelcome attention. He wished he had brought someone else with him to look after the horses while he snooped around but that had not seemed necessary; it was not supposed to have happened like this. He had been told to keep himself and the horses in constant readiness on the first night and to expect a flying start with a long hard fast ride back to Bonoriacum. It had neither been the first night nor the second night and he had been beginning to think it was not going to be third night either.

But then had come the alarm bell.

Dare he hope that was good news?

Bonitius had chosen the hide-out well. There was a gently-running stream of clear water from which the horses could drink and there was also good grazing. The animals all needed exercising however and Eluhan could not do that for fear that while he was away the remaining horses would be stolen.

He was hungry too. They had brought only a limited amount of food and some of that was supposed to be for young Helgot but Eluhan had already eaten most of it and he had no idea how much longer it would be before they turned up.

He decided that if they did not come tonight the best thing he could do would be to give it another couple of days. If they did not arrive by then he would have to do *something*. The trouble was, he was not sure *what*!

--o--

Clarisse helped her mother up and put her arms around her. Her heart was full too.

"You were so brave mother."

"Yes - but to what purpose? I hoped this was going to be so quick and easy," she said. "I hoped that I would just have to show these two monks how to open the trap-door and that we would be in and out of here in a trice, but that bastard Fauve has put paid to all that."

Botolph winced at the archdeacon's wife's language but, in the circumstances, decided to let it pass.

"Fauve?" said Bernard.

"Yes, Fauve. It was he who locked us in."

"How can you tell that?" said Luka. "I could only see a shadow."

"I'd know that bastard anywhere. I'd like to see him drowned in boiling oil. He's the most evil man I know."

Once started, she was clearly going to continue this tirade but Luka intervened.

"So what do we do now?"

"What *can* we do?" said Botolph, "except to return to the trap-door and open it again and wait for the morning."

The black cloak of despondency folded around them all and Clarisse joined her mother in weeping. One of the lamps went out but nobody noticed it. They huddled miserably outside the iron door.

And then the other lamp went out.

CHAPTER 46
Lubaia's last hope

Perversely, the sudden lack of light had an illuminating effect and jolted them into action. *Something* needed to be done, even if it was only to light one of the other lanterns. Botolph had been silently uttering what he felt were empty prayers but decided that he had better take the lead.

"Right, - stand back everybody," he said.

Once he sensed that the pitch black area in front of him was empty, he knelt and put the lantern in front of him. He pulled a strike-a-light and flint from his scrip and placed them on the floor. Feeling carefully he pulled a small quantity of dried grass tinder from his scrip and placed it to the right of the lantern. He leant forwards and struck the flint with the strike-a-light. The sparks of hope briefly illuminated the group but missed the tinder. He re-felt the position of the tinder and tried again with the same result. On his third attempt his aim was more successful and the grass started to glow. He crouched forwards and blew gently until a flame flickered up. He quickly pushed the wick of the oil lamp into the flame and it readily ignited. Taking the second lamp he lit that too and passed it to Luka.

He stood and put his foot on the tinder to snuff out the little glow that remained.

"So, - that's the first stage. Now Lubaia - what's next? Are you *sure* there is no other way out of here except that iron door and the trapdoor?"

"None," she answered, - a little too quickly.

He held his lamp to her face as he peered into her eyes.

"None?"

She faltered and then whispered something unintelligible.

Botolph felt himself begin to get irritated and threw up a prayer asking his Lord for composure. His original 'Speak up woman' condensed to "Come on Lubaia, - it's our only chance."

"But such a slim one," she said. "There *is* another way but it's almost certain death. I'd rather wait and accept the consequences in the morning than face the ..." - her voice tailed away.

"Face the what?"

"The *Furies*," she whispered as if speaking their name out loud might invoke their actual presence.

"The Furies?" laughed Botolph. "What on earth are they?"

"On earth?" she said. "They are the *devils on earth*."

She turned to Clarisse. "You tell him."

Clarisse nodded.

"They live deep down under these tunnels and feed on the food scraps that are thrown down the Beggars Hole."

"Ah - I know that," said Bernard, "- that's the thing that looks like a well just outside the kitchen but instead of drawing water *from* it, the cooks throw waste food *into it*."

"Exactly."

"Well if there are devils down there, wouldn't it be a better idea to stop feeding them so that they all died off?" said Luka.

"If the devils got hungry, legend says that they'd climb out of the hole and start eating *us*."

"Right," said Botolph impatiently, "we can't waste time talking about Beggars Holes, - Christ's power is many times stronger than any devil so show me where they are Lubaia and let me, through Christ, protect you from them."

She looked at him with astonishment.   Far from being intimidated he was relishing the idea of confrontation. It gave her just the little bit of confidence and hope that she needed.   She shook her head violently as if just waking and ridding herself of a persistent nightmare.   She looked at Clarisse and then back at Botolph and said "Come on then."

--o--

She led them back to the chamber containing the trap-door and raising her lamp she pointed to a round stone held in place by a wooden bar resting on two iron hoops.

"In there," she said.

Botolph wasted no time in lifting the wooden bar and he and Luka heaved on the stone but it would not move.

"It's not that large," said Luka kneeling down and feeling all around the stone.   "I can't see what's holding it."

He stood up and kicked savagely at the lower edge with the under-surface of his heel.   A cylindrical shaft of flint fell out and the stone rolled obligingly away.

"Ah! *That's* what was holding it," he said.

The others did not know whether to laugh or cry.

Botolph knelt down and thrust a lamp into the hole and then crawled through after it.   His face reappeared at the opening.

"The tunnel's higher this side," he said.   "You next Bonitius because if you can get through then everyone can."

It took a bit of huffing and puffing and some quite unseemly cursing but Bonitius made it and the others followed immediately afterwards.

Luka said "It's a bit pongy.   Smells like an open sewer to me."

"Well the smell's not going to kill us," said Botolph, "perhaps that's what devils smell like, - come on," and, holding his lamp in front of him, he led the way down the steeply sloping tunnel and followed round a sharp right hand bend.   Another steep slope took them to some rough-hewn steps whereupon they entered an enormous cavern with a soft wet sandy floor and stalactites hanging down from the roof.

"The rest of you stay here," said Botolph.   "Luka, - you come with me and we'll see what we can find."

"Wait," said Lubaia.   "Let me refill your lamp first or you might never find your way back."

--o--

Bernard tried to find a reasonably dry piece of rock for Lubaia and Clarisse to sit on and they lit their second lamp and refilled the one that was in use.

Bonitius unlaced his sandals and walked up and down on the sandy floor to cool his feet.   After a few moments he returned to find that only one sandal remained.

"Helgot," he called crossly, "what have you done with my other sandal."

"I ain't got it," came the sulky reply.

"Well you must have it.   It was here a moment ago," and he cast about wondering where it might have got to.

Suddenly out of the corner of his eye, he saw the other sandal move.   Bonitius was quick for his size and his great paw grabbed the little pink arm that had come out from between some rocks and hauled it into the open whereupon the attached body set up a frenzied screaming and yelling. The creature was pulling and dancing and trying to bite at his hand but Bonitius had no intention of letting it go.

The others stood and backed away leaving the two contestants in centre stage. The creature was bucking and gyrating so fast that it was difficult to make out exactly what it was. It looked like a naked human child but seemed to have an excessive amount of legs. It had a larger than normal head and a wide mouth which persistently squealed.

The others turned as the light from Botolph's lamp re-appeared on the other side of the cavern. He and Luka had turned back to see what all the noise was about. They made to rejoin the group but suddenly became aware that they had more company. A line of creatures silently appeared at the back of the cave.

"Let it go," said Bernard.

"What?"

"Let it go."

"It's got my sandal."

"Do as I say, - let it go."

Bonitius reluctantly released the arm and the creature scampered off and merged with the others. Silence was restored.

There appeared in the midst of the creatures a tall thin man, naked except for his long beard and dirty grey hair.

"It's not often we have guests. What do you want of us?"

Botolph and Luka started forwards to re-join the others and the creatures who were nearest them moved away a little to ensure that the gap between them remained a large one.

"Stop!" called the bearded man urgently.

Botolph and Luka froze.

"What's the problem?" Botolph called back.

"Go any further and you'll fall in the crater."

Botolph raised his lamp and to his horror saw what the man meant. At that same moment there came the sound of rushing water from the cavern's ceiling and then a few seconds of silence before, somewhere deep below them, a resounding splash as fluid hit water. This was accompanied by a repulsive stench of sewage.

"Uugh!" said Luka. "What a smell."

"Smell?" said the bearded man. "I smell no smell."

Botolph and Luka looked over the edge of the pit but could see nothing but blackness. They carefully skirted the danger and walked along the line of creatures until they faced the man. Botolph saw that the creatures were human. They were mostly young but all were monstrously deformed. Many of the eyes were dead and did not reflect his lamplight. Other eyes reflected the light and looked wild. Some seemed more normal and looked as if they were in charge of the others who were little more than pitiful animals.

"What *is* this?" said Botolph. "Who are these ... people?"

"They are your sons and daughters," the man replied.

Botolph began to wonder if he was really asleep and this was some foul nightmare.

"What do you mean by that?" he said.

"Just what I say," came the answer. "These are the children of the nobles and gentry of Meaux who have nothing better to do on dark winter evenings than to fornicate with their daughters, grand-daughters, sisters and mothers. Sometimes the children are born healthy but often the mother gives birth to a monster and when she does the baby is thrown straight down the Beggars Hole. Most of them die. Some survive. Those that survive I care for."

"But what are *you* doing here?"

"Ah," came the answer. "Atoning for my sins. I too was a monk like you but I fell deeply in love with a beautiful nun. We were both very young unable to resist the temptations of the flesh; so we too fornicated."

"Go on."

"My heart's desire became pregnant. We tried to escape to start a new life together but we were betrayed and captured. I was tortured and beaten but when they told me they'd killed my darling and her baby I wanted to die anyway. They tortured me for days and then finally locked me in a cell to rot."

"So why didn't you rot?"

"I was beaten unconscious and when I woke I couldn't stand. I dragged myself around in the dark and nearly fell through an open trap door. At first I assumed that it was the entry to another deep pit like the Beggars Hole but when daylight came some light filtered through an air vent and I could see a platform below. When I was strong enough I lowered myself through."

He paused.

"It didn't help. There were two tunnels, one of which led to an iron door but it was locked. The other led down here where I was at least able to find fresh water and food. Later I went back up the tunnel to have another look at the iron door but I couldn't reach it because the tunnel had been blocked ..."

"... A rock had been put across the entrance held in place by a wooden bar," Luka finished for him.

"Yes indeed. Of course - that was the way *you* gained access too. Was the iron door locked again?"

"Not initially. Someone locked us in."

He nodded. "History repeats itself. When I first entered this cavern I thought, like you, that it was deserted. I too was surprised to find friends. There were only three and they were in a bad state and one soon died but the other two survived for a couple of years. I had to work hard clearing the stack of rotting food and bodies but once that was done the place became reasonably habitable and I was able to find untainted produce to feed babies that survived. They never live for long but they've become my responsibility. They're my family. I wouldn't leave now even if I could."

"Your *first* family didn't die Samuel," came a voice out of the darkness.

"What? Who's that?"

"Lubaia," she said, stepping into the pool of light issuing from Botolph's lamp.

"*Lubaia*?" he said, taking a pace towards them.

"And this," she said, "is your daughter Clarisse."

The man slumped forwards onto his knees and shook with grief. As he did so the confused creatures crowded round him intent on comforting the leader they loved.

A short distance away Clarisse and her mother embraced each other and sobbed likewise.

Luka looked up at Botolph and then shook his head and as he turned it sideways, beads of moisture flickered away in a fine spray.

--o--

When the old man had recovered his composure Botolph made an attempt at addressing the problem of their escape.

"Oh, there's no way out," said Samuel, "except through the iron door."

"What about the Beggars Hole," said Luka. "What comes down can surely go up?"

"You can go and look," said the old man, "but the hole is wide at the bottom and narrow at the top where there is a grill and a lid. You'd have to be a skilful climber to manage that."

"How about the sewer pipes?"

"Huh!" he said. "You couldn't even get into those, - they finish right over the top of the crater."

As he finished his sentence, right on cue, another lot of effluent came pouring out of one of the pipes and, after a period of silence, could be heard splashing below.

"There is …" he said thoughtfully.

"Yes?" said Luka and Botolph together.

"There is one other possibility but I've no idea if it's feasible."

"What's that?"

"The water level in the crater changes every few hours and I can only assume that it depends upon the level of the tide in the river. Sometimes the lake completely fills the crater whereas a short while later it's empty.

"Aah - I don't like the sound of this," said Luka.

"Go on," said Botolph.

"If I'm right there must be a tunnel out of which the water flows and exits somewhere in the river. It is conceivable that you could get through that but you'd have to follow close on the water level as it dropped because there'd only be a short stand before it started to fill up again."

"That's it," said Botolph.

"Oh no," said Luka.

"Ah," said Botolph, thinking of a snag, "Would there be a grill at the end?"

"I don't think so," came the reply and the man looked embarrassed.

Botolph raised his eyebrows questioningly.

"I am afraid that a lot of bodies of all shapes and sizes have passed that way and it never seems to get blocked."

Seeing his obvious distress at the things he had had to do, Botolph changed the subject slightly.

"What is the state of the water at the moment?"

"Well," said the old man, "it's falling. You might not have noticed but that last lot of sewage did not fall into water but onto the rocks at the base of the crater; it makes a different sound you see."

"So now would be the time to go?"

"Well, - err - Yes I suppose so."

"Come on," said Botolph. "I'll go first and you follow after me Luka."

"But we're going to be walking in shit," protested Luka.

"Have you a better idea?" retorted his friend.

The others crowded to the edge of the crater, holding their lamps out to try to give some illumination as Botolph eased himself over the side. He was pleased to find rock edges to get his feet onto, which at least was better than sand. The rocks were slippery and slimy though, - both to the pressure of his feet and the touch of his fingers and he slipped more than once. Gradually he felt the steepness of the sides decrease as he approached the bottom of the bowl and it was not long before he could stand unaided except for holding his hand against the side. A grumbling Luka soon joined him.

"Can you pass me down a lamp?" he called up to the others.

This caused some consternation because the watchers had no rope and the lamps had to be kept level or the oil would run out. Eventually Luka had to climb back up the side again until he was just above Botolph and supported by him, while Bernard clambered down to Luka before taking a lamp from the watchers and passing it down to Luka who in turn passed it to Botolph. Once that was successfully accomplished Bernard continued his journey downwards and the three of them gazed around the crater in the new light.

"Poo!" said Luka holding his nose, - and then wished he hadn't.

There was a central sump which consisted of a foul smelling mess which they each mentally decided to avoid falling into. As they moved around the bowl they found the entrance to the tunnel which looked just tall enough for a man to walk through in a crouched position. When Botolph held the lamp inside they could see that it fell away steeply and they could just manage to make out the water level far below them. Putting the lamp safely down Botolph led the other two carefully back to a position beneath the watchers.

"Come on," he said. "There's not a moment to lose. Quick as you can."

Helgot was handed down first, followed by Clarisse. Then it was Lubaia's turn.

"I'm not coming," she said.

"What?" said Botolph angrily. "It's not that bad down here I promise you."

"It's not that," she said. "I'm staying with Samuel."

"Why?"

"I love him. I've always loved him. I have yearned for this moment for years."

"But the conditions ... "

"I don't care about the conditions. I can help him. I can help these poor children. I can be happier than I have ever been. Don't force me. Don't take that away from me."

"Mother!" called Clarisse. "*I* need you too."

"No you don't, - not now. You have your own life to lead and I know Luka will make sure you are safe. Go now. Remember me. Pray for me and your father ... now go before the water starts coming back. As your mother I am *telling* you. There's only one thing I ask."

"What's that?" said Botolph.

"Leave me the jug of oil and one lamp."

"Done," said Botolph. "Come on then, - who's going to be next?"

The lithe Alfrid made it easily to the party.

"Your turn Bonitius, and careful with that lamp."

When Bonitius was over the edge, the lamp was passed from hand to hand as before and soon the whole party stood below.

"God bless you both and all your family," called Botolph upwards.

"God be wi'ye," came the replies.

Clarisse blew a silent kiss to her mother and then could look no more as she suddenly crumpled, sobbing, into Luka's ready arms. She half-walked and he half-carried her across the rocky surface until they reached the queue at the beginning of the tunnel.

"Now my girl," he said gently. "I know this is hard but you're going to have to pull yourself together for this bit."

She nodded and wiped the tears away.

"I'll go ahead with the first lamp," said Botolph, "and Bernard'll bring up the rear with the last one. There's a fair amount of sewage in the middle of the tunnel but if you walk with your feet apart you should be able to avoid it and be less likely to slip. The tunnel's quite steep and if you feel yourself slipping, push up with your back on the roof. What we don't want is for someone to fall at the back and then push all the rest of us into the murky water. All understood? Right, here we go."

The descent was challenging and they were slithering and huffing and grunting and retching at the foul smells. Helgot actually vomited which added to the unpleasantness.

Botolph was in the lead followed by Luka; then came Clarisse followed by Helgot behind whom was Bonitius and then Alfrid with Bernard at the back.

They made steady progress for the first part but then Botolph reached the water level and could go no further so all they could do was to wait as the water sloshed and gurgled into and out of the tunnel.

Breathing became difficult in the confined space. Helgot started to complain and Bonitius cursed at him.

"Keep yourselves calm," called Botolph. "Save your breath because you're going to need every bit of it."

Every so often they moved a little forwards as the water level dropped further but it seemed to be taking forever and they were all getting weaker and feeling dizzy. Botolph began to wonder if they should try to back out of the tunnel and wait until they could perhaps hear that the water level had dropped beyond the tunnel entrance.

Then came the noise that he had been dreading and another mass of sewage came flooding under them causing them to cough and choke anew.

Botolph's lamp went out and he felt that he was losing consciousness. He shook his head to try to keep awake.

"How're you doing Luka?"

"Great, - having a lovely time. Why don't we do this more often?"

Botolph grinned to himself. The irrepressible Luka. He pushed his lamp back behind him and said

"Hold on to this will you? I'm going to dive for the entrance."

"What?" said Luka. "Through *that* muck?"

"I think we're all die waiting otherwise."

He wanted to say more but dizziness was overcoming him so he untied his belt and stripped off his habit, both of which he thrust backwards in the general direction of Luka, took a deep breath, closed his eyes and pushed off into the unwelcoming mess.

To his surprise it took less than a couple of strokes before he felt his back scrape across the edge of the tunnel and his body popped up to the surface. He retched a couple of times and took several long gasps of fresh air. He could see that he was at the river's edge. Quickly he knelt down in the water and felt for the rim of the tunnel. When he found it he pushed his arm through right up to the shoulder and felt his hand emerge into the air on the other side. He waved it frantically and felt Luka's hand grab at it and was unsurprised when the grasp changed to their double grip and he heaved his friend firmly but gently through.

Like Botolph after *his* exit, Luka similarly coughed and spluttered and gasped at the cold night air. They seemed to be making a lot of noise and Botolph hoped that it was not attracting unwelcome attention but there was nothing he could do about it. The cold November mist was helping to mask their activities but Botolph began to shiver. Luka handed him something.

"Here," he said, "your habit, belt and lamp."

Botolph tossed the bundle at the shore and then said, "Quick, - let's get the others out."

Having already had the experience and having longer arms than Luka, Botolph repeated the process and soon felt Clarisse's little hand; he pulled her through; then came Helgot. By the time it was Bonitius's turn the water level had dropped even further. Botolph repeated the process for Bernard but there was no response. He splashed the water repeatedly with his hand but to no avail.

He turned to Bonitius. "Was Bernard still behind you?"

"Well I think so, but he didn't say anything. His lamp had gone out."

"I'm going back in," said Botolph and before anybody could object he dived out of sight.

He found Bernard slumped on the 'muddy' floor. He poked him and shouted but there was no response. He could not tell if he was breathing or not. He rolled him onto his back and then grabbed the hem of his habit and backed down the tunnel into the water, pulling Bernard behind him until he judged that his head was just clear of the water. He then backed right out of the tunnel himself still clutching the hem of Bernard's habit loosely in this hand. He surfaced and took two deep breaths and then with the aid of his other hand he pulled hard on the woollen cloth and Bernard's body came slithering down the tunnel like a ship down a slipway whereupon Botolph leant forwards, grabbed his shoulders and hauled him out of the water.

Strong hands took the two of them and Bernard was carried to the bank and laid face down where Luka slapped his back while he coughed and vomited and choked and vomited more water again. They could do nothing but hold him, they were exhausted themselves.

The first few words he managed to say were "Alright Luka, - that's enough - get off me."

Luka put his head down close to Bernard's and said "Well there's gratitude, - I was saving your life!"

Alfrid had been exploring and found that they were hidden from the bridge by a bend in the river. He had also managed to wade right across the river which was now hardly flowing at all.

"Well there's no time to be lost then," said Botolph.

Luka groaned. "Not again, you're always rushing us about."

"Well I'm sorry," he replied.

"Joke! It was a joke Botolph, - don't get so touchy - the world's wonderful, - we can breathe again - enjoy it!"

Botolph relaxed. "Well unless you wade across this river fairly soon you're going to have to swim for it again so I suggest you get going."

Luka laughed. "Of course you're right brother. Thanks for leading the night's entertainment. Good luck in heaven." They embraced. "Ugh you smell awful."

"That's not me, - that's you," said Botolph laughing.

Bernard was by now sitting up and breathing normally but feeling rather weak. Botolph hustled the others along ensuring them that he could manage Bernard and it was to his great relief when they took their leave and waded off into the dark swirling fog, disappearing … perhaps for ever?

Botolph recovered his habit from the water's edge and, with his teeth chattering violently, waded into a deeper part of the river where he washed it. Returning to the bank he enlisted Bernard's aid to wring it dry as best they could. He was shivering violently and pulling on the wet habit did not make him feel a lot better.

Bernard's habit was also sodden so the process had to be repeated. At least with less water in them their clothes were lighter.

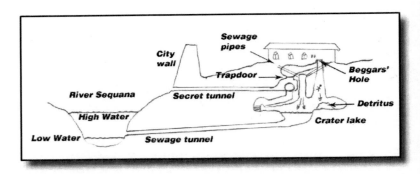

Fig. 6. How the escape was accomplished.

The two exhausted monks struggled up the river bank until they came to a grassy path and made their way round the corner towards the bridge. They climbed as close as they could to the city wall and found the wicket gate. Once in the precinct grounds they managed to slide through the south door without being seen … or smelt!

"Where's your spare habit?" whispered Botolph.

293

"Rolled up at the head end of my pallet," he answered. "I use it as a pillow."

"I'll get the spares then. D'you think you can make it to the laver on your own?"

Bernard nodded. "I'll see you there."

Botolph crept into the dormitory and found the two habits. It would be quite a while before Prime. The others were still sleeping deeply, their night having been disturbed more than usual.

He slipped out and made his way to the laver where he found Bernard stripped off and washing his tunic for a second time.

"I don't think I'll ever get this smell out," he said.

"I know what you mean," replied Botolph following suit.

They were soon dried off and clad in their spare clothes. They left their wet habits hanging over a line to drain and headed back to the dormitory arriving just as the Prime bell began to ring.

"We can't go in now, - they'll be awake. We'll have to go straight into the chapel."

Bernard groaned, "All I want to do is sleep."

"I know, I know, but I'm afraid sleep'll have to wait a bit longer. Come on."

They were the first to arrive but they tucked themselves away behind a pillar and waited for the church to fill up before they moved out and made their way towards the centre.

They saw Abbess Fara and she turned and caught their eye and nodded. She did not look perturbed so Botolph dared to hope that they had not been missed.

Fauve came in with the archdeacon and they took their position close to the front. Nosey as always Fauve started to look around to see who was there and, as was bound to happen his gaze reached Botolph and then passed on as he scanned the congregation further. Suddenly his brain seemed to realise what his eyes had seen and to Botolph's amusement his head suddenly jerked back and his eyes refocused on the tall monk, his face going visibly pale as he did so. Botolph gave a wry smile and inclined his head in acknowledgement. Fauve's eyes bulged and seemed disinclined to look anywhere else. He clutched at the archdeacon who said "Get off Fauve, - what's the matter with you?"

The office then started but Fauve paid little attention, constantly glancing backwards in disbelief at what his eyes were telling him.

CHAPTER 47
Marriage

They gradually managed to recover their equilibrium through the rest of that day which was the last day of the synod.

The next day after Prime, there was a meeting in the chapter house to close the synod and then all repaired to the refectory to breakfast before departure. An hour later they were crossing the river on their way back to Evoriacum.

As their horses waded through the water behind the wain Bernard looked downwards and said to Botolph "I certainly prefer going *over* the water rather than through it."

"What's that?" said the Abbess swinging round.

"Oh nothing mother, - just idle chatter," said Bernard, reddening.

"Well find something more worthwhile to chatter about or don't chatter at all," she snapped.

The boys' horses trotted along behind the dray, their riders talking quietly but carefully avoiding mention of details of their recent adventures knowing all too well how long the ears of the prioress were. Most of the time they were heading to the south-west and the winter sun had been in their eyes since they had left Meaux. By the time they reached Evoriacum the golden globe was just settling on the tree-line and when they entered the monastery Collation had just begun.

The ostler took the horses and they entered the refectory and thankfully collected their soup and bread.

Everybody was pleased to see them back although they discovered later that it had been 'holiday time' in the abbey while it was run under the auspices of Brother Antonio.

Bernard and Botolph easily fell back into their monastic duties. Indeed it seemed to them both that their recent experiences made them value even more the protection that the abbey provided. The best thing that had happened was the creation of a strong bond of friendship between the two monks. They had shared secrets and triumphs that very few people would ever know about and that nobody could take away.

--o--

Bonitius and his group also had a good ride home. Eluhan had convinced himself that something had gone wrong in the city and that he would be riding back alone so he had the fright of his life when his erstwhile companions burst into the camp. His discomfiture was, of course, much to Luka's joy.

"Jesus!" he said when he smelt them. "What've you been doing, - rolling in a dung heap?"

"Worse than that," said Luka. "Clarisse, - meet Eluhan."

The horses were more than a little frisky and were easily spooked during their ride in the darkness. Clarisse sat behind Luka and he relished the feeling of her warm body nuzzling up against his and her arms around his middle.

The guards at the Gateway heard them coming half a league away and were alert to the possibility of a dawn attack. When they realised that it was their leader and his squad who had come home, they gave them a triumphal welcome.

Clarisse was amazed at the warmth and friendship she received and felt *very* blessed to have escaped the acrimonious rigours of daily life under the control of her stepfather. She was well looked after by Aliz who was overjoyed at having her surviving son Helgot back again and remarked how much he seemed to have grown up since his imprisonment. Bonitius just sighed.

--o--

Fauve and the archdeacon had watched very carefully as Abbess Fara and her party left the city. They even arranged for the dray to be stopped at the gatehouse to make sure nobody was hiding under cover of the nuns' habits.

Fauve was intrigued to know what had happened after he slammed the iron door shut. His nature was such that he needed to know everything about everything and he was constantly tortured by the fact that others knew what had happened that day in the footing vaults but he did not.

The archdeacon was confused about his marital status. He had hoped to become a widower but he was now unsure if he was one or not. For moons afterwards he kept expecting Lubaia to pop up somewhere. He began to assume that she was dead but he felt that she tormented him in death even more than she had tormented him in life. Fauve noticed that no signs of grief had clouded his face.

It seemed to Fauve that he was the one person who had lost out in this incident. He was disappointed that all the ingenious plans he had made for young Helgot would no longer be implemented.

The archdeacon was also disappointed that his prisoner had escaped. Still it could not be helped. His revenge could wait until another day and might be all the sweeter for the delay.

--o--

The celebrations at Bonoriacum were soon over and Helgot's experience at Meaux stood him in good stead as Bonitius gave him more responsibilities in the running of the camp in an effort to turn him into a man.

Much to the delight of Aliz and her two daughters, Clarisse continued to live in Bonitius's farmhouse. It did cross Aliz's mind that the hard-working and ever-cheerful Clarisse might make a good wife for Helgot. It soon became evident however that Clarisse's loyalties and affections lay with Luka who, Aliz noted, was forever lurking near the house.

Much as she loved him, she could not resist teasing him. He would come and look forlornly over the picket fence like a young lamb that had lost its mother.

"She can't come out today," Aliz would say wickedly, "She's too busy doing the cleaning and the cooking." Luka would splutter that that was not why he was there anyway, - he just happened to be passing. He would then turn and continue on his way up into the woods.

Behind the open wind-vents, the three girls would giggle at the banter and then Aliz would come through and say, "Go on Clarisse, - you'd better put that broom down and go and find him or he'll have that hangdog look all day."

Clarisse would hand the broom to one of her two smiling 'sisters' and skip down the path with a grateful grin and then go scampering up the hill and into the woods behind Luka.

He would pretend not to see or hear her until she flung her arms around his shoulders at a run and they both collapsed onto the forest floor.

The first time it happened it *did* come as a genuine surprise to Luka but for several weeks after that it became a regular event until one day Clarisse told Aliz that she believed she was pregnant.

Aliz questioned her about her body's natural functions and felt her stomach and placed her ear to it. She then stood up smiling with a tear in her eye. "Yes, my dear, it's pregnant you are so we'd better get you and Luka wed."

Luka of course was delighted at the prospect of being a father but he was also a little fearful.

"What if the child's a dwarf like me?" he asked Clarisse.

"What do you mean?" she said.

"Well," he said, "you can't have failed to notice that I'm about a cubit shorter than every other man."

"You're the same size as any other man when you're lying on top of me," she giggled.

"Be serious," he said.

"How can I," she replied, running her hand up the inside of his thigh, "when I find you so adorable," and she flung her arms around his neck in a passionate embrace.

One day after they had made love again, he raised himself up on one arm and looked adoringly down at her. "So," he said. "How would you feel if our baby turned out to be a dwarf?"

"Oh Luka," she said, sitting up and taking his serious face in her two hands, "I'd love it and cherish it and enjoy all its funny little ways, just as I do yours," and she started to kiss him passionately again.

He took her hands by the wrists and held them softly, "Really?" he said.

"Really!" she replied.

A few days later all the woodland folk rejoiced when Luka and Clarisse were married and moved into their own hut. Luka was sad that he had not been able to invite Botolph and Bernard to the wedding but it was just not practicable and he felt sure the two monks would understand. He resolved to try to get a message to Evoriacum at the earliest opportunity.

CHAPTER 48
Luka and Bonitius

And then came terrible news: King Dagobert was dead.

"How did he die?" Luka asked Bonitius.

"The Plague apparently."

"What's that?" asked Luka naïvely.

"It's a nasty illness that kills you off in a couple of days. There was word of it spreading round the country before New Year. Much as Dagobert and I were on opposite sides of the fence, I'm sorry to hear he's gone. I suppose young Clovis is our *only* king now. I can't see myself fighting a three-year-old!" He grimaced.

"He was in the coach with his mother when we attacked and Helgot was captured," Luka reminded him.

"So I believe," said Bonitius. "My memory's very hazy about that day. How in God's name did Queen Nanthild get out of that mess alive? You never told me."

"Well, you were halfway between life and death and talking a delirium of nonsense for over a moon," said Luka, "and as soon as you were half-recovered our time was taken up with rescuing Helgot. Anyway, - it seems that Scarface caught her. She somehow managed to kill him and escape. She found her way to a farmer's cottage and he took her back to Lutetia."

"Hmm," said Bonitius, "that must have been Farmer Arnaud. He must've got a good-sized bag of gold for that. What about Scarface though? I thought he was dead. What was *he* doing there?"

"Ah," said Luka, "that's another thing you missed out on. As far as I can make out we were set up by Gaubert and Scarface. When Scarface vanished from the camp he went to Meaux and contacted Gaubert because he knew that the archdeacon wanted to get revenge on you for sending him off naked on his horse."

Bonitius laughed at the memory.

"Scarface also wanted *his* revenge on *me* for his disfigured face, so the two of them plotted together to leak word of the gold consignment, knowing that you'd be short at this time of the year and guessing that we'd take the bait; which of course we did."

Bonitius nodded.

"What neither of them knew was that Queen Nanthild and Prince Clovis would also be travelling on the coach and so the guard would be even heavier than usual."

Bonitius grunted. "So those masked horseman who arrived after we had the gold and had killed most of the guards, were ..."

Luka nodded, "... Yes, they were the archdeacon's men in company with that miserable little weatsop Scarface."

"And she killed him you say?"

"Yes, Scarface got his just desserts so we won't have to worry about him trying to take *his* revenge anymore."

"Just the archdeacon eh?"

"Well yes. We thwarted the archdeacon's plans by rescuing Helgot. Gaubert's going to be rather aggrieved about that 'cos I think the treatment he had in mind for him would not have been pretty."

"He won't give up," said Bonitius.

"No, I'm sure he won't," agreed Luka, "but we can look after ourselves."

303

CHAPTER 49
Botolph meets Erchinoald

The word of King Dagobert's death soon reached Evoriacum. Botolph was upset for two reasons: firstly because he liked and respected the king and secondly because he had had high hopes that the king would have granted Luka a pardon so that he would be able to come to Evoriacum and continue his training as a monk.

Little did he know that, as Luka was now married and expecting the birth of his first child, his becoming a monk was out of the question.

In ignorance of these facts Botolph reflected that he would have to try to get to see Queen Nanthild because he felt sure that she would be sympathetic to getting a pardon granted for Luka. He guessed rightly that it was she who was now regent and running Neustria on Clovis's behalf.

Botolph made regular attempts through his abbess to try to arrange an audience with the queen but his requests were constantly turned down. He was more than a little hurt at this but assumed that her duties were so all-consuming that she had no time to see him. He wondered if he might have more luck if he contacted Eligius again.

It was not until late August that Abbess Fara at last came to tell him that his request for an audience with the queen had been granted.

"How will I get there?" he asked her.

"Would you walk?" she replied.

"Aye, willingly," he answered.

She laughed at his earnest expression. "Yes I'm sure you would but there'll be no need. You may take one of the horses and you may also take your friend Brother Bernard for company. I wouldn't see you murdered by footpads for your horse."

This was good news indeed and it was a glorious late-summer morning when the two monks turned their mounts towards Lutetia.

--o--

On their arrival in the city they went first, as had become Botolph's habit, to see Eligius whom they found in his usual quarters. After formally introducing Bernard, they sat in company with the great man and brought him up to date with the various trials and tribulations that they had endured at Meaux.

Eligius told them of a journey he had recently made with Queen Nanthild and Clovis to Peronna in the north.

"After the king died," said Eligius, "the queen was at first distraught and seemed almost unable to move, and then so filled with energy that she was rushing about, giving orders for this to be changed here and that to be altered there. The servants and slaves didn't know whether they were coming or going. In the spring, the whole palace was opened up and gales of air allowed to blow through so that we nearly froze in our beds. It wasn't 'til she'd made sure that all was fresh and clean-smelling, that her energy suddenly left her again and she collapsed into a fit of depression.

Our liegeman Erchinoald had, for many months, been inviting King Dagobert to go and visit his palace. Our previous visit there was on our way north before we met you at Sithiu.   Erchinoald has a wonderful household and we were well entertained, so I suggested to Queen Nanthild that she might like to go there for a change of scenery; perhaps without Prince, ... I mean, *King*, Clovis.   She wouldn't hear of leaving him behind and was insistent that she'd only consider going if her whole retinue came with her.   She's very nervous that someone might try to kill the young king. Anyway, she was persuaded to go.   It was a great burden to put on Erchinoald but he maintains that it was his pleasure and he and *his* retinue are now back here and staying with *us* for a while so you will, no doubt, meet him later tonight."

Botolph, whilst listening quietly, had been furiously wondering where he had heard the name of Erchinoald before but the answer to his question stayed stubbornly in the back of his memory.   "Ah, so *that's* why I've had such difficulty in getting to see the queen earlier?"

"Indeed."

"So what can we do now about Luka's pardon?"

"I've discussed it with Queen Nanthild and she *has* agreed to it in principal but it involves a fair amount of work and diplomacy, not the least of which is trying to get the authorities at Meaux to append *their* name to the parchments."

"But they'll *never* do that," said Botolph, instantly horrified.

"No, probably not and she's agreed that if they don't, she'll still issue a formal royal pardon from here and then they'll just have to accept it but she feels it's in Luka's best interests to at least *try* to get them to cooperate."

"Anyway Botolph my son, I'll do what I can, rest assured of that."

"I will my Lord."

The two monks went to their new quarters and shook off the dust of their travels before heading back to the royal rooms where they were ushered into the presence of the queen regent. Sitting next to her was little King Clovis who was pleased to see Botolph but full of questions as to where Luka was and when would he see him again.

They were introduced to Lord Erchinoald who Botolph had some difficulty in assessing. He was an elderly gentleman of about six decades who had a serious face but mischievous eyes.

He greeted Botolph with "So, young monk.   I hear you've met both my daughter and my grand-daughter!"

Botolph was lost.   "Have I my lord?" he said, "I'm afraid you have the advantage of me.   Who might *they* be?"

"Why now," said his tormenter, keen not to let him off so lightly, "You know of Folcanstane do you not?"

"Indeed I do sire."

"Well then.   Who is the queen there?"

"Why, Queen Ymme my lord."

"Well there you have it then.   It is she who I sired."

"So Princess Eanswythe is your grandchild then?"

"The very same."

Botolph felt himself start to melt under the mocking eyes of the nobleman as the colour rose from his neck to his cheeks which he felt burning like a soss-ball at Samhain.

"Aah," said the perceptive Erchinoald looking wickedly at Queen Nanthild "I trow the good monk and my grand-daughter share more than the love of God."

Botolph courted silence, knowing that whatever he said would betray his feelings. He looked sheepishly away but the wicked Erchinoald would not let it rest.

Unfortunately for Botolph, there were not many places his averted gaze could freely go and it landed on two young handmaidens who were standing to the queen's right. The older visitor was clearly about to start his teasing again when the queen came to the rescue by announcing that it was time for dinner.

Clovis wanted Botolph to sit near him and by virtue of the fact that the handmaidens were charged with looking after the young king, they fell into conversation with the two monks.

"Good evening, Brother," the taller one said with a mischievous twitch of her lips. "I'm Feya."

Botolph suddenly recognised her: "Feya," he said "my word, - but how beautiful you've grown."

She blushed. "It's ten moons since you brought us here in the cart and I've been fed well since then. This is my friend Balthild, - we share the same birth date of 6th September although she's one year younger than I."

Balthild smiled and said, "Feya's told me all about the last time she met you. Your friend Luka must be very brave to have killed the man who attacked her."

"He's brave alright," agreed Botolph, "but I can assure you young lady, that his bravery gets him into more trouble than it's worth."

Balthild changed the subject. "I'm helping Feya," she said.

"Are you now?" said Botolph, noting that Bernard was taking care to keep well back and remain a silent observer leaving Botolph to do all the entertaining of the chattering girls.

"Yes," she said pertly, "I'm come with Lord Erchinoald from Peronna to help look after and play with

King Clovis," and she bowed her head prettily to Clovis as he turned and smiled up at her.

The conversation was cut short by the arrival of the palace food and all were called to order as the palace chaplain led them in grace.

--o--

The next day, being the Lord's day, was not for longer travel. Botolph and Bernard joined the royal party at Clovis's Abbey of St Maur, after which they returned to Lutetia to sleep.

The following day, immediately after breaking their fasts they clambered onto their horses and took the Pons Magnus out of the city and crossed the marshy ground towards Bonoriacum.

Botolph had explained to Bernard about the bandits' lair but Bernard was looking rather nervous in spite of Botolph's assurances that they would be quite safe.

They trotted up to the 'Gateway' and stopped.

"Why've we stopped?" whispered Bernard.

"Ah, well," said Botolph. "This *is* the tricky bit where you have to know what you're doing. Go further and like as not you'll get an arrow through your neck."

"Quite true," said a voice and Bernard spun round to see a khaki-coloured figure where a few moments earlier no figure had been.

"Wassail Brother Botolph and friend."

"Pax vobiscum, Alfrid," replied Botolph. "You remember Brother Bernard?"

"Aye I do, so Wassail Brother Bernard too then," said Alfrid. "I guess you have come to see Luka and his fine young son."

Botolph felt as if he had been struck by a lightning bolt. He sat with his mouth open wondering if he had heard correctly. He gathered his wits and closed his mouth and said "Luka has a son?"

"Aye he does and a fine lusty voice the youngster has too."

"But with whom? Ah – no, - don't tell me. He's wed Clarisse hasn't he?"

"Aye he has and a lovelier couple you couldn't hope to find. Tie your horses here and I'll lead you to their hide."

As Alfrid ran on ahead, Botolph's emotions were overflowing and so many questions were vying to enter his head at the same time. Luka a father! And a husband! And, it would appear, never to become a monk. How our plans and aspirations change. Botolph felt so happy for Luka that there was no space to feel sad that their lives were splitting apart even further.

They heard the baby's cry even before they left the confines of the wood but then the cries suddenly stopped; they rounded the corner and there was the family. Clarisse was sitting outside the hut with the baby suckling at her left breast. Luka had his back to them and was hanging newly-washed raiments over a hedge.

As they arrived, Clarisse jumped up and cried joyfully, "Botolph!" and Luka swung around. He strode towards Botolph and they clasped arms in a fond embrace. Clarisse came over too and the three hugged each other delightedly with the little one in the midst of them, still sucking hungrily at his mother's nipple.

"I daren't take him off 'till he's had his fill," she said, or his cries will scare the birds out of the trees.

"What have you called him?" said Botolph.

"Ash," said Luka.   "We were going to call him Botolph but decided there couldn't be two Botolphs so we settled on Ash."

They spent a happy interlude with the young family during which time Botolph told Luka about his attempts to arrange a pardon for him and his hopes that Nanthild would be able to persuade Bishop Faro to agree.

Luka was circumspect. "Well," he said, "It would be good if it happened but I won't raise my hopes too high. Archdeacon Gaubert and I hate each other with a passion and I suppose he carries great sway with the bishop.   If it happens, it happens, but don't lose any sleep over it my friend.   I'm happy enough here working for Bonitius and now that I have my lovely wife and son I couldn't be more content," and he put his arm round Clarisse and hugged her; she responded with a smile and a loving gaze.

They looked so right together that Botolph could not wish more for either of them.   "Well, my friends," he said, "much as we would like to tarry longer, we must press on while we still have daylight.   God's blessing on you all and may He guard and keep you and bring us back together again soon."

With that, they all strolled back to the 'Gateway' and Botolph and Bernard mounted up and, with a wave, headed for Villa Calae.

On their arrival, the first thing Botolph did was to search out his old friend the Master Ostler to whom he introduced Brother Bernard.   They passed a pleasant evening chatting over old times and then, after a good night's sleep and their early-morning devotions, Gurnard had their horses brought round for them and waved them off to Evoriacum.

"Well, I'm sorry I'm not going to have the company of your friend Luka," said Abbess Fara when Botolph told her of his friend's new family commitments, "I was looking forward to meeting him. I thank you for your news from Lutetia and Villa Calae but, in exchange, I also have something for you: next week mark's the anniversary of your arrival here and although I have from the start regarded you as a loyal servant of Our Lord, the time has come for you to cease your life as a novitiate and to take the first vows of your four-year training as a dedicated monk. Do you feel ready for this Brother Botolph?"

Botolph looked up with sparkling eyes and said "Oh yes, Mother Abbess, I have no doubts."

"Good," she replied, "Go and pray about it then and we shall pray for you and it will be done."

CHAPTER 50
Eanfled

It was a year later when the abbess sent for Brother Botolph and sat with him in her cloister.

"I'm afraid I've some bad news for you," she said.

His first thought was for Luka, Clarisse and the baby.

"What is it?" he asked and, heavy-hearted, gripped the arms of his chair.

"I'm sorry to have to tell you that many of your friends in Folcanstane are dead."

He caught his breath, "Not ... ?"

She nodded, "Yes ... I'm afraid that both Abbess Eanswythe and her father, King Eadbald have gone to join Our Lord. I know not who else but we'll soon have a visitor who'll tell us all."

"But, how? What happened? When?"

"I know not how or why Brother Botolph," she said, coming over and placing a comforting hand on his shoulder. "All I can tell you is that King Eadbald died at the beginning of last month and Abbess Eanswythe joined her Maker in Heaven two weeks ago on the last day of August."

Botolph leant forward and placed his face in his hands. He visualised the pretty nun as he first saw her in the fisherman's hut when Luka was close to death; and then again at his chapel on the hillside when she brought the good news that Luka had recovered. He recalled his feelings towards her. He was young then of course but he remembered the passion he felt for her and the joy when they talked and how she just seemed to understand his feelings so fully and he hers.

He thought of Luka and *his* family and knew now how much he had wanted to lie with Eanswythe and have his own family - just like Luka now had.   But then he remembered their talk that evening as they went round and round the courtyard of the fortress and he knew that their decision had been the right one. Even at that young age they had both dedicated their lives to God and there had really been no other question than that it should turn out the way that it did.   It was because of Eanswythe that he had left Britain to come to Evoriacum so that he would never be tempted to kiss those sweet lips;   and now the temptation was for ever gone.

He looked at the floor feeling miserable.

The abbess said, "Shall we go into the church and pray about it?"

He nodded, unable to speak for feeling so full.

Once in the church, she took the lead and intelligently voiced every prayer he would have wanted to make had his constricted throat allowed him to do so.   All he had to do was to intone the "Amens" and when she had finished and they walked out into the sunshine together he felt infinitely better.   Eanswythe was at rest and would now be forever in his company.   She was truly a saint and he would be able to pray to her and talk with her and ask her to intercede for him with their Lord Jesus Christ.   He felt the warmth of her soul and, indeed the warmth of her love, since he knew that she had loved him too but had wisely managed to push him to one side for that greater love they both shared.

--o--

A half-moon later a new entourage arrived at the abbey gates and after a few days Botolph was summoned to the abbess's cloister once again in order to meet a somewhat short and stocky young lady with ringlets of long black hair.

"Eanfled," said the abbess, "this is Brother Botolph and, now that you have rested after your journey, both he and I will be interested to hear news of Folcanstane and Cantwarebury and what brought death to the dear Saint Eanswythe. Ah ..." she said, a thought passing through her mind, "... perhaps you two have met before?"

"I have *heard* of Brother Botolph," said Eanfled, "but as far as I remember, we've never actually met. My mother, Abbess Ethelburga, founded the abbey of Liminge, after we fled to Folcanstane following the death of my father, King Edwin of Deira."

"Yes of course," said Botolph, "I met your mother when she came to visit her brother Eadbald in the fortress at Folcanstane when we celebrated our victory over a raiding party. I then met her again at Liminge abbey when Luka and I were walking from Cantwarebury to Folcanstane."

"Victory over a raiding party?" said Abbess Fara. "Were you a soldier before you became a monk then, young brother?"

Botolph shuffled a little uneasily. "Er, well no not exactly. I didn't actually do any fighting, I left all that to Luka," he said ... and then wished he had not ... as the abbess replied somewhat sniffily:

"It sounds to me that it might be just as well that he's decided not to become a monk then. So, Eanfled, you and Saint Eanswythe were cousins were you? ... Let's sit down and make ourselves comfortable." They sat in a circle.

"Yes indeed Abbess, we *were* cousins. When we arrived in Folcanstane, both my mother and Uncle Eadbald were afraid that enemies of my late father might be sent from Northumbria to kill me or my two brothers."

"So it was the three of you came down to Cantium with your mother?" said Botolph.

"Yes, but the two boys were sent straight over here and I remained at Liminge with my mother."

"The boys came to Gallia?"

"Yes, King Dagobert took them into his court."

"Really? I'm surprised he didn't mention it," said Botolph.

"Ah. Well he might not have liked to, since within a year they were both dead. Nobody knows quite what happened. Perhaps agents from Northumbria got to them after all. Anyway, sadly they have left us but now no doubt they are living in joy and happiness with Uncle Eadbald and Cousin Eanswythe."

"Yes," said Fara, "pray, tell us what happened there."

"It all started," said Eanfled, "when the nuns took into their infirmary a foreign sailor from a boat which called at Folcanstane. The man was constantly coughing and hardly able to breathe. Later he developed evil black stains under his arms. The nuns thought at one point that he was getting better but then he suddenly died.

It was after that that other people in the town started to get sick and then Uncle Eadbald fell ill. Abbess Eanswythe nursed him in the infirmary and did all she could but he died at the beginning of last month. They called it the Justinian Plague."

"So I presume Eanswythe's elder brother Eormenred is king now?" said Botolph.

"No ... Eormenred fell in love with a girl somewhere far away to the west and has gone to live with her there. Apparently Uncle had a furious row with him but he

316

wouldn't listen, so it's Cousin Eanswythe's *younger* brother Eorcenberht who's taken over the kingdom."

"How old's he?"

"Nineteen summers."

"And is he married?"

"No, nobody will have him!" she laughed. "But he is basically a good man. It was he who insisted that I should come over here in order to avoid the plague. My mother wasn't very pleased, saying that she'd already lost a son and a grandchild to Gaul, but King Eorcenberht's word is now law ... so here I am!"

"But what about Eadbald's brother Aethelwald?" said Botolph, thinking back to his conversation with the twins. "Surely he should have taken over as king?"

Eanfled laughed. "Uncle Aethelwald doesn't really even want to be king of *West* Kent," she said. "He's old now and doesn't have any sons to help him but he's agreed to carry on for as long as he can."

"And how old are you?" said Botolph, thinking to himself that all the nuns and monks seemed to be getting younger every time he saw a new one.

"I'm fourteen summers," said the child confidently.

"And have you decided to become a nun and be a bride of Christ and live here with us forever?" he asked.

"Oh, no. My mother said she will call me back as soon as the sickness leaves the land and then I shall go home and get married."

"Oh will you indeed?" said Botolph. "And who, pray, are you proposing to marry?"

"I haven't decided yet," she said, pouting, "but he'll be tall and strong, and ... and ..."

"Yes?" said Botolph and Fara together.

"... He'll *smell* nice!" she finished.

317

30th September A.D.640.

So Eanfled settled into the monastery and Botolph and the twins were pleased to have another British soul amongst them. Indeed it was the twins who were called upon to be mentors to the young princess and to educate her in the ways of Evoriacum Abbey which shared many similarities with that of her mother at Liminge although there were also subtle differences between them.

Abbess Fara enjoyed hearing about the British monasteries, although it gradually became more and more clear to Eanfled that her abbess was convinced of the infallible superiority of her Evoriacum.

Botolph and Bernard the Pot-stirrer, as he continued to be known, often reminisced privately about their adventures in Meaux. One day, one of their conversations was overheard by the ubiquitous Irish gardener Brother Abraham who suddenly popped up from behind a bush that he was pruning as they shared a conversation on a sedilla.

He wanted to know all about this and that and about all the details that it was possible to absorb.

Botolph asked him if he did not consider eavesdropping a sin.

"Oi do, Oi do, indeed Oi do, to be sure, to be sure," said the old monk gleefully, "but Oi'll ask forgiveness tonoit 'n' Oi'm sure the Good Lord will grant me redemption."

Clearly, to Brother Abraham, the story of the boys exploits in Meaux was one of the most exciting things he had heard in years. Since that day, whenever the three found themselves alone, he would constantly badger them for more details or even for simple repeats of what they had already told him many times before.

--o--

Back in Bonoriacum, Luka, Bonitius, Helgot and Alfrid were having the same problem. Whenever there was a feast and legendary tales of their forebears were told, there was now always a great clamour for the four heroes to tell how they had escaped the clutches of the Furies of Meaux.

Otherwise, Luka and Clarisse were enjoying a happy and loving life together. As he grew and thrived, young Ash's antics gave them endless pleasure.

It was sometime in the spring that Clarisse fell pregnant again, but she kept her own counsel until mid-summer's day when she made the announcement to Luka.

"Are you sure?" he said.

She nodded, biting her lip and giving a shy smile as she gazed into his eyes. He opened his arms and she fell into them. They grasped each other in a joyful embrace and Luka was the happiest man in the world.

Later that night as they lay side by side, he moved down and pressed his ear to her belly, raising himself up shortly afterwards saying, "I can hear her heart."

"Her?" she said, "Her? What makes you think it's a 'her'?"

"I don't know," he said, "I just get that feeling. Still, her or he, - who cares?"

"Not I," she laughed.

Clarisse blossomed and flourished and Luka fondly watched his wife turn into a little dumpling and marvelled that she could still find a hip upon which to tuck Ash. He loved to watch them both as she stood with the wind blowing through her red hair gazing proudly into the distance.

He adored her sweet face. The laugh that came from her lips was like a rivulet running down the hillside and chuckling as it crossed stones and boulders.

"Round every corner I see your face," he said to himself. "From every crowd I hear your laugh. Each ray of sunshine reflects the colour of your hair. I love you so."

The beautiful summer was spent bathing in the lake and playing and working in the forest.

Bonitius had returned from Meaux with a new outlook on life. He had decided that his gang of ruffians could just as easily put their energies into farming as into robbing; although he found himself unable to totally rule out their traditional occupation. He did feel however, that the camp should be as self-sufficient as possible so in spite of grumbles from some of the bandits, he started his own farm and encouraged his men each to have a small-holding.

It gave Luka great delight to see his vegetables grow and be freshly ready for the table. He also had a couple of pigs and some chickens which Ash 'helped' to look after.

Clarisse was due to give birth in September, and it was in the middle of the night that the pains began. Aliz came to her together with some of the other women from the camp. All the noise had woken Ash and, it being a clear moonlit night, Luka took him down to the lake away from the screams which he guessed would come.

He was keeping Ash amused by throwing stones at an old log that was floating close to the water's edge when he heard one of the women approaching at a run and swung round with a hopeful smile. Before she spoke he knew something was wrong.

"You'd best come quick," she said, beckoning and turned to run back. Luka scooped Ash into his arms and ran back after her.

When they arrived at the hut, all was ominously quiet. One of the women took Ash from him and Luka went in to where a deathly white Clarisse was lying, covered in blood, Aliz was still doing her best to staunch what little remained of the flow.

Luka knelt down by the side of her and scooped he into his arms. She opened her eyes and recognised him.

"I'm so sorry," she said. "I couldn't ... she wouldn't ... Oh, Luka – I love you so much ..."

"Hush, hush now," said Luka, "I love you too. It'll be fine ..."

She looked straight into his eyes and held his gaze as she shook her head slowly giving him just enough time to understand before "I'm so sorry," escaped her lips and her head fell to one side.

He pulled back, horrified. "No!" he cried. "No, Clarisse, don't leave us," and then he fell forward, nuzzling into her still warm neck and sobbed as if there were no tomorrow which, for him, he felt there never would be.

Strong, gentle hands eventually pulled him away and guided him to the door. He didn't know who it was, but he remembered later that someone was trying to take him to Bonitius's house, but he was suddenly imbued with energy and rage. He hated the world. He hated Bonitius. He hated Gaul and most of all he hated God. He shook himself free from whomever his carer had been and ran off into the darkness of the forest and ran and ran, cursing and swearing and ranting and raving until he broke out the other side of the woodland where the lake gently lapped another grassy shore. He threw himself down and his body was again wracked with sobs until he had no more tears left to cry.

The lack of sobbing gave him time to think which resulted in his emission of another cry of agony and a pounding on the muddy grass with his fists followed by more sobbing which continued until, exhausted emotionally and physically, he slept.

When he awoke it was daylight. He was still lying face down on the soggy ground and something was nudging the part of his neck which had last nuzzled Clarisse. He pushed it away. It was wet. It came back again.

As he turned to sit up there came the sound of startled hooves and through hazy morning eyes he saw a pretty deer with a new-born fawn. The hind had a pelt of the brightest red he had ever seen. She was looking at him in a concerned way and it was obvious that it had been her nudging curiosity which had awoken him. The youngster was skittling about beside her but she ignored it and, hesitatingly she moved closer to him where he lay stock still. He felt her warm breath and then her moist muzzle touched his forehead for a moment before she turned as if her duty had been done and, closely followed by the fawn, trotted off into the forest.

Luka suddenly understood and was up in a flash. He ran to the trees calling "Clarisse, Clarisse!" And as he reached the first tree he saw a flash of brilliant red disappear in the distance. He listened and all was quiet. No birds were singing. There was no sound of a hind and fawn pushing through the undergrowth. Nothing stirred. He started to run. Not in panic. Not in need. Not with ever a view of trying to catch up with the elusive deer. He just wanted to follow the path she had taken and as he ran, the birds started to sing and the forest came alive again.

--o--

Back in Meaux, archdeacon Gaubert had adapted to the loss of his wife. He reasoned that, since his sexual needs were non-existent, all he needed was a cook and housekeeper and both of those were readily available. As far as companionship was concerned he and Brother Fauve had become closer and they shared many sinister interests.

Bishop Faro was far removed from these activities and was pursuing his own agenda of collecting around him as many as possible of the aristocracy in order to counterbalance and, ideally overcome the influence of royalty over church and trade affairs.

--o--

In Lutetia, various other dramas were being acted out on an ever-changing basis.

Queen Nanthild's mayor, Aega, had been her comfort and support since her husband had died, but then, suddenly, Aega died too.

Erchinoald, the widower from Peronna, had made no secret of the fact that he wanted to fill the gap left by Aega's death.

He was in a strong position having sponsored his former slave, now known as *Princess* Balthild, as handmaiden to the queen and companion to King Clovis. Queen Nanthild had been delighted with the arrangement and took pleasure in seeing how placid and happy her son was when in Balthild's company. She had even made it known that, despite the eleven year gap in their ages, she believed Balthild might one day make her son a good wife.

In spite of this, the queen was reluctant to give Erchinoald as much power as he wanted. By way of a compromise however, she made him Mayor of Neustria.

Erchinoald was disappointed. He wanted to be Mayor of Burgundia too - but, with Eligius's advice the queen offered the position elsewhere and with great pomp and ceremony the new appointment was confirmed. Mysteriously however, the new mayor suddenly died and shortly after that, to the Gallic court's horror, so did Queen Nanthild.

Her demise came soon after she gave in to Erchinoald's demands and made him mayor of both regions. This, together with his position as leader of the new five-year-old King Clovis's household, made him the most powerful man in the country.

CHAPTER 51
The Grand Baptism.

Luka could not settle after Clarisse's death. He tried. Oh how he tried but every walk in the forest, every corner of the hut, every smile from Ash reminded him of her and broke his heart further.

"Round every corner I see your face. From every crowd I hear your laugh. Each ray of sunshine reflects the colour of your hair but you're not there. I love you so."

Their unborn child had died in its mother's womb. They would have cut her open so that he could see it, but he did not want his poor Clarisse's body damaged further and she was buried with the dead child still inside her; he never knew if it was a girl or a boy.

He worried about Ash.

The little fellow had not asked to be brought into the world and now all he had was a worthless father who felt guilty about the loss of his mother.

It was not right to bring the boy up as a bandit. Much as everyone in Bonoriacum loved him, Luka had to get him out of there somehow.

He wondered whether they should both leave the camp and he would just travel with Ash until he could find somewhere else to set himself up. But he had become notorious because of his exploits with Bonitius and was a marked man who could not, because of his stature, disguise himself effectively. There was a price on his head and if he left the security of the camp there was no doubt that he would soon be served up on a platter to the archdeacon. It was one thing risking his own life, but, if he were to take Ash with him, the boy's life would be at risk too.

He thought about Evoriacum. He supposed there might be the chance of the abbess giving him work there and he and Ash living in one of the cells but again he thought ruefully, a monastery seemed nearly as bad a place in which to bring up a little boy, as a bandit camp.

The palace was another possibility. Maybe he could arrange for Ash to be fostered there. There would have been a chance of this if Dagobert and Nanthild had still been alive. He trusted Eligius but Erchinoald was another matter altogether. Feya and the other children would look out for Ash, he was sure of that but once he had handed him over, the chances of seeing him ever again were really quite remote.

He did not want his son to grow up a stranger to him. He wanted to teach him to fight and ride and swim and play ... he wanted to be there when he fell, ... to comfort him ... to bandage his shins ... to laugh and cry with him but it was hopeless. They were trapped.

Whichever way he looked there seemed to be no answer other than remaining at Bonoriacum. He felt sure that Clarisse would have wanted him to keep the boy near him. By so doing he *would* be able to teach him all those things. And besides, ... there were worse things than growing up in a bandit camp.

--o--

Eanfled returned home in the autumn. Botolph was sad to see her go in spite of her precociousness but she had been with them for eighteen moons and during that time had learned to mingle the virtue of humility with her failings.

326

One moon later came another wrench for Botolph when Brother Bernard the Pot-stirrer took his solemn vows and became Father Bernard before leaving Evoriacum to travel north and join Bishop Amand at Elnone.

It was shortly after this that, one morning in the chapter house, the abbess announced that there was to be a large baptism service the following Easter. Bishop Faro and his entourage would be coming from Meaux and the ceremony would be performed at the water's edge of the nearby River Moran.

This sounded exciting to Botolph although he was less than enthusiastic about meeting Fauve and the archdeacon again. Baptism had been one of the subjects that had been discussed at the synod four years earlier.

"My," he thought. "How those four years have flown."

He remembered the chapter house meetings after they had returned, when the abbess had discussed the resolutions made at the synod. There had been some talk of new-born babies being routinely baptised but those who objected pointed out that it is impossible to prepare such a young child adequately. Nevertheless it had been decided that any child in danger of imminent death could be baptised by any other person who had themselves been baptised as long as they followed the proper rite by anointing the head with water and saying: "I baptise thee in the name of the Father, the Son and the Holy Spirit."

As a result of this there had been a regular flow of distressed parents arriving at the abbey gates with nearly-lifeless or febrile bundles in their arms begging for the sacrament to be given before the light went out in their lives.

Adult baptisms had always been routinely performed at Evoriacum and the waterside ceremony was

327

familiar to all. This event was going to be different however. The Bishop was hoping for over a hundred catechumens and they were going to be drawn from all over the area. All would have to receive 'Divine Instruction' which would take several weeks and Botolph wondered how the abbey would cope with so many. It came as a great relief when the abbess said that those who came from Meaux and neighbouring regions would receive instruction at their local churches and abbeys.

There were nevertheless nineteen catechumens who would have to be taught at Evoriacum and most of this work devolved on the novice monks and nuns.

In the event Botolph found it rather fun. Two months before Easter, he and four other novitiates were given their own private instruction by Abbess Fara; at the same time five novice nuns were receiving similar tuition from Prioress Pedra.

Once they had received their training they were let loose on the catechumens.

Botolph was given charge of the young son of one of the abbey's tenant farmers. He was a polite lad and eager to please so his weekly visit proved no hardship. His name was Godefroi. When the sixth week came he was well-versed and ready.

Two weeks later it was Easter and during the week before, the abbey was turned upside down as it was spring-cleaned and thoroughly dusted in anticipation of the arrival of nearly two hundred overnight guests.

It was only dignitaries and monks who would be staying in the abbey; the rest would be put up in the neighbouring farms and outbuildings.

Easter Day started with Matins and Lauds and then, after Prime, as the sun was rising and the bells were ringing, everyone met at the abbey gates.

The crucifer lead the way down the well-worn village track.   He was followed by chanting monks who in turn were followed by chanting nuns and behind them came the tall, imposing, elegant and unsmiling Bishop Faro.   Botolph was a member of the first group which comprised the monks and nuns of Evoriacum.   Behind the bishop walked Archdeacon Gaubert and then came the cathedral dignitaries together with Abbess Fara, Prioress Pedra and Prior Antonio.   Following them were the monks of Meaux amongst whom was Fauve.   Then came the catechumens all dressed in their best attire, no matter that it was due to get wet in the muddy Moran.   Behind them came the menfolk followed by the women and bringing up the rear were several dogs, two goats and a stray donkey.   In all there were over 300 souls.

On their arrival at the river the group spread out into a pre-ordained crescent-shape with the Bishop in the centre. Botolph found Godefroi and they joined the queue that was forming behind the Bishop. The boys with the monks were at the head of the queue with the girls and the nuns at the back.

Prior Antonio had taken charge of the proceedings and, at a nod from him, the singing began again and Bishop Faro, with Archdeacon Gaubert on this left and another cleric on his right, walked along a causeway.   This led out towards the centre of the river and then swept towards the left so that it ran parallel to the bank.   Towards the end of this had been placed a high-backed wooden chair and the bishop took his placed in this.   Behind the vanguard walked Abbess Fara and the rest of the local worthies and they spread out on each side of the bishop in a line which faced the still-chanting monks on the river bank.

Once everybody was in position to his satisfaction, Prior Antonio gestured to the first monk and he and his catechumen descended the hardened path into the water.

Looking at the bishop's party in front of him, the thought crossed Botolph's mind of how much he would enjoy seeing the archdeacon slip over the edge and he could not stop the corner of his lips twitching as he envisioned the scenario.

Unfortunately Godefroi noticed and whispered, "Why do you smile, brother?"

Botolph flinched guiltily and said "I was sinning by thinking idle thoughts."

He looked upwards and said "Please forgive me Father," and then he looked down again and said to the boy, "You see, - even monks sin, - make sure you don't emulate me my son."

"Who should I emulate then brother?"

"Why, - Christ, my son. Emulate Jesus of Nazareth for he's the only one amongst us who's without sin."

"Is he among us now?"

"Of course he is. Don't you remember? 'When two or three are gathered together in my name, there will I be amongst them'."

"Yes I remember, brother, but which one is He?"

"None of them my son, - they are, I am sad to say, all sinners like me. Jesus is the one you *can't* see, - but he's there, - he's near us, - he promised to be and he always will be. You must have faith."

"I will brother. I will."

The queue had moved forwards during this interchange and they were now close to the front and had a clear view of the baptisms. Each monk and his catechumen waded through the water until they came to a stone arch above which sat the bishop. In front of the arch, but underwater, were some steps. Because these were invisible beneath the murk, a vertical strut had been fixed to each step and the struts joined to a sloping handrail which offered support in the event of potential disaster.

By the time the candidates reached the bottom of the steps they were more than waist deep in water and facing the Bishop.

Botolph had rehearsed what he must do but, even so, he carefully studied the actions of the two couples in front of him. Suddenly it was his turn.

"Here we go then Godefroi. Are you ready?"

The boy nodded and, as the others had before them, Botolph stood on his catechumen's left side holding the boy's left upper arm with his left hand. He placed his right hand on the crown of Godefroi's head. In this fashion they walked slowly into the water and stopped half way between the bank and the previous baptism that was still taking place.

Suddenly it was their turn. The water suddenly became deeper and both Botolph and the boy gasped slightly as the cold water took hold of their bodies. They approached the steps.

Botolph was determined not to look at Gaubert but he felt the archdeacon's eyes boring into him as the boy stood in front of the bishop.

"What is your name?" asked Bishop Faro loudly.

"Godefroi of Evoriacum," answered the lad equally loudly.

The bishop leant forwards and asked more quietly, "Who brings this soul for baptism?".

"I, Brother Botolph of Evoriacum."

"Have you versed the candidate well in the Catechism?"

"I have my Lord."

"Is he ready for baptism?"

"He is my Lord."

He leant back and loudly called again: "What is your name?"

"Godefroi of 'Voriacum," the boy answered enthusiastically.

"Do you renounce the devil and all his works?"

"I do."

"What is your name?"

"Godefroi of 'Voriacum."

"So be it."

Botolph squeezed the boy's arm whereupon Godefroi fell backwards onto Botolph's supporting right hand which he let fall away into the water until the lad's head was fully submerged and then pushed him upright again.

"What is your name?"

"Godefroi of 'Voriacum."

"Come forward, Godefroi of Evoriacum."

Botolph and the lad carefully climbed the steps up to the bishop who leant forwards again and, taking a pinch of salt from a golden bowl used it to make the sign of the cross on the youngster's wet forehead, saying, "I baptise you in the name of the Father, the Son and the Holy Spirit."

"Amen," said all who were in earshot and Botolph and his charge turned to their left, climbed the rest of the steps out of the water and made their way behind the bishop's party and back along the causeway to regroup with the other newly-baptised candidates.

Once the baptisms had been completed they all returned to the abbey for Holy Communion. Then came a feast followed by blessed sleep. The bishop and his group left after Prime the following morning and Evoriacum breathed a sigh of relief.

--o--

Nearly a year had passed since the departure of Eanfled and Bernard. Oblates and Novitiates came and went but there was nobody special in Botolph's life until the arrival of two British princesses from East Anglia. Their names were Saethryth and Ethelburg and he was delighted to discover that they were the offspring of his one-time sponsor King Anna.

Abbess Fara had of course known of their impending arrival for some considerable time but had not shared the news with Botolph, partly because she had learned never to expect people until they arrived and partly because she hoped it would make a pleasant surprise for him.

The next day she invited the girls and Botolph into her quarters and introduced them.

Saethryth was tall, slim and elegant and aged about eighteen whereas the other was much younger. They were clearly united by a spiritual bond in spite of the differences in their ages. Everything they did seemed to be in unison.

"How old are you Ethelburg?" asked Botolph.

"Twelve brother," she answered primly.

"You share the same name as a dearly-beloved friend of mine who's the abbess of Liminge in Cantium and whose daughter was part of our order until a few moons ago."

"I know of the Abbess Ethelburga and I'm honoured to bear her name and, in fact we bring news of her daughter," she replied, looking up at Saethryth who smiled lovingly down at her.

"Indeed," said the elder girl formally to Abbess Fara, "We're pleased to tell you that, in the spring, Princess Eanfled was married to King Oswiu of Northumbria and so is now *Queen* Eanfled."

"Well then," said the ever-practical abbess, "that liaison will have strengthened the kingdoms of both Cantium *and* Northumbria. And where pray does your kingdom of East Anglia stand Ethelburg?" she said, with the intention of testing the intelligence of the younger maid.

"We stand fair, mother," replied little Ethelburg confidently, "in fact we too have a close liaison with Cantium, as my sister Seaxburg is married to King Eorcenberht."

"Ah yes indeed. So with all these alliances, Britain must now be a peaceful place. It can do nothing but good. I wish Queen Eanfled well."

"How many brothers and sisters do you have?" asked Botolph.

It was the tall Saethryth who answered: "King Anna is actually my step-father; my mother was a widow when King Anna married her and took me on as his daughter."

"You're half-sisters then?" said Botolph and received more nods in unison.

"Brother Botolph has been with us for nearly five years now so we've learned a great deal from him about British habits and customs," said the abbess. "He's told us much about your father's kindness to him and to his friend Luka when they escaped from the fighting at Cnobersburg. Have you heard the story?"

This time the heads *shook* in unison.

"Well, no doubt you'll hear it one day soon."

She stood suddenly and clapped her hands, realising that the day was slipping away from them.

"Now away with you all. There's the Lord's work to be done."

Of course Magburga and Nelburga were delighted to see the quaint newcomers who in many ways were younger mirror images of themselves. As they came to know them better they learnt the story of how the bond had formed between the two girls from the day that Ethelburg was born. Saethryth had been six at the time and had become a 'little mother' to the extent that they became inseparable.

They had grown up in a fiercely Christian family which eventually consisted of seven children, - six girls and a boy, who all enjoyed a happy, loving, family life. When the time had come for Saethryth to consider marriage she had professed her desire to become a nun and arrangements had started to be made for her to enter a monastery in East Anglia. Young Ethelburg had become so distressed at the prospect of losing her 'little mother' that the idea had had to be put to one side. Six years later came the time that Ethelburg too was of a marriageable age. Predictably she chose the same vocation as her 'little mother'.

They had already heard wonderful stories of the joys of Evoriacum from others who had served there and they pleaded with their father to allow them to follow the same path. At first he and Queen Saewara were reluctant to lose them but finally they relented and the arrangements were made.

--o--

It was in September of the same year that Botolph's novitiateship came to an end and he was called to the abbess's office to be told that his status as a monk would be confirmed in a special service which would be attended by Bishop Faro and clergy from Meaux.

"*Another* visit from the bishop, mother," said Botolph questioningly.

"Indeed," she replied tersely, "it seems my brother has taken such a liking to Evoriacum that he can't keep away."

Botolph himself dreaded the prospect of having to meet Gaubert and Fauve again. He felt he had escaped lightly at the baptism sacrament but wondered if there was something more to this next visit than was immediately apparent. There was no way around it however and he decided that it was a cross he would have to bear. The prospect brought his thoughts back to Luka. He prayed every night for his dear friend and his family. He had not heard a word from them for the past four years but he pictured Luka surrounded by a brood of offspring with his pretty wife, Clarisse, - probably pregnant again - looking on.

--o--

Luka had wanted to take Ash to visit Botolph but he had decided that it was just too dangerous. Travellers who visited the bandit camp were always delighted to meet Luka who had become a legend in his lifetime. Sadly it was this legendary reputation that made him and Ash prisoners.

He gradually became resigned to this as well as to the death of his dear wife although never a day passed when he did not think of her.

Gradually the sadness that had engulfed him was replaced by the joy of nurturing and rearing his young son. As they rode through the forest or swam in the lake, the boy's chuckle would come rippling back towards Luka and

336

was always reminiscent of Clarisse's ... *"From every crowd I hear your laugh."*

At the flash of his son's auburn hair a voice in the back of his mind would inevitably and tantalisingly trill *"Each ray of sunshine reflects the colour of your hair ... but you're not there ... I love you so ..."*

He would stall slightly for a moment but then see her soft smile and he would smile back again as if she were really there. He would continue with his task. Each time, it became a little easier.

He took Ash with him wherever he went and the other members of the commune were amused to see how similar the two were becoming. Ash even assumed Luka's unusual but characteristic dwarf-gait and Aliz and Bonitius wondered if he would lose that as he grew taller. It was abundantly clear that Ash had acquired none of his father's other dwarf-like features.

The smallholdings at Bonoriacum had developed into an ever-growing farm of which Luka had become the manager. There were times that he bent his back to ploughing or sowing but most of his time was spent supervising the others. The camp was still kept well-protected and Bonitius continued to extract protection money and tithes from other farmsteads round about.

CHAPTER 52
Father Fursey

The day came when Botolph was to take his solemn vows. Bishop Faro was determined to make this visit a longer one and he and his party had arrived during the previous week. Other candidates from the monasteries of St Maur and Jouarre, including Sister Bertille, had drifted into Evoriacum over the previous couple of days.

In some ways it had the potential of a family event but Abbess Fara had been jittery for several days before the arrival of the bishop, feeling that his presence was not so much for the sake of the ceremony as to inspect and criticise her administration of the abbey.

Botolph was pleased to welcome Mother Theodochilde and pretty Sister Bertille from Jouarre. It was not, he insisted to himself, the fact that she was *physically* pretty, - in fact he had hardly noticed that, it was her pretty personality and pleasant and holy manner that he enjoyed.

In spite of these internal protestations of innocence he still felt the need to linger longer over his confession that day.

When they met after the ceremony, Bertille gave him a somewhat cheeky look and greeted him with "Pax tecum Father Botolph."

He laughed and gave back "Et pax Mother Bertille."

"So," she said, "shall Gaul be losing you now? Will you return to Britain?"

"I think not," he said. "There's still much for me to learn here and to be honest I so enjoy the company of my brothers and sisters that I'd be loath to leave them. Will you stay at Jouarre?"

"Mother Theodochilde has plans for me to move to Villa Calae."

She spoke with such disarming innocence that, in spite of the mischievous smile that ever-so-slightly curled the corner of her lips just below the dimples on her cheeks (which of course Botolph did not notice) he was caught off-guard by her words. He was coming to the conclusion that she was quite aware of the effect that she had upon him and that she was not such an innocent as she first appeared.

"Villa Calae?" he spluttered, having always felt that there was more to the villa than he knew about.

"Yes," she said. "Have you not heard that it's to be turned into a monastery?"

"Is it?"

"Yes.   Just before her death last year, Queen Nanthild had suggested the change and Mayor Erchinoald and Bishop Faro are now working towards its conversion and, if I live long enough, I'm to be its first abbess."

"If you live long enough ... are you ill?"

She laughed gaily. "No I didn't mean that. It'll take maybe a year or two for the building work to be done. Then we'll need to stock it with monks and nuns, so it just depends upon whether or not the Good Lord spares me for so long."

A few days later, Fara called Botolph back to her quarters and told him that she had it in mind that he should become her chaplain.

"Ahah! The 'capellanu'!" he cried. "I shall carry the cloak!"

The abbess was lost, "Whatever do you mean?"

Feeling a little sheepish about his spontaneous outburst, he related the story of when he and Luka had met

King Dagobert's capellanu on their journey from Sithiu to Lutetia and how they had first heard the story of St Martin's cloak.

"Well Father Botolph," she said, "it's the cloak of care that I shall want you to spread over God's people here at Evoriacum. It will be your job to ensure that their welfare's looked after. I have no doubt you'll want to pray about it but if you decide that it's God's will then the position is yours."

Botolph did indeed pray about it and give the matter a great deal of thought. Again he wondered if he should stay in Gaul or go home or whether he should move to another monastery; maybe join Bernard at Elnone? Luka was always at the back of his mind and that was perhaps the factor that swayed the balance and led to his final decision to remain closer to him at Evoriacum.

During his prayers he did however come to the conclusion that one day God would call him back to Britain and that meanwhile his duty was to spend his time wisely at Evoriacum and prepare for whatever may befall him in the years ahead. A week later he returned to the abbess with his answer.

--o--

Further to the north in the port of Gesoriacum, a flamboyant character with a long white beard and a thick Irish accent had just landed from a British boat. His arrival in Gaul was the result of an invitation from a local nobleman called Duke Berchar who was waiting on the dockside to greet him.

"Salve et pax vobiscum Fursey," said the Duke.

"Et in terram pax," replied Father Fursey and the old friends grasped each other's arms affectionately.

"I see you've not left your great walking stick at home then?"

"Never in y'r loif, Oi'll not go anywhere widout it. It can do miracles on its own these days!"

The duke laughed and they strolled down the quayside to join the carriage that was to take them to the palace at Lugdunum Clavatum where Fursey was looking forward to resting.

"So I hear you're pushing on to Rome when you leave us?" said the duke. "I'd hoped that you were going to make your home here in Gaul after the way they treated you in Britain?"

"Ah well, ye know me," said the big man with a twinkling of the eyes and a shaking of the great white-bearded head. "Oi've not made up me moind yet. Oi'll go where de Good Lord takes me.

"So what of your brothers?"

"Ah, now, would ye be talking about me holy brithers or me family brithers then?"

"Well I'm happy to hear of both but let's start with Foillan and Ultan."

"Well to be sure, Foillan's looking after de monastery at Cnobersburg ..."

"Was it easy to build it up again after the attack?" interrupted the duke.

"Indeed, yes. We had to start from de very beginning again of course. Dat devil Penda had burned a lot of de huts and of course half de monks disoided to stay here in Gaul so we had to build up de numbers again but 'twas alroit. Foillan, with de Lord's help did a woonderfu' job.

"Now Ultran! - *he* disoided to become a hairmit. Oi t'ought dat was a bit indulgent of him so Oi've bin stayin' wid him for de past year or so to make sure he wasn't enjoying it too mooch. Eventually Oi got fed up with him and him with me so here I am!" and he slapped his thigh and gave a great roar of laughter.

Some hours later after a lot of shouting the horses suddenly came to a standstill. The occupants of the carriage clambered out, as much to stretch their legs as to discover the reason for the disturbance.

"I should have known," groaned the duke to Fursey. "It's Haymo! Trust him to upset my journey and find some pretext for introducing himself to you."

"And who, moit one ask, is Haymo?"

"Here we are, you'll be able to see for yourself."

Fursey turned to see a forlorn figure staggering towards him waving his arms and moaning, "Dead! Dead! My son is dead!"

"For Heaven's sake," said Berchar irritably, and then, remembering his manners and supposing that he should apply them properly he said, "Haymo, this is Father Fursey, Abbot of Cnobersburg in Britain. Fursey, this is Duke Haymo of Ponthieu."

"Father? Abbot? Oh Praise the Lord," said Haymo. "It's a sign. It's a sign. You must come quickly Father. You'll be able to restore my son to life. I know you will."

He took Fursey's arm and propelled him along the track to a gateway and thence into a palatial hall where a crowd of people consisting mainly of women were surrounding a table on which lay the body of a young man. The women were wailing and crying but some looked up and made a space as the duke led the party of travellers to the body.

Fursey went to the side of the table and raised his great arms in the air, the right one bearing his massive walking stick. At this the crowd fell silent.

Berchar looked doubtfully at the body, convinced that it was a trick fabricated by Haymo simply to get himself introduced to the abbot. The body certainly looked dead enough though. He poked it. It did not respond. Perhaps he had done his rival an injustice?

Father Fursey had been standing perfectly still with arms raised for what seemed to many a long while and it became clear that he was intent on waiting for absolute silence and stillness. When such silence duly arrived he started to pray and raised both his hands further until they touched at a point above his head whereupon he transferred his staff from his right to his left hand finishing his prayers at the same time with an 'amen' that was echoed by the others present.

To a gasp from the crowd he brought his right hand swiftly down in a clenched fist and struck the body in the centre of the rib cage.

The crowd's gasp was followed by a short period of intense silence where the watchers saw the body's previously white face suddenly flush pink. This was followed by the 'corpse' contorting as it gave a single protracted violent cough and opened its eyes.

There was a scream from the boy's mother and she rushed forwards and grasped the child in her arms pulling him up and off the table. Duke Haymo turned and, for a moment, stared incredulously at Fursey and then, with tears streaming down his face, fell onto his knees and, taking and kissing his hand, thanked him as profusely as his cracking voice would allow.

"T'ank de Lord. T'ank de Lord. Don' t'ank me," responded Fursey. "Oi'm merely de instr'ment of His divine will. Praise be to God."

"Praise be to God. Praise be to God," came the response as the crowd made way for the great white man with the great white beard to regain his carriage.

Haymo would not hear of it though and in spite of protests from both Fursey and Berchar, they and their whole retinue were turned around and imprisoned for the night to enjoy as best they might the great feasting and celebrations for the return from the dead of young Haymo.

Fortunately the following day was a comparatively short journey to the House of Berchar where Fursey spent several more days alternately giving audiences and resting. After this he travelled on to the city of Peronna where he had a standing invitation to spend time in the palace of the once-new but now more-than-well-established Mayor of Neustria, Erchinoald.

The potential for performing miracles seemed to shadow Father Fursey wherever he went and his companions were to witness two more before they arrived at Peronna. The news of this charismatic figure and his activities preceded him and it would have been difficult to discern which of the two was most honoured when Erchinoald finally welcomed him to his house.

During the following days at Peronna his host concentrated on doing all he could to encourage Fursey to make Gaul his home on a permanent basis. To that end he offered him land and labour to build himself a monastery wherever in Gaul he might choose.

There was no shortage of recommendations and Fursey, after some days of thought and prayer, eventually came to the conclusion that it was God's will that he should remain in Gallia for a while.   The villa at Latiniacum, with its proximity to Lutetia and its shady glades and vineyards, sounded like a place which might convert to an idyllic abbey.

Erchinoald was delighted with Father Fursey's decision and it was agreed that, once he had completed his tour of the kingdom, the Irish abbot would move into Latiniacum for a few months and make his final decision then.   Once he was comfortable, the building works would start.

Little did he know the consternation this would cause to the existing occupants of the villa whose professions were rather less than holy.   There would be a great rush to expel many of the inmates and expunge all evidence of their activities before the arrival of the famous patron.

CHAPTER 53
Hereswith

When Botolph next met Abbess Fara, he also had, with the Lord's help, made a decision. He would remain in Gaul until God moved him elsewhere.

The abbess wanted him to start his chaplaincy straight away in spite of the fact that he had not yet been ordained. He would, she told him, spend the next year under the tutelage of her brother Bishop Faro at Meaux.

"I see a cloud pass over your face Father Botolph," she observed.

"I'm sorry Mother. I have of course great respect for your brother Bishop Faro but my experiences at Meaux during the synod were fraught with difficulties and even the name of the city now makes me feel uneasy."

The abbess smiled. "You misunderstood Father Botolph. I didn't mean that you'll transfer your living to Meaux. How could you be both there and - spreading the cloak of your chaplaincy over our people here - at the same time? No, you'll remain at Evoriacum. Bishop Faro will arrange for your tutelage by a series of priests and bishops who'll visit our abbey from time to time. Indeed it's likely that it'll be Father Ouen from Rebais or his brother Father Adon from Jouarre who'll be providing most of your supervision".

At the mention of Jouarre Botolph's thoughts turned again to Sister Bertille. He wondered if God might perhaps send him into her company at Jouarre.

As it turned out there were instances over the next year when Bertille and Botolph did indeed meet again but to his disappointment their meetings were rare and short-lived.

CHAPTER 54
Botolph's future unravels

Twelve moons later, in September 644, Father Botolph took Holy Orders as a priest and felt that he was at last fully-fledged and able to fulfil his duties properly as chaplain to Abbess Faro's monastery.

It was while carrying out those duties that he was thrown into the more frequent company of the twins Nelburga and Magburga. He still enjoyed reminiscing with them about his days in Britain and they asked him one day if he was homesick or had any plans to return.

Up until that point he had not really given the matter any thought because he had had so many other things to occupy his mind. Their words struck a chord and he silently mused on the matter wondering if his parents were still alive and how his sister and brother had fared. Was Adulph still abroad or had he returned to Britain? Did Matild and Atheran have a large family or had they, like Princess Eanswythe, succumbed to the plague? It was a long time now since he had flown his family's nest and he supposed that it was normal in such circumstances for folk to lose contact with their kin. But even so ...

The twins noticed the faraway look in his eyes and did not disturb his reverie until he turned his head towards them again. They asked him if he had ever considered setting up his own monastery in Cantium.

Botolph was astonished.

"My own monastery?" he spluttered.

They smiled up at him from the wooden bench upon which they sat, and nodded.

"Aren't you happy with me as your chaplain then?" he teased and their smiles immediately vanished.

"Oh no, we ..."

"... didn't mean ..."

He laughed. "There now my sisters, I was only teasing. It's a nice thought but with my own monastery I'd be unable to travel ..."

As soon as the words were out of his mouth, he knew what their reply would be.

"But you don't travel now Father."

It was true. His spirit wanted to fly like a bird and see new places and minister to new people and to bring the gospel of Christ to all and to spread the word of God throughout the land. But he had seen twenty-five summers already and for the last four of them he had hardly moved out of Evoriacum. He had been happy, it was true, and fully occupied and felt fulfilled but maybe the time was coming when he should move on.

He had learned so much since he had been in Gaul and now that Eanswythe had died, the reason for his self-imposed exile had passed and there would be no danger to his soul by going home. Indeed, he admitted ruefully, there might be more danger to my soul if I stay here and am thrown into the company of the beautiful Bertille! He would ask God.

The twins persisted in bringing the matter up from time to time but not so often that it appeared that they were intent upon his departure. They too had been praying for him and wondering what God's decision would be.

Finally it was to them that he first admitted that he was seriously considering the prospect of serving God back in Britain.

"We could write to our brother," said Nelburga. "I'm sure he'd be able to provide you with some land upon which you could build an abbey." Sister Magburga nodded enthusiastically.

"Well, that's a kind thought," admitted Botolph.

He remained silent, thinking quickly. Eastern Cantium was quite well served by monasteries now and he would not want to tread on the toes of the abbey of Liminge or Folcanstane's nunnery which he assumed would been taken over by another abbess. The twins' brother, being king of *West* Cantium, might be able to provide him with new pastures where he could build his monastery without any undue influence from Cantwarebury or anybody else for that matter - except God.

"*Are* there any monasteries in West Cantium?" he asked.

The girls looked at each other and shook their heads slowly.

"There's one at Hrofsceaster I think," said Magburga but nothing closer than that - although ..."

"Yes?"

"Well, not far away from us there's an ancient site they call 'Springhead', close by the River Tamesis. It's been a sacred place for as long as anyone can remember but we've never been there."

They shook their heads in unison.

'Springhead?' The name had an interesting ring but it didn't sound like the sort of place for a monastery. Still, everything depended on the reluctant king, Athelwald. He made his decision.

"I would be grateful," he replied. "Thank you."

A moon later the sisters were embarrassed to receive the reply to their letter and they wondered how they were going to break the news to their chaplain.

--o--

Father Fursey in the meantime, was living as a guest of the Gallic aristocracy. He moved from palace to palace, performing miracles on the way and the news of his multitude of successful conversions spread widely.

It came as no surprise therefore when a message arrived at Evoriacum saying that Father Fursey from Ireland would be arriving at the abbey in late Autumn.

Brother Abraham was of course delighted to hear the news and for days before his arrival was eagerly looking forward to discussing the joys of his garden with his famous kinsman.

And Fursey, when he did arrive, was no disappointment. Ever the showman he was soon charming the whole monastery with his presence. He was delighted to meet again all those he had met before as well as those who, like Brother Abraham he had not met and yet with whom he had some connection on a higher plane. He had special words for everyone and Father Botolph was no exception.

"Ah t'be sure, it's *Faither* ye now are whereas when las' I saw ye, ye were but a young obedientary. And your brither Adulph now? ... Hav' ye herd fram him?"

"I've heard nothing Father, since Luka and I saw you set sail from Cnobersburg. I have no idea where you landed even, so I'm hoping that it's *you* who will be able to give *me* some good news."

They were in the presence of Abbess Fara at the time and after so many years in her company, Botolph had come to realise how she loved to hear a well-told story so he was unsurprised when she arranged for time in the misericord when they could hear the tale in comfort and share it with other members of their community.

It transpired that Father Fursey, Adulph and the other former residents of Cnobersburg monastery had had an uneventful voyage in the *Manigfual* under the skilful direction of the ship-master Torrel and had arrived safely at Gesoriacum.

The party had then split up. Adulph and some other monks headed to the northeast and Father Fursey and his cronies headed south. Torrel and Betta and a few others stayed with the ship in Gesoriacum.

Several months later, Torrel received news that all was now quiet at Cnobersburg again and that it was safe for them to return. He relayed the message to Father Fursey and to Sithiu where he had heard that Adulph's party had gone.

Fursey received the message and returned to the boat but there had been no word from Adulph. They delayed their departure for a few days while they made further enquiries and discovered that he and the monks had only stayed at Sithiu for a few days before pressing on further east to Mosaetraij – a fortified town on the banks of the river Mosa.

The listeners in the misericord were enthralled, - and Fursey paused for breath before continuing. It was only later, he told them, that he had heard that it was in Mosaetraij that Adulph had been professed. After that apparently, he joined another group travelling northwards and finally settled in a town called Traiectum. When he arrived he apparently found that the Christianity there was in some disarray and he instantly and very successfully set about putting it in better order.

Botolph was proud to hear of his brother's success.

"So what of Cnobersburg?" asked Botolph.

"Well t' be sure, we got back safely and found 'twas all in a terrible mess but within a couple o' weeks we'd built it all up again and me brithers Foillan and Ultran took over de running of it. Oi'm gettin' too auld for dat sort of ding. Aifter a while, Ultran decided de Lord was callin' him t' become a hairmit, so we left Foillan t' run de monastery n' Ultran n' Oi went off t' be hairmits."

The longer he spoke, the thicker Father Fursey's accent seemed to become and Botolph was having difficulty understanding it himself so he could not imagine how the abbess was able to follow the conversation at all. She was however smiling and nodding and making the odd comment in all the right places so he assumed she was managing somehow.

"I thought hermits were supposed to live on their own," said Botolph rashly.

"Indeed dey are, indeed dey are; bait Oi know me brither Ultran, n' Oi knew he'd benefit from me presence so Oi went along t' give him some advice ye see."

Botolph did not see at all and thought the others probably did not see either but he decided against pressing the point.

"So then you decided to come back to Gaul?"

"Dat's roit. Berchar was very upset t' see me go n' invited me t' come back whenever Oi wanted to. So Oi thought Oi was duty bound t' do so ... n' here Oi am! Oi did originally plan t' go on to Rome. Alwez been an ambition o' mine dat.   But what wiv' Berchar, Haymo n' Erchinoald all bein' on at me t' stay ... what chance has a body got?"

They laughed at his apparent frustration.

"So what happens next?" asked Botolph.

"Well, Oi've jus' been t' have a look at Latiniacum n' 't seems t' me a good place t' have a monastery so Oi tink Erchinoald n' me will be startin' work on 't pretty soon."

"We'll be neighbours then?" said Abbess Fara.

"Well oi'll not be far away dat's true, - so ye'll be able to keep an eye on me," and he slapped his leg and let out another of his great belly laughs.   "But what about you, me foin fella?   What does Faither Botolph have in mind for de future?"

Botolph made to answer but Fursey continued, "Dis country of Gaul ye know, is foine for auld folk like me but thrustin' young priests like youse 'r needed in Britain.   De country is ripe, ... *ripe* fer missionarying.   Dere's no call fer dat here.   People in Gaul are oither Christians or Pagans. Dere's no way ye'r goin' tae change 'em, but in *Britain* ..."

Thus for the second time Botolph had the prospect of returning to Britain waved in front of his face. He had not mentioned the first occasion to Fara and he looked across at her now.

She was already watching him and as their eyes locked she gave a sad half-smile and an almost-imperceptible nod.

So she too had seen it, Botolph thought; it seemed more and more likely that the call was there. He turned back to Fursey.

"Well, Father, I am the Lord's to command so I shall pray about it and await his directions."

"Do dat, me boy. Do dat 'ndeed. 'N if ye do decide n' 'r not too sure where t' go, den head up t' Cnobersburg n' give Foillan a hand ... Oi know he'll be pleased t' see ye."

Their conversation was cut short by the sound of the Vespers bell. Father Fursey left the monastery early the following morning.

--o--

A few days later the twins plucked up courage and came to see Botolph again.

"What is it, sisters?" he said immediately sensing that they were troubled.

"I'm afraid we have bad news from Britain," said Nelburga.

Botolph's heart sank, fearing that the news would be about his parents of whom he had been thinking a lot lately. He braced himself for whatever words might come.

"Let's hear it then," he said.

"I'm afraid our brother Athelwald's scribe's written to say he's not prepared to give you any land to build a monastery on," Nelburga blurted out, feeling at the same time the colour rising in her cheeks.

Botolph suppressed a desire to laugh; he was relieved to find that the news had been so inconsequential. 'When you have never had something, losing it's not too much of a problem,' he thought.

Sister Nelburga mistook his intake of breath as being a gesture of annoyance and she continued quickly, "All's not lost though, our sister-in-law Queen Sarre tells us she'd *so* much like you to minister in Cantium and ... and ..."

"Hush sister," said Botolph bending towards her benevolently. "Hush now. If the Good Lord wishes me to go and minister in Cantium then your sister-in-law's pleas will prevail but if not then He'll either keep me here or send me somewhere else."

"You're not cross then Father?" she said.

"Never in your life, no."

The tension visibly drained from her face and, turning to her sister, she grasped her hands and they hugged each other in relief, no words being necessary.

--o--

The next year saw the re-consecration of Villa Calae as the Abbey of Chelles; Abbess Fara and Father Botolph were invited to the installation of Mother Bertille as abbess. Both she and Father Botolph had grown in spiritual stature since they had first met. Botolph had come to realise that although it had at first appeared to him that the Bertille bore him a special fondness, it had now become clear that no matter to whom she talked, she always made her listener feel special.

On his arrival at the abbey, Botolph made his excuses to Abbess Fara and went to find the stables. As he walked down the path he saw a leather-aproned individual busily pitching fresh hay through an open door. The man looked up as he heard Botolph's step and then his rugged face broke into a delighted grin.

"Father Botolph. How good it is to see you."

"You too Gurnard. How's it going? Do you *like* working in an Abbey?"

"I do," he replied. "It's good. The life's not so exciting of course but I'm getting old and to be honest I was beginning to feel that too much excitement was bad for me. I was beginning to worry about how I was going to cope in my old age.   Here however I do my best and in return I'm well looked after.   Busy today though, - with all the coming and going."

"Yes, I'd better get back to the celebrations," Botolph said, turning.   "Take care of yourself Gurnard.   Stay happy and healthy and trust in the Lord."

"Thank you Father, - I'll try.   Come and see us when you can."

Whilst at Chelles, Botolph was introduced to a recent arrival from Britain by the name of Sister Hereswith. Mother Bertille told him excitedly that another member of Hereswith's family, her sister Hilda, was also expected to join the abbey within the next few weeks.

Botolph remarked to Hereswith that it seemed customary for British obedientaries to arrive in pairs.

"We have the twins, Sisters Nelburga and Magburga from West Cantium," he said, "and Sisters Saethryth and Ethelburg from East Anglia.   Now Chelles will have Sisters Hereswith and Hilda from ... ah ... from *where* may I ask?"

"It's a long and complicated story but we originally came from King Edwin's household in Northumbria.   He looked after us both when our father died.   We became Christians when he married Queen Ethelburga. We were all baptised at the same time by Bishop Paulinus in one grand ceremony."   Her eyes shone.

"Ah yes, King Edwin, God rest his soul," - both he and Hereswith crossed themselves.

"Ethelburga returned to Cantium after he died and I came to know her quite well," he said and his thoughts immediately moved sideways towards thoughts of Princess Eanswythe.

"You did?" said Bertille interrupting his thoughts.

Botolph had been day-dreaming and when he looked up into Bertille's face it was replaced for an instant by that of Eanswythe. He shook his head slightly to clear the vision.

"You didn't!" said the abbess.

"No, no, - I *did*," said Botolph, himself becoming confused by the confusion he was causing. "In fact her daughter Princess Eanfled joined us as an obedientary at Evoriacum a few years ago."

"Of course," said Bertille. "A sweet young girl who went back to Britain and married King Oswiu."

"The very same," said Botolph.

"What a complicated patchwork our lives weave," said Hereswith, "but each thread somehow manages to touch all the others in its passage through the cloth."

"So does that end your story?" said Botolph.

"Well almost," she replied. "After his conversion my lord king was keen to forge an alliance and bring peace with his neighbours. I was part of the peace-making process and he married me off to Prince Aethelric, the brother of King Anna of East Anglia."

"Ah - I know him too!" said Botolph and then wished he had not, realising that this was beginning to sound rather too much like conceit. The comment however was lost in the listeners' enthusiasm and interest in the remainder of Hereswith's story.

"My husband died last year. We had a son who's just come of age and now serves King Anna in the East Anglian court, so my sister and I are now free to do as we wish and, after much prayer, we felt that God had called us here to Chelles."

"And here you are," said Botolph, "but what of your sister?"

"Hilda will join us in the Spring," said Bertille. "Hereswith tells me she's been spirited away to the island of Lindisfarne by the redoubtable Father Aidan, but she assures me that it's only a passing fancy; her sister has a passion for visiting desolate places."

A cloud passed over Hereswith's face. "We've never been apart for as long as this," she said. "She received the offer from Father Aidan just before we were due to leave and I couldn't deny her the joy of her heart."

The story being complete, the group divided and went to pray. Botolph surmised that Hereswith's prayers would include supplication for a speedy reunion with her sister.

CHAPTER 55
Finding a Boat

Nelburga and Magburga were ecstatic.   At last the news had come; the news for which they had been hoping and praying for the past year. Their sister-in-law had finally managed to persuade their brother to agree to granting some land for Botolph to build an abbey.   They immediately requested an audience with their chaplain and presented him with the news.

Botolph was at once amazed, thrilled and perplexed. Where should he start?   What should he do next?   He thanked the twins for their kindness and they returned joyously to their devotions. He in the meantime went into the abbey church and attended to his.

After all his prayers were spent. he spent a long time staring up at the carved wooden cross in front of him.

This was going to be a massive undertaking. A knot of panic and excitement started to build up in the pit of his stomach.   Simply *leaving* Evoriacum; simply *leaving* all his friends and acquaintances; simply *leaving* this shrine where he had been nurtured, taught and protected for the past nine years; all these things would make a huge change to his life.

Was he competent?   Did he have the ability to work on his own?   For the past nine years he had relied so much on the guidance of Abbess Fara; she was the rudder who had steered his ship of life.   Would he be able to sail that ship single-handed?   He had already helped to build a monastery at Lutetia. Had this been God's way of preparing him for his future, he wondered.

There again, building a monastery was one thing (he presumed he would have the help of King Athelwald and his workers for that), but gathering together enough monks to form a community. Could he *do* that? Were there enough people out there who would follow him? What was Britain like these days? Had it changed in the past nine years?

So *many* questions. It would all be so much easier to stay where he was where he was comfortable and happy and ... yes he had to say it ... 'buried'. Yes. He had not thought of it before but - yes, he was buried. This made him think of Jesus' parable of the talents and he remembered the one servant who had simply *buried* his talents and then returned them to his master when he had come back from his long journey.

'Long journey': that would be the next thing. The prospect itself caused a shudder of excitement. And then there were the new people he would meet and the potential he would have for spreading the word of God.

It was time for him to become unburied. To dig up his talents and expose them to the world. To invest them in the Lord. To move on. To start accumulating some interest on the talents he possessed.

And then he realised again. He had many more talents now than when he had arrived at Evoriacum. He had not been idle. He had learned much. He was ready.

The abbess looked up as he entered her office but, for a while, neither of them spoke; he because, in spite of his prayers, he did not know where to start and she, because she knew.

She was the first to break the silence.

"So the time has come?" she said.

"I think so Mother," he said.

"You *think* so?"

361

"I *know* so."

"That's better."

They smiled sadly at each other.

"When?"

"When may I?"

"In the Spring?"

"Spring it will be."

--o--

Like wildfire the word buzzed around that Father
Botolph was leaving. In the same way that he had become
comfortable with them, so they too had become comfortable
with him and would be sorry to see him go. Indeed how
would they manage without him? He assured them that
with God's help they would manage very well.

One day he received a visit from the two young nuns
from East Anglia, Saethryth and Ethelburg. They expressed
their sadness at his forthcoming departure. They wrote
regular letters home and in one had told their father of
Botolph's intention to return to Britain. They had received
a letter in reply in which King Anna had expressed the hope
that, on his return, Botolph would visit his court at Exning.
Botolph was touched by such friendliness and resolved to
write directly to his former patron.

A few weeks later he received a letter in return in
which King Anna made him an offer of land to build a
monastery in East Anglia should he not find West Cantium
to his liking.

Botolph was a little overwhelmed by this but not at
all intimidated. On the contrary, he saw the prospect of *two*
offers as providing scope for missionary work on a scale that
he had never imagined. Cantium, - particularly *West*

Cantium and East Anglia were relatively close and travelling between the two would provide great opportunities to serve the Lord. His excitement and enthusiasm were increasing ever further and he began to expand his plans.

--o--

Spring came quickly for Botolph and Fara in AD 647 and the abbess arranged for a special service and feast to be held on the Sunday before his departure. This gave everyone the opportunity to express their love and admiration for him and gave him the same prospect in return.

The following day he arose at his usual hour and, for the last time, joined the rest of the monastery for the offices of Prime and Lauds. Instead of the usual meditation, the whole community escorted him to the abbey gates and to a chorus of "Pax tecums" and a cloth-wrapped bundle of food to eat on his journey, he headed on his way.

The ground was flat. The weather was cool but dry. The land smelt sweet. The fields were colourful. The next stage of his life had begun.

He arrived at Villa Latiniacum in mid-afternoon. He had wondered if he would be early enough to wade across the river before the water became too deep but the flood was already well underway. He had no alternative therefore but to spend the night at the villa where he was welcomed as one of the many monks who travelled the area. The villa showed no signs of any conversion into a monastery and Botolph wondered if Father Fursey had changed his mind or perhaps, in the way of the Irish, he had just not got around to starting it yet.

Although he rose early, the earliest time he could cross the ford would be an hour or so before noon so he strolled out into the vineyard and found himself a sunny place out of the wind where he and God could communicate undisturbed. When the sun seemed high enough in the sky, he made his way to the river's edge and watched as the mud banks which were lurking underwater gradually made their appearance. On the other side an impatient and adventurous traveller was already entering the water and Botolph watched him as he struggled across. He stumbled once or twice and at the deepest point the water nearly reached his neck so Botolph decided to delay a little longer.

"T' water's cold today," grumbled the traveller as he came ashore.

"Well you've been deeper into it than I was planning," replied Botolph.

The fellow laughed. "Alwez hate havin' t' wait," he said as he sloshed past.

The tide fell rapidly and it was not long before Botolph could venture across.

He arrived at Chelles nearly half a day later and went straight to the abbey stables to find Gurnard; the two old friends greeted each other warmly again. Gurnard was surprised to hear that he was returning to Britain but people came and went in Gurnard's life so he took the news in his stride.

As he left the old ostler, the Compline bell started to ring and he joined the throng of monks and nuns entering the chapel. At the end of the office he was able to have a short talk with Abbess Bertille before making his way to the dormitory and bedding down.

Another early start the next day saw him at Bonoriacum by noon and, upon enquiring at the 'Gateway', a young thug whom he did not recognise, led him to a field where an ageing Luka was tending his crops. He had a young boy by his side.

Luka's joy at the meeting was evident but Botolph saw that it was restrained. He noticed the deep lines on Luka's face and his prematurely-greying temples.

"How's things?" said Botolph brightly.

"Oh, so-so," said his friend. "Ye heard 'bout Clarisse I s'pose?"

"Clarisse? No? Why? Is she ill?"

"Dead," came the blunt reply.

Botolph stood, stunned, not-knowing what to say.

"Dead? When? How?"

"Dead these past five and a half years. Died in childbirth so she did."

"Oh my poor Luka. I'm so sorry. I didn't know."

"No reason you should. Nothing you could do. This 'ere's Ash who you met as a babe. Come and say 'ello to Father Botolph me lad."

The boy came over shyly and took Botolph's proffered hands. He was a scrawny but wiry little chap with auburn hair and a thin smattering of freckles. As he looked into his eyes Botolph saw that they were an iridescent green.

He and the boy made an instant bond and they chatted away, the child's rippling voice dancing brightly like Clarisse's used to, while Luka led the way to the farmhouse to find Bonitius and Aliz.

The four adults stretched themselves out in a sunny corner with some loaves of bread with cheese, fruit and beer and Botolph told of his plans and prospects for the future.

The word had spread about Botolph's arrival and many of the community adjusted their schedule so that they could walk past the group and offer their greetings to the reverend visitor. As soon as Bonitius realised the purpose of Botolph's visit and that they would probably never meet again, he immediately started making arrangements to have a feast that night.

Luka had stayed uncharacteristically silent during all the various interchanges but he now turned towards Botolph and said, "Can we come with you?"

All heads, including Ash's, turned to Luka in silent astonishment.

Luka looked at Bonitius. "I'm sorry, Bondy," he said, "but I think this is the answer I've been looking for."

"But you won't get ten leagues before the authorities'll have you," said Bonitius, "and then we'll see you strung up on a gibbet and that will be that. Besides which how'm I expected to run the farm without you?"

"I know," said Luka, "but the boys'll do it. I've trained 'em all up. You've just got to get them organised and it'll run as smooth as a river. Believe me."

"Huh," said Bonitius doubtfully.

Luka turned to Botolph.

"Which way're you going?"

"Well I hadn't decided really. The same way as we came I suppose. Northwards up to Gesoriacum."

"Yes, that's what I thought," said Luka, "and that would be certain death for me. But there is another way."

"What's that?"

"Well first – would you take us?"

"Us?"

"Me and Ash."

"Well ... Yes ... and gladly so long as there is a chance we could get you home alive."

"It's my only chance you see."

"How do you mean?"

"When Clarisse died, all I wanted to do was to move on; move away from the memories of the happy times that'll never come back and from the memories of the saddest of all times. But I couldn't go. There's a price on m' head and m' height makes me too recognisable.

"And then there was Ash. I thought about trying to get Eligius to have him accepted at court in Lutetia but that meant I'd see him rarely if ever. Again I thought about just going - and fighting m' way out of trouble wherever I could, but then I realised that one day I'd probably make a mistake and then Ash'ld be on his own, so the answer seemed to be to stay here.

"We've been happy here. I've taught him all I know. He can ride and swim and shoot a good arrow. We've learned farming together. He knows how to handle swine and sheep and horses and cattle. We've been together and it's been great but he's now eight and I don't want him to grow up outside the law."

Botolph nodded. "So what's your plan?"

"Well I hadn't really thought about going back to Britain but it's the one place we'd be safe, especially if we were with you. It'd be like the old days except there'd be three of us." He was looking intently at Botolph as he spoke. "How do you feel about that?"

Botolph considered. Building an abbey. Collecting his people. Managing a team. Running a monastery farm. How much easier that would be with Luka by his side. He detailed his thoughts to his friend and saw the relief flood into his face.

"I was afraid we might be an imposition on you but if you put it that way, then maybe I'll end up doing God's work and being an asset after all!"

"So what's your plan Luka?"

"A boat."

"A *what*?"

"A boat from Lutetia."

Botolph laughed. "The last two times we tried a boat as a method of escape it nearly killed both of us."

"Ah yes, but we've learnt a lot since then haven't we?"

"Maybe so. What d' you have in mind?"

"There are always ships coming up the Sequana and unloading cargo at Lutetia. We could get one of those to take us back to Britain. That way the only part where I'm risking capture is between here and Lutetia."

"Right," said Botolph nodding. "But who's going to find a suitable boat?"

"You are."

"Me?"

"Well none of us here can go anywhere near Lutetia unless we take an armed guard and that would attract too much unwelcome attention. It'd be quite logical for you to want to go back to Britain by ship and you could make quiet arrangements. I've some valuables saved up which you could use to pay the master to take his ship a little further down river to a spot that I can tell you about and Ash and I'll come during the hours of darkness and we can just slip away."

"Easy?"

"Simple!"

"Well it sounds a good plan. What do you think Bonitius?"

"I think it sounds awful."

"Awful? Why?"

"Well firstly, you can't just '*slip away*' because it'll depend on what the tide's doing - and secondly, how're you going to let Luka know that you've been successful in *getting* a boat?   He could turn up and find no boat was available.

"The first part of Luka's plan's alright.   By all means go and find a boat and get the master to take it down river. I know the spot Luka's thinking about, - the Landing Stage eh Luka?"   Luka nodded.

"Right - well you can't miss that. It's quite obvious. It's a mud berth so if necessary the boat could stay there over low water.   But the whole scheme's going to depend on the tides.

"Botolph'll have to agree with the ship's master about a boarding time and then get a message back here telling Luka what time to get there."

There was silence for a few moments while everyone reflected on the good sense of this.

"He'll never get a messenger who'll be brave enough to come anywhere near Bonoriacum," said Luka.

"Yes he will," said Bonitius, "Fulkh'll do it.   We'll pay him well.   He'll do anything for money!"

"How do I find *him*?" said Botolph.

"Oh he'll be sculling around wherever there's activity going on in Lutetia," said Bonitius.

"I thought he was outlawed from Lutetia."

"Ah - that was in King Dagobert's time.   Fulkh's still a scoundrel but a respectable scoundrel these days."

"That's it then," said Botolph.   "I'll leave at first light tomorrow.   I'll get a message back to you as soon as I can, with a view to sailing as soon as possible after that."

"Sounds good to me," said Bonitius standing up. "Now - I've got a feast to organise to celebrate the peace and quiet we're going to have once Luka's gone," and he clapped Luka's back with a rare grin.

Botolph woke the following morning with a sore head but he had broken his fast by daylight and was on the road at dawn.

Before he left, Luka had given him a golden ornament in the shape of a beautiful little bird with garnet eyes.

It took him nearly half a day to get to Lutetia and he relished the sight of the city as he crossed the Pons Magnus. It had, over the years, become very familiar to him and it was with some sadness that he thought that it was unlikely he would ever see it again.

He wondered whether to go and find Eligius but decided to leave that duty until later and concentrate his attention on finding a boat. There were several at the town quay and he stood back and surveyed them for a while. A couple of them were big heavy dirty old things. Another seemed better but the skipper did not inspire confidence. Tucked at the back of the line was a pretty little vessel that was tidy and well-kept and looked as if she should have a good turn of speed for her size. She was only carrying light cargo consisting mainly of vegetables and the skipper and his boy were unloading them carefully. Botolph went and sat on the dockside and watched their progress.

There eventually came a natural lull in the activities and Botolph caught the skipper's eye.

"Wassail Father."

"Pax vobiscum my son. I've a favour to ask of you."

"I thought you might. What can I do for you?"

"Where are you bound?"

"Portus Reginorum on the other side of the Gallic Sea. Why do you ask?"

"Could you take me and two other passengers with you?"

"I'm always pleased to help men of the cloth Father but three monks would be rather an encumbrance."

"The others aren't monks. One's a child and the other's a man."

"Can they pay?"

Botolph brought the little golden bird out of his scrip. "This is yours once you've delivered us safely."

The skipper took it and held it to the light and then bit it gently. Botolph wondered why they all did that. It must tell them something but he had no idea what it was. Still he was not used to dealing with gold or silver, only men's spirits and consciences.

"That'll do handsomely Father," he said, handing it back to Botolph. "Now what'd you like me to do?"

Botolph explained the plan and pointed out that he could not decide on the day of departure until he had managed to get a message to the other passengers.

"Aren't they in the city then?" asked the skipper thinking that this was beginning to sound a bit odd.

"No - but they're not far away," said Botolph. "Err, one more thing ..."

"Yes?"

"I'd be grateful if you'd keep the plans to yourself. I don't want others knowing about them."

"Trust me Father," said the skipper.

As Botolph swung his feet back onto the dockside and heaved himself up on a stanchion, a figure in black moved away from the wall behind him.

--o--

Eligius' usual rooms were occupied by somebody entirely unknown to Botolph and on enquiring he found that he had not lived in the palace for the past five years.

"Five years?" thought Botolph. "Is it really as long as that since we met?" Somehow the news that Eligius had been made bishop of Noviomum must have entirely missed him. He would be sorry to depart the country without taking proper leave of his old friend.

He was more successful with Fulkh who looked as disreputable as ever but seemed to have acquired more than a smattering of Latin. Combined with that and the fact that, since they last met, Botolph had become reasonably adept at speaking the local patois, meant that communications between them were much easier than previously. Once Botolph had assured him that Bonitius would pay him well, he did not hesitate in agreeing to take the message. They went together to the dockside to see the skipper again.

"When d'you think you'll be able to leave?" asked Botolph.

"Whenever."

"Ah, I forgot to tell you. You'll need to go down river and wait at a landing stage where I gather there is a mud berth where you can stay at low water."

"Yes I know where that is," said the skipper "I've picked people up there before."

"I'll come with you when you go," said Botolph. "I need to know what time to tell my friends so that they can just step aboard and leave."

"Ah, I see," said the skipper slowly, beginning to think that now he really *did* begin to see. That golden ornament was not going to come to him quite as cheaply as he had thought. He looked up at the sky. "Well there'll be a good moon tonight and there's no cloud to obscure it so we can slide down to the landing stage at about midnight on the ebb if you like?"

"That'll be ideal I should think," said Botolph.

"And then we'll be afloat and ready to go as soon as there's some flow in the ebb. Say about noon on the morrow? How does that suit you Father?"

"That'd be wonderful. So Fulkh, the message is 'Noon on the morrow."

"Right you are. I'll be off then. Good luck on your voyage Father, I hope we'll meet again."

"God bless and keep you Fulkh and thanks for all your help."

As he watched Fulkh thread his way back through the crowds on the quayside, he saw a dark figure fall into step behind him. A nasty feeling hit the pit of Botolph's stomach.

He spent the next couple of hours saying his God be w'ye's to as many of his friends in Lutetia as he could find although most of those he knew were away in Peronna with King Clovis and Erchinoald.

When he heard the Compline bells ring out he made his way back to the quayside and went aboard the boat and acquainted himself with it. The kitchener at the palace had been kind enough to give him some food wrapped in a cloth bundle and a couple of flagons of sweet water which he gave to the skipper for safe stowage.

Before long the previously calm water started to ripple against the hull and the boat tugged at her warps as the ebb tide picked up. The skipper let the bow warp go and slackened the stern one as the boy pushed the boat off the quayside. As the tide caught her the skipper threw off the stern line and sculled her out into the river using the

steerboard oar.   Once the tide had her she drifted silently
away into the darkness silhouetted by the rising moon.

It took no time at all to glide down-river to the
landing stage where the skipper coaxed her into the slack
water and the boy hooked a loop of stern warp over a bollard
before jumping ashore taking the bow line with him.

"Well then," thought Botolph.   "Just a few more
hours and then it will be the old team again, with an eight-
year-old for company," and he settled down under some
sacking to get some sleep.

CHAPTER 56
The Race

Fulkh made his way to the stables, hitched his horse to the wagon and walked her over the bridge. Once they were on the grassy track to Bonoriacum he shook the reins and she broke into an easy trot.

"Noon on the morrow." he said to himself and wondered how much he could persuade Bonitius to pay him for this easy message. The sun was still high in the sky and he would have no problem making his call and getting back to Lutetia before nightfall.

As the wagon rounded the corner of a wood he saw that a young tree had fallen across the track. It was not large but he could not go round it because of the ditches on each side of the road. Muttering a curse, he reined the horse in and locked the wheels as he jumped down from the cart, grasped one of the branches and started to haul the tree to one side.

Suddenly he felt his arms grasped from behind and locked behind his back. He looked up and sideways to see the unwelcome faces of two men-at-arms who hauled him off his feet and bundled him into the wood where an even more unwelcome sight greeted him.

"Fauve," he said.

"*Brother* Fauve to you, Fulkh. Now where are you going?"

He did not answer and received a kick to the back of his legs which brought him down to his knees from whence he was pushed onto his face. Somebody knelt on his back while his wrists were lashed behind him and he was then hauled to his feet again. One man stood behind him gripping his shoulders while another came and faced him with a smirk.

"I'll ask you again," said Fauve.

There was still no answer. Fulkh waited for the punch that he felt sure was coming but nothing happened. Fauve smiled. That was worse than a punch.

"Come with me."

Leaving one of the men-at-arms to look after the wagon, the other man-handled Fulkh along after Fauve as he walked deeper into the forest As they entered a clearing Fulkh was horrified to see his wife and daughter being held by two other ruffians. Both of them had knives at their throats.

His captor held Fulkh back as he spat obscenities at the men.

"Now, now," said Fauve, "There's no need to get all upset. Just cooperate and your wife and daughter will be unharmed. All you need to do is tell me what your errand is. Now. Let's try again. Where are you going?"

Fulkh looked at his family. His daughter squealed as her guard tightened his grip. He had no choice. Fauve would think nothing of killing a child. In fact he would probably enjoy it.

"The Gateway."

"Good. What for?"

"To give Bonitius a message."

"Well done. I'm glad you're seeing sense now, but in fact you've told me nothing that I don't already know. So what's the message?"

Fulkh hesitated but not for long as his wife's face contorted with pain.

"Noon on the morrow."

"Good," said Fauve. "Well we will help you to deliver your message but you will change it to '*Daybreak* on the morrow'. Do you understand?"

He nodded.

"Do you also understand what will happen to your wife and daughter if you fail to carry out these instructions?"

"You'll kill them."

"Precisely. Now you'll be restored to your wagon so that you can go and perform your duty. We'll stay here and await your return. After that you and your family'll be our guests overnight and until our business with Master Luka is completed. Then you'll all be released to carry on your daily lives as if nothing has happened. You got all that?"

Fulkh nodded, thinking furiously.

Fauve read his thoughts. "Don't bother yourself thinking about it Fulkh. You're not bright enough to think. You are a 'doing' man, so just get on and *do* it."

He motioned at the guard to take him back to the wagon and said, "When you've set this scum on his way, ride back to Meaux and tell the archdeacon 'Daybreak on the morrow'.

When his wrists were released Fulkh considered his chances of a successful attack on the man-at-arms - but then of course there was still the problem of his wife and daughter. He released the brake and sadly frapped the reins. His mind was still in a whirl. What should he do? Should he tell Bonitius everything or would that be jeopardising his family's lives? He was really having difficulty in thinking straight. Fauve was right, he was a 'doer'. Anyway it was not really his problem. He was only the messenger. Why should he care if Luka was killed? He decided to stop worrying and play it as it came. His family were his first priority.   That, and getting paid for delivering this pesky message which did not seem such an easy job now.

He was greeted by Alfrid at the Gateway but he knew he had to take the message directly to Bonitius if he was going to get paid.

"You alright?" said Alfrid as they walked towards the farmhouse.   "You look a bit pre-occupied."

"What?   Nah, I'm fine," said Fulkh relapsing into silence.

He gave the message to Bonitius who said, "Daybreak? Christ, I thought the tide 'd be later than that," and he gave Fulkh his money.

Fulkh looked at it, "Is that *all*?" he said.

"All?   Well you've only delivered a bleedin' message, it's hardly a matter of life and death!"

Fulkh looked up at him and opened his mouth but then closed it again and turned away.

At the Gateway he clambered onto his wagon and drove it back to Fauve's hideout.   By the time that he arrived the sun was setting.   His wife and daughter were hauled roughly out of the wood to the roadside and then thrown into the back of the wagon.   Two men-at-arms sat one on each side of him and Fauve and four other guards formed a mounted escort while two riderless horses were attached to the back of the wagon.

This imposing posse took a little-used track through the woods keeping well clear of Bonoriacum and skirted round until they came to a series of huts.   These were deep in the forest and atop a hill.   Darkness had fallen by the time they arrived but the full moon gave ample light for their needs.

Fulkh and his family were placed in one hut where he was at last able to console his sobbing wife. His daughter by contrast seemed cross rather than upset and the youngster had no need of his consolation. They settled down on the floor and one of the guards came in with some food and beer and an oil lamp and then went out bolting the door behind him. They could hear the constant sound of low voices from which they gathered that they were guarded by two or more men. There was nothing for it but to eat and drink. All three settled down on a pile of straw cuddling together and eventually entered a fitful sleep.

In the middle of the night they were awoken briefly by the sound of shouting. Fulkh recognised one of the voices as being that of Archdeacon Gaubert. He guessed that he had just arrived with another posse of men. The disturbance only lasted a short while and then all went quiet again and they assumed that the new arrivals were sleeping.

--o--

Luka and Ash were also awake in the middle of the night and hitching the horse to the dray. Bonitius had organised two outriders to go with them for protection and to bring back the wagon. The party left the Gateway several hours before dawn in order to cover the three leagues to the landing stage by daybreak.

It was at the same bend of the road where Fulkh had been ambushed that Fauve's party struck. They even used the same branch to block the trackway. There was a furious fight where Luka used his seax to good effect but they were overcome by the sheer volume of numbers and by the time Luka and Ash were trussed up like chickens, four of Fauve's men were dead and two badly injured. Bonitius's two outriders had fought like demons but they had also been killed.

Fauve came and stood above Luka and Ash where they were lying in the forest clearing, the setting moon casting its oblique white rays across them.

"So," he said. "We meet again my little dwarf. And with a dwarf dwarf to boot." He laughed shrilly at his own joke which Luka did not think at all funny but as his face was being pressed into the leaf-mould earth, he was in no position to offer a quip in return so he stayed silent saving his energy for when he could get at this rat-pig properly.

"Guard! Back in the wagon with them and let's go and see the archdeacon. Push those bodies into the undergrowth so that they won't be found for a while."

--o--

Dawn had just broken when Fulkh and his family heard a great deal of shouting and swearing. Fulkh guessed the hut must be quite isolated because nobody seemed to worry about making a noise.

The door was thrown open and Fauve strode in.

"Well done Fulkh. Our little ruse worked perfectly, and, as I am a man of my word, you're all now free to go."

They stood up and walked cautiously to the door where Fauve seized Fulkh by the shoulder and passed him to one of the guards who grasped him similarly.

"Take these three down to their cart and send them on their way," said Fauve.

As he was being frog-marched down the hill, Fulkh felt a pang of conscience and regret as he saw Luka and Ash, their hands tied behind them, being marched in another direction. At the bottom of the hill the two carts came into

380

view, both of them with horses still hitched to them. Tied to various other trees were the soldiers' horses.

Well before they reached the carts the guard pushed Fulkh forwards with an "off you go then" and stood watching them as they completed the distance.

Their horse gave a welcoming whinny and they wasted no time in getting away. His wife climbed in the back while Fulkh unlashed the reins from a tree and handed them to his daughter while he took the chocks off the wheels and then joined her.

He took the reins himself and gently slapped them while clicking his teeth and the cart started to rumble down the track. Fulkh looked behind and the guard nodded and unfolded his arms and then turned and started back towards the camp.

As soon as they were round the corner and out of sight, Fulkh pulled the horse to a standstill.

"Get off," he said to his daughter as he moved to one side and raised the flap on the seat upon which he had been sitting. He peered in and rummaged around before finding what he wanted. It was unwieldy and rusty but it was better than nothing. He slammed the seat back shut.

"Up you get again," he called to his daughter and handed her the reins.

"What're ye doin' now?" asked his wife in a whining tone.

"I'm going back. You're going on."

"Whatever for? Why're ye going back?"

"Unfinished business. Don't argue. Off you go. I'll see you at home later," and he handed the reins to his daughter and slid down to the ground.

"How ye goin' t' get back?" she persisted.

"Mebbe walk. I don't know, - now don't waste time. Be off with you," and he slapped the horse's rump and leapt back to avoid the wheels as the startled animal took off.

He ran back to the corner and peered round to where the guard had been standing earlier but now it was only the horses which remained. He continued cautiously up the track. When he reached the point at which he had seen Luka and Ash being taken along a side path, he took it too, moving as quietly as he could, alert for signs of life.

--o--

Luka was trying to keep as close an eye on Ash as he could. The boy was not crying. In fact on his face he had a defiant look that Luka recognised from somewhere. Luka was proud of him. They caught each other's eye and that gave them both hope. Seeing the action a guard gave Luka a rough push making him stagger. He bit back a comment. He was in no position to make one at the moment.

The archdeacon was at the head of the procession with Fauve close behind. They were both dressed in some weird robes that Luka had never seen before and they wore tall white hats. They climbed up a hill and reached a flat summit, in the centre of which stood a large rectangular stone.

Luka's heart dropped. There was no doubt. It was a *sacrificial altar.*

The procession stopped in front of it and Fauve motioned the guards to put the boy on top of it. Luka moved forwards in spite of the restraining hands.

"No," he said, - "Me. It's *me* you have the argument with. Take *me.*"

"You're no use little dwarf. *You're* not a virgin. Never mind, your turn'll come, - don't you worry. Blindfold him."

Fauve realised that Luka thought it was he who was going to be blindfolded and the depraved monk let out a burst of his crowing laughter and said, "No, not *you* my little dwarf. We want *you* to be able to see *everything*. *Don't* we archdeacon?"

A leer passed between them.

In spite of his biting and kicking Ash was blindfolded and spread-eagled across the altar, his wrists and ankles lashed to each corner of the slab. The archdeacon was standing at the head of the table and to his horror Luka saw him pick up a knife. *His* knife. His seax which had been taken from him after the fight.

Fauve placed a large lavishly-decorated golden bowl on the table close to Luka between Ash's legs. He then turned and walked up a slight slope to a point where there was a tree on a ridge overlooking the stone. He motioned to four of the guards to bring Luka up to him.

Luka's wrists were cut free but he was still kept firmly held. He was forced back against the tree and, leaving him in a standing position his wrists re-tied backwards around the trunk and his feet were lashed similarly.

"Go and light the fire," commanded Fauve to his men. For the first time Luka noticed a stack of firewood with kindling set below it. On each side stood a tripod made of three stout branches bound together at the top. Lying against these with its handle on the ground was a large spit skewer.

The archdeacon joined Fauve at the fireside. Neither of them seemed to be in a hurry. They each had a drinking horn from which they continually sipped. They talked animatedly in low voices whilst apparently waiting for the kindling to set fire to the logs. At last a delicious smell of wood-smoke pervaded the air and Fauve dismissed all the guards sending them back down the hill to the huts.

The archdeacon, seax in hand, walked with Fauve across to Luka. He aimed it at Luka's head but in spite of his bonds Luka managed to duck out of the way and the blade stuck in the tree. Both white-robed men laughed.

"Good job you moved little dwarf," crooned Fauve. "We wouldn't want to kill you just yet."

Leaving the blade in the tree, the archdeacon suddenly snarled and curling his hand into a fist smashed it into Luka's jaw. Luka was not able to duck this time and took the full force of it; the archdeacon was no boxer though and Luka had been hit a lot harder than that many times before. Nevertheless he thought he would play their game so he groaned realistically. Scenting blood, Gaubert tried another tactic and, taking a run at him, pounded his fist into Luka's abdomen. Luka saw it coming and tensed his ample musculature so that the punch hardly had any effect at all but Luka nevertheless gave a realistic moan as he sagged forwards. The archdeacon tasted the sweet joy of satisfaction.

He pulled the seax free of the tree and held it threateningly. The archdeacon assumed that Luka's look was one of fear and he waved it in front of his nose saying "Like Brother Fauve says, we don't want you to die before you've enjoyed our entertainment." A breeze came up and a cloud of wood-smoke blew over them making the archdeacon cough.

When he had recovered, he continued, "Today's your lucky day. You're going to have the privilege of helping us celebrate 'Alban Eilir'."

"That's a *pagan* festival," spat Luka.

The two men laughed humourlessly.

Fauve answered, "Well spotted my little dwarf. You're right. We *are* pagans. Christianity is for fools."

The archdeacon took up the dialogue, speaking unnaturally slowly: "I wonder if our little show today might persuade you to become pagan too with your dying breath ...

"What you are about to witness will make you pray with all your heart to the God you worship ... You'll plead to your God for help ... But he *won't* help you and you'll hate Him for failing you.

"Your very own knife will travel from your son's left ear to his right ... and his blood will drain into the golden bowl ... His body'll turn as white as marble. He'll become a thing of great beauty.

"The knife will then split him from his navel to his manhood ... and his guts will spew on the ground ...

"His head will be pulled back and the spit-skewer will be run through his mouth to his arse ... and he'll be turned over the fire until nightfall.

"The second part of our ceremony will then begin and it'll be your turn to provide the entertainment."

Luka tried to remain expressionless.   He was working away at his bonds but they had been efficiently tied and he could not move them.   He had been in a few desperate situations before but never in one quite as desperate as this.   He had already lost one child and he certainly did not want to lose another but what could he do?"

He decided that the use of delaying tactics might be his only answer.

"So you only sacrifice virgins then?"

"That's right."

"How often do you do that?"

"Every month, close to the full moon."

"There's a plentiful supply then is there?"

Fauve's face clouded over.

"There is when idiots like you don't get in the way."

"Ah, - the consignment of slave-children?" said Luka.

"Yes indeed. The girl Feya was going to be our next sacrifice and the other children were to be put in store."

"But Feya wasn't a virgin."

"She was before that one'eyed idiot and his gang got at her," said the archdeacon.

"But ... but that was many years ago," ventured Luka as he struggled to find ways of keeping the conversation going.

"Indeed it was, but today's work will be all the sweeter for waiting."

"What about the blood? What does that do?"

"Ah, well we offer that to Alban Eilir and he blesses and fortifies it. As we hold it up to him it bubbles and froths. When the bowl becomes hot the nectar is ready and it is time for us to drink it," said Fauve.

"Enough talk," said the archdeacon, "it's time for you to watch your blade do its work. It's appropriate, is it not, for the father's blade to be the instrument of his son's death? Watch closely because this is certainly something you'll never see again."

Fauve gave a short howl of laughter at his archdeacon's wit and they turned and walked back towards the altar

Fulkh heard the guards coming towards him and he pressed back into the bushes as they passed. Once the last one had gone he moved up the hill again. He smelt the wood-smoke and wondered what it meant. When he reached the top of the path he could see between the trees to where Ash's body was lying on the altar. To his left were the two white-robed figures and a tied-up Luka.

He ducked back into the forest and crept up the hill in the opposite direction, carefully making no noise. He hoped there were no outer guards.

Once he guessed that he was in the right position he pushed through the scrub climbing back up the hill towards the ridge at the edge of the clearing. He had judged it well and came out directly behind Luka's tree. He could see the two figures talking to Luka but was too far away to be able to make out what they were saying. When they turned and started to walk towards the altar he ran to the tree. The sword, though rusty, was still sharp and it sliced easily through the captive's bonds.

Once he felt himself released, Luka did not waste time wondering why or how but shot from the tree like an arrow from a bow. He caught up with his two persecutors just before they reached the altar and leapt onto their shoulders putting an arm around each neck. They collapsed in a heap. Luka recovered quickly and grabbed Fauve with his left hand whilst issuing a pile-driving punch to his jaw with his right fist. Fauve's inert body fell to one side.

Luka, still filled with rage and venom, turned his attention to Gaubert who had got up and was attempting to run towards the guard house but a little man with a rusty sword suddenly sprang out of the bushes in front of him.

"You!" Gaubert hissed at Fulkh.

"Yes it's me, - you perverted lump of lard," and with that he thrust the sword deep into the archdeacon's belly.

"Christ," said Luka, arriving on the scene. "That wasn't exactly what I had in mind."

"Had to be done," said Fulk. "It would've been him or me. I was hoping to get out of this without being seen but once he knew it was me who released you, my life wouldn't have been worth nothing."

Luka knew what he meant.

"Well you'd better make yourself scarce now before Fauve comes round then. Leave me to deal with him and see if you can find some horses for us."

"Right," said Fulkh - and then, bending down to pick something up from the ground near Gaubert's body, "Here, - you'd better have this."

He handed Luka the knife that the archdeacon had been carrying. Luka looked at it and nodded gratefully. "It keeps coming back" he muttered. "Off you go now."

He ran to the altar and cut Ash free, removing his blindfold as he did so. The boy rolled sideways and lithely jumped down without a word.

Fauve was still unconscious and between the two of them they lifted him onto the stone slab and secured him with the remains of Ash's bonds.

"Right, - c'mon - let's get away from here" said Luka "but take it easy, we don't want to attract the attention of the guards, - quietly and quickly now."

They made their way stealthily down the path towards where they had seen the horses. As they passed the soldiers' huts they could hear the sound of singing so they hoped that they were all engaged in merrymaking and had not posted any guards further down.

In the event there were none and they found Fulkh ready with the three good horses.

"C'mon," said Fulkh, "let's go. There's just enough time left for you to catch the tide".

"There's more than enough time," said Luka gloomily, "the next one won't be until sunset."

"Noon." said Fulkh, "Come on!"

"But you said ..."

"I know ... Fauve forced me to ... Long story ... Trust me ... We must go - *now*."

They started at a brisk trot, knowing that they had at least an hour's ride in front of them but wanting to keep some of the horses' stamina in reserve.

Luka thanked Fulkh for rescuing them.

"Think nothing of it," he said. "'Twas my fault in the first place."

"How's that?"

He told him the story of the ambush and how he was forced to give Bonitius the wrong message.

"Heigh-ho," said Luka, "you can't be blamed for that and you've done us a good service today. That's the second time you've saved my life."

"Yes," said Fulkh, "It'll be a relief to me when you're back in Britain."

They both laughed.

A quarter of an hour later they rounded a corner of trees and reached a spot where Lutetia was visible in the distance.

"I must leave you here then," said Fulkh. "God bless you both and give you safe journey home. Hurry now, the ebb will have started running."

They waved and carried on westwards as he turned to the south.

"Home ..." thought Luka, "Home!"

As he turned a little to glance again at the retreating form of Fulkh he saw a movement out of the corner of his eye. He turned further and saw dust rising from the galloping hooves of six horses.

"Come on," he shouted to Ash, digging his heels in to his own horse's flanks. "Ride like the wind!"

The ground flew by and his horse stumbled a couple of times. That's *all* he needed, to be thrown off now. He could see the landing stage in the distance and there *was* a vessel tied up against it. He hoped it was the *right* vessel. He looked behind. They were gaining on them rapidly. There was no chance of stopping at the landing stage. They would never get the boat off before the soldiers arrived.

As they came closer he could see Botolph standing amidships and gazing towards him. He wondered if he had noticed their pursuers.

"Cast off! Cast off!" he was shouting, well before they reached the boat.

"Don't stop Ash. Keep going as far and fast as you can. I'll catch up with you."

The boy surged ahead as Luka slowed at the boat. "Pick us up at the point," he yelled as he dug his heels in again and surged after his son.

He looked back. Botolph was already on the quayside and throwing off the warps. Luka saw him heave the boat out into the stream before jumping back aboard but then he lost sight of him as he concentrated on spurring his horse to one last extraordinary effort as the thunder of the pursuing hooves vied with the sound of blood thrumming in his ears.

There was no way back and Luka would not be able to fight all seven of them so he hoped this was going to work. He was close behind Ash again now.

"Drive her right into the water and then swim as fast as you can out into the stream," he called.

The young head turned as he pulled alongside him, "What?"

"Drive her right in and swim for it."

No sooner were the words out of his mouth than both horses were over the edge each one giving a great splash before their forward motion was suddenly arrested as their hooves left the ground and the deep water stopped them dead.

Their momentum pitched both riders over their horses' heads and they made an ungainly entrance into the Sequana but both recovered rapidly and pulled strongly towards the middle of the stream. Moments later came more splashes as the pursuing horses hit the water but were blocked by the other two animals endeavouring to clamber out.

Loud neighing shouting and swearing came from the bank side but the cacophony rapidly faded into the distance as they reached mid-stream and the tide picked them up and swirled them away down the river.

Luka caught up with Ash. "Alright son?" he said.

The boy nodded and they looked back. Nobody was following but around the bend of the meander came the beautiful sight of a black hull above which a cloth sail was drawing bravely in a fresh south-easterly breeze. A brilliant white Saxon moustache of cascading foam marked where the prow joined the water and as the craft bore down on them they could see Botolph's grinning face peering over the side.

The skipper stepped forward and doused the sail and gasketted it and the swimmers saw the moustache dissolve as the boat slowed in its approach. Luka pushed Ash ahead of him and the boat boy made a grab and nimbly hauled him over the side.

Luka was a heavier prospect but as Botolph clasped the wrist of his friend a surge of elation gave him the power to heave the sodden horseman aboard ... whereupon they both fell into the bottom of the boat and started to giggle helplessly.

"Here we are again then!" said Botolph as he sat up.

"Here indeed brother ... or should I say, 'Father'?"

The skipper threw off the sail's gasket and the sail filled strongly making the craft heel over as she surged forwards, picking up speed in a sailor's wind for Britain.

Here endeth Volume Two of the Botolph Trilogy.

Abbey   A building inhabited by a religious
                     institution of monks or nuns governed by an
                     Abbot or Abbess.

Amblethuys Ambleteuse near Boulogne, France.

Apuldre   Appledore near Tenterden, Kent.

Atrebatum   Arras, France.

Austrasia   Ancient part of Northwest France including
                     today's Boulogne.

Beltaine   Celtic festival held on 1st May.   Devoted to
                     the god Bel and involved the lighting of
                     fires.

Beodricsworth   Bury St Edmunds, Suffolk.

Beorgh Asc   Burwash, East Sussex.

Bloomery   Strictly a primitive type of furnace used in
                     the Iron Age but in this series of books is the
                     fictional name of a Saxon village in the
                     Weald devoted to iron-making.

Bourn   A stream.

Burel   Natural undyed wool. Varies in colour
                     between white and brown.

Burgh Castle Near Great Yarmouth.

Burgundia   Ancient part of Southeast France.

Caesaromagus Beauvais, France. Stronghold of the
                     Bellovaci tribe.

Caleton   Sands off that part of the coast of Gaul which
                     eventually became Calais.

Cantium   Kent.   A province in England.

Cantwarebury   Canterbury. Known in Roman times as
                     Durovernum Cantiacorum and later as Burh.
                     Although the latter would have been the
                     correct choice of name for Botolph's time, I
                     have chosen not to use this in order to avoid

I

confusion between Burh and Burgh in East Anglia. Occupied **by** Roman forces until c.400 AD when they were recalled, after which little is heard of the town until c.590 AD when Ethelbert became king. By the time Augustine arrived in AD 597 via Ebbsfleet on the island of Tanatus, Cantwarebury had become well-established again. In this book, a monastery/abbey under the control of ArchbishopHonorius and Prior Peter.

Capellanu   The guardian of reliquaries.

Celts   Celts were polytheistic animists. That is to say that they had many gods and goddesses and also venerated deities existing in aspects of nature such as streams and trees.

Cnobersburg   A monastery near Great Yarmouth, under the control of Abbot Fursey and, in this book, Prior Matthew.

Coenobium   A religious institution of monks or nuns following a communal rule of life.

Colneceaster   Colchester, Essex – the original Roman capital of Britain.

Contubernium   Roman term for "Tent erecting party".

Convent   From Latin "Convenire" meaning "To come together". A religious institution, usually (but not necessarily) consisting of nuns.

Cubit   An ancient measure from the tip of an adult's middle finger to the elbow. 18 inches (45.72 cms).

Dofras   Dover (also at other times called Dubris).

Ebon's Island   Ebony, Kent.

Eveqcomte   Special title for the Bishop-Prince of Beauvais.

Evoriacum   The name of Faremoutiers before Fara's death.

Exning   10 miles south-south-east of Ely in Suffolk.

Faremoutiers   Moûtiers (in the Albertville region of France) was the capital of the Ceutrones, a Celtic tribe of Gaul. The town was previously called "Monasterium" and the two names became interchangeable. Thus "Faremoutiers" and "Marmoutiers" represent Fara's and Martin's Monasteries respectively.

Folcanstane   A town in Kent, now known as Folkestone, at the narrowest part of the English Channel. Site of the first nunnery in England founded in A.D. 630 by Princess Eanswythe, daughter of King Eadbald.

Francia   That part of Gaul populated by the Franks (following the collapse of the Western Roman Empire).

Fyrd   A militia band called to fight in times of danger

Gallia   Gaul. A large area comprising the southern part of the Netherlands, Belgium, part of Germany, France and northern Italy subject to constant alteration of sovereignty.

Gesoriacum   Boulogne. Also known as Bononia and Itius Portus.

Greynose   Cap Gris Nez, France.

Gippeswic   Ipswich.

Hide   Originally a parcel of land of a size suitable for supporting a family and its dependents.

III

Later a specific size of 60 to 120 acres used for assessing taxes.

Heartburst Hill Crevecoeur in France.

Hrofsceaster Rochester, Kent. Also known as Durobrivae.

Imbolc Celtic festival held on 1st February. The spring festival dedicated to the goddess Brigid.

Laver A washroom with running water.

League Three miles (the distance a man or a horse could walk in an hour).

Ligugia 8 km south of Poitiers, France.

Liman A bay or harbour (the Turkish language still uses the same word). In the 4th century, the Celts used this word for an "elm-wood" or "marshy" river. Before that time, the wordmay have been used to describe the whole Romney Marsh area when it was a lagoon.

Liminge Lyminge. A village in Kent which took its name from the tribe who lived by the Liman (see above). The site of England's first mixed-gender Monastery (under the control of Abbess Ethelburga).

Longseaxe A large Saxon fighting knife.

Lotha's Croft Lowestoft

Lundwic London. As mentioned in the Pronounciation Section, the "c" here is pronounced as "ch". Thus "Lundwi*ch*" or "LundCity".   When the City became large and divided into two, Lundwic became "Ealdwic" (or "old" city) which eventually became the more familiar "Aldwych". During Roman times, the capital was called "Londinium" and this name was used for many centuries after the Romans left, but "Lundwic" was in common use in Botolph's time.

Lugdunum   Lyon, France.

Lughnasadh   Celtic festival held on 1st August. Dedicated to the three-faced god Lugus.

Lutetia   Paris. Originally the home of the Parisii tribe.

Luxovium   Luxeuil, Burgundia, France. Site of monastery, founded AD 585 by the Irish monk Columbanus. Became one of the largest and most important monasteries in Gaul.

Manigfual   Cnobersburg sailing vessel. (Name "borrowed" from Frisian legend)

Meaux   Cathedral city 25 miles north-east of Paris.

Mettis   Metz, Northeast France. Important Roman city.

Mile   A Roman mile was 1,000 paces, i.e. 1,000 "yards".

Minster   Any large church originally connected to a monastery.

Misericord   As well as meaning a seat, this word is also used in Benedictine Monasteries to indicate a 'room of relaxation' where the rules of the monastery are not so strictly observed.

Mithras   God popular with Roman military between 1st and 4th centuries A.D.

Monastery   From Greek "Monos" meaning "Alone"; a religious institution living in seclusion from

	secular society and bound by religious vows. Usually (but not necessarily) consisting of monks.
Neustria	Ancient area of Western France including today's Paris.
Niwendenne	Newenden, Kent.
Noviomum	Noyon, France.
Novitiate	A person who has entered a religious order but has not yet taken their final vows.
Nunnery	A religious institution consisting of a community of nuns.
Ox Island	Isle of Oxney, Kent.
Painter	Rope tied to the front of the boat for mooring it with.
Pax in terra	Peace on earth.
Pax vobiscum	Peace be with you.
Portus Limanis	A Roman port near Lympne, Kent. Functional c.130-350AD. Site of Studfall Castle.
Priory	A religious institution governed by a Prior. Sometimes subordinate to an abbey.
Prior	The deputy head of a monastery or abbey, ranking directly below the Abbot. In certain religious orders the Prior is the actual and only head of the community.
Remi	Cathedral city of Rheims, 80 miles north-east of Paris.
Rhee Wall	Raised land-wall on Romney Marsh, running from Appledore to New Romney. Origin controversial but may be Roman.
River Limen	A stream, running along the northern edge of Romney Marsh, consisting of a tidal saltwater creek at its eastern end and a

narrow freshwater tributary from the River Rother at its western end.

River Rother   A river running from the Weald to the Marshes of Rumniae.   The river's name was not in fact acquired until the later middle ages.

Romney Marsh   Marshes of Rumniae in Kent.

Sandgap   Sandgate, Kent.

Samara River   River Somme, France

Samarobriva   Amiens, France.   City where Saint Martin gave half his cloak to the beggar.

Samhain   Celtic festival held on 1st November.   Starts at sunset on 31st October and finishes at sunset on 1st November.   The day when spirits of the Otherworld become visible. Generally hoped to be the day of the first frost after the harvest has been gathered in. The first day of the new Saxon year. Customarily a place was set for the dead at the Samhain feast and the night was notable for the telling of tales of ancestors.   A westerly door or window would be opened to invite the dead to attend. A candle would be placed nearby to guide the spirits home. It was the time to take stock of supplies - in terms of both grain and cattle. It was the time when decisions had to be made regarding how many and which animals were to be slaughtered.   After the slaughter, the bones were placed on the bonefires and once these were alight (often two bonefires side by side) the rest of the village fires were extinguished and then re-lit from the new

	fire and people and livestock walked between the bonefires as a symbol of purification.
Scrip	A leather pouch typically carried by a pilgrim.
Seax	A Saxon fighting knife.
Sithiu	Saint Omer, France.
Sixmile	Hamlet on Stone Street, Kent, six miles from Canterbury, and also six miles from Portus Lemanis, Folkestone and Ashford.
Stade	A name of ancient derivation used in southern England for "quay" or "strand".
Stone Street	Roman Road between Canterbury and Portus Lemanis, Kent
Tanatus	Isle of Thanet, Kent. The royal base chosen by Hengist and Horsa, 455-488, and probably subsequently by Octa and Eormenric. "Thanatos" was a minor Greek God; the daemonic personification of death.
Tenetwaraden	Tenterden, Kent. (Thanet-men's forest den).
Tervanna	Therouanne, France.
Thury	Meadow Town near Beaumont-sur-Oise.
Thwart	A structural crosspiece in an open boat. Used as a seat.
Tonsure	The partial shaving of the head to leave a "halo" of hair to indicate membership of a monastic order.
Venta Icanorum	(Also, later, Norwic) Norwich.
Whitenose	Cap Blanc Nez, France.
Wic	Suffix meaning "Trading Station".

Meaux Cathedral.

Although, uncannily, I found that Meaux Cathedral did bear many resemblances to the building I had imagined, the seventh century cathedral of this book is entirely fictional. Today's 12th century cathedral is actually situated *north* of the loop in the River Marne rather than at the *centre* of the loop as portrayed in the book. The French historian and hagiographer Monseigneur Duchesne (1873-1922) dated Meaux's first bishop (Medovechus) as being in office between AD 549 and 552 and Abbess Fara's brother, Faro, as bishop from AD 626 to 672.

Accuracy of the story.

In case it is not abundantly clear, these stories of the activities of Botolph and Luka are entirely fictional. As far as I am aware, no synod was ever held in Meaux. However I have attempted to ensure that the *time frame* and *many of the characters* as well as the *circumstances of the cities, towns and villages* are historically accurate.

Faremoutiers Abbey (originally known as 'Evoriacum').

Faremoutiers Abbey still exists although today (2014) it is occupied by only eight nuns who are under the leadership of Prieuse Clothilde. The foundations of the seventh century monastery can still be seen but the building was destroyed during the French Revolution. The present abbey was built in 1931. Everything that I have read during my research suggests that this was indeed the monastery that Botolph attended although this fact is still subject to scholarly speculation.

Slaves.

In Botolph's time, slaves were often the descendants of Britons who, years previously, had been taken by raiding Saxons who subsequently settled in the country. From then onwards they and their offspring would be bartered as the mood took their owner. In times of famine and severe hardship, a husband or wife might find that their only hope of survival lay in choosing *voluntary* enslavement. In such circumstances they were known to sell their families and/or themselves into slavery. Slaves were ubiquitous, even being found in religious institutions.

The value of a slave was set at one pound which was the price of eight oxen. This was the price that anyone who killed a slave would be expected to pay to his aggrieved owner. There was no law against anyone killing their own slave. Owners had to treat the acquisition of a slave with caution since they became responsible for their actions. The dress of slaves was however indistinguishable from free people but they were expected to do all the heavy manual labour and anything that was remotely unpleasant. It was within the right of an owner to grant a slave his freedom. This was usually done at a holy place or at a cross-roads, symbolising, for the newly-freed person, his or her right to choose their own pathway in the future.

King Dagobert and his counsellor Eligius (also known as Saint Eloi).

In about 1786, over 1,000 years after his death, a poem was written called "Le bon roi Dagobert". This eventually became a nursery rhyme which is still familiar to most French schoolchildren.

The original purpose of the poem was to poke fun at the aristocracy in order to further the causes of the French Revolution. King Dagobert is portrayed as a bumbling selfish fool who relies heavily on Saint Eloi to get him out of many scrapes.

The twenty-two verses of the poem refer to the same King Dagobert whom I hope we have grown to know and love in the preceding chapters; it must be clear then that these libellous accusations are quite unfounded. I attach just four (liberally translated) verses for your amusement, together with one example in the original French:-

Le bon roi Dagobert.

Le bon roi Dagobert
A mis sa culotte à l'envers ;
Le grand Saint Éloi
Lui dit : Ô mon roi!
Votre Majesté
Est mal culottée.
C'est vrai, lui dit le roi,
Je vais la remettre à l'endroit.

The king wrote some verse,
But the rhymes were bad and worse,
The Arch Saint Eloi
Said "Oh mon roi!

Leave some other smelly swine
To write for you the awful rhyme."
"Good idea" said the king,
I'll get *you* to write the thing.

The good king Dagobert
Went hunting in Antwerp.
The Arch Saint Eloi
Said "Oh mon roi!
You do seem left
Quite out of breath."
"It's true" said he, "I am a bit",
"I've just been chased ... by a rabbit!"

The dogs owned by Dagobert
By spots became "covaired"
The Arch Saint Eloi
Said "Oh mon roi!
To get them sound
You must have them drowned."
"Oh well, if that's what's to do,
You 'd better drown yourself too!"

The pretty queen of Dagobert
Took a lover, - Oh so fair.
The Arch Saint Eloi
Said "Oh mon roi!
You are cuckold
I'm reliably told."
"It's good,"(to him said the King),
"My father was the very same thing!"